Queen of Sorrow

by

Y D Jones

About the Author

Y D Jones lives in the North East of England. Leaving school turned just 15 following a Secondary Modern education in cooking, sewing, netball and singing, and yearly school visits to the ballet and historic locations, she went on to be offered unconditional places at university 3 times in adulthood. Realising this wouldn't happen indefinitely she embarked upon a BSc Psychology (Hons) degree, culminating in her dissertation being published in The British Psychological Society's journal, The Occupational Psychologist.

Her interest in creative writing began around the age of 8 until her mother decreed, 'Stop wasting your time and do something useful'. She would happily agree, it was a different time. In 2018 *Alice and George* was published in the first local literary anthology as "Highly Commended" and another, *Ashes,* has been broadcast as a play on BBC local radio.

Love After Life, three short story representations of the affectionate link between the living and dead will be published shortly with *The Erdinger Project,* a dystopian short narrative begun in 2017. More recently, a pile of writings and short yarns from across the decades was discovered in the attic, which are also to be revisited.

Information and news can be found at email:- queenofsorrow715@gmail.com.

Quote

'**S**ometimes, when writing you need to go off piste,' said the writer.
    'I agree,' said the reader. 'And thereby you can find adventure, exhilaration and sometimes, fun.'
                            Anon

Printed and distributed by Amazon.co.uk

First printing edition 2023
Book Design by Jaguarpoem
queenofsorrow715@gmail.com

Dedicated To

Women of the world who do what they must to survive in conflict or damaging situations, and good men everywhere who choose to make the right decisions. Also to my wonderful family both here, and gone.

Acknowledgements

Respect to historic and military sources providing background information of WW2 in Italy, one of the inspirations for this novel. Thanks also to the lovely people who read the story before publication, fellow author Peter Townend, and friend Garry McNaughton who gave positive feedback and gratitude to Barbara Bonas and Diane Mickey who, in the early days, eased me into the process. And finally to Sarah Haigh, who unlocked the document from my pc when technicians were unable to.

Contents

PROLOGUE

South of England, early January 1947

Her head rocked gently against a grimy railway headrest, eyes sore from smoke and lack of sleep.

Departed a traitor, arriving in England an enemy; at least here an enemy with food coupons. In this new world she would be spat upon, hated, and distrusted by women as much for her looks as any other reason. But men showed no such concerns. She was a seductive beauty with misty-grey eyes and a tempestuous pout that worked as well in lust as anger, and wore an impressive fur coat. Her styled and waved hair was flat and tired, stockings laddered from the journey, the best saved for arrival.

A nine-carat gold ring had committed them on a cool, autumn day in Italy, coat made then from an army blanket pressed to look like felt until her arm had ached.

Darling Ted, her Teddy, saviour from the madness and terror, he would be there wouldn't he? Or would he even remember her? In Italy they had spoken with soft eyes and tentative touches, the fewest of words and a mutual attraction uniting them.

Alighting onto the platform at her final destination, an unfamiliar figure swaggering towards her, cigarette cupped in the palm of his hand - old habits die hard.

Hesitating, she drew upon hellish experiences, heart racing in her malnourished chest, no coping space left as the stranger approached. She rallied to play the situation to her advantage. Having lived off her wits for so long and exhausted to the core she observed his contemptuous stare, her mind racing to act.

Twisting her frame showed her figure to its best advantage, stretching her legs to show the curve of her calves, and throwing open the fur revealing the cut of her jacket around her tiny waist.

She raised a gloved hand to the side of her neck, gently resting it on her imitation pearls, running her fingers slowly round her throat, then rested her fingers, spreading them seductively across her breastbone and sighed. Men liked that. The gesture said nothing, but everything to him. Uncertain how long she could maintain the air of mystique, of superiority, if she were in danger with this unfamiliar man, she would take whatever advantage she could.

'You're late.' His voice matched his frame, deep, flat, menacing.

She lightly flicked the other loose glove on his arm, speaking carefully, 'England train', and looking away unconcerned, walked slowly down the platform.

He flicked away his tab end, drew back his shoulders, and picked up her cases, beside her within two steps.

The guardsman on the train who had observed her too closely throughout her journey for her liking, watched solemnly, as the two strangers disappeared.

Part I

Chapter 1

Trieste, Italy, Summer 1922

Travellers shoved and milled about the cool train concourse, some knowing immediately their direction, others hesitant. Dark, darting eyes searched the crowds for familiar faces, others wavered before facing the blistering heat outside.

Passing the arrogant, self-assured young man in his twenties, several noted his languid posturing, not unusual in 1922 Italy. Confident conceit was a popular attitude amongst virile young men, how else to demonstrate their stallion mentality and masculinity? Posters of Il Duce, Benito Mussolini, led the way, his star rising on a wave of nationalistic rhetoric after the depressing years following the Great War. Superiority now was measured by a straight back and up-tilted chin and it wasn't unusual for youths to peer down their nose, though this alone did not mark this young man out. His expensively cut suit set him apart, and an indefinable ominous presence lingered in the onlooker's mind.

A woman, as tall and broad as any man, followed him onto the platform. She wore a respectable, understated, expensive silk dress, an iridescent string of pearls radiated around her neck, a neat felt hat clung securely to her distinctly middle-class crown, obscuring conservatively styled hair. As she turned to address him a small leather case was placed next to his on the concourse and her gloved hand, already prepared with a modest gratuity, deposited the coins seamlessly into the porters' hand.

Brief, snapped words passed between the two, the name *"Vittorio"* rising from her lips above the hubbub with clipped words spat back in reply. He picked up both cases with a brooding manner that bellowed, the task was beneath him. Stepping out into the stinging light he slung the cases down near the road. As they prepared to wait for transportation to Monfalcone, the sun caught the exquisite diamond clasp at the base of the woman's neck, dazzling spears and sparkles splitting and cracking the light.

In the shade of the station façade, a dead-eyed eighteen-year-old boy absently marked the couple's arrival. Born originally in Trieste, returning now from Vienna to train at the old hydroelectric plant, on the quay of Porto Vecchio. His name was Odilo, and already planning his destiny elsewhere. As like recognises like, he noted the young Italian man as a kindred spirit. After a short wait a chauffeur-driven car appeared, and picked up Vittorio and the woman. Odilo's cold gaze followed them as the vehicle disappeared.

The day drifted on in steamy heat as more modest transport arrived and Odilo's superior signalled that he too should pick up their cases. The young man's fathomless, forbidding eyes responded with icy darkness.

*

Vittorio and the lady showed no interest in each other on their journey, sitting back to back, gazing through open windows at their side of the car. The woman considered the rough limestone landscape of the devilish Karst above her, shuddering at its' reputation for brutal treatment of careless travellers. It was a wilderness, pitted with narrow, overgrown openings to deep inescapable caverns, and sinkholes. Despite the horrifying stories she had heard, she didn't seek comfort from her unemotional companion, his silence slicing through her discomfort.

Vittorio lazily cast his eyes upon the calm, beautiful, azure sea to his left, occasionally considering a minuscule spec or crease to his attire that required attention, his image pristine, even in the dense heat. He idly observed the charming fairy-tale Castle Miramare, perched precariously on the lip of the Adriatic, unmoved by its beauty until it disappeared, and they neared their destination, Monfalcone.

Mothers nurtured the next meal of the day, the eternal labour of love in every home, as the strangers entered the fishing village. Their impressive vehicle attracted curiosity, with children running behind daring to touch the fine paintwork when the driver stopped for directions. It pulled through increasingly narrow lanes, three-story houses shuttered against the heat, washing lines draped across from one house to another, hampering their way. The chauffeur finally pulled up outside a plain two story fisherman's house by the shore, dazzling white in the heat with a pair of small square windows looking out over the courtyard wall, onto the lane. Whoops and yells from the boys informed the inhabitants that visitors had arrived.

A large man appeared at the sun blistered yard doorway in a collarless shirt and well-worn waistcoat, covered by a mismatched striped jacket, too small for his frame. He stepped aside as a bent old woman clothed entirely in black hobbled uncertainly across the threshold into the light, offers of support swiftly dismissed with snapped crone retorts, a collection of muscular young men spilling out behind her.

Prolonged respectful greetings were made by the large woman as she stepped from the car. Vittorio, disinterested in pleasantries, lent against the vehicle, assessing his surroundings with barely disguised disgust until his companion snapped instructions. Following protocol, he reluctantly acknowledged the old matriarch.

The refined lady retired with the family to the house as he sat among the geraniums and potted herbs in the courtyard, comfortably watching rays chase around the top

11

of the whitewashed wall. As the afternoon slipped to even-time, his gaze fell to green, white, grapes grasping at weakening rays of sunlight, ripening as best they could.

Eventually, his travel companion stepped into the waning light. Lack of siesta, prolonged travel, and protracted niceties had worn her energy. Vittorio followed her to the car as she moved a discreet distance from the faces at the wooden door. He surveyed the scene with lacklustre vigour as she turned to see his sullen expression, her wearisome work of the day finally fracturing open with hissed, long-suppressed emotion.

'Your deeds are in the grave with the girl in Verona,. Make sure you tend only to your own business here,' she snapped. Vittorio stared back unmoved.

'Attend to me cretino! Why did you ever touch that girl?' her coarse words so out of character, incredulity flitted briefly across his face, the fishing family picking up the tone. Suppressing her anger she continued.

'Mark what I say, boy. You think you're a man but have the selfishness of a child. Your despicable acts have disgraced the girl and our family too. Do you hear me? Every one of us is tainted by your actions. Remember, Verona society is aware and does not forget.' Her stare chilled the air between them. 'Your indiscretions have ruined many reputations apart from your own. Removing you from our city is just the beginning; we all have to work to mend your recklessness. Ignorant, fool!' She caught sight of the curious faces a short distance away. A vein throbbed on Vittorio's neck, a muscle twitching at his jaw. She lowered her voice.

'We have done what we can, and your life now is dependent on you alone. Verona, will not look favourably on your return, there will be no welcome until you make amends for your shameful impulses.' Raising her voice, 'Do you understand?'

Vittorio dropped his head, everything he saw or touched at home had belonged to him, the world, his playground, people, his toys, as some semblance of understanding seemed to dawn. Banished to this outpost of classless simplicity, abandoned and isolated, cut off from the finer things in life was to be his existence now. Wealth, position, society, the things he valued, gone.

The woman's eyes flickered; a trace of humility hovered on his face. *'Is there hope?'* she asked herself, *'Can he be rescued from his animal wants? Be saved from his scandalous, heinous deeds?'* she wondered.

'Your overheads are dealt with. Upkeep and future are up to you now.' Hesitation held her to the spot. 'Remember Vittorio, you walk the earth, the girl cannot.'

'Thank you, Zia.' For a moment she imagined there was genuine regret in his deep blue eyes. As she turned, reason leached back into her consciousness; it was remorse for himself alone.

Reaching the driver, she quickly instructed him to take her to the exclusive Savoia Excelsior Palace Hotel in Trieste, then turned to kiss the hand of the old matriarch, bidding farewell.

Chapter 2

Monfalcone, Italy, Summer 1922

Vittorio's lazy manner and mysterious arrival provoked more questions than answers wherever he went.

'What do you make of this new Adonis here?' an aged matron cackled, following her granddaughter's gaze, as the straight shouldered stranger sauntering along the dockside, proffering her comment a little too loudly.

'What are you saying Nonna?' the girl mumbled, dropping her eyes, a crimson flush rising up her slender, tanned neck. The old woman smiled, she hadn't lived a long life without knowing how to quash inappropriate interest in a young girl, embarrassment being a very useful tool.

Rumour had spread of him being deposited with the fishing folk by a distant family member, and speculation was rife. Usually, purchase of a new sail, or net, had been news, but the striking new man inspired much more entertainment. It was suggested he was escaping an unsuitable marriage, or was in hiding from jealous comrades from the Great War, given his tales in the local trattoria of wartime heroism.

In truth, Vitorrio had been in Italy's 5th Engineering Regiment, supporting Alpini soldiers in crevices and craggy escarpments above sheer drops in the northern mountains. To lose the peaks would have been a devastating blow to Italy so, despite the weather, they swiftly carved 52 tunnels through the soft limestone. Around bars, he inferred fighting mercilessly and of bitter stories of waking, frozen to the ground. Then of comrades who perished from the arctic blasts that induced the lightheaded tendrils of sleep, lulling them to hypothermia, and death.

In reality, Vittorio had had no intention of slipping to icy oblivion like his comrades, watching who struggled to endure the incessant icy air by laying their blanket without care. It was a simple exercise to spot weakness; consider who to edge out of their comfortable spot, establishing an advantage as fundamental as breathing itself to him. Death had no place in his destiny and only he and Death knew how equipped he was to survive. *"Paulo, fool, have you no sense?"* Vittorio's cutting remarks stung the rustic labourer's dull mind as night after night he humiliated him. During the day they worked side by side, striving towards the same outcome for their country. Vittorio had taken the young man under his wing, a little extra food here, a kind word there, yet every night the lad struggled to understand the jibes. A couple more nights of negative direction and Paulo's space in the tunnel shifted little by little closer to the opening, Vittorio's position gradually more protected, and Death blessed Vittorio for his offering.

But around the fishing village, he made no admission of shortcomings as engineer, soldier or man, his tales expertly reinvented into modest heroism.

At the onset of the Great War, Italy had been lured by promises of great lands at the end of hostilities, but disregarded in peacetime. Now stirrings were being awakened in Italian hearts by Mussolini as his star shone brighter, unifying the country with national pride, and a little self-promotion on Il Duce's shirt-tails did Vittorio no harm.

Of average height with good physical proportions, Vittorio's smooth, lightly tanned skin displayed well defined aristocratic features, above pristine, carefully pressed shirts and a gold collar pin. A straight, distinguished nose and high cheekbones completed his image, an ideal candidate in the new emerging world he considered. Observing his effect on their womenfolk, the men of Monfalcone preferred to point out his self-important attitude and woeful lack of work ethic.

Unease developed within the family in Monfalcone. He was an intruder, his features as alien to their rough weathered faces as a foreigner, openly slouching about with resentful disdain in their humble home. They were quickly out of their depth with this tricky character. But the shiny gold coin went a long way for simple fishing folk in post war Italy.

It transpired it was impossible to occupy him. Every trade found for him resulted in a woeful lack of enthusiasm on his part, his sharp collared image screaming, he did not belong. Cunningly he determined employment would reject him, rather than he be seen to reject it and he was swiftly sacked from all positions for laziness. Eventually no longer tolerating his presence gnawing away at their gold coin, they decided to send him to Opicina, a predominantly Slovenian commune on the edge of the Karst, near Trieste.

Chapter 3

Opicina, Italy, Summer 1922

Vittorio was delivered to family associates, industrious folk, away from Monfalcone and nearer to Trieste. No need to mention the gold coin to these good people. On arrival, Mamma and Papa were joined by their three sons, perfect specimens of manhood, unable to conceal their interest in their new houseguest.

When the fisher folk departed, a slight figure peered around the kitchen door. Unruly earthy hair, roughly styled by her mother fell over her eyes. She warily slid along the wall into the room, moist palms flat to the rough white-washed stone. Peering through her curls, Mia marvelled at the remarkable being in their midst, clutching nervously at her dress - her mother's remodelled - feet bare. Vittorio's jacket was cut to show his slim athletic build, the gold collar pin catching a glint of afternoon sunlight through the open door.

She looked at him as if a movie star were in their midst, the most beautiful creature she had ever seen.

*

Mia and her parents had lived in Parenzo, a beautiful old fishing town on the Croatian coast before moving to Opicina. Three boisterous brothers had quickly followed and Mia withdrew into the background.

Her brothers would watch as Papa took the tram down to Trieste and when he returned, he would regale them with tales of his day.

'Can you believe what happened boys?' he would say.

Large childish eyes would look baffled until one would ask, 'Papa please tell us.'

When he had their undivided attention the story would emerge.

'Trieste is the Gateway to Zion,' he declared.

The three looked one to each other.

'Today, three hundred Hebrew folk arrived from Austria. Yes, men, women and children came by train and moved to hotels near the Jewish quarter. They are going to Palestine by ship, the land of their forefathers'.

This story had something of familiarity about it; hadn't their own Mamma and Papa had to leave their home in Parenzo?

'Is it a holiday, are they going to see relatives?' Claude the eldest had tried to fill in the gaps.

'Maybe, but it's not a holiday'. The boys looked blankly at each other.

'But why would anyone take a ship to see strangers?' Claude asked.

'It is dedication; they will be nearer to their God, that's why they go.'

The information had hung in the air between them, and though not always sure of the facts Papa would still carry the story as far as he could.

'So is their God different from our God Papa?' their youthful curiosity stirred with anxiety. At times like these the boys would glance at their mother for reassurance, as she worked at the table, the crude wooden crucifix, looming down from the wall behind her.

'Of course, we haven't lost our God, what nonsense' her words had flown as she hastily crossed herself. 'Monsignor, the Pope, and the Holy See will make sure of that.'

Looking sideways at his wife, her expression would usually tell him if he was getting out of his depth, but memories were stirring.

'When we lived in Parenzo.... I worked the fishing boats then....' Papa said.

'Why did you move, Papa?' Claude urged the story on.

'Others wanted to live there son, so we moved here to Trieste, but I could only get work on the quay.'

Rocco the youngest had been shoving a shoe around the floor making hooting sounds as Salvo, middle son, slow and brooding spoke. 'But we don't live in Trieste do we, we live in Opicina?' He beamed at catching his father out.

'Opicina is a commune of Trieste son, a neighbourhood.' Papa shook his head, teasing his wife. 'Mamma, do you teach these children nothing?'

She slammed the bread down into her rising bowl indicating the story had spiralled out of control and he quickly wound it up.

'So we moved here and I took a job on the quay at Trieste, as close to the sea as I could get,' looking covertly in her direction, 'until you get jobs as close to the sea as possible too,' checking he was back on the right track with her. 'It is the best job in the world. You just have to look at a fisherman to see honour and integrity running through their veins,' and swiftly wound up the tale.

*

Time had moved on, but the stories continued as Vittorio sat by the window bored.

Mia's brawny, inquisitive brothers were a contrast to her seemingly dim, bashful ways. Most of the time out of sight, she studied the stranger, head to one side eyeing him with deep brown, almost black eyes, he transcended any man seen in her world before.

On the odd occasion when they were alone, he would suddenly swing round and thump the table, laughing as she jumped.

19

'Oy Bambina!' he would yell to make sure she jumped again. She loved that he didn't call her *"Little Bird"*, like others, that he had his own pet name for her. These were special moments to treasure when they were alone, just the two of them. After the initial shock, nervous giggling would burst out sending her scurrying to the sanctuary of her kitchen to catch her breath.

They had both been born the same year, but everything else about them was opposite. Her skin was almost the same colour as her gold brown hair, bleached from washing clothes in the midday sun, outside in the stone sink, always working the hardest to prove her value, knowing she was different. Children had mocked her by making bird noises as they ran past. Her delicate nerves would jangle at their screams of laughter, self-doubt crawling through her like a worm as her mother had watched on sadly. No suitor had ever pursued her, no man noticing her modest, kind, gentle heart.

After Vittorio arrived, Mamma noticed a change; she was no longer content to wear simple remodelled old clothes. When mending she looked for trimming to put on pockets, or neatly shortened hems a little. Vittorio observed too, she started anchoring her unruly curls down with a conspicuous new tortoise-shell hair slide.

He considered her gauche, but with nothing else to occupy him, he studied her too. Her manners at the table were impeccable. She was obedient, hardworking, and comfortable in the company of her elders; she displayed respect, patience and was quick to obey. With a straight nose and blemish-free olive skin, her face revealed high cheekbones sweeping down to a jaw-line and lightly dimpled chin, her lips becoming fuller.

*

Times were changing. Claude and Salvo joined their father daily on the early morning trip to Trieste's Porto Vecchio to unload cargo on the huge new wharf. They cautiously eyed the glamorous haughty cosmopolitan ladies in their spare time. Rocco made room for Vittorio by joining the fishing folk at Monfalcone.

Nationalistic posters multiplied in all locations, discharging fascist persuasive slogans. It skimmed over the conscience of bohemian, cultured individuals who lounged stylishly in the smartest Trieste cafes.

Chapter 4

Opicina, Italy, early Autumn 1922

'Ciao Mamma, come va?' She spun around
    'Hello mother, how are you, what kind of way is that
to greet your mother?' arms raised to the Lord, for safe
deliverance home of her youngest.
    'Hey, cara Mamma, I've only been away a few weeks,'
as she grasped his head and kissed his forehead.
    'I'm well son, very well. Better even at seeing you,'
running her hands over his hair and shoulders, leaning
back to better assess his well being, outside the jurisdiction
of her care.
    'Your brothers will be home soon with Papa'.
    'I've brought fresh cod, caught by my own hands this
morning.' He yawned, thinking of the pre-dawn and shoved
the package at his mother. She fell upon his bag, finding
sardines and calamari too, wrapped in paper nests amongst
his clothes.
    'Ay, ay, ay, fish in your clothes? Cooking or washing -
what to do first?'
    'Mia, dirty clothes, your brother sleeps with fish and
wears them too.' She threw her hands to heaven and rushed
to the kitchen ushering her daughter to action.
    Rocco's venture into independent life had matured
his instincts, and instantly he noticed a difference in his big
sister. Over the next few hours he observed Vittorio,
hanging around the kitchen door more than any man
needed to, and decided to put his thoughts to Claude before
returning to the fishing village.

*

After evening meal he and Claude strolled towards the old
Obelisk on the outskirts of Opicina, falling into comfortable

conversation of his new life. The impressive pillar was a popular meeting place erected to commemorate the grand opening of the road to Trieste, establishing the firm intermingling of Slav and Italian communities. As they wandered, Rocco noticed the entrepreneurial endeavours of local traders and shuddered at the growing conflict between the communities, quickly diverting his thoughts to matters at hand.

'Claude, what do you make of Vittorio?' Claude stopped at the base of the grand monument, raising an arm to lean nonchalantly against the straight flat base, contemplating his query.

'Vittorio?' he rolled the name around his thoughts.

'Of course Vittorio! What, you don't know him? He lives in the same house as you?' Rocco's new life had liberated him from family hierarchy daring to challenge his elder brother, as Claude casually observed a girl with a bicycle turn into the lane to Prosecco.

'Won't be living with us for long,' Claude drew on his cigarette. ' After you left he found himself a job as an engineer at the hydro-electric power station on the old dock no less.'

'How did that happen?' Rocco asked.

'I don't know. I suppose Papa mentioned something to him, like when he got Salvo and me work unloading the ships, and of course the cranes are all operated by hydro-electric power now,' Claude replied.

'I thought he was hanging around under Mamma's feet all the time?' Rocco's concern for Little Bird Mia resurfaced. 'When will he be moving?'

'I don't know I'm not there all the time, am I?' Claude's interest was elsewhere, and in typical Italian masculine manner made his irritation felt. Rocco raised his hands in submission, hunched his shoulders and cursed with equal drama.

A short exchange of oaths followed as the girl with the bike travelled out of sight. Claude ground his cigarette into the floor and turned to follow her down the lane and Rocco put the discussion aside. The stir Vittorio had caused in the local female population hadn't gone unnoticed by Claude either it seemed.

They sauntered in the direction of the girl, finding her struggling to get the chain back on her tired old bike, shaken loose by the rough lane. Rocco wondered at the direction of their walk, and now all was revealed. Claude casually wandered over to her as if by chance, as she gracefully stepped aside.

Rocco looked down the rocky escarpment towards Trieste; the conflicting rough terrain represented the growing tensions between the two communities more and more, and remembered how his own parents had been refugees once, safer they thought in this Slav community.

A lick of cold air blasted the back of his head as without warning an icy eruption shunted air from his lungs. The first thrust of autumn's Bora wind rammed down from the Karst above, before barrelling over the precipice towards the city. The girl delicately held her skirts and Claude consolidated his chance by graciously protecting her with his jacket, and taking the bicycle, he started to wheel it back towards the Obelisk.

The vicious airstream, having arrived for its' annual terror, had assisted Claude with the meeting he'd been seeking. Rocco followed in their wake, unsettled still. As the handsome lodger was moving on, hopefully Mia would return to her usual domestic serenity.

Chapter 5

Opicina, Italy, late Autumn 1922

When Vittorio arrived in banishment to Opicina, he adjusted smoothly, seeking to make this stay as comfortable and short as possible. He adopted politeness personified to Mia's mother, was respectful to the father as head of the family and indicated any suggestion of chasing local girls, far from his thoughts to the brothers. Any interest in Mia was deflected by the bond he manufactured with the rustic brothers; it was surely unthinkable he would pursue a friend's sister?

Recognising he was no physical match for her protectors, and considering their intellect no match for his, he considered the youngest and most gullible. Rocco, usually last in line, and heard the least, appeared only too happy to be picked as his new confidant. The other two followed like dominoes until Vittorio felt they were sufficiently under his spell to manipulate as he wished.

Mia remained in the kitchen with Mamma most of the time, to protect her from boisterous conversation. She took her meals alone to save the embarrassment of eating in front of a stranger, while the men gathered around the scrubbed wooden table in the front room. Mamma would bustle in and out with different dishes and join her when the men were satisfied, to shield her from uncomfortable new experiences.

After a while, inexplicable emotional outbursts from Mia started to draw attention. Dropping something in the kitchen would result in sobbing; making a mistake when mending resulted in her harshly reprimanding herself.

'Child, what is the matter with you?' Mamma admonished. ' All you did was lose your thread,' which resulted in more snuffling as her mother watched cautiously. Initially, outbursts were explained by the anxiety of sharing her home with a stranger, until she recognised her daughter's shame, by which time, Vittorio had left to take up his impressive employment at Porto Vecchio, and lodging in Trieste.

Claude and Salvo thought Iva's outbursts were a sign she missed the brief tokens of attention Vittorio had given her out of pity, baffled when teasing her resulted in crying. Reality set in after a meeting with Mamma. There could be no wavering, father must never know of Mia's shame and dilemma, and an urgent message was sent to Rocco requesting his immediate attendance back home in Opicina.

In Monfalcone the memory of the haughty interloper still hung like a whiff of distaste with the fisher folk, and he was given immediate leave from employment.

*

Mia's predicament, and the collective preservation of family honour, determined the brothers stop at nothing and force Vittorio to do his duty and marry her, no matter how much it might displease. Ruining her reputation would destroy their standing in the community and her life forever. Simple and un-worldly their ambitions, haughty their morals, failure was out of the question in forcing a marriage. Claude considered the implications would reverberate throughout the town, and on his long sought after association with the bicycle girl.

Unless for work, they avoided travel to Trieste, roaming only as far as the Prosecco track to watch fine liners taking travellers to Israel, as Papa had told. Sometimes cargo ships came from the four corners of earth, laden with luxuries, or they would gaze down at Castle Miramare teetering romantically on the edge of the sea. Strapping men, they were more comfortable with a simple life, the city held nothing they chose to entertain. Visiting involved stepping side to side, nipping in and out of crowds of people to get anywhere. There, men donned their finest attire, ladies their most elegant hats and promenaded from stylish cafe to smart hotel, partaking in coffee or aperitif, exchanging pleasantries with acquaintances or making contacts with persons of influence and interest. A sophisticated centre of music and literature, the rich and famous residing comfortably alongside the wealthy influential Jewish community; it wasn't for fisher-folk like them.

*

Not wishing to cause gossip, the brothers made their way to Campo Romano on the outskirts of Opicina mid morning to travel down to the city. Waiting for the tram, they avoided eye contact as they contemplated the imminent confrontation. Salvo dragged the dust back and forth at his feet as they waited, a vicious kick accompanied the arrival of the tram.

They hung back to sit as privately as possible, and having already talked tactics found a certainty of outcome in revisiting their plan until Salvo erupted.

'When I get him in front of me, I'll smash his brains,' hacking the wooden slats of the tram floor with his boot. The others shot hasty looks around checking passengers' reactions, alarmed at the rapid clenching and unclenching of his mighty fists, until Claude spoke.

'Salvo, quieten yourself. That old woman at the front is not a deaf as she pretends. Hold your temper.'

'I'll break his scrawny neck,' he muttered.

'Be quiet. We have a cunning snake to challenge and it's decided, we confront him at his workplace where he can't ignore us and won't want to have a scene, make him face his responsibilities,' he reasoned.

Rocco, better at handling his rustic brother added, 'Salvo, if all else fails you have permission to beat him to a pulp if you like.'

Claude shot a look at the youngster of the family, taken aback at his lead, but remained silent, it wasn't the time to act on being usurped, and Rocco continued.

'We use diplomacy if we can. Remember it is our sister's future we have to think about, and that means his also. We need to make him do the right thing,' He paused. 'Our aim is to make Vittorio become Mia's husband, and our brother-in-law too remember, so dial down the strong arm stuff, yes?'

Claude leaned back against wooden seat rungs of the bench, looking moodily at the city below, the motion of the tram rubbed the slats against his spine. So much was to change. His sister would acquire a husband; his youngest brother had become a man. Salvo, still the brawny hulk who thought with his hands, rising to anger too quickly. They fell silent, each regarding the rocky incline with clutches of scrub here and there.

'Those bushes cling to rocks as precariously as we cling to hope' Claude thought. *'So many futures on our shoulders'*, as he considered the unborn child.

Chapter 6

Trieste, Italy, late Autumn 1922

One thousand feet later they had descended into Trieste alighting at Piazza Oberdan. It was lunchtime as they briskly made their way toward the twin brick towers of the hydro-electric station that powered Porto Vecchio. Disappointment sapped determination, resolve evaporated, when they discovered siesta had already begun. Most of the workforce were home for lunch and rest, Vittorio included and the custodian of the entrance was irritated by their unwelcome interruption to his break.

A gust blew around the cuffs of their simple clothes, as they stood on the quay deflated at the deserted entrance. Not yet winter they had hardly noticed the Bora wind gathering but the icy blasts fused with their anger and resentment. Thwarted and disappointed they took to surrounding streets to find an open cafe. Prominently displayed in the window of one, ensuring no one misunderstood the proprietor's position, yet another poster of Il Duce Benito Mussolini, chin stone-square, the personification of authority.

The owner leant forward over a newspaper spread before him on the counter as they clattered into the empty space. He eyed them carefully sliding forward several well-fingered pamphlets championing Trieste's Italianization, asking if they would like to read while waiting for their coffee. One celebrated that only two years previously the huge modern Slovene National Centre in Trieste had been destroyed by fire. The act of nationalistic purification had been praised by Mussolini at the time as *"a masterpiece of Triestine fascism"*. The brothers were aware of the Black Shirts' deeds, yet in Opicina, Italian and Slovene still lived side by side, squabbles resolved quickly and privately, but their parents ethnic flight from Parenza was never far from their minds.

'Grazie,' Claude sensed the importance of accepting the proprietor's gesture and took a leaflet. Life was becoming too complicated all round, but he knew the action would mark them down as untainted Italian stock, and enemy of the Slovene, and he could see that refusal would not get them served.

They took the table in the furthest corner, hunching over coffees still retaining the wary eye of the owner as he idly re-positioned to listen to their conversation as best he could. When *"hydro-electric station"* rose out of their whispers, the owner asked if they were looking for work. Claude took the opportunity to engage in conversation about local workers, especially new ones as the proprietor declared there wasn't anything he didn't know about the area. He had cleared tables and washed dishes there since he was eight he declared, and enjoying his audience began to pontificate on the rise and fall of different commercial enterprises in the area.

'Take the rice factory, Risiere di San Sabba for example, a great employer of locals in the rice husking business,' hoping to urge them towards employment as prospective new customers. 'It was built twenty odd years ago but it's expanded now.' He scrutinised them hunched in the corner, as he turned newspaper pages without looking at them.

Getting no response, he returned to the original subject declaring the hydro-electric plant an example of superior Italian industry, but couldn't vouch for the workers adding, 'Now then, there is talk of a new electricity plant to be built up the hill, only a mile away.'

Claude hoped he wouldn't turn his attention to Il Duce Benito Mussolini again as the proprietor persisted on his theme.

'Italy must surely be thriving in these economically uncertain days, for Trieste to have two power stations.' The brothers stared blankly, uncommitted.

'Doesn't it only validate Benito's philosophy? King Emmanuel lll inviting him to form a government was a masterpiece of intent,' the man obviously an enthusiastic exponent of the growing fascist regime.

'What would we have done if Benito hadn't taken steps to unite the country, make it independent, and promote self-sufficiency to feed the state? Five governments since 1919 and not one able to rid us of the economic strife the Great War left us with? Strikes and riots? Ha!' Claude's head drooped, as the man addressed Il Duce in first name terms, firmly affiliating himself to his hero.

'What happens when the workers move around so much, and I have my livelihood to think about?' he continued. Sweat and blustering dialogue gave way to a confusing conflict of interests, as he bemoaned the loss of business when the Slovenes were driven out of work by the Black Shirts.

Claude's patience was growing thin and they left, he needed to get the brothers moving towards the old port and heading for the main entrance. The stress and delay at the café had only heightened their urgency, as rounding the corner, they spotted Vittorio's unmistakable saunter a short distance ahead.

'Hey you there, Marchetti, wait!' Salvo's deep, rough tones cut through the blasting wind. His shouts went unheeded yet a noticeable stiffening of Vittorio's back and shoulders propelled him swiftly into the mingling crowd. The brothers broke into a run, Claude reaching him first, yanking his arm back within yards of disappearing through the entrance.

Chapter 7

Trieste, Italy, late Autumn 1922

Vittorio turned, throwing his arms up in welcome, straight white teeth bared, his handsome features cracked around an unnatural smile. For a second the younger two grinned back, their quest momentarily forgotten. Smile widening Vittorio patted them on the shoulders, and excused himself from the scene.

'Hey boys, it's wonderful to see you. What a life, work, work and more work. I would tell you but....' He shrugged, hands spread in resignation at his predicament to return inside, adding dismissively, 'I cannot be late for business of this nature,' and turned away.

Claude's large hand pitched forward again, swinging him around, foiling his crafty escape. Vittorio cast his gaze at them for the briefest moment. Assessing further attempts to brush them aside to be futile and unexpectedly pulled Claude towards him in embrace, patting his shoulder heartily, regaining the commanding position and continuing conspiratorially.

'There are things about which I must talk with you my friend, delicate things. I have wanted to ask you for some time....' The intriguing pause hung in the air between them as he re-assessed his position.

'But as you see, and I know you will understand, any man worth his place with a family, he paused, 'must provide a good living and prove himself,' he whispered.

Claude was not the rustic fool Vittorio had assumed and stood firm, dark brown eyes drilling back, not to be brushed off so lightly.

Vittorio continued, 'Although I haven't been in touch these past weeks, as you can see I am working hard to establish myself with a good income. Time and exhaustion separated me from my intentions and now, here you are,' he attempted further delay and avoidance, in the game of thrust and parry. 'I cannot, no, no, I will not disgrace myself in the eyes of my good employers, draw shame or distrust upon myself, so I must beg to leave you now.'

Three pairs of angry eyes stared back. 'I will call upon you when I next have time off work.' Self-assured, confident, a friendly pat on Claude's shoulder indicated the brothers were dismissed.

Vittorio supposed simple fishing folk like these would not be able to hold their resolve or confidence for Mia's honour, could be put in their place, and turning to go anticipated this time his discharge absolute.

Claude immoveable, presented the game still on, he would have no release yet. Vittorio looked down at the huge weather-beaten fist, fingertips overlapping around his arm, in his smart new winter coat. It didn't escape the brother protector he had been spending handsomely on himself, thinking nothing of Mia, in her re-knitted woollen jacket.

Their adversary bared his teeth, as a gust of wind whipped away hissed oaths. A simple twist and his arm could be snapped like a twig.

He considered for a moment. If he allowed them to use strength and fists he could play the victim, they would be incarcerated by the Carabinieri, never in a position to trouble him again, probably lose their jobs too.

It wasn't difficult to grasp why they were there. He had completely beguiled Mia with his dashing looks, sophisticated ways and persuasive charm, her seduction had been an easy diversion in the boredom. Resting a hand on her arm a little too long or casually breathing on her neck as he passed her had broken her noble resolve. Taking a flick of hair from her face as her doe eyes looked up through curls, then gently running a finger down her back for the briefest moment, stirring her work-weary body to a quiver, it had all been so easy. But he considered now, gossip about her ruin would soon dictate her shame, and reflect on his character too.

He employed stealth and guile to restore the upper hand, the brothers taken aback when no further argument came. Flinging an almost celebratory embrace at Claude with one arm, the other around Salvo he proclaimed sincerely to be free the very next weekend, a trip to Opicina already planned, begging to speak with them alone before visiting their father. His detached cold stare merged with blasting squalls of wind as he assessed their reaction.

The brothers fell back, agreeing to meet at the Obelisk where he was to ask permission of them, something of the greatest importance regarding Mia, before speaking to her father, and confident he'd regained control, departed.

*

They passed the railway station in silence and deep contemplation.

'Let's wait in the public garden for the tram,' Rocco first to speak.

They made their way through narrow streets until the huge Synagogue loomed. Its bold grey and white exterior rose majestically, completed only ten years previously, a symbol of Trieste's respect for their Jewish friends as much of the city's wealth rested on their shoulders and initiative. Only three years before the Hebrew community had rallied to the unification of Italy, had used its illustrious business, academic and high political office to the cause of Il Duce.

The Great Temple's huge rose window regarded them solemnly as they passed below, uncomfortable wisps of unease rising in them in its presence and they abandoned the park, turning towards the tram terminus.

Salvo always preferred to contemplate rather than agitate the air with words looked back over his shoulder recalling his childish question about how the Jewish God might be different to theirs. As a man, he had learned how their community had been established in Trieste for centuries, hundreds of pilgrims passing through the port every year visiting the synagogue; was it not even the fourth largest in Europe. Certainly their God was popular but then, he pondered, so was the Pope's.

*

On the tram, Rocco spoke first about the ramifications of the day.

'It sounded as if he is going to ask for Mia's hand,' he paused for a response. 'Certainly, he's gone out of his way to get lucrative employment.'

Claude reminded them he hadn't said as much, simply implied it, and their sister knew nothing of any promise.

Sitting on facing benches they leaned toward each other. 'We have to keep the secret and remain vigilant.' Rocco moved to speak as Claude cut him off reasserting his seniority.

'We can only hope and pray that marriage is his intention and he'll keep his word. It all depends on this weekend.' He reminded them of their sister's honour, the secret from their father, they must not lose sight of marriage at the earliest opportunity, time was of the essence.

When Rocco suggested the Monsignor be informed Claude remarked, he probably already knew if Mia had dared to meet her sacred commitments.

Hearts heavy, limbs tired from battling weather and confrontation, they returned to Opicina stopping at the first trattoria, a change of behaviour for the temperate men, and a first for Rocco. There was hope, it was all they had. Flushed with events of the day, and inauguration into a man's world he bought the wine. Salvo pondered in silence as he mulled over their first uncomfortable encounter at the café and the image of the stately Temple of Jerusalem lingering in his consciousness.

For Claude, there was only one standpoint - to save Mia's honour.

Chapter 8

Redcar, England, late Autumn 1922

Roy couldn't forget the words, his prosperous Baptist family frequently uttered to him, _"The easiest way is not always the right way,"_ no matter how hard he tried. With his liberal character, he fell in comfortably with the people of Redcar, zealous Chapel upbringing out of mind, back in Wales.

When he met Rose, life took an unexpected curve. For a small north-east fishing town she was different, eyeing him brazenly with unwavering, hooded stares, more confident than a young woman should be. She thought nothing of telling him he was wrong, giggled at his Welsh accent, mocked his clothes, her boldness leaving an unaccountable craving when she flicked him a last glance and moved on.

It was entirely baffling to him, he thought her far too familiar. From a large family, she knew most of the people in town, easily holding her own with a mischievousness he didn't expect. Catcalling and sniping she soon had his attention, then chuckling, was off leaving his head reeling.

Not the best-looking girl he thought, eyelids heavy, nose straight, perhaps a little too long, lips not full. Her stare said she saw straight through him and didn't hang around waiting for favours or attention, simply took what she wanted of his time and left. Her clothes were simple, her figure more fleshy than comely, but her daring eyes had him smitten.

Both born in 1898 the similarity ended there. Rose's father from London, mother from farming stock, the two had come together around the new ironstone mine near New Marske and they rubbed along lovingly together, ten of their thirteen children surviving. Hard work, enterprise and application had elevated them to a modest confectioners business on Redcar High Street, though Rose's nature left her untroubled by status, more interested in fun and cheeky vexation.

*

Roy and Rose gravitated towards each other in decreasing circles, culminating in an enforced marriage, a baby boy born a month later, only to die within a week, and so their mismatched union began.

Despite Roy's displeasure, Rose continued her boisterous friendships and when their second child, Cissy, was born he insisted they honour his preacher forefather, the Reverend Michael.

'The girl gets his name as well, every child in the family does.' Roy's Welsh brogue had lost most of its' romantic fascination for her, but despite declining interest in each-other she never abandoned an impish argument.

'Michael?' she would retort, 'Give a girl a man's name, that won't happen.'

'We all got it, the lad that died, he got it.' He thought of the poor mite who'd joined them for all eternity. 'So she gets it too,' he was determined.

'You're so la-di-da,' she'd reply, gauging her words to raise Roy's temper a notch.

*

Four years had passed since Cissy Michel was born and he still couldn't believe the woman. She was about to give birth to their third child and the same arguments resurrected.

'Rose, you know too well it's our tradition. You know how my family would view it if the baby didn't honour Reverend Michael.'

'So your family wants everyone to have the Reverend's name? What's so special about your family...?'

'It's a privilege you lazy mare.' The words echoed around the bare room. 'We've been through all this with the lad that died and Cissy already,' he glared. 'And it'll be bestowed whether it's a girl or boy, it always is,' he paused, 'especially if the marriage isn't expected to last.'

Rose's mouth hung open.

'At least not by the father?' she added.

For once she fell silent, her eyes following his back as he slammed the door behind him.

Despite continuous quarrels the family was growing, the baby due and they were about to be evicted. Roy declared she lacked interest in the home, she argued his work as a groom journeyman didn't bring the money in and the rift grew.

*

Torrents of rain flew sideways as they dragged their wretched belongings through the streets that night. Rose yanked young Cissy by one hand, with pots wrapped in old blankets under her other arm, bedding and clothes bundled under Roy's canvas duster coat for protection.

Cissy whined, dragging her feet as cold rain pricked her face, running down her neck until a thump to her back spurned her on. Even at this young age, she knew she couldn't get a proper clout from her Mam with her hands full, but rankling her relieved the trudge and she was satisfied with the small triumph.

They reached the horse trader's big house behind St Peter's Church, trekked across the mud, down Bum Alley passed the donkeys, to the abandoned railway carriage in the far corner. A sullen lithe fellow barred the way as Roy opened the door attempting entry without invitation. Rose and Cissy stood in the downpour as Roy slung clothes and bedding into the middle of the floor. They looked up at the streaked window where a faint light flickered, as rain splashing the mud, splattering the back of Cissy's legs. Irritation seethed as she contemplated the chance of getting

39

away with another annoyance to break the tedium until loud voices and scuffling inside the carriage grabbed her attention.

Roy appeared at the door, 'Your father's promised it to me, and that's it. You're out and I'm in.'

The shouting had drawn an older man from the house, making his way towards the commotion. As a part-time groom, Roy wasn't entitled to the carriage but he had played his cards hard, needing somewhere for Rose to have the baby, the boss finally giving in.

'Get you stuff kiddo, you're in the house,' he said to his son.

'I'm not budging dad, you said I was to be staying here, my own little house, like. I'm not going no-where.'

'You don't need it son. Get your stuff and skedaddle.'

'He's only here now and again,' the lad protested, 'and you don't know 'ow long he'll stay, or you mightn't even be able to get rid of them.'

The disgruntled occupant wasn't going without a fight but eyeing the dripping couple in the mud, his argument was getting thinner. 'And what if they do a midnight flit?'

'He's here and he'll stay as long as I say,' the farmer ordered. 'Journeyman he may be but he's got a family to feed. Now get your things for the morning and get back in the house.'

The boss's gaze wandered to the carriage smeared with rain and muck. He knew his son had been sweet on Rose once, and despite loyalty to his own, he would let them stay; and observing her swollen belly, held his boy had made a lucky escape. A cheery girl she may be, but a right handful too.

'Get going now.'

The lad was stunned into silence by his father's tone as he added, 'Roy get your wife and the girl in here quick.'

The boss stepped forward and as a matter of decency threw the rest of their things in and passed Cissy up for them. His son shot Rose a look he hoped would sting like the rain, hoping she would have to haul herself and big belly up on her own, and satisfied it would be no easy task, sloped off.

Roy's wiry frame heaved Rose up the three-foot in one pull and for a moment the three of them sat where they could, exhausted. A small pot-bellied fire warmed the carriage more than Cissy thought possible. Soon layers of wet clothes were coming off as she started to nod off in the comforting heat, Rose throwing less damp layers over her as she slid to slumber.

Rain stopped the next day, the outlook misty and cold, with Rose greedily burning wood stacked in the corner, relishing the warmth that had worked through to her bones, and complaining to Roy when the boss expected her to pay for more. Nine months pregnant, being damp and hungry had done nothing to pacify her lively tongue or lessened her amusement protesting her sorry state to him.

*

Roy was in and out all day and much of the evening, grooming and butchering for the boss, some of the time just avoiding Rose. Cissy made a game of making a bed for herself on a raggedy pile of hay sacks, and Roy found some money for wood when the baby boy was born early the next October morning.

Rose cheerfully accepted hot tea, bread and cheese sent from the boss's wife, begrudgingly delivered by the evicted son. The horse trader's wife knew Rose well and secretly admired her cheerful, emancipated attitude, nonetheless hoping complications would be avoided with the sorry tribe off elsewhere soon. Meanwhile, Roy assisted with a complicated birthing for the boss's best mare, cementing their mutual respect.

However, in the railway carriage, the discussions continued.

'I'm not calling him Edwin Michael. This baby's name is Ted. You can call him what you like, but I'm calling him Ted, so stick that in your pipe,' Rose had spoken.

'I'm calling 'im Sonny 'cos he's your son and I think he's like the sun in the sky,' young Cissy was learning fast at her mother's knee.

*

By the time Rose's fourth was due she had rubbed the horse trader's back up the wrong way one too many times. Roy said he would stay to see the baby born safely, but would then be off, throwing doubt over the child's parentage, and stuck to his word. Before Stanley's birth, Roy's trips south looking for better work had become longer and longer, Rose regarding his growing absences with disdain.

'Bet it's not just work yer getting,' she would say.

'Pot calling the kettle black woman' he growled back slamming the door for the last time. Rose and her three surviving children had to leave the railway carriage and Roy was never seen again.

Chapter 9

Opicina, Italy, December 1922

Blasts of air skirled and snatched at clothes as the cold downdraft of the Bora collided with the warm air edging Trieste, whipping at the waves below. Little Bird Mia, eyes modestly cast to the ground, held down the hem of her skirt as best she could. Flanked by Mamma and Papa, and followed by her brothers, they walked through the narrow streets towards the 13th century church, the icy wind stinging their skin.

The Church of San Bartolomeo Apostolo sat amid a snake nest of roads, all named Via Prosecco,spewing out from the plain towering walls that rose heavenward towards retribution and consolation. Neighbours and friends followed the wedding party, respectfully proceeding to the church with its' semi-circle of grass at the rear, one lone tree at its centre. Mia's eyes lifted as they neared, hesitating as her line of sight locked upon the battered solitary shrub, a reflection of her morally distressing predicament.

A knot of tension grasped her as blood rushed behind her dizzied eyes, palpitations exploding, her heart pounding. She swayed.

'Mia,' Mamma whispered, 'don't let your spirit fail you now child,' catching her elbow.

Her tender grasp on the dried wedding flowers in her hands loosened, as they whipped away on the wind. The Bora gaining strength as hers dissolved, the bouquet now mere sticks in the air.

The little procession hesitated as Claude turned to her.

'He's here Mia, he waits for you,' grabbing her elbow. They progressed ever more slowly around the side of the church, the old trees at the front shaking their brittle branches as if in admonishment at her shame. As the group gathered at the front, Claude raised his eyes to the clock high above the door. He rested his hand on his sister's arm, eyes warm, love unconditional, whatever. It was time.

*

Vittorio sat alone, his head dutifully lowered in pious, composed demeanour, eyes cast down as if in prayer as he played with the diamond signet ring on the little finger of his left hand, admiring the stone. His future was mapped out and he twisted it round and round violently until the skin ran smooth and red. Removing it he placed it on his right hand in readiness for the wedding band.

Saints looked down gravely on the finely attired man in the silent empty church, his life as family provider and protector now foretold, inconceivable his actual thoughts. Mussolini had declared *"The state of the nation is bound up with their powers of reproduction"*, and sitting impassively Vittorio considered himself the very embodiment of Italy's nationalistic future. The marriage would make him the archetypical family man, a symbol of stability. He was already turning the situation at work to his advantage, laying down plans for his advancement in fascist Italy, all born of this folly. An imperceptible, wry turn at the corner of his mouth, could be observed by the apostles alone.

A shaft of light cast down the central aisle as the old wooden doors scraped open. Vittorio raised himself in one dignified movement turning to glimpse the slight figure at the entrance. The intense light in the door-space behind her quickly filled with muscular, serious figures, heads straining, assuring themselves of his presence. He stood alone, no member of his family had been prepared to join him on the memorable day. Relief surged through the brothers' tense muscles at his presence, the very air of the church lightened as the saints looked down kindly on

44

innocent, naive Mia who never doubted her handsome paramour. Hadn't he respectfully asked her brothers' permission before approaching Papa for her hand, and they attested to her father of the innocence of their relationship? Only Mamma's creased brow, eyes glistening, hinted at a different tale.

Mia advanced half way down the aisle towards her beloved, crossed herself, kissed her well-worn rosary and curtsied to the cross behind the altar whispering,

'Lord you have brought us together and will guide us through life.'

Borrowed shoes pinched her feet and grazed the stone slab floor, her best dress stretched tightly across her middle.

Reaching the statue of the Blessed Virgin Mary, Mater Dolorosa, the Sorrowful Mother, she paused. Looking at the beloved figure, seven swords of sorrow piercing her heart, gazing heavenward in abject misery, pleading for blessed relief, left hand clutching her breast, Mia clutched her rosary to her stomach, hastily crossing herself again. Having spent many hours in devotion to the Sorrowful Mother, her prayers had been blessed, she had been delivered from shame, her love for Vittorio sanctified.

Turning, the congregation scattered among the pews, throwing a blinding shaft of light across the Tabernacle from the empty door space, casting the groom's side into shadow, cloaking Vittorio from her sight. Peering into the dim light she began to sway again, as if her next step would take her into a black void, a disorientating unfamiliar world without him. The Monsignor chanted Latin verse, and a soothing cloak of gentle familiarity washed over her, the moment of dark trepidation, a caution for the future, forgotten.

Chapter 10

Opicina, Italy, August 1923

Ophelia was born, at their house with a little balcony in Opicina, August, 1923, a snub-nosed, round-faced beloved darling. Long perfect fingers grasping and inquisitive, flawless olive skin enhanced by white, hand-made lace dresses, sewn by Mia herself. Giggling and squirming, the blessed child that bound them, even entertained Vittorio with her bright antics, until she began to grow pale. Her little body frightened Mia as she slowly stopped feeding, laid lethargically, moaning and crying. The doctor diagnosed leukaemia and her little angel died after only one birthday.

*

Nothing could transport Mia through her grief. Weeks turned to months, then seasons; Vittorio's romantic manoeuvres no longer enchanted, and not even his beauty could persuade her to accept his nightly affections. At every opportunity she visited her mother, staying for days, Vittorio sitting at the kitchen table, back to her, demanding, *'When will she ever stop? The child is gone,'* his patience depleted.

Mia's mother, no stranger to grief for a lost child, realised she would lose not only her husband, but her home and standing in the community. Vittorio had none of the kindness she had hoped for her daughter, concerned only with his star rising in Mussolini's new world. He had aspirations, was moving through the ranks, tactically positioning himself to attain a prestigious new post, available only for the right stock, and all there for his taking. Weakness was not an option for Mia as she drifted towards life as a spurned wife, disgrace and embarrassment for them all.

When Ophelia died, Mia continued her devotions to Mater Dolorosa. She believed the Sorrowful Mother had protected and saved her from shame when Vittorio married her, but his brutal demands revealed the darkness within him, and with no concern for their baby's death, her spirit wilted and she turned to her mother. She was the commanding force within the family directing all towards good decisions, maintaining respectability in the community, her husband, a good man, believing every decision was his own. When he spoke all fell silent in respect, reminded of her words, *"Father is the soul of the family"*. Her mother knew Vittorio would not wait forever for his absent wife, her mission was to cajole Mia back to the world of the living - with another baby.

She coaxed her to believe a babe in arms would cure her malaise, enlisting neighbouring mothers to feign a need to leave their offspring in her care, as she watched cautiously from the kitchen. Vittorio considered his wife should uphold her domestic and wifely duties, and came to take their home. Awareness of her surroundings began to creep back into her numb, wounded, heart, shrunken from her loss and in time a second daughter was born in 1926, the same month, almost to the day, beloved Ophelia was lost. They named her Bianca. She had beauty and purity Mia's Mamma declared, and would bloom at her breast.

But her agony was unquenched by the innocent child who could understand nothing of her mother's tears. Somewhere within her innocent little heart a kernel germinated laying down the awareness she would come to know, that in her darkest hours, she would always be alone.

Bianca would lay untouched in her cot, as empty eyes looked down, bitter tears dripping at Mia's barely audible words, *'I want my baby, not you,'* and the wailing would begin. *'Where is she, my lovely, my darling? Not you,*

never you.' slumping to her knees, to be lifted from the
floor again, put to bed, again.

Chapter 11

Redcar, England, 1926

'Come on, your turn now Ted, up on the stool.' The little boy with wavy, angelic hair, chubby cheeks and a sweet mouth looked up at his mother Rose, eyes wide with concern.

'Get yerself up there,' she, no time for messing, edging a look towards the front door of Gale's Photography Studio. No more than four years old, in smart brown leather shoes, he stumbled awkwardly in the direction of the wicker stool, the photographer swinging him up to his seat as his mother snatched another furtive glance at the door.

'Now then, Ted?' The photographer stepped back and surveyed his timid little model, eyes brimming. Kneeling before him, Mr Gale looked at the terrified boy, 'No need to worry so much lad, this is going to be fun, you watch.'

'How long's this gonna take?' Rose had sidled even closer to the door, looking up and down the High Street. Sister, Cissy, in peril of being squashed against the wall, expertly dodged aside.

'Mrs Jones it takes as long as it takes, this is an artful process, and it'll take less time if you stop interrupting.'

Having put up with her interference for half an hour while taking young Cissy's portrait, he was about ready to call an end to proceedings. It had been awkward verging on impudent; their mother agitating no end and the girl had a smart mouth too with the session now running late. She would just have to wait.

'He's not called Ted.' Cissy's voice sliced through the photographer's nerves adding to the urgency, his frustrated expression thrown heavenward. Mr Gale sighed and turned to eye the little madam.

'He's not called Ted, we call 'im Sonnie. That's 'is name to us, that's what we call 'im,' she clarified.

'How long is this gonna take?' Rose piped up again.

He turned, ready to lay down the law, moisture welling up in the child's eyes ready to spill, and appreciated the boy's discomfort.

'Please, be a little quiet so I can finish properly.' His words were lost, her back to him now as he heard the familiar click of the key in the door.

'Mrs Jones what are you doing, unlock the front door right now?'

'It's alright,' she dismissed his request, ' it's just to keep it closed, it was rattling terrible like, letting a draught in,' her face, a vision of innocence.

'Unlock the door, Mrs Jones. How is a customer supposed to get in?'

'No bother, I'll stand here and let anyone in.'

'Madam, I'll say it again. Unlock the door.'

'Just do the photograph, I'll watch the door, and the sooner the picture's done, we can go.'

Mr Gale couldn't argue with the logic. The quicker he photographed the child, the three of them would be out the door, and turned back to the youngster on the stool.

'Ted, I mean Sonnie, look at me child,' the big blue eyes looked up in apprehension, one hand nervously picking at the corner of the stool the other grasping the edge with vice-like fingers.

'Just one moment.' Ever the perfectionist he nimbly knelt before the boy and crossed his ankles at the smart leather boots, completing the pose.

A clattering at the door drew his attention as a woman outside frantically tried to get in. Rose, having turned her back on the door, hung on to the handle behind her for dear life, eyes cast to the ceiling in flawless piety.

'Ow long's it going to take Mr Gale? Need to get on you know,' a sudden, unexpected deference to her tone.

'What are you doing Mr Jones? There's someone at the door, let her in at once.'

'Mam, missus from next door's outside. Ow!' Cissy's practised expertise at avoiding a clip around the ear failing her this time.

'It's nothing Mr Gale, everyone admires your pictures. She just wants to interfere,' adding conspiratorially, 'gets herself all worked up you know - I know her well,' laying praise and blame in equal proportions while earnestly demonstrating an expression of wide-eyed virtue.

'Mrs Jones, let her in now,' he demanded again.

An ominous click of the key preceded a tirade of abuse and commotion entering the room, a certain amount of scuffling finally pinning Cissy to the wall as the two women squashed bosom to bosom in the tight entrance.

'Mrs Jones, what is happening?' He turned toward the pair in the doorway, thought twice, and stepped behind his nervous model.

'What 'ave you done with my son's boots?' the woman yelled.

'Don't worry, she's always a bit like this. Too excitable by half; it affects her health it does.' Rose's voice rising easily above the hubbub.

'I want my boy's boots; he needs them for Sunday school tomorrow.'

'There, isn't that what I told you? Lent me the boots she did, and now wants 'em back, right off.'

'I did not lend them!' the woman squealed.

'Is that when you went round yesterday, Mam?' Cissy wiser from her first clip, nipped behind the intruder and continued. 'Thought you said you didn't like her much.' A boggle-eyed glare from her mother, enough to end her fun.

'Lent them you did,' Rose declared righteously. 'I said to you, *"Would be lovely if my boy could borrow them for the photograph."*'

'And I never said you could borrow them. I said, *"my husband wouldn't like me lending things, 'specially to you".'*

'There you are, never said you wouldn't did you?' Rose crossed her arms below her plenty some chest, satisfied at regaining the upper ground in the dispute.

'But, I never said.... I never thought... you.... Just give me my boys' boots!' the interloper fairly yelped.

'Take the photograph quick Mr Gale, she's gonna blow.' Rose viewed the photographer over her shoulder, virtuous satisfaction emblazoned all over her face. 'Hasn't got a leg to stand on has she?'

The photographer looked at the child, who hadn't moved a muscle from his pose, looking up with confused, pleading eyes at Mr Gale, the only haven in the maelstrom.

The boy's knitted, woollen, romper suit and matching knee socks completing the image, he took his chance. Click. The one and only picture, snapped.

The woman pushed through the doorway, yanking at the neat little boots laced tightly around Sonnie's ankles.

'How's he gonna get home with no shoes on his feet, poor mite?' Rose shrieked comfortably over the hullabaloo, barring any easy exit with her well-covered frame. The tableau of characters all looked to the four-year-old child, clear blue eyes glistening, Mr Gale retreating, very much hoping he was surplus to requirements.

'He can wear 'em home but I'm coming with you to make sure I get 'em back, do you hear?' the woman declared.

'You can please yourself,' Rose tightened her arms under her abundant breasts, and shrugged, head to one side.

As the small crowd spilled out through the now unguarded door, Rose's utterances carried cheerfully over her shoulder, 'See you next week then, to pick up them photos.' She paused looking at her neighbour, saying, 'Eee, what you like?'

The flushed expression of the invader, hat askew, exhausted from a fight she'd always suspected there was little chance of winning, cautiously eyed her back.

'Back to mine for a brew then?' Rose declared unconcerned.

Her opponent, attempting magnanimity in defeat, with more than a little uncertainty in her eye, looked into the middle distance and replied.

'Aye, alright.'

Chapter 12

Opicina, Italy, 1929

Vittorio decreed a daily regime to be followed to provide a comfortable clean home, his right to enjoy the best of everything. Mia was dutifully available to his whims and desires, her misery at losing Ophelia detached her from his coldness, while his arrogance and disinterest allowed him to pursue his career undisturbed.

The baby that died had touched him, certainly, but there wasn't anything he could do about it, and a wife distracted from his needs could not be tolerated. However, his honourable act of marriage and reproduction, and resilience at the subsequent loss of a child, attracted the attention of his superiors at Porto Vecchio. He was observed to be dutiful and reliable under any circumstance, and his attitude commanded authority over the common man. The loss of Ophelia did not interrupt his work, and was interpreted as strength of character, an example of fascist superiority, and as Benito Mussolini had moved to make Trieste a showcase for modernity, it offered an opportunity not to be missed. The city was to be an icon of nationalistic superiority standing firm against neighbouring Slovenia, presenting prospects for the right man, and despite Mia's lack of refinement, she carried out her duties to his satisfaction. With Mussolini's help and the unexpected inconvenience of marriage, he was turning it to his advantage.

*

Days flowed from weeks to years as Mia obediently completed her domestic responsibilities in his household. Memories of Ophelia's emaciated body remained as Bianca was nurtured in an environment of parental distance. By the age of three years, she had grown into an isolated, lonely little girl, understanding nothing but sensing much, quiet and withdrawn, viewing the world through a mesh of lonely acceptance. She didn't affect delight in her mother's eyes, she didn't rouse attention in her father; she was a presence, a cause, an addition in the family. Fine clothes mismatched an expressionless face, the big bow on top of her head a counterpoint to her wide eyes, observing all, experiencing little.

Mia engaged vigorously with home obligations, striving to keep to the stringent criteria dictated by her husband, as her daughter started to enter her consciousness.

Watching her below their little balcony, Bianca squinted at the doll in her hands, gently grasping her only friend, and something in Mia's heart shifted. A wash of cool waves seemed to rush across her mind. Stunned, aware for the first time it seemed, of the lonely figure her daughter made. She had just retrieved her doll for the umpteenth time, grubby and broken, abandoned where the other children had left it after wrenching it from her fingers. Bianca didn't try to hold on to it anymore if they wanted it - she hadn't learned how to.

Mia came to the front door, 'Bianca, bambina, come to your Mamma,'

Immobile, she looked back damply.

'Come here child, I have something to tell you.' Bending before her, Mia's arms stretched towards her,

'When you received this doll for your birthday, she was just visiting,' she said.

Curiosity seeped through Bianca's watery eyes.

'There is another one waiting for you in Trieste when we go this week.'

Bianca looked into her mother's steady gaze; she had never been further than Nonna's house before, and never been so close to her mother's face, as Mia clasped her little hands between hers, palm to palm, as if in prayer.

'My bella bambina, you deserve a special trip to the city and we will go together,' she whispered.

As a shy smile formed hesitantly on her daughter's face, Mia clutched her to her breast, whisking her inside before onlookers might see her tears.

*

They made their way down to the city by electric tram, Bianca's initial alarm met with loving reassurance.

'Cara, don't be frightened. This is how the tram travels, downward, bump, downward bump.' Bianca's pale eyes looked up to her Mamma.

'Look sweetheart, look at the trees, soon you will see the ocean, and the beautiful fairy tale castle.'

The juddering tram descended, wooden seat slats no discomfort on the adventure, as stunning Castle Miramare came into view, seemingly hovering on the aquamarine sea below.

'Can we live there Mamma?' Wide eyes shone at the glistening white building.

'It was built for the old Archduke dear, but it's not to be lived in,' her mother answered.

Puzzled, Bianca looked up through her shiny fringe as her mother passed the time telling the story of his death in a far off land, his lonely wife imprisoned in the castle before going mad and dying herself. Bianca's eyes sparkled at the fairy tale and descriptions of opulent furnishings, rich interiors and exotic parklands until suddenly the whole spectacle disappeared out of sight.

'The place is cursed,' Mia whispered, 'But is as beautiful and magical as you are,' a fateful oath, predicted with the tale.

Bianca listened, soaking up her first memory of the white turreted loveliness of the fairy tale, so close.

Chapter 13

Redcar, England, 1930

Sunshine drizzled and streaked through the window, barely covered by worn, flowery material stretched across. A thin stream of snoring from mother Rose's bedroom drilled into Sonnie's head. Another day had begun.

Barely 5 o'clock in the morning, he'd already heard the front door close, as "Uncle" Fred slipped onto Muriel Street, on his way to Warrenby steelworks. Rose thought he and Cissy believed everything she told them about his occasional lodging there and he at least had, until Cissy put him straight.

Turning his back to the window his gaze fell to little brother Stanley next to him. The toddler lay on his back, arms flung above his head, gently murmuring as he inhaled. The sound never bothered Sonnie, the soft hum reassured, a warm confirmation he was not alone.

'Did you hear him?' The words came from Cissy's mattress at the bottom of the bed; she lifted an arm across her eyes. 'I know yer awake our Sonnie. Did you hear them come in last night?' An eye peeped out, 'Cheeky blighters, laughing and singing, waking up the street.'

'I heard.' Sonnie answered as he did every time she brought the subject up, which was every time Uncle Fred stayed.

'Wonder what 'is wife thinks,' Cissy's disapproving tone rose from her sleep-deprived drift, 'about 'im coming over 'ere every time they have a row? And I wonder the row's not about 'er anyway.' She nodded towards Rose's room.

Only eight years old, he realised his sister was getting into the swing of her favourite subject - disapproval of their mother's relationship.

'If they liked each other so much, why didn't he marry 'er in the first place, 'stead of carrying on like they do.' Sonnie lifted his head wearily to gauge whether she was set to continue with his most hated topic.

'Course "Roy the Rat Catcher" was true to his word wasn't he. stayed until Stanley was born, leaving the very next day you know, not that he was ever around much then anyway,' she chuntered on.

'Why do you call him "Roy the Rat Catcher", Cissy?' Sonnie made a feeble attempt to divert her.

'I don't know, just because he worked on farms I think. Back and forth to Wales he was, searching for groomsman work he said. Anywhere we weren't, our Sonnie.' She raised her head to check he was fully engaged. 'He claimed our Stanley wasn't his, even said the baby looked more like Fred than 'im, and so Fred could look after 'im, and he's never been back, and that's what happened our kid.' There was a moment of silence as Cissy covertly wiped her eyes.

The first time she had let the cat out of the bag, she regretted it immediately, looking at her darling brother's eyes fill up. He had lived in ignorant bliss, but no longer a secret she regurgitated it every time she was angry or annoyed with their mother, releasing some of the pain, Sonnie's lack of confidence a receptacle for her ire, and this time she continued.

'You know 'ow Uncle Fred's really little like, don't you?' Sonnie considered the strange image Fred presented next to their mother, no taller than her shoulder.

'Well, have you ever wondered why she calls our Stanley, Titch'?' Leaving this latest nugget of information to hang in the air.

Chapter 14

Opicina Trieste, 1930

Bianca's full fringe and short brown bobbed hair was brushed until it shone, a popular style for Mussolini's little mothers of the future. She and two neighbouring girls stood in a line below the little balcony.

All three presented in knee-length cotton pinafore dresses and aprons. Bianca stood out in a well-fitting dark waistcoat dress, mimicking Il Duce Mussolini's boy soldier uniforms, with four large buttons simulating the waistcoat. The whitest, finest, tulle sleeves, gathered at the edge, were trimmed with velvet ribbon; her pristine apron had two circular pockets, a little flower at the centre of each, completing her outfit. The day was to be commemorated with a photograph.

Vittorio arranged them, positioning his daughter rightfully at the centre. Bianca was relaxed and comfortable gazing into the camera as her Slav friends scowled, unaccustomed to such indulgent luxury, playing their part just as accessories.

'You there, hold hands he barked, producing obvious resentment from the girl with an aesthetically displeasing square apron. He was moving up in the world, and not just a little, a final photograph of the family against the lowly Slovene backdrop marked the occasion. Opicina had been a mere stopping off point in his life, the majesty of Trieste to be his domain. On the edge of the Karst, the rough, untamed, sparsely distributed communities, who scratched a living in the treacherous terrain were to become a faint memory. Mia complied obediently with her husband's needs and had produced a male heir named Benito. With the family and wealth increasing, they were poised to ride the crest of General Mussolini's provocative commercial future, among a higher society in Trieste.

Another photograph was required, family only this time.

'Position the boy above the girl,' snapped Vittorio.

Mia nervously jumped to accommodate familiar barked commands, and placed Bianca below Benito.

'Too far away, I can't see their expressions.'

Impassively they stood before the concrete, pseudo-classical columns supporting the portico of their old home. Attired perfectly in mock fascist military uniforms his children obeyed, it marked the day the family would move to more appropriate, modern, surroundings.

Slav names in Opicina had already been Italianized under the swiftly developing nationalist regime. Croatian and Slovene businesses were being absorbed to become Italian owned, their newspapers dissolved, finances converted to Trieste savings banks - living among them was no longer viable. The family was to be collected by automobile, and at last he would distance himself from the unpolished surroundings he had endured too long, his exit from the backwater recording with appropriate grandeur.

*

They travelled south of the Karst plateau towards Trieste. Vittorio gazed dismissively at Opicina in the growing distance, the moment savoured, a dividing between ancient and modern worlds, the past no longer relevant. He was building his future upon Il Duce Benito Mussolini's forward-thinking nationalistic fervour and had elevated the family above Slovene society.

'Look below,' he instructed as they passed along the narrow road above Trieste commanding 'now!'

Mia, unfamiliar with chauffeured travel, clutched one-year-old Benito on her knee. She scanned the view, uncertain what reaction was required, eager to please her husband. Bianca, wedged between her parents, could see nothing, content with the breeze on her face. Winding down from the desolate Karst, trees and vegetation grew thicker, it was an adventure.

As the vehicle slowed, Vittorio viewed with satisfaction a large, bright angular building ahead, crunchy, decorative white stones scattering below the wheels of the car. Huge steel lattice pylons towered over the building, connected to wires running flat and straight through the air.

Bianca stood to see the enormous, strange new structure through the car window, much longer than tall. with small windows below a flat roof, all painted a pleasant light shade.

The driver spoke over his shoulder to Vittorio, a clipped reply directing him to pull up on a raised platform overlooking a smaller building in front of the larger, with views of the city. This structure differed considerably with walls plastered and painted in smart wholesome colours. Six modern, wood shuttered windows on the upper two levels, a large square window each side of double ground-floor doors opened to a large flat courtyard in front. Next to the domestic building, furrowed earth had been churned by large machinery entering the huge gaping entrance of the work building, the height of a small house itself.

Excited, Bianca was first out of the car clambering over Mamma and young brother, she ran along the modern iron-work fence overlooking the courtyard below.

'Mamma I can see into the windows from here,' jumping up at the rail. Mia stepped nervously out of the car with Benito.

As the family gathered at the fence, Vittorio took his time to disembark, walking first to the driver as jarred words drifted on the warm breeze.

61

'.... Slovene anti-fascists slaughtered... four of them .... Special state Defence Tribunal ....'

The driver cleared his throat and spat on the ground, '.... violent anti-fascists.'

Vittorio dismissed him and stood back, eyes trained above the small family group, demeanour demanding, they joined him. Mia, ever attuned to his humour swiftly moved to his side.

'It's magnificent Papa,' she gasped nervously, 'You are so clever my dear to acquire such a home for us.' She looked anxiously at the domestic building at the front of the complex. Vittorio spoke.

'You observe, to the front I have had the men plant fruit trees for you.' Two rows, some cherry, others peach line the passage from the lower gate to the front door.

'Husband, you are too clever, too generous. There is so much I can do with the fruit, my dear,'

'Tomorrow the men will place gravel around the entrance to enhance.' Vittorio's right hand swept in grandiose circling gestures, his other ostentatiously upon his hip.

He led the way down to the house, hand sliding along the smooth, newly painted modern wrought iron railing, the family following. At the bottom, he gestured to the slope rising at the right of the large building, behind and above their new home.

'This area you will cultivate for olives and grapevines.' Alarm and confusion leapt across Mia's face, surveying the vast expanse.

'Maybe the men will help' Vittorio dismissed his wife's timid display.

Unlocking the entrance doors Vittorio led the way into their new home, on each side, work and storerooms. Ahead a modern cream tiled staircase took them up to the main living area. On the first landing, the house divided, an office straight ahead with a new desk and business paperwork already carefully stacked, to the left looking out over the courtyard an impressive dining room. To the right, a large kitchen suite took up the corner and rest of the floor. At the sink, one of the modern shuttered windows looked out over the fruit trees to the front; another to the side gave an expansive view over Trieste. Bianca stretched to see the wonderful vista below. Down the hill a railway line, and a large building with soldiers, the whole city spread beyond, and then, white sparkling flecks of sun glistened on a most perfect blue sea, flat like a flawless painted plate.

'I wish I could fly to the sea,' she cried enchanted.

'Bianca here' her father's order awoke her from the daydream.

'My dear you can sit there all day later if you wish,' her mother said, stunned at her own authority. Trembling, her heart bouncing in her chest, knowing her husband's dictates the only ones to be heard.

Off the kitchen, a cool airy store room housed crockery and state of the art modern equipment, everything necessary to keep a home of the highest calibre. A second cool room prepared with stores of food.

Bianca joined the family on the top floor. Above the kitchen the largest bedroom was furnished with a handsome carved bedstead, already made up with the finest quality white linen, boarded in pale blue. A matching chest and wardrobe housed her parents carefully placed clothing. From the landing, and above the kitchen storeroom, a pristine, modern white tiled bathroom, then a bedroom for herself looked out over the city.

'Oh Vittorio, this is most beautiful, how extraordinary. We are to live here, how could we be so lucky?'

A glance was all it took to remind her of his position and hers. She tried to make amends and began to babble.

'You are so clever dear, I never imagined....' He turned on her.

'You never imagined what? You never thought I could provide a home like this?' he levelled her a cold stare and even young Benito fell silent, the air still, her excitement drained.

'Why would I not?' He turned casually away, the day was too good, his achievements too great, to spoil with rebuking the timid creature.

They dutifully followed him along a wide polished corridor, enthusiastically examining two further bedrooms at the other end of the corridor.

When they returned to the kitchen, Bianca dragged a stool to the corner overlooking the city.

'Mamma, I can see down the hill. There is a little house, and a train, then a big building, and a street, and lots of other streets,' she sighed, 'and then the sea. It is wonderful.'

Vittorio announced the arrival of a woman.

'Bianca be quiet. This is Carlo Primavera's wife, Maria.' The woman that stood before Mia was of similar age, not beautiful, but her eyes shone with a kind heart as Mia's discomfort melted cautiously away.

He had talked of Carlo Primavera many times. They met when he started work at Porto Vecchio and Carlo had smoothed many ripples he had created for himself, and in return had not been abandoned in his progression. Now one of his workers in the ultra-modern electric power station, he was rewarded with work and his own accommodation just down the hill.

'Buonasera Signora Marchetti. I live down the hill from you,' the woman waved in the direction of the little house. The two stared at each other silently, darting a look to her husband.

'Maria is to work for you in the home, he said, 'she is to be your housekeeper.' Mia's anxious eyes widened in surprise.

'My wife will instruct you fully in the morning at 6 o'clock sharp.' Maria proffered an uncomfortable curtsey.

'I've prepared food for your first night, Signor, it is ready at my home. I will bring it now if you wish, Maria said.'

'It is acceptable to bring in half an hour.' Vittorio redefined the suggested schedule making his point, he was in charge, then arbitrarily dismissed the second person of the day, those present fully comprehending their new positions in his life.

Chapter 15

Trieste, Italy, 1933

Gone were the long lonely days among Slovene girls in floral pinafores, and rough boys stealing her toys; Bianca had always been awkward in that world.

Mia and Maria prepared fine dishes for Vittorio's wealthy associates, life progressed so well, children of the rich and influential played with Bianca and Benito in the coolness of their small orchard. One day Signor Hertzfelt, a pillar of Trieste's Jewish commercial enterprise, was entertained in Vittorio's plush dining room to discuss general business and brought his little daughter to play with Bianca. Initially shy, they quickly formed an attachment as they concocted affectionate games, she the baby, the older girl her mother, filling playtime with cosseting and cuddles.

In due course she and Benito were enrolled in Fascist Party summer camps, a nursery for housewives and soldiers of the future, boys and girls alike, running, playing games, healthy limbs glistening in the sunshine. Times were changing as Il Duce brought Italy's children together, happy, carefree, and barefoot, boys and girls together in romper suits and sailor hats, growing strong in the nurturing sunshine.

*

'Benito come here, come to your mother,' Mia called her sullen son. The baby in her stomach was stretching again, its feet firmly wedged against her ribs. Cupping the mound with her hand she reached for the new uniform on the scrubbed kitchen table.

'I washed and ironed it again Mia,' Maria called cautiously from the storeroom. 'I'm so sorry I spilt milk on it this morning. I've made it as good as new.'

'Don't fret Maria, it's fine, as long as Signor Vittorio doesn't find out,' she shot a cautionary glance at the door to the landing. Maria peeked out, having spent most of her time hiding away, cleaning and tidying, hoping being out of sight kept her out of mind.

Resting against the kitchen table, Mia carefully stretched her back, closing her eyes for a peaceful retreat.

'Benito!' The boy appeared slowly at the kitchen door as she called.

'Papa doesn't like you to raise your voice,' he leaned lazily against the door frame. His insolent attitude, growing in proportion to his height spurt. Colour flushed his mother's already warm cheeks.

'Come to your mother, your uniform is here.'

'I don't want a uniform,' arms crossed he gazed up through a sun-streaked fringe, dragging his feet to put his arms around her swollen waist, resting his head on the bump. Engulfed in motherly love she thought, '*No-one can ever take this from me. No authority will ever break the bonds that tie my children to my side. I am their Mamma, they love me.*'

Benito stared up into her dark brown eyes, something indefinable made her uneasy.

'Son we have your first uniform for Il Duce General Benito Mussolini's little army, it came today, you can wear it and attend the summer camps with your friends properly attired.'

'It came yesterday and was covered in milk this morning,' his words jarred. If her husband found out, Maria would be sacked, and she herself punished. '*Why does this boy work against me?*' she thought, an uncomfortable uneasy jangling within her.

67

'No child, they were other clothes, things that don't fit anymore.' Benito calmly considered his mother's discomfort.

'Those old clothes are going elsewhere, these are new,' she faltered.

Like a cat at play, he carefully watched her, a glint in his eye. Accepting the uniform, he let the mouse go.

Maria emerged from the store "ooing" and "ahhing" as he returned in dark shirt imitating Il Duce's famous Black Shirts. Grey-green shorts, two white belts crossed his chest, another around his waist, fez type hat, fascist wood-bundle emblems and blue handkerchief completing the outfit.

The women stood back and admired the little soldier, and pleased with their response he took turns, marching around the kitchen table.

'Il Duce's Son of the She Wolf, he will soon become a fully fledged Balilla' Maria cried as she saluted him at every turn. Mia shuffled uncomfortably to select a set of clothes for donation to the poor to cover the tale, before her husband's return.

*

When Vittorio arrived, Mia had already donned her best two-tone leather shoes. The string of pearls he had presented to her upon Benito's birth glowed with a late afternoon, honeyed, radiance, her hair styled by Maria in the latest fashion, attempting to enhance the best of her tender condition. He appeared pleased with the effort. Life was good, they were no longer the thin angular individuals of youth, and wore their good fortune on their bones. He wore a blazer and cotton twill trousers with turn-ups, a small company medal and chain to his lapel. He would not bite the hand that fed him.

The family gathered on the empty land behind the power plant as Carlo carefully took the camera from

Vittorio's hands to record another auspicious moment. Bianca watched as Benito was placed in the most prominent position, denoting the first in the family to wear the full fascist uniform. Mussolini had rewarded Vittorio's diligence well, and he made sure it was repaid with family loyalty.

'Are you ready?' Carlo looked at the wincing twitches on Mia's face. She straightened her back producing a grimace of a smile, the lens clicked as Vittorio placed his right hand upon her shoulder. No affectionate touch for a dear wife and mother as their expressions were captured for all time. Benito's sullen stare bore through the hot heavy afternoon towards the camera, Bianca an addition at the side.

Maria appeared behind her husband, knowing Mia's time was close, recognising her strains and groans throughout the day. Dedication to family and domestic duties had united the two women as firm forever friends, Carlo's connection to Vittorio bonding them further. Despite the many advantages of working for him, Maria's heart went out to Mia on many occasions, not least this one. She had put aside the growing contractions to meet her husband's expectation of the photographic event, and her own clumsiness with the milk had delayed that further, she wouldn't let her down now, and whispered,

'Carlo, tell Signor Vittorio his wife needs the doctor now.'

He looked from his wife to Mia understanding the situation, and informed Vittorio she needed to retire immediately. He took a moment to retain command and instructed he would send a man to collect the doctor, Carlo to ensure Maria escorted Mia to the delivery room safely.

*

'Hush cara, hush' Maria dressed Mia in a plain cotton shift as she leant forward against the high bed, and rubbed her back, then neatly folded her clothes, placing the necklace in her pocket

Vittorio arrived and gave superfluous instructions, stamping his authority on the situation and made to depart, Maria rushing after him into the corridor.

'Signor Vittorio. The jewellery, take it and make it safe,' ensuring he took the pearls. She had learned quickly to take no chance where he was concerned, no-fault or mishap would be found with her. With no reprimand forthcoming she returned to the birthing room, ignoring his ineffectual instructions. No wailing from Mia, only a meek simper as she clenched her friend's hand, restrained even in birth, ensuring her husband's peace should not be disturbed even by her painful predicament.

Within a few hours, another child was delivered; the family's commitment to Il Duce's Battle for Births met with a boy child, to be named Luca. Vittorio, buoyant at his wife's commendable provision of sons, issued a bottle of local Prosecco to Maria and Carlo to salute his success at their evening meal. The following day his men were instructed to begin cultivating the area above the power plant for vines.

Chapter 16

Redcar, England, Winter 1934

The night was like so many, as Cissy, Sonnie and Stanley
huddled together in the cold front room, Rose sang a cheery
song as she put on her coat, declaring she would visit a
friend. It only took a moment for Cissy to decide she was
probably going to end up in the Red Lion Inn.

'Right then, Cissy, you make sure those two boys get
to bed. I'm just popping round the corner.'

'You mean to Betty's, who's brother's on leave with a
pocket full of money and having a knees up?' The words out
before she realised.

'You what? Come here you little madam, don't you
speak to me like that,' Rose lunged at Cissy, across the
table.

After a short burst of chasing her around, Rose
chuckled, ruffled Sonnie's hair, abandoned her ire and
went, adding a slammed door for effect, leaving the
children to take stock of the skewed table and fallen chairs
left in her wake.

The three huddled before the dying embers in the
hearth, crunched up against each other for warmth in the
darkness. In the diminishing glow Cissy went to the
window furtively looking up and down the road.

'Come back Cissy it's cold,' Stanley's plaintive
whimper cut through the dark.

'Bugger her,' she declared.

'Don't say that Cissy it's hard for her on her own.'
Sonnie, always a counterpoint to her quick tongue.

'Hard for her? It's worse for us. Said she couldn't
afford a proper tea again, and then off out and about.'

'I don't blame her,' he muttered.

'You should, our Sonnie, when she takes your farm wages off you, and you hate it there,' she said.

His thoughts dragged to the long slog up West Dyke Road to Ramshaw's Farm. He loathed it, the sting of the farm girls' words were firmly engraved in his brain, reminding him of their pitiful existence, painful shyness and lack of confidence.

"Poor townie boy, need the money do ya?" The taunts were unrelenting *"Did you get yer coat off a tramp?"*

'Look Sonnie, she takes every penny off you, you don't need to feel like you're letting her down. It's not your fault we end up sitting here, on our own, in front of a dead fire, it's her. She could leave you some earnings, and anyway, you're supposed to be at school not missing days on the farm,' Cissy continued.

Sonnie peered at the last glimmer in the grate.

'I just want to help, that's all,' he said.

After a pause too long to pass unnoticed, she asked, 'What is it Sonnie, what's the matter?'

He broke down.

'I pinched a couple of boiled potatoes out of the pantry. They were only little 'uns Cissy, honest.' Liquid eyes pleaded forgiveness. 'I feel so bad, I was just so hungry and tired when I walked to Ramshaw's, no food there and then it was too late for tea when I got back. I just couldn't help it. I didn't mean to, really I didn't.' A tear ran down his tortured face.

The longest time passed as Cissy stood, her back to the street window. Silence slashed the darkness, light radiating around her from a street lamp, piercing his conscience until she spoke.

'That's nowt our kid, I pinch tuppence out 'er purse whenever I think she won't notice.'

Stanley curled on Sonnie's knee for warmth and slept, as Cissy caught his astonishment.

'Wait here,' Cissy said, 'I thought she'd be out and about tonight. Now, don't move, or look, the less you know the better.'

Cissy disappeared out back to the outhouses, returning with a little jingle in her pocket.

'Make me clean out the privy would she? I thought - I'll make it worth me while missus.' She winked and with a cheeky glint in her eye, looked up and down the road again.

'Reckon she'll be there by now, I'm off to the fish shop. Fancy a bag of chips, our kid?' and in a flash, she was out, dashing by the front window towards Lord Street.

*

Later, satisfied from chips and scraps, laced with salt and vinegar, Cissy and Stanley slept as Sonnie laid wide awake, Sunday school guilt refusing him rest, *'Never forget your misdemeanours'*. Concern for his mother's predicament, and duty to family, always at the forefront of his mind. The short time they had spent with Roy's Baptist Chapel family in Wales after they had been abandoned had left its' indelible mark.

Maybe it was in their blood, perhaps in every fibre of his body; Cissy's righteous indignation, and his sense of duty; it was the only thing he had left them.

Chapter 17

Trieste, Italy, Spring 1937

'Come along, time to get yourselves ready boys.' Bianca turned to her brothers,

Benito sullen as usual, Luca always looking for his mother's side, neither exhibited much joy, but fussing over two small boys developed a flourishing confidence in her.

From a solitary lonely figure, she had become confident and self-assured with well-heeled friends, growing into a natural resident of Trieste's cultured streets.

'Boys, you are to wear your sailor suits, all three of us are to be ready for Papa's visitors.'

Benito rattled expensive metal cars across the sparkling landing floor as he slid behind on his knees. Luca's rarely heard voice rose above the racket.

'Where's Mamma, she always dresses me?' he asked.

'She put me in charge, I will dress you,' she informed.

Maria smiled as she passed the group on her way from kitchen to dining room, immaculate white linen in her arms thinking, _'That girl will sort those two out, she's growing into a formidable little Mamma.'_

Bianca briskly ushered the reluctant boys upstairs to change.

The three reappeared at the kitchen door to intense activity. Benito sidled idly towards the kitchen table laden with delicious food, a single finger casually sliding towards the nearest plate. A hand caught his shoulder pulling him to the corridor, Bianca reprimanding.

'You are not allowed to go in there. Don't you know how important this is to Papa?' Surly eyes stared back, then withdrew the challenge to her authority.

Mia arrived, hair coiffured, pearl necklace glimmering against her moist dark neck, smoothing a fine knit short-sleeved jumper belted at the waist. Vittorio procured the finest styles for her, such as the elegant ladies of Trieste wore, but always considered, she was what she was, home and baby maker. At least Il Duce would approve.

'Ay, ay, ay, my babies, look at them Maria, look at these fine children here,' Mia enthralled at her sons.

Maria clattered back along the corridor stopping to examine the children's immaculate shoes, socks, shorts, Bianca's white pleated skirt, all topped off with perfectly ironed sailor tops and neckerchiefs.

'Come here Benito, come to Maria you have a smudge on your face.'

Well practised at avoiding wet, sticky, thumbs of matriarchs, he twisted under her arm. Out of reach she settled to correct non-existent smudges on Luca.

'Excellent Mia, your daughter has done you proud, getting your little soldiers ready,' Maria said.

Bianca beamed at her contribution to the event. Her father's position was highly respected, he was the gatekeeper to economic potential, his innovative state-of-the-art electric power station the lifeblood to successful industry. Every tycoon's business, industry potential, household comfort, rested in the palm of his hand, his friendship and alliance regularly sought.

*

The luminaries arrived, ferried in expensive automobiles. Some of the dignitaries directed their own staff to occupy key posts, at the front entrance below the open dining room windows, and at the dining room door. To provide the highest service, waiters from a prestigious hotel had been engaged. From the corridor, Mia nervously instructed Maria in the kitchen to direct a chef from Excelsior Palace Hotel as to when to prepare dishes. Despite the two women's insistence, the guards refused all refreshment;

their serious demeanour enough to send the ladies scurrying.

When waiting and kitchen staff were finally dismissed, the visitors embarked upon private discussions, the dining room door firmly closed, Maria calling her dear friend to the privacy of a kitchen storeroom.

'What's the matter cara?' Mia relieved to at last spend time with her friend.

'I overheard one of the waiters as he left, he said he recognised the group.' She nervously looked over her shoulder. 'They are of the Grand Lodge!' Wringing her hands, colour drained from Mia's face, as her friend flushed crimson. Mia spoke.

'The FreeMasons, they're illegal! Il Duce has banned them. What are we to do? Anyone who is a...' she hushed realising her panic. Maria drew her closer.

'Don't fret Mia, no-one is aware we know. If that stupid waiter is overheard it's nothing to do with us. I never heard it and you weren't there. If your husband says anything, we are innocent. Even this conversation never took place.' She stared into her friend's terrified eyes, shaking her gently.

'Do you understand?' She rubbed Mia's trembling hands, emphasising again, 'Do you understand?'

Mia thought of earlier days when her husband had been proud to be welcomed into the Lodge, and had boasted of his achievement. But everyone knew now, how the fascist party had abandoned those who had brought it to power, high chiefs of the Lodge imprisoned or exiled, any association strictly prohibited.

Mia poured a coffee and sat at the corner overlooking the lights, scattered like diamonds across Trieste, contemplating the new information. If her husband was caught what would become of them, how would she care for her children, separated from her home and husband? Her thoughts turned, eyes revealing nothing as Maria finished at the sink behind her, until bold thoughts took her.

'It will rest upon his head alone, I will take no part. If he goes to jail I will not wait in exile. My brothers will protect me. I'll take the children and live with my parents. It would be a hard, but I will fight like a She Wolf myself to separate from him and protect them'

Satisfied at her conviction, surprised with her daring resolve, she determined if she needed to leave his ivory tower and return to her roots, she would be free, stronger than she thought she ever could be. Perhaps even hopeful it might come to that.

The evening business continued, only the guards in their smart suits remaining when Maria finally took her leave. As she passed, she squeezed Mia's hand.

'I will see you tomorrow as usual. No change here, our life continues as always,' she whispered.

No revealing glance exchanged to alert the guards. If anyone overheard their innocuous comments, it was no more than two domestics, speaking of their daily toil, no indication of their furtive conversation earlier.

Chapter 18

Redcar, England, June 1937

Morning began, as usual, Cissy off to work, Sonnie delivering Stanley to West Dyke School. But that day was to be different. He didn't turn left to James Mackinlay Secondary School, instead turning right he walked directly out of town along the Trunk Road opened the year of his birth. He wasn't thinking, his feet simply took him that away, an average boy with uncertain crystal eyes drawing no-one's attention, beginning the ten-mile trek to Middlesbrough.

Passing the huge Pleasure Park, tucked behind Stanley's school, he looked up at the Giant Racer ride. It was the largest outside of London he'd heard, and the wooden construction now unsafe, it was due to be dismantled, and he would never get to experience the thrill of the ride like everyone else in town. Cissy had ridden it, sneaking her wages away for treats, but for him, the anticipation and magic was over, no chance to join in the excitement like the rest.

He had walked around the Park so many times, only watching, poverty keeping him apart, one eye on the floor for lost pennies, only ever enough for candy floss on a stick. A fist of disappointment gripped the pit of his stomach, reaching up and wrapped around his heart. As The House of Fun disappeared behind him, he didn't look back.

Like him, the day was average, people going about their business no-one noticing the boy in a crumpled jacket until, near Eston, the farmer from Ramshaw's pulled his truck over in front of him.

'Lad, what are you up to, where you going on a school day, not to my farm that's for sure?'

Used to Sonnie's blank stares in response to almost any conversation, he recognized the painful shyness behind them.

'Need a lift son?'

Too bashful to ask where the farmer was going, Sonnie nodded.

'Get yourself up here then lad, give yer legs a rest.'

Sonnie was thrilled with the ride, window open, light summer air blowing in his face, he enjoyed the boss's company. When the farm horses were too old for the job, the farmer had invested in a magnificent mechanical beast of a tractor, getting Sonnie to help him tweak the engine, anything to get away from his daughters. He had been drawn to the surrogate father figure who appreciated him, no matter how temporarily.

'So lad, where are you off to then, you gonna tell me?'

'Just Middlesbrough,' he replied.

'Not saying then.' The farmer tried again. 'Lad, I won't tell a soul, not 'til it's safe to,' he shot a glance at the badly cut, home trimmed hair as Sonnie looked away.

'I know it's not easy for you lad, and I know them girls of mine give you a hard time, but know this,' clear blue eyes turned towards the farmer.

'Lad you're a good worker and I think you've got a knack with engines too,' he paused, 'you're not a farmer that's for sure.'

The last comment stung, doubtfulness rushing in to occupy the space swiftly vacated by the compliment.

'Look lad, I don't know what you're up to, but life gets better, yes it does.' He looked at his silent companion. 'I know what your life is like son, but you need to know, every man has a glove that's a perfect fit, and you'll find yours, I promise you.'

The rest of the journey to Middlesbrough was spent in embarrassed silence with occasional safe conversation about the few vehicles on the road. On the outskirts, it became apparent the farmer had driven out of his way and as Sonnie prepared to climb down the farmer leaned forward pulling his arm back.

'Always held a bit of your wages back, I did son, in case you didn't turn up regular like. Here,' Embarrassed, he yanked at Sonnie's hand, dropping coins into his palm, and curled his fingers around them.

'Get on with yer lad, and look after yerself mind. Alright?'

Avoiding eye contact, each turned away. Sonnie ran his fingers through the money in his pocket without daring to look, a full five shillings he estimated excitedly.

*

He finally made it home about 9 o'clock at night, Rose's crimson cheeks damp, meeting his eyes as he tried to sneak in the back door.

'Where you been, what you been up to?' a flush of anger drying her face. 'Been worried as sick as a dog, I 'av, 'aven't I Cissy? Been up and down the High Street to everyone I could think of. What you been doing?'

Before he could edge towards the safety of the stairs another sudden volley erupted.

'Here, you 'aven't been up to no good 'ave you?' angry indignation spurting from every pore of her body, almost masking the concern in her eyes.

'No, I 'aven't Mam, I've been to Middlesbrough.' He braced himself for outrage, continuing cautiously.

'I've joined up,' met with stunned silence and confusion from Rose and Cissy. He continued, 'I'm in the Army now. I leave next week. Got to get myself to the barracks and start training. I'm going to be a soldier.'

For safety, he slid closer to the stairs.

His mother flumped onto a kitchen chair, wrap around pinny stretched to the limit.

As Cissy squeaked, spitting out incomprehensible sounds, he ventured another step into the room.

'It's good Mam, I'll be able to send money home, more than I get at the farm. It'll be for the best you'll see.'

For once in his life, his mother was silent; her hair-netted head flopped forward, managing a barely audible mutter,

'Aye lad, you know best. Recon you'd better get some sleep.'

He clumped up the carpetless stairs, confusion and relief competing for attention.

Downstairs the only noise was Cissy's raised voice arguing, 'Why don't you say something? He's only 14 years old!' mostly to herself it seemed.

She ran up to join him, young Stanley was already asleep.

'What are you doing Sonnie? Why did you go and join up? You didn't need to; you could get work around here.' Cissy was his little mother, the one he could always rely on, her face wet with tears. 'Don't go, our kid, we can sort something out, you could still get out of it, maybe,' she pleaded. Silence rested between them for the longest time.

'Cissy, I can't take it anymore. I have to leave,' he finally said.

This bold move from her timid brother was a huge statement. In an instant, she realised how unhappy he must have been, moving away from everyone and everything he knew, finding the courage to go as far away as he could.

'Oh, Sonnie, I'm so sorry,' she cried.

'Don't be Cissy. There was a talk at school last week. You get your food, clothes and a wage. They teach you a trade, and there'll be more to go around here with me gone. Anyway, you'll be married soon I expect.'

'Edwin Michael how dare you,' outrage demanded his full name. 'I'm never getting married, I'm not looking after some man,' she quickly reverted to her forthright, confident approach to life.

'You say that now Cis but you never know.' In a moment of tenderness, she gently squeezed his hand.

'You look after yourself, our lad, and make sure you come home often, do you hear?'

As he drifted to sleep a muffled whimpering drifted up the stairs.

'*All the women in this family have turned into someone else today,*' he thought.

*

Rose ensured everyone in Redcar knew her son had joined up, and the night before was due to leave, the party started early. Cissy invited Arthur, her new 'friend', a big, bold, brave young man with eyes only for her. As he entered, Rose looked him up and down taking his measure, curling her lip to be on the safe side. Untroubled, he followed Cissy around all night, while she stayed close to her brother.

As everyone crammed into the front room at Muriel Street, jollities began. Rose's friend Mrs Dent arrived with her husband, beer bottles in hand. Mrs Dent with her prim respectable manner drew quizzical comments in corners, as to how the most unlikely of women had come to be so close. Uncle Fred's wife arrived as he ducked into the back yard for a Capstan light-up. Even the horse-breeder and his wife came with roast chicken, bread and beer.

Fred's wife was singing gaily by eight, table and chairs out front in the street as dancing in the little room began. Rose's skirt merrily flicked as she swung around to the Gay Gordons, pale pink bloomers flashing above her knees with stockings tucked into knicker elastic, instead of rolled down round her ankle as usual.

At a quiet moment, she pulled Sonnie aside and handed him a glass of beer.

'Here son, puts hairs on yer chest,' checking over her shoulder. 'Don't let Cissy catch you,' all mischievousness returned.

Gasping at the acrid hops he sneaked into the back yard to practise this manly new pursuit with the men. By the time the singing had grown to full belt, of dubious content, he decided he quite liked it.

Neighbours who had protested the noise were quickly drawn into the gaiety, even "missus" from next door joined in for a modest tipple or two, all animosities forgotten in Rose's convivial company.

By midnight, Sonnie's opinion of beer had dramatically changed.

*

In the early hours, he crept up the stairs on hands and knees, incapable of keeping up with the exuberance of the party, as sweaty bodies staggered and laughed. Uncle Fred and a couple of others congregated in the yard, their women scurrying home to check on children and Cissy returned from saying goodnight to Arthur, sneaking to bed herself.

'What do you see in him Cissy?' Sonnie's slurred words emerged out of the gloom.

'He's got something about him that's all, but I'm not interested, he's just a friend.'

An intoxicated, strangulated giggle came out of the dark, 'Yea, that's right,' he said.

'You're drunk you great narna.' she said. 'You've got to be gone early tomorrow our kid, you can't be late you know.'

'All packed' were the only words he could manage.

After a while, he whispered, 'Cissy, you can't be calling me Sonnie anymore.'

She spluttered in reply. He continued, 'I gave them that as my name when I joined up, and they laughed at me.

83

It's Ted now, you know from my first name Edwin. That's what they said I should call myself.'

Choking back comments Cissy fell unusually silent.

'Not just losing my little brother, and me being more of a mother to him than Mam's ever been, but not even able to call him by the name I gave him as a babe? I won't admit how much it's upset me.'

In the dark Cissy struggled with her emotions.

A moment went by as she continued thinking, 'But there has been a change in him since he signed up. Doesn't he walk a bit straighter, head not so bowed, eyes not counting the cracks in the pavement so much? And there's nothing you can do about it Cis lass, he's leaving us and that's it, and truth be told maybe I won't be around forever myself either, now Arthur's here,' and she spoke.

'Aye, you're right our kid, you'll be mixing with all sorts now, from up and down the country and all over the place.'

'How do you think Mam'll be Cissy?'

'Don't you worry about her, lad, I'll make sure she's okay.'

Cissy had never heard her mother cry before, she'd taken it hard at first, but true to form had bounced back. The easy come easy go character that had sustained them through so much had propelled her up and down Redcar High Street, proud as punch, telling everyone of her eldest son's new adventure, a young lad on the brink of manhood.

*

Next day started with clattering and curses as the family made their way through the party debris. Rose, bleary-eyed, adjusted her hairnet, pushed the others aside to hug her lad for a markedly long moment, as Ted tried not to focus on his headache. Rose, eventually prised off by Cissy, pushed a parcel into his hand, with pie, bread and lard, for the journey.

They proudly watched him make his way down the road toward the railway station bag in hand, a few early risers patted him on the back and wished him luck as he walked towards his new life, and new family, the British Army.

Chapter 19

Trieste, Italy, June 1938

'Carlo, come here!' Vittorio's command demanded instant attention and Carlo's back stiffened.

'I said now!' he bellowed from his office.

Carlo remembered when they'd met at Porto Vecchio, suggestions of his transgressions with an unsuitably young girl in Verona trailed behind him. Already established, he had chosen to believe gossip is just that and had befriended the precocious new man with a high opinion of himself, despite most thinking Vittorio ludicrous and harbouring attitudes above his station. Outsiders trained regularly in the new electrical technologies, usually passing through unnoticed, but when Vittorio overplayed his position Carlo would interject, make light of his superior manner and diffuse situations with his easy manner. A quip here or gentle comment there broke the tension with the workforce and they learned to ignore this newcomer's self-importance. It left Vittorio free to exploit his position as self-promotion propelled him through the ranks. Carlo trailed behind him in the work hierarchy, but secured an income suitable to marry Maria. Vittorio invited to attend, but retreated at the earliest opportunity to enjoy the stylish bars of the city, to flex his arrogant self-importance in surroundings more befitting his ambition.

Having slipped from Vittorio's inner-circle, Carlo's hunched shoulders spoke volumes, his mind piqued at every new humiliation. Recalling their early bond, he realised their friendship had been no more than Vittorio's need for a useful colleague, a stepping stone in his journey to the top.

'Carlo, what's the matter with you? You drag your feet when your boss calls? Think of your position here, it is not set in stone.' Vittorio's tone stung.

'Your daughter, Sofia, is twelve years old, yes?' Vittorio asked.

Sharp words twitched in Carlo's throat as he tried to make sense of the query, recovering,

'Sofia is a good girl. You know her... her mother and I are very proud....'

'Business at the power station progresses well, with increasing electrical provision to outlying areas coming online shortly,' Vittorio continued.

Carlo was impatient. 'Why do you speak of my daughter Vittorio, what does she have to do with work?' His eyes narrowed, concern tightened his jaw, recalling the rumours that had hung around his boss.

'You address me as Signor. Take a lesson from your wife.' Vittorio's eyes darted to the lowly workman he saw before him, and resumed.

'Maria works well in my home, and Signora Mia speaks suitably of her,' he paused, 'at the moment.' The hold he had on Carlo's family came sharply into focus.

'Sophia will attend senior school with my daughter Bianca at the best academy in Trieste. She will enjoy the finest fascist education, accompanying my daughter as her friend,' levelling a steely gaze at him.

Carlo's indignation quickly turned to confusion as he said, 'Sophia is Bianca's friend already, they've played together for years.'

Vittorio rose from his desk and started to pace around his office, head high, right hand gesticulating his authoritative generosity.

'I have identified, my wife and daughter have attachment to your family, and they in turn provide efficiency and comfort.' He, Signor Vittorio Marchetti, was the puppeteer, demonstrating his control over all he surveyed, maybe even prepared to keep Carlo's lips sealed where his past indiscretions were concerned. Appreciating the importance of image, he had decided to present Carlo's daughter, Sophia, as an embellishment to Bianca as she began senior school.

For a moment, Vittorio contemplated the chubby-cheeked attraction Sophia held as a little girl was faded now, apple round cheeks disappeared, no longer the beauty he had expected, but she would do. He proceeded.

'The child is bright,' he cast an authoritative eye at Carlo, 'and you and Maria have a value to me.'

Carlo recognised, his boss was finally abandoning their friendship, compensating his family in a way which would hold his loyalty. They had known each other for long enough, confided much, and he knew secrets that would not sit well with his new social circle. He stood dumb as Vittorio informed how transport and uniform would be supplied by one of his new associates, his concerns oscillating between delight, anxiety and loss, when Vittorio looked down at his desk, reaching for his pen.

'Bring her to me,' he commanded.

Blood drained from Carlo's face, what was he thinking; that he would peddle his daughter for a prestigious place at school? Carlo feared the depths of his depravity, his bitter gaze drawing Vittorio's attention.

'Bianca, bring my daughter to the workshop on the left, then you can inform the family.' Carlo turned away, relief washing through him.

'And,' Carlo stopped short at the door, 'when we're alone you may call me Vittorio. In front of the work-force, I am Signor Marchetti,' and without looking up, 'good, you understand.'

Chapter 20

Trieste, Italy, September 1938

'Sofia you are late, the car is here,' Bianca called to her friend as she ran up the hill ahead of her mother.

'My little brother had a toothache; we were trying to treat it with cloves, but the yelling and screaming! He's such a baby,' Sofia laughed at the image of her Mamma trying to compress ground cloves and cayenne pepper paste onto the elusive, affected area.

The driver opened a rear door and the girls quickly settled on the back seat, new leather satchels carefully placed on knees, ready for their first day of school. Giggling, they looked into each other's eyes, giddy with excitement and trepidation. Together since their mothers met, the truest of friends were ready for their adventure.

Weeks previously, Mussolini had visited Trieste, and now this excitement, attending one of his finest schools. Light-headed memories of his tour spilt out on the journey down the hill.

'Did you put the photographs from Il Piccolo newspaper in your folder Bianca? I'm sure that was you right at the front in Piazza Unita d'Italia.'

'No, no, I told you Sofia, we passed around the edge. Papa was in the banqueting hall, Mamma and I in an antechamber.'

Sofia was reminded of watching the family, leaving for the event.

'Oh Bianca I'd never seen such finery, you and your Mamma in fine silk dresses of the most delicate pattern, and your Mamma's magnificent orchid corsage pinned just above her heart,' the tale still excited the girls.

'And Papa with his new silver-handled cane and splendid straight-sided fedora, and you will never guess how much his suit and shirt cost, all hand-made,' Bianca added.

'We definitely saw Il Duce where we were standing by the road,' Sophia, thrilled at her own noteworthy experience. 'We had to walk back up the main road to be in a good position, it was so crowded anywhere near the Piazza.'

'I finished my folder last night,' Bianca said, 'I've included my invitation. Do you think they'd like to see the menu from Papa's meal too?'

Preparation for the new school was competitive; every girl would have a story. It all depended on subtle details to establish status in their new elevated world.

Arriving at the impressive building, they took a deep breath, flattened their dark pleated skirts, checked leather waist belts, smoothed the fascist insignia on their left breast pockets, all ready for induction into Il Duce's world.

Chapter 21

Trieste, Italy, Spring 1942

Bianca and Sofia happily attended school, housed prominently among impressive modern architecture of Mussolini's benevolence. Smart lady teachers dressed impeccably in white suits, badge of the administration proudly emblazoned on the left breast completed with regimental style tie. They were in the care of an elevated class, supporting their country, training to rule the known world.

'The photographer is coming today Bianca.' Sofia's voice rose in excitement as they walked through the city, as young ladies, now allowed exposure to their cultural metropolis.

'Signor Photographer - of Via Carducci? Papa is an associate of his; they attend the same meetings I think, I've seen them talking,' Bianca replied.

'The secret meetings?' Sofia's eyes rolled, teasing, 'What do you think they talk about?'

'I'm not allowed to discuss that,' Bianca hissed, as if the very buildings would overhear. Guilt clutched Sofia seeing the terror in her friend's eyes, the photographer making a good distraction,

'I wonder if he will just photograph the school?' Sofia checked her friend's expression relaxing.

'Last year he set his camera in the classrooms. Do you think he will photograph us?' Bianca asked.

'Oh just like movie stars. I could be Olivia de Havilland.' Sophia threw her head back in a dramatic pose.

On the brink of womanhood, and allowed a little independence, they were preparing for their roles as domesticated, fertile mothers of the future, ready to swell Italy's population with battalions of little soldiers. They had been taught the art of cooking, sewing and house-keeping to support the nation's valiant soldiers they were to marry; it was their only duty. Their men would impose their superiority upon lesser nations, which was every nation they had been instructed, except perhaps the Arians.

Bianca's skill as a seamstress was her proudest boast.

'Did you bring your white ribbon in case we are to model our confirmation dresses Sophia? Mine's a little tight now, I sewed it last year.'

Sofia linked her arm; she knew she could out-cook her best friend in any kitchen.

Bianca was pretty, and popular with classmates and their siblings, hardly perceiving how much she loved her life, comfortably enjoying entitlement and privilege. Her family was wealthy under Il Duce's leadership, a situation sanctified by His Holiness the Pope himself.

*

In the classroom, dress patterns carefully drawn by students were pinned on the walls. White confirmation dresses placed over them, rippling gently in the early summer breeze that drifted through the open classroom window. The garments were perfect, unsullied, pure, and unblemished as the girls who created them. Convivial groups of girls had chattered while they had sewed them, sitting around tables, embroidering white organza, stitching lace collars, eager to impress and be rewarded with their revered teacher's approval.

'Bianca' the teacher cast a critical eye over her pristine uniform, 'I have selected you for an image of female physical superiority, throwing a javelin. Go join Signor Photographer in the court.'

When she returned the tutor commanded, 'Sofia, direct the girls who still fit into their confirmation dresses to change quickly and attend back immediately for a photograph.'

The girls quickly clipped back disobedient curls of hair, assembling for the moment their purity would be recorded as Bianca joined the group.

'Come, ladies,' the teacher clapped her hands imperiously, as the photographer began to perspire. The proximity of so many refined examples of femininity, budding on the verge of womanhood seemed to unnerve him. His presence seemed to disturb her immaculate image as she fussed and darted around the girls and garments, her disquiet seeped into the girls' humour.

'In front of the blackboard, you six... ,' he managed to stop himself saying, "virgins" recovering just in time, 'ladies in white.'

Losing himself in artful design, his manly urges mercifully contained, he arranged baskets of flowers around their ankles, suggesting a tableau of tender female perfection, pristine in Godly garments, hooped flower garlands on the classroom wall enhancing their image of wholesome fragrance.

Ushered together, shoulder to shoulder in a clutch, glimpsing apprehensively through bowed heads and thick eyelashes, he separated, prodded and poked the girls into position, while lips pouted sullenly. The girls failed to relax or smile in his presence, growing ever more uncomfortable.

By the time he finished, the dresses, intended as spotless representations of youthful innocence were grubby and snagged, and were rolled and dumped unceremoniously. Only Sofia carefully recovered her lovingly constructed garment, folding it delicately, to save and hang in her bedroom at home.

Chapter 22

The English Channel, Spring 1942

As the ship heaved sideways, Ted looked for something to occupy his mind. He thought of his mother Rose, how she didn't have much, never expected anything, but cheerfully took any opportunity life offered with little consideration for consequences; a moments' fun was worth a week of hopes. She'd had to. Money was always short, times tough. He, Cissy and Stanley were bound closely together in her wake as she ploughed her furrow through the hardships of life, a mother abandoned by the cold-heartedness of an absent husband.

He turned to consider the latest adventure the Army had presented him with. Appointed Artificer of the Royal Artillery, Class 11, not so bad he thought, and now three years into the war he was on his way overseas at last. The ship listed violently as he tried to re-engage with thoughts of home.

Cissy said Rose could start an argument in an empty house, but what she lacked in domestic commitment she more than made up for with survival instinct, getting what she could, however she could, keeping a roof over their heads. He pondered her cheerful temperament, single-handedly skivvying and conniving to keep her children by her side.

She was warm and welcoming, perhaps too much with sometimes a price to pay. He considered the stream of people who had knocked on her door in times of trouble, often through their own indiscretions. She made no judgments, welcoming all into her home, always room for one more. The draughty ship was awash with waves but thoughts of Rose's escapades buoyed him, viewing his job now akin to that his mother's had been, to be there in hard times for the Army, to do what he had to for the greater good, whatever.

Rose wasn't sentimental, and he would have to put emotions aside himself in the days to come. He remembered when his father walked out, she was living off her wits, cleaning at a big house, and vaguely described herself as a "nurse", with him sent to Ramshore's Farm to bring in a few more pennies. On sunny days he would distract himself in West Dyke Beck, running along the road from town to farm, but when the vicious north-sea wind blew in, or it rained, his thin mismatched variously sized clothes and shoes, just added insult to injury. As the ship tilted, he recalled the reluctant long drag up past Easson Road and its big posh houses.

Reflecting on his condition now, huddled between two puking sappers, wearing waterproof boots, warm, clothes fit for the job. Even at sea, life seemed a definite step up from back then. If only the farm girls could see him, ready to fight for King and country, their cruel jibes would count for nothing. He had a valued skill, a place in the Army team, a part to play, all working together, and as the eldest male in the family, was proud to send money home to support his Mam.

When Roy went, the only things left were his family's Welsh Chapel ethics; right and wrong, duty and responsibility, respect for your elders. He should have used them himself, Ted reflected sadly.

His last thought as he drifted to sleep, in the only spew free spot he could find, was the one shining light of his young life, strong-willed, outspoken, upstanding, Cissy, and she loved him back.

Chapter 23

Trieste, Italy, Autumn 1942

Vittorio's career advanced with his indisputable grip around the workforce, his opinion widely sought; he examined the newspaper before him, freshly ironed by Mia that morning as every morning.

As expected the synagogue was desecrated, the Jewish community no longer an influence in Trieste, administrative or financial as Il Duce's fascist squads established brutal control. He sighed, considering the Hertzfelts, his former friends and associates, but party-line was primary, discarding concern for their welfare.

Turning the page, other matters were not progressing as expected either. Hitler's forces had been obliged to support Italian troops in Greece, with the eventual surrender of the Greek nation. Neither was there triumphant news of Italian troops in Africa. Irritated, he shook the newspaper, training his gaze on another page. Slovene youths had formed into partisan clusters, responding to Germany's invasion of Yugoslavian states and he had been informed that Communist Slav boys were being blindfolded and executed and yet, they still continued to form.

Dissatisfied, he threw the paper on the floor, no mention of total annihilation of the pale, wretched, British either. Mia scurried from the kitchen sensing somebody would pay for his annoyance.

Chapter 24

2nd Battle of El Alamein, November 1942

The Brits were better equipped than Rommel's Afrika
Korps during the First Battle therefore Germany and Italy's
3 Corps' efforts went badly with many prisoners from
Trieste and Trento motorised divisions taken. Yet, the
British 8th Army failed to smash Axis forces despite the
British commander's wish to attack immediately as he
wasn't given permission to proceed. Being exhausted with
many casualties, the Allies took a month to regroup as Ted
was mustered, preparing for war.

Cissy had teased him about his war contribution
while stationed in England, though secretly relieved at least
one of her loves was out of harm's way. When Ted had left
in 1937, her admirer Arthur had just returned from fighting
Franco in Spain, then when war declared in England had
immediately enlisted in the RAF, taking his place in the
perilously dangerous position of rear gunner.

'Our Cissy, you can't half pick 'em,' Ted had said.

Now he was twenty years old, six-foot-tall, bashful
and handsome in equal proportions with manly expanded
chest, artificer qualifications and commendable reports.
Each month he sent Rose her money. As her children
drifted away, he felt she needed his support. Cissy chided
him about it upon discovering that after paying Army dues,
all he had left was a few pennies for a box of broken
biscuits. Ted ignored her protestations. He had mates, a
roof over his head, regular food and a bit of a treat, what
more could he want? Welsh Chapel values still coursed
through his veins.

The regularity of Army life comforted him, learning
new skills to excel and please his commanders, he had a
purpose in life and was happy with his lot. Originally in the

Royal Artillery, he'd achieved a good basic education and the Army had given him focus, like a family he could rely on every day. He had transferred all over the country, even as far as Wales, there were no limits to the experiences the Army had bestowed, and he was eager to do his duty in the field.

*

By the time he disembarked in Tunisia, part of 1st AGRA, the enemy had withdrawn from Agheila, employing delaying tactics. Soldiers recounted extraordinary experiences. A patrol rushing back to camp, having been lost in the desert, had screeched to a halt behind a roadblock. When young German troops turned to see the Brits behind instead of in front of them, the two patrols had nervously eyed each-other, neither willing to make the first move. They had gingerly put their Land Rover into gear, no response. Edging forward slowly, still no response, young men, face to face, too many similarities between them. Nearing the roadblock the Germans fell back, waving them through, pointing towards the Allied camp. It was Ted's first experience of how unclear the lines of war could be drawn, how unwilling to kill their fellow men could be.

*

Given leave in Cairo, creased, sweaty soldiers thronged the streets as Ted had his photograph taken with mates, all wearing a precariously perched fez, displaying the universal two-fingered sign of victory.

A voice suddenly rang out, 'Oy, Ted!'

Plenty of men from Blighty milled around, it wouldn't be him.

'You there, Sonnie!'

He couldn't ignore that. Turning, he saw two large hands waving above the crowd, the cheerful, fleshy, face of Cissy's Arthur grinning from ear to ear. Out of the hundreds milling around, two men from home, joined by

Cissy and the war, found themselves feet away in this foreign land. Embracing they slapped each other's backs, *'I can't believe my luck'* Ted thought.

'Me old mate, what're you doing here?' Arthur, man of the world, took charge. ''Ow long are you on leave for?'

A mate from Ted's Army camp shouted above the hubbub, 'I'm off to the brothel old son, you coming?' drifting away in the crowd. Arthur, surveying Ted's bashful expression, flung an arm around his shoulder and directed him towards the nearest bar.

'Here for two days Arthur, unless I don't find my way back,' Ted couldn't believe his eyes. 'What are you doing here Arthur old son?'

'Just a bit of R and R, that's all,' he punched Ted's shoulder.

'Cissy said you were RAF, and you made it as a rear gunner. Is that right?'

'Aye.' Arthur quickly changed the subject. 'How is she? Still sweet on me? I 'aven't seen her for,' he paused, 'it seems like years.'

Uncertain how his strong-willed sister would take him commenting on her feelings, Ted asked, 'Aren't you writing to her? She'll have told you herself won't she?'

Arthur noticed the increase in confidence, and sat back and stretched, enjoying his friend from Redcar, with satisfaction.

Overwhelmed at a little bit of home in Cairo, they made a toast to Cissy, then one to Rose, adding Stanley, then everyone in Redcar they could think of. They turned then to salute those back in camp, and those who hadn't made it, and then, through an alcoholic haze, just about anything that came to mind. As Ted had declined the suggestion of joining the man at the brothel Arthur recognised that some things just hadn't changed; he was still agonisingly shy with the women.

Chapter 25

Trieste, Italy, November 1942

The upper echelons of society called less and less, a decrease in confidence or triumphant outcome for Italy at the forefront of everyone's mind; it all seemed a distant vision. It was suggested though never uttered freely, for fear of retribution, that the nation was disintegrating like Il Duce's fragmenting mind.

Still, Vittorio's standards had to be maintained. Sixteen years of age and no longer at school, Bianca spent her mornings assisting Mamma in the kitchen, scrubbing the same clean floors she had scrubbed the day before.

Mia placed a light lunch on the table. Freshly baked bread rolls, eggs from their chickens, and a selection of cheeses, decorated with mint and parsley to enhance and disguise the meagre fare. Provisions had become rare and sporadic. As Bianca reached for a crumbled corner of cheese, her father dragged the plate towards himself with his knife. Inwardly she berated herself, hunger had made her forget the procedure; father first, then her brothers, Mamma to distribute the remains.

'Not eggs again.' Benito's sullen tone rumbled into the uncomfortable silence as her father placed her cheese back onto the serving plate.

'Here Benito and Luca, you take it,' he pushed the plate of cheese towards them, tossing a morsel across the table towards Mia. The boys sat, uncertain, eyes darting from plate to Mamma, then back to Papa. Luca, still permanently tied to his mother's side, asked, 'Mamma?' silenced with a look. Muttering, she stammered,

'That's fine, I'm not so hungry. All that baking ....' Trailing off she viewed the six feeble bread rolls on the white linen napkin in the breadbasket, quickly being removed by husband and sons, '... it puts me off my food.'

Food on their plate, the boys hesitated. Vittorio threw his knife on the table, casting a commanding eye at wife and sons. 'If you want to eat again boys, finish the food on your plate,' then demanded, 'coffee!'

Mia scrambled from the table reaching for the coffee pot, covertly stroking her daughter's shoulder as she passed, placing his cup at his side.

Bianca sat, silently, screaming inside, *'What about me? Why am I treated with such regard? I do everything I can to maintain his standards and please him.'*

As the lifeblood of Italy drained away with mismanagement and defeats, the effects on everyone was beginning to show. She remembered the lavish tables her mother had once prepared, and looked at the single remaining roll, leaned forward to pick it up. A hot cup of coffee flew through the air, scalding her hand.

'If you do not provide, you do not eat,' her father blasted.

Then she heard her own voice,'The boys don't provide anything and they get to ....' Her father exploded,

'They have their place, they don't scavenge,' he yelled. Not for the first time she held her hands over her ears shrieking inwardly. She tried to block out the sound, but still the words burrowed into her head.

'Get out of this house,' her father slammed the table. 'It's a woman's work to find food; there will be plenty around, and when you bring it here, then you eat.'

Benito opened his mouth to speak, and with the most imperceptible movement Mia shook her head. Biting his words, he shot a disdainful look at his sister, Papa's authority undermined by her disagreeable nature, again. His age commanded his sour attitude towards Bianca, but he knew the kitchen was Mamma's domain, and it was good practice to imply she influenced his behaviour. His father continued.

'It is all you are good for, useless spawn, get out of my sight,' Papa screamed as Bianca dashed to the stairs, 'and do something useful,' reverberating through the empty, spotless corridors. 'Life has changed!'

From Italy's bold 1940 position in Egypt, to the unwise invasion of Greece the same day they assaulted Albania, Italy had needed Germany to buoy its troops. It was whispered, their increasing reliance on Nazi forces to sustain disintegrating efforts, enraged Hitler.

In her bedroom Bianca took down her memory book, cartoons and verses drawn by admirers and friends' brothers covered the pages, with declarations of love and bravado before leaving for distant countries. She turned the page to a boy, so confident of victories he had drawn a picture of them both as children, he in military uniform, she a little housewife, hugging him. She ran her finger along the inscription, "Dearest, Soon a stripe for my uniform for Bianca's affection". It was dated 19 January that very year, but he'd never been heard of again, just like brave Uncle Salvo. All vestiges of the life she had lived and enjoyed, had disappeared.

She crept out, a stone of torment in her gut, resolving to prove she should, and would, eat. Walking down to Sofia's home halfway down the hill, a memory of Indian literature from her prestigious school came to mind; an abusive father, "Papachi ", beat the mother "Mammachi" to "put her in her place". It flitted through her mind briefly, and never truly left.

Sofia saw her from the kitchen window at the front of her home, recognising the now familiar look on her face, guessing she had been verbally abused again. She grabbed a late tomato from the plant in the window, and bread from a tray, and ran to meet her, asking, 'What's on the agenda today?'

'I think I'll go to Trieste.' Bianca couldn't bear to explain fully.

'Here,' Sofia thrust the morsels into her hand. Bianca's up-bringing necessitated she refuse as a matter of politeness, but the aroma of warm bread seduced her overriding her gentile manners, and the fragrant, fulsome fruit tempted. Her brow furrowed as she took a juicy bite, catching the ripe liquid with the delicious absorbent interior of the bread.

Maria listened at the window as the tale unfolded, and joined them on the bleached bench outside, presenting Bianca with warm milky coffee as a distraction, suggesting, 'Why don't you girls go into town and explore places where food might be sought?'

Markets had become unreliable, sometimes even empty. Shops from whence they had purchased the finest cuts of meat, were open for limited periods, displaying cheap slices of mutton or pork.

'Don't forget girls to mention the name "Marchetti". It was good for the most expensive wares before the war, and the shopkeepers should not forget this.'

She reached out a hand to Bianca. 'Come gather yourself cara, you can get a feel where your Mamma and I can shop. Or maybe tell us which café proprietors can be coerced for supplies.'

The adventure inspired the girls, and linking arms they proceeded down the hill, under the railway bridge, and turned left away from the army barracks, into the city.

They gravitated to Rialto's Cafe, in Piazza dei Foraggio, the proprietor, father of their friend Roberto. Only a short time previously the girls had enjoyed delicate cakes and delights among prosperous customers. As the conflicts progressed, his father shrewdly diversified, adding more hearty foods, as the decadent ingredients of his exclusive menu became scarcer. Roberto's mother, more enamoured by her former well-heeled customers was not enthusiastic but finally bent to his resolve, and a pizza oven was built. As the tides of war ebbed and flowed, his wisdom proved to be their salvation as earthy odours pervaded the salon.

Nervously the two girls peered through the large front window, nudging each-other into action. Roberto's mother recognized Bianca, guessing their aim, and having seen the darkness in her father, was prepared to indulge her a little. She deduced there was a benefit to staying on his good side and sent them to the back entrance to see her husband.

Roberto's father was more affable, and the girls gained courage. As he affected disinterest, they attempted nonchalance, leaning against the wall, singing to each other to attract his attention. Eventually he considered their request, giving them salami cut-offs, agreeing with mock irritation, they may call again.

*

They developed a practised performance with Roberto's Papa. He would feign disinterest, then, absentmindedly join in their ditty seemingly unconscious of their presence, suddenly spinning round to demand what they knew of this lady or that old esteemed customer of his. Sometimes he would pretend they leave him in peace, only to give in to their crestfallen looks by passing prepared parcels containing dregs of olive oil, smears of butter or rinds of parmesan, claiming to rid himself of their nonsense.

After their first tentative successes, repeating their girlish act became a given and they became more self-assured and artful as the weeks passed, ever-increasing their network of suppliers. Each small item contributed to the ever more ingenious meals their mothers created, all from the haphazard collection of food-stuffs.

Part II

Chapter 26

Trieste, Italy, early December 1942

A more advanced system developed. Meat and sophisticated foodstuffs could be found in the city, and they would meet at the railway bridge below Sofia's house. If vegetables or country fayre were required, they would make their way behind the power-station and travel up to the Karst.

Early morning sun drizzled through the trees, as they set off up the hill, and despite their youth, the trek was arduous with infrequent vehicles passing for possible lifts. Bianca's dissatisfaction at the injustice of their task never stifled.

'I can't believe we have to do men's work, but I suppose complaining isn't going to get us there any quicker.' She looked at Sophia. 'What does your mother think of us going to the Karst?'

Sofia was silent for a moment struggling for a reply.

'Mamma is reserved in her thoughts, but I know she doesn't like us to be under your Papa's spell.' Uncomfortable she had repeated her thoughts out loud, she turned around to see Bianca kicking the dirt at her feet.

'Don't worry Sofia I know what you mean, he's a tough master. He wants what he wants, and will accept nothing less. Look at how he sends me out to put food in front of him; it can be so frightening at times. I don't know why the boys can't do it.'

'You know why Bianca, it's not safe for them.'

'But what about us?' Silence fell between them, continuing, 'I'm so grateful you're with me Sofia. He still expects me to walk the streets and hills on my own when your Mamma will not allow it, and I don't think he would care if anything happened to me,' tears glistened in the rising sun.

'I'm sure he would be Bianca. The city depends on the power station to provide power. There are many that need him.'

'I need him too. I need to know that I'm not just one of his workforce. I am his daughter; I need to know that he cares. He orders Mamma and I around like servants, Benito and Luca lounge around like princes or Luca follows Mamma like a little dog and Benito stares at film magazines with blank eyes. I wonder if he thinks anything at all.'

They stopped to catch their breath at the top of the steep road. Sophia called out.

'Look out Bianca, you're sliding all over.' She bent to tie her friends' shoe laces, snapping upright. 'What's happened to your shoes?' looking up at her dear friend, eyes swelling with tears again. Bianca sank to the roadside.

'Papa's work shoes needed mending; he had the leather sole of my winter footwear removed to patch his,' auburn hair tumbled over her contorted face as wet cardboard fell through the hole in her shoe.

Sofia sat beside her, taking off her shoes, 'Here, we'll take turns. Let's look for something to put in your shoe. I can't believe he expected you to climb all over the flinty Kart in footwear like this, it's dangerous. All those over-grown hidden bottomless potholes, plenty of people have been lost to them, never seen again. I can't wait to tell my Mamma, she isn't frightened of him.' She searched around for dry, rough grass to line the shoe sliding her socked feet over the lumpy soles.

'There, that'll do for now; put mine on.'

They continued walking, hand in hand through deserted lanes, Bianca's spirit lifting as they made up a song about "Papachi", a father so cruel to his daughter, ending with expletives shouted at the top of their voices, until they came to a small hamlet. Despite regular visits, the Slovenes watched them with curiosity and distrust, their well-bred Italian bearing difficult to disguise. Eyes darted shiftily and disgruntled muttering rose as they passed. *'Why are city girls around here stealing our food?'*

In the wake of Mussolini's Slav persecution they had to watch their backs, but hunger, and Vittorio's relentless directives required they take their chance, their sensibilities replaced by cunning and guile.

Bianca ignored the taunts, launching snippets of conversation into the air. *"Happiest days of my life when I lived in Opicina,"* knowing the locals would pick up on the Slav reference, followed by chatter of having been born in the, her life ruined when torn away to sordid Trieste. This usually cultivated safe passage, fending off the most malignant comments as they competed for foraged food.

*

Finally, picking their way among the rocks, Bianca saw them first, the shoddy clothes of the two male figures blending with the winter vegetation lying motionless in long grass. Sofia quietly climbed onto a small escarpment to get a better view, receiving a crude motion from the nearest lad.

Having wandered the rough edges of the Karst for weeks they were accustomed to oaths and abuse, but the way he gestured drew special attention. Almost a sixth sense for food alerted the girls to a good opportunity, the juices in their empty stomachs churned.

Without warning, he leapt, like a thin, long-legged bird, silently and swiftly gliding through the air with a corner of a net in each hand. It was hardly visible as he manoeuvred silently, bringing the corners down in well rehearsed synchronicity.

He sprang around, rocks and his feet covered the edges of the net giving the squawking prey little chance of escape, fragile wings flapping, the odd beak poking out as desperate birds fought to flee. One corner badly secured, a couple of sparrows took their opportunity, wings catching in the netting.

Finally satisfied that the prey were secured, the nearest boy had time to pay attention to his audience, pulling shoulders back, chest out, he strode around, pulling a stalk of dried grass and hanging it from the corner of his mouth, like a gangster's cigarette in a film. Silently, another figure arose beyond; older, black eyes silently observing the girls as they swapped shoes again.

Bianca and Sofia carefully approached the younger grass chewing boy who attempted nonchalance, reclining against a large pitted limestone boulder. Nearing, they saw the netting encased various birds, tangled and flapping hopelessly as their energy ebbed away.

'Why are you doing that?' Changing times demanded instant decisions, Bianca's direct approach could invite trouble, but she'd learned taking the upper hand had an advantage. Or a flick of her hair, or pout, provided a distracting escape.

'Mamma makes an excellent rabbit stew,' the boy with the grass was Slav and grinned. He was about their age, and Bianca noted his affected casualness as an attempt to impress.

'What are you talking about? They're not rabbits,' she replied.

The Bird Boy sighed.

'She doesn't like people to know they're birds so we have to say she's cooking rabbit,' eyeing the girls carefully. 'When there's plenty it makes a good ragu, if not, they add to a tasty pizza rustica,' he laughed.

The man with dark narrow eyes, barely visible under furrowed brows, sliced a glance at the youngster.

Bianca surreptitiously studied the brooding fellow. He was older and surly. Hunger had stunted development of his larger frame, as barely disguised hatred lurked beneath his sullen exterior. Following his instruction the Bird Boy left them and gathered the birds tight in the net, flapping wings crushed together.

Sofia pulled Bianca away, reminding them they needed to get to a hamlet where provisions were expected, neither of them sorry to miss the final outcome for the poor flightless creatures. Glancing over her shoulder as they walked away, Bianca caught the full uninhibited animosity of the older one, while the Bird Boy strained for one last glimpse of the girls, straw still in place. His older companion spat foul words in their direction and, despite the sun's brave attempts to beat back the winter chill, a shiver ran down her back.

On return home, they received a reprimand for their late appearance, the atmosphere changing when spinach, broad beans, polenta flour and late autumn mushrooms were displayed across the kitchen table. Mia rushed for onions and a precious scrap of carefully wrapped parmigiana as Bianca emptied her purse to demonstrate her excellent bargaining power.

The girls' secret delight was their scheme to catch "rabbit".

Chapter 27

Trieste, Italy, late December 1942

Recently every trick Bianca and Sofia tried had failed.
Despite girlish cajoling and emerging womanly wiles,
Bianca engaging proprietors with bright eyes glistening
while Sofia adopted a wholesome distraction with their
wives, times were hard. Anything would do for their artful
mothers who could take a scrap of stale bread, a crust of
cheese and eke out a meal with home grown supplies.

Trailing behind Mia down to Sofia's house, Bianca's
attention was taken by sparrows hopping between rough
grass near the gate, plucking at grubs and insects. A couple
of starlings swooped down to join them, the rest of the flock
soon outnumbering the small birds. She thought of the
similarity with food supplies, only the strongest and most
determined took the spoils. She and Sophia had been quick
learners, and the halcyon days of school taught how to
position a young lady to advantage.

'Sofia, come quickly,' Bianca called from outside as
her mother disappeared into the kitchen with Maria.

'What's the hurry, we have a day of rest, except your
Mamma had us wash your linen, as you can see,' she
flashed a hand at the ballooning sheets blowing on the line.
'What do you have in mind?'

A rare shaft of winter sunlight skimmed off blinding
white sheets and tablecloths, flapping almost dry in the
wind.

The young women put their heads together as they
took their regular place on the bench outside the kitchen
window, gazing up the hill towards the electricity stazione.

'I saw you dragging your feet, ' Sofia said.

'It was my silent protest Sofia. I am sick of the
demands made of me. Why should they be so exacting

about every moment of my time? Do this, wash that, wash it again. I do everything. I've already been to the garden today, ironed yesterday's washing, cleaned the vegetables, and sluiced the floors.'

'I'm sure it's just as hard for them Bianca....' she recognised her friend's agony. Her own life was so happy; she was cherished and nurtured by kind loving parents making the burden of the times so much easier to bear.

Blinding flashes of sunlight cast slivers of sunlight on thrashing laundered sheets. Bianca ran a few seeds from grasses by the path, through her fingers. Protected from the wind they watched the last damp on the laundry disappear, all white crispness now, as an idea took them both.

'The boy,' Sofia whispered.

'The birds,' hissed Bianca. Furtively she shot a glance at their mothers in the kitchen, making a circle of thumb and forefinger and nodded. Their attention darted around the garden to beyond the blowing laundry where muted chirruping was detected. They nudged each-other, moving slowly.

Quietly, they crept to the washing line, surreptitiously checked the kitchen window, and carefully took down an old checked table cloth.

The swiftness of the Karst boys had fascinated them as they leapt through the undergrowth, working together, expertly signalling "straight ahead", "go right" or "left" to secure their prey; it couldn't be too hard. They slunk around the edge of the dry grass, within feet of the feeding birds. It looked easy, the birds were stupid and hadn't even noticed them coming. Bianca scattered the few seeds she had on the ground before them to draw the birds closer. Sofia stretched for a stone to put on her corner of the cloth, picking a large useless pebble instead. At that same moment, Bianca lunged at the birds, table cloth in full sail. The resulting shrieks drew their mothers to the window.

111

Seeing chaos and the unexpected spectacle of a squawking tablecloth they stood open mouthed.

Bianca's leap had resulted in a scream possibly audible at the railway station as Sofia, gripping her edge of the tablecloth, was dragged from her crouching position, falling on her face onto the fabric. Resulting immobility yanked Bianca's clutching arm back. In full creeping mode, she proceeded to stagger sideways, leg over leg. Sparrows in a state of confusion under the material, flailed and squawked in all directions looking for escape. Times were tough, even for birds, but nothing in their short lives had prepared them for this. Sofia rolled over the cloth whilst trying to get up; it moved beneath her, shifting and squirming as the birds sank into vegetation below, some wriggling free. Bianca, regaining her hunting position hovered over their trap which undulated and screeched in protest.

Their mothers watched bewildered as the confusing scene unfolded, spluttered laughter escaping tight fingers clutched across their mouths.

Bianca's position was interrupted as a lone starling made a brave attempt at freedom, flapping out of the edge of its' prison, and attempting ascent to blue sky safety, but taking any route available, flew up her skirt. With no deference to modesty, motivated by alarm and panic, she hopped about, flapping her skirt around her chin in a passable imitation of the bird itself and waft the creature free. Unfortunately, her other hand still hung to the corner of the tablecloth enabling the liberation of a confused collection of small bedraggled birds as they flapped, tripped and tumbled out.

Their mothers ricocheted from confusion, to alarm, to hysteria, shrieks of laughter adding to the mayhem. Sofia was on all fours with birds avoiding flight risk dashing between her legs as she still attempted to get up. The resulting bizarre hopping from one hand and foot to the other, in all combinations to avoid hurting them, added to the ridiculous scene.

Running, flapping, attempts at flight subsided, most of the birds gone, a couple of sad casualties remained in the tangled dusty tablecloth.

Their mother's retreated from the window with muffled gasps and giggles, attempting to regain their composure as the girls surveyed the scene. Scratches, dirty socks, a raggedy tablecloth, and a quick look at the kitchen window to check - no-one to be seen, it seemed they had got away with it.

As they picked the twigs out of their shoes and tried to rub the dust off of the cloth, Mia and Maria emerged calmly, chatting, Bianca quick to explain.

'Oh, Mamma, you should have seen it, the wind! Such a sudden gust tore the tablecloth from the line and it landed on some birds; they were so frightened, flapping around, they tore a hole in it, and when we tried to save it, the birds were so big they just made it worse.'

For the slightest moment, everyone looked at each other then Sofia stepped forward.

'Even I wouldn't believe that. Big birds? What are you saying, they were Eagles?'

Their mothers with hands on hips and unwavering eyes gave no clue to their reaction. The girls stood bedraggled and dusty, grass in their hair, mouths dry, eyes wide, waiting for the inevitable reprimand.

'What an amazing thing to happen Bianca,' her mother's tone surprisingly stern, 'how could a thing like that happen?' For a moment, silence seemed the safest option, until; 'Well....' an idea was developing in Bianca.

Sofia cast a panicked look in her direction. Surely she wasn't going to reveal they had consorted with wild boys on the Karst.

'....well, we saw some boys catching birds with a big net ....' she was. 'Their mother made rabbit stew with them.'

Sofia gulped. Maybe punishment could be halved if both involved, and added tentatively, 'And probably the birds saw the cloth when it blew off the line and thought someone was trying to catch them, and they were trying to escape?'

Their mothers stood silent, Bianca filled with confidence at their combined ingenious explanation and ventured a casual stance, leaning her weight on one leg, kicking the earth with the other as if attitude would add validity to the explanation. She looked sideways to check their reaction.

'Strange the wind should affect only one item on the line,' Mia stated, then, linking her daughter's arm, began marching her up the hill, 'but a good tale nevertheless.' Bianca grimaced as she was paraded past her friend. 'Amazing, birds can be made into rabbit stew,' Mia added, 'and that these particular birds knew they too would be made into stew, ingenious animals.' She looked into her daughter's eyes. 'Well I suppose they fly a long way and talk to each other.' Mother and daughter understood, the subject was closed.

*

Shortly afterwards however, boys on the slope down from the electricity station were seen employing the same trick to catch birds. No-one mentioned where they got the idea, it was just boys doing what they did in the brutality of war. But occasionally, rabbit stew started appearing on the table in local homes, and sometimes, the girls dared to credit themselves for the unusual foraging method.

Chapter 28

Trieste, Italy, early 1943

What food rationing that existed was ever more erratic. Bianca and Sofia continued to approach shopkeepers and restaurateurs, who themselves were under continuing pressure, and explored ever wider sources for supplies. A rumour of a whole truck of fresh vegetables arriving inland had them set off early into unpredictable Slovene territory; never their favourite destination but every possibility had to be explored.

Bianca wore a pair of her brother's boots to tackle the trek across the winter Karst as they set off for the long hike, backpacks empty except for a bottle of water and an apple each, money sewn into secret compartments in their jackets.

'How are things at home?' Sofia hazarded the sensitive question, relieved to see her friend a little more light-hearted.

'Oh you know how it is Sofia, it all depends on his mood or business or who has called on him, what is in his stomach.' She was making light of things, a good sign.

'Is it Opicina today?' Sofia asked.

'Do you need to know exactly where we will place each footstep along the way?' her good humour brittle it seemed. She looked away.

'I'm not always sure where we will end up, so at least I like to know where we are going,' Sophia's laughter tinkled in the still early morning.

'Shush, we don't want to attract attention if we can avoid it or we'll end up with a trail of hopefuls behind us,' Bianca said. Smiles settled on their faces as they held hands and ascended the road towards Draga in Slovene territory, Bianca continued, 'I just know we are to make our way to

Wolf Valley, and it's called that for a reason she warned.'
Sophia looked concerned.

'Don't worry,' despite everything, Bianca was
protective of her friend. 'If we find anything else on the
way, we'll fill our bags and return home as soon as we can;
would that suit you cara? We don't have to tell anyone the
truth.'

Sofia was uncertain; she didn't keep secrets from her
mother but understood how different Bianca's life was.

An old vehicle rumbled up the road behind them,
stopping a little way ahead.

'You girls, where are you going?' A gummy smile
below a bristly, uneven, moustache belied the flint eye of
the driver. The girls knew better than to give away too
much information, attempting vague explanations.

'We're going to see our aunt,' Sophia replied.

They looked at each-other, it was obvious they
couldn't be sisters. But situations could be complicated. On
more than one occasion they'd had almost everything
stolen by hungrier, more desperate travellers on the road,
and assessing possible adversaries on their travels, was
their life now.

'Get in girls, I'll give you a lift.' He slung open the
passenger door.

'No thank you, we don't have far to go,' Bianca said.
He had generated a flicker of distrust in her, so eager to
make their acquaintance.

'But where are you going, there is nothing around
here for miles?' his eyes narrowed.

'We know the landmarks,' Sofia piped up. 'We don't
need an address.'

'You take a dangerous road girls, you're asking for
trouble. Go on, get in.'

They were usually able to talk themselves out of
unwanted attention, but this one was craftier, too helpful
and insistent, eyes cold. Excuses depleted, and with him

parked across their path, they couldn't refuse or turn back, it would belie their story. There was no avoiding it and they slid onto the front bench seat of the truck.

He continued probing, suggesting people who would know their aunt, they mumbling replies. Eventually, Sofia discreetly nudged Bianca, indicating the narrowing road ahead and the edge of a steep ravine on the driver's side, preventing any opportunity for him to disembark. Just before, a rough cart-way turned off to the right. As he slowed to negotiate the swing along the gully edge they threw open their door, and jumped out.

'This is where we turn away,' they shouted, better be polite, just in case. The man could neither reverse nor get out of the vehicle on the narrow pass above the steep drop, his curses and oaths travelled after them as they ran up the cart track away from the gulch, a new sound throwing them into panic. They threw themselves into the undergrowth ignoring the danger of any unseen pothole, and lay as flat as possible fearing their thudding hearts would reveal them. Boots crunched on stony ground beyond a bend ahead of them. Sofia mouthed, 'What are we going to do?'

'Lay quiet,' Bianca mouthed back, closing her eyes in pretend sleep to calm her friend, as the old truck drove away.

As time passed their hearts beat slower, muscles relaxing a little, there were men just around the curve of the trail. Bianca thought she could lie there all day if need be, warm in the foliage, content not having to strive for anything for anyone, for just one moment in her life.

An ominous crack of a twig above them snapped, her eyes split open to gather every detail, each sound analysed, calculating danger. She slowly raised her head through the vegetation instantly dropping to the ground.

'What is it?' Sofia mouthed.

'It's the Bird Boy, the one catching sparrows with a net,' she shook her head in disbelief.

'What's he doing here?' asked Sophia.

Bianca shrugged her shoulders.

'Tst!' a hardly audible sound came through the undergrowth. Sofia raised her head. There eye to eye, not far away, Bird Boy lay, his face a warning.

'Get down' he matched their silent communication.

Bianca slithered through the plants until she was behind him. Unseen heavy boots began making their way down the path; she looked at Bird Boy, his hand clenched in the small of his back above, sitting in a crevice, coolly observing the strangers.

He flicked out a thumb from his fist, then fingers one, two, a pause then three and four. She turned silently towards the pathway; her heart froze as rifle barrels appeared above the plants by the track. Looking again at Bird Boy one thumb and finger closed, she realised two men were gone, then two more fingers closed. Listening to the drag of boots from her leafy hide she caught the profile of the rough one who had been with Bird Boy that day. As he trudged by, a ruthless chill emanated, having lost none of his menace. She didn't breathe or move for the longest moment, then, carefully turning to the boy's fist, the fifth digit closed. A moment, and he wiggled them as if walking. There must have been five men and they had all left. If they waited long enough, if God was on their side, they were safe. She looked to Sofia, eyes still tightly closed, hands over her ears in silent prayer. More moments passed.

'Well, well what do we have here?' Bird Boy crept into their den, 'It's fine for you to come out now,' grabbing Sofia's coat collar he dragged her from her position, 'just as long as you don't stand up. I can still see them down the hill, but best you don't advertise yourselves, eh?'

'What were they doing, why didn't you leave with that bruto?'

'You mean my brother? Because, I am not him.' His congenial face darkened, 'we don't think the same, or do the same things. I just wanted to know what he was up to.'

'Why were you hiding?' Bianca asked.

'It's best not to anger him,' he searched for a suitable piece of grass to chew. 'Anyway, what are you doing up here?'

'We've been sent for vegetables, over at Draga, you know Wolf Valley?'

'You're lost and way too late, that was yesterday and it was nothing but rotten leaves. It's always the same, by the time you hear of it, it's gone.' The girls looked disappointed.

'We'll have to go back with something,' Sofia moaned.

'You spend a lot of time up here don't you?' Bianca began a little gentle interrogation. Still lying on the ground below the vegetation line, the boy stuck a finger in his mouth, wetting it and tentatively raised it above the brush and plants around him.

'What are you doing now? She sat up, and he yanked her back down with his free hand.

'Now what?' she asked.

'My brother can detect odours like a dog, if he gets a whiff of a girl out here he'll be back in an instant. Anyway, he won't want anyone knowing what he's been up to.'

'What has he been up to?' she pressed. *"Knowledge is power,"* her father said, and she wanted to be armed with as much information as possible about the frightening creature.

'All I can say, is if he knew I was here he'd batter me into next week at the very least. It doesn't do to know too much, or get too involved these days,' thoughtfully he scanned the earth they were holed up in. 'Don't worry though, we are downwind of him,' he grinned, wiping his finger dry on his jacket.

119

'So what are you doing?' Bianca asked, innocently. 'It's always nice to know what your comrades are doing,' for safety's sake.

'Don't call me that again, ever! Don't you understand how dangerous it is for an Italian to know a communist for both of us? Just keep me out of it anyway, I want nothing to do with any of that anyway,' he scowled.

'Sorry, I won't ask your name then,' Bianca apologised.

'Now you're thinking clearly,' he shot them both a friendly grin.

'But what were you doing?'

'Hunting. I've rabbit traps all over the place, how was I to know he was going to turn up here with some of his meat-heads. He hasn't seen the traps though, or he would have been looking for me.'

'Can we come with you while you check them?' Bianca adopted her biggest wide-eyed gaze. He didn't respond. 'Or maybe you would teach us how to trap?' he looked defeated.

'Well, you haven't caused me trouble yet, and took instruction well,' he considered, then running his eyes over the pretty faces, 'why not? You can come while I check the traps and I'll show you how to set them too, but you have to do it regularly to make sure the catch doesn't rot. There's nothing more dangerous than infected meat, except perhaps my brother,' he chuckled, jumping to his feet, the girls scrambling after him.

*

After an hour he had retrieved a cache of animals in various states of rigour. 'These'll be fine,' he said, handing some to the girls.

'Are you sure, don't you need to take them all back to your family?' Sophia, in awe at his kindness.

'It won't matter, we're all out trapping today; they'll probably have plenty too.'

Deep gratitude replaced the girls' usual reserve and they flung their arms around him. Surprised and embarrassed he managed to extract himself.

'Come along, let's see what you can learn and remember about setting traps.'

He walked them back towards their home, pointing out animal runways, identifying droppings of edible creatures like rats, anything that would provide food, directing them across the dangerous ground.

'Look now at that rivulet,' they glanced at the clear water running beside them. 'Listen to the sound, can you hear it?' The girls stood silent, concentrating. 'Do you hear it?' he repeated.

'The tinkling of the stream, it's mixed with a kind of whooshing sound?' Sofia hazarded a guess.

'That's right, that stream disappears underground around here somewhere' he poked at the grasses with a long staff, 'it will be emptying into a foibe, and that's the rush of the water as it lands way below ground.'

The girls grasped each other, unable to move. Everyone knew about the foibes, the Karst's cavernous holes, sometimes as big as a cathedral below ground with tiny openings hidden by vegetation. They stood as if they feared the earth would open up and devour them.

'You look so funny,' Bird Boy laughed. 'Do you think I don't know what I'm doing? Nothing's going to happen to you,' he nearly fell over at the sight of them.

'Alright, you caught us out. Did you enjoy your joke?' Bianca regained her composure first, 'just give us more tips to keep us safe. What do we do if we get lost?'

'Just follow your trail back.'

'What if it's dark?'

'Don't be on the Karst at night; sometimes even wild boar from Wolf Valley come this way,' he replied.

'We're not supposed to be this far from home when it gets dark anyway,' Sofia remembered her parents' careful instructions.

'If you ever do get stuck out here at night and you're not sure of the ground, just hide yourselves underbrush and wait until it starts to get light when you can better see where you're going. Or if you can see, you could track yourselves back to where you came from.'

'How do we do that?' Bianca, keen to learn.

'Every animal on the Karst leaves a mark, maybe emptying bowels or peeing. Use your noses, sit still, smell the air, and if you detect a stink avoid it. But, if you are lost and have a general idea which direction you should go, zig-zag a path from side to side until you pick up your trail. You two would leave a clear route of crushed vegetation for sure' The girls took it all in enthralled.

'Now you know everything I know, but not as well,' he grinned again and made his way to the road.

As they tucked the rabbits in their bags, he offered final advice. 'If you see any of us, Slovenes I mean, stick the rabbits under your clothes, keep your head down and don't draw attention to yourselves, unless you want a lift and you can barter a rabbit for the trip.'

They turned to go, waving.

'See you again,' he cheerily shouted, returning up the steep hill.

*

That evening there was much praise for the catch, and the next day, from the power station down to the railway line, traps were laid.

Chapter 29

Trieste, Italy, early 1943

'**P**apa has a gift for you.' Bianca's mother scuttled to meet her daughter, taking the hessian bag of groceries from her stringy limbed grasp.

'What are you talking about Mamma?' She was weary, exhausted from carrying potatoes up the hill. Sofia's little brother had met them at the bottom, and relieved her of some of her burden, but as usual, no such assistance was forthcoming from Benito or Luca.

'Don't pout dear, he has a surprise for you.'

Her mother's excitement piqued her interest. Could it be true? Was she to be rewarded for her hard work and dangerous quests at last?

'He has made an appointment for you. Here is the name and address,' her mother confirmed.

Adjusting her vision from the windy weather outside, she squinted at the card before her, wondering, '_Am I to get a new outfit; I've outgrown most of my clothes?_' Lack of nutrition hadn't prevented her womanly development.

The gift was that she was to have her portrait taken by the photographer of her school days, when life was luxurious, and he recorded the glorious development of the fascist girls academy. Now she realised it was as dangerous to be a fascist as not to be one. How times had changed and she thought of their new good friend, the Bird Boy.

*

On the appointed day, she approached the studio, thrilled and excited. Her father was finally showing his appreciation for all the hazardous journeys she had taken, and encounters with the most desperate, and rewarding her with a portrait. In the times they now lied, a photographer's

123

services would be expensive, and an honour. Her Papa must really care about her. Making her way through the city she pondered why Sofia had been forbidden to know of, or accompany her to share in her excitement.

'Hey Bianca.' Her voice called from across the road, her dearest friend emerging from an apartment block.

'War and events are making Nonna very weary,' Sophia said, 'she's dismissed me from my visit, Where are you going cara?' Sofia was delighted to see her friend and they quickly connived no harm could be done if she joined her at the event, and arm in arm, they set off excited together.

'You remember when Signor Photographer took our academic pictures at the end of term. The one of me holding a javelin was crazy, as if I could throw that.' Bianca laughed happy to have her friend by her side, 'and then those of us in confirmation gowns?' They fell silent for a moment, transported back to the heady days of promise before war ripped through their lives.

They reached the address and rang the bell. The photographer looked flushed and confused when presented with the pair, glancing furtively up and down the street ushering them in quickly. A passing old man called to Sophia before she disappeared, requesting the health of her Nonna as the door slammed shut, leaving him muttering in the street. They were steered swiftly up the stairs to a room where thick dark curtains hung at the window, immediately drawn closed by the photographer.

Their excitement ebbed as they stood together in the dark, gradually making out details. He still hadn't spoken as he anxiously started positioning cameras and equipment. Exhaustive nervous energy flooded his pores, sweat forming on his palms making adjustments to lenses and stands difficult.

The girls huddled closer in the middle of the room, Sofia's little finger curled around Bianca's, gradually tightening, and whispered, 'What's he doing?'

'I've no idea,' Bianca replied.

'Why isn't he talking?'Sophia asked.

'I don't know Sofia' not the answer she was hoping for.

The photographer turned his shirt sleeves up to his elbows, tie loose now, collar undone, but sweat still ran down his shiny forehead, wet patches forming under his arms, a world away from the professional performance of their school days. Bianca grew ever more apprehensive.

Eventually, he seemed to gather some semblance of self-control. Some twenty minutes had passed before he seemed able to bring himself to look at them. The girls had been rooted to the spot by the bizarre situation, unable to move or query his authority, tightly clutching hands.

*

A few days previously.

His daughter! His very own daughter! What was the man thinking, if he was a man at all?' He wouldn't, couldn't take such a job, not even in these tough times.

'Signor Marchetti, it is out of the question. I responded to your commission under the assumption that a family photograph was required. This is quite outrageous.'

Emotionless eyes rose slowly from his desk, the darkness within them pinned the photographer to the spot for the longest most uncomfortable moment.

'Don't take such a high hand with me,' Vittorio spoke, ice blue eyes drilling into him.

'I know of your side-line producing revealing photographs for local whores to advertise their wares,' he levelled his gaze, 'in exchange for a little fun no doubt, taking advantage of their business, as a friendly gift ?'

The photograph wilted visibly before him.

'You will comply with my request or your dealings will be exposed. I am sure your wife, the priest, and I would add, the community, would be very interested, and,' he paused, 'no more lucrative commissions with schools.'

A fist clenched the photographer's chest. It had only been a little fun. Why, any man would have done the same, life was so very hard now, and a little light flirtation helped ease the stress of troubled times. He reflected how everyone's pre-war lofty principles had crumbled all around them, Marchetti was no better.

'So my friend that is the deal,' Vittorio, unconcerned, looked from his paperwork to regard the defeated man before him, and laid down his pen, continuing.

'There are no boundaries my daughter will resist, I assure you.'

He had seen a couple of flirty cartoons among the lyrical verses in her memory book, penned from hormone infused brothers of her friends before they went off to war during Mussolini's hay day, and that was sufficient excuse.

He was furious. His daughter had dared to develop a network of friends and acquaintances outside his control, and she would pay. There would be no place she could go, nothing she could do that would prevent his power, she was developing far too much confidence. His grip had loosened when she had started making her own decisions out on the road he reasoned. She was asking for trouble, and he would make sure she got it, from him. She would learn, he was the only one who conducted her thoughts, her behaviour.

'There is no reason to expect her to resist,' he continued. 'You will take the images as I have instructed, and expose every part of her with no concern for resistance or pleas of her reputation, no compassion required.'

The photographer's mouth was dry, he couldn't speak, dared not move, disbelief and horror frustrating words. Nothing could express his shock; what kind of madness was he being drawn into. He couldn't do it, what would become of him?

Vittorio continued casually as if ordering a meal from a menu.

'Make her as a girl, and yet desirous of deflowering,' he gazed heavenward in consideration then to the photographer again.

'You lay a finger on her at your own cost.'

Reeling, the cameraman left the office, sunlight confusing his brain. As he stumbled light headed back to his studio, he could see no way out of the sordid trap.

*

When he had opened the door to the two girls, it had thrown him and the already unthinkable dreaded situation into complete disarray. As he fussed around the studio, inwardly he lamented his plight; he was a simple man who had taken what work he could, to make ends meet. The flirty photos of the night girls had become an oasis of fun in an otherwise bare-boned existence. He was not prepared for truly smutty photography and the threat of his pious wife finding out horrified him; she would think it unforgivable he had associated with women of the night but he had panicked, confronted by the dark terrifying soul of Marchetti. His directive was inconceivable, cursing himself he'd gone to see him at all. Why hadn't he known better? Now it was too late, he was sucked into a conspiracy to defile the poor girl's character.

By the time equipment adjustments came to an end, he settled on a course of action. Bianca was a beauty with expertly plucked eyebrows and loosely curled dark brown hair swept back from high cheekbones, all speaking of style not shameful wanton lust. As he ran his artistic eye over her, he detected nothing of the lust her father had talked of and decided to photograph both girls together in the main, then concentrate on Bianca.

As they relaxed into the experience, his eye fell to her full pouting lips, a touch of arrogance there maybe, or was it defiant self-protection? She had a look men wouldn't ignore, but no heedless sexuality, simply a beautiful young girl on the brink of womanhood.

'What was that evil beast of a father up to trying to rain such damage upon his daughter?' he thought. What could she have done that would make a man devise such a punishment? He knew Vittorio wasn't a man to be crossed, but this plumbed unfathomable depths. Could it be an act of revenge upon his daughter, but for what? Or was it something she had not done for him? The question spread through his mind like a virus.

He had to think fast, plan carefully. He posed them standing together, back to back, holding hands, then sitting. Skirts outgrown, too short now, riding up over flawless knees, giggles indicating they had relaxed into the session. Now to introduce something else.

He asked them about their travels gathering food on the dangerous roads and some of their terrible experiences, suggesting portraits to show vulnerability, while demonstrating the strength of an Italian woman, the idea well-received. To demonstrate his ideas he showed classical pictures of heroines from history, limp-wristed delicate hands resting lightly on naked necks while plunging Renaissance necklines revealed as much as possible to engage the viewer. When he produced the Venus of Urbino, they recoiled, and he gauged their limits.

So together, and separately, he took photos of them naked at the shoulders, eyes looking into an indefinable distance, alert to danger. Starvation had already accentuated Bianca's bone structure, gently resting lips

128

spoke of a young woman proud but dignified as she looked over her right shoulder into an imagined place.

*

Without revealing the original despicable nature of the commission the photographer decided the images were to be delivered to the two mothers in their kitchen, who quickly brought their daughters to account. His adapted version of the commission now revealed, it left him no longer at risk of blackmail, especially, with so many people becoming involved.

Maria had to be ejected from his studio screaming her daughter should not have been exposed to such an experience, without her permission. Thankfully, he was able to cite the old gentleman witnessing the girls' attendance of their own accord, and the photographs and film were instructed to be burned by the girls themselves to teach them a lesson.

At the end of that fateful day, all but one image remained, a single piece of evidence of the alarming and exhilarating experience, hidden by Bianca.

*

Within a few days, Bianca witnessed the photographer's irate wife marching her husband to her father's office to seek payment for the task, evidence, she claimed, of his involvement of a purely professional nature.

As she waited outside, workers within the power station witnessed money being flung in the photographer's face. Bianca heard the real sordid story unfold from an adjoining workshop while looking for Luca. Hungry and worn down by war, no longer proud, the photographer scraped the bank-notes from the floor. As he rose, Bianca heard every word the workmen couldn't, as her father coolly walked around his desk towards the photographer, almost hissing.

'Useless cretino,' she heard, as her father's vicious hot breath spat in the photographer's face. 'You think you can disobey me?'

He took a long cool look into the man's very core, reaching deeper still, holding him tight by his collar against the wall. 'I will bring the hordes of hell down upon you, insignificant pile of filth.'

From somewhere deep within, the photographer seized courage, quietly choking a reply.

'You had better be careful old man. That you could wish me to visit such a malignant dishonour upon your daughter, display her body so? Have you never looked into her eyes? She harbours no lust there, just a lonely weariness at having experienced things no young girl should ever have to. Her life is hard, she's been braver than you ever have, and you wanted to subject her to such degradation, displaying her womanhood as filth.'

Released from his grip she heard the photographer stumble to the floor, and turn at the door.

'If there ever was a reason you would want such photographs of her, it's conceivable you were spawned by the devil himself. Watch your back old man, God doesn't pay his debts in money.' He turned and left.

Bianca, on the other side of the wall could not have said when she next inhaled. The unspeakable things her father had contrived to happen to her, the consequences and horrors of the mind she would have endured for the rest of her life, echoed around her brain. Her head throbbed. Desolate, she tiptoed from the workshop.

Memories of "Papachi" came into her thoughts again; the wicked father symbolising the most grossness of behaviour. Her own father's malignance, augmented by his arrogance, left no more room for affection in any corner of her being. Berating and bullying satisfied a need in him, her

130

mother no protection, brothers no inclination to get involved; she was alone.

Lying awake that night, a veil descended upon her, shrouding her heart, wrapping tightly to protect what few thoughts she could still comprehend; it was the foundation of a barrier between her and the world, begun.

No-one else would enter her life and harm her again.

Chapter 30

Trieste, Italy, early 1943

'*Such a great man!*' Bianca watched her father walk across the courtyard. '*Every man knows his word to be followed without question, the same in this house*'. That day he had decreed a workman, with six children, had looked at him wrongly, and been unceremoniously dismissed with no sympathy or compassion; his security withdrawn, no longer in a protected occupation conscription his only option.

Despite shortages, he commanded and rebuked, barked and snapped at her mother if food was not laid to his satisfaction. He took whatever he wished, her brothers next. Benito enjoyed his privileges, taking at leisure, or demanding items she and her mother had helped for themselves. Mamma and she, the main provider, always last. Mia saw her daughter's pain and saved scraps in the pans to allocate to her when her husband left the room.

Bianca's dissent grew in proportion to her growing hunger, and depleted energy. Her emaciating body raged with growing resentment for "Papachi" as she struggled with the daily challenge of her dangerous life. Then one day her father came upstairs, taking his place at the head of the kitchen table to dominate again in the heart of Mia's domain. 'Serve the food!' he barked.

The two boys sat next to each other at their fathers left, Mia at the opposite end to her husband, Bianca always to her mother's left opposite Luca. They had waited for his arrival for an hour, eagerly eyeing the forlorn collection of plated provisions. At his arrival, the boys sat, heads bowed out of sullen indifference rather than respect; Mia fluttered around the kitchen as her husband settled, nervously rearranging the dishes, as if movement would disguise the paltry offerings again.

Bianca considered how they always waited, eyes devouring paltry mismatched ingredients. They were weary, yearning for siesta, and prolonged staring at food only worsened their distress.

'This is what we have today, husband,' Mia trailing off. 'It's all we could manage my dear,' she stumbled as she tried to take her place opposite him.

Dead eyes scrutinised the meal.

'You give me pig swill?' he glared at Bianca.

'I could set my watch by how long you make us wait, 'God almighty!" she thought. *'No matter what time it is arranged, we always wait for you, as if you punish us for the shortages.'*

She jumped as his hand slammed the table

'Pass the putrid dish in the middle,' he growled.

Mia rushed to her husband's bidding, scraping her chair in the rush. 'It's a soup of sausage, with preserved tomatoes, and herbs from our garden husband dear, it's very nice'. She ladled half of the tureen onto his plate. 'Pass your father the bread Benito.'

He briefly tasted it and grabbed her wrist, 'The rest!'

'I was going to share it, Vittorio, they are growing boys,'

'I said, the rest.'

'But the children?' she twittered, 'I'm not having any and there's an egg salad from our hens dear, fresh and tasty.'

'I'm not interested in eggs,' his voice rising. Mia's eyes swept around the room, all three children alarmed.

'Here husband,' she started spooning more into his bowl and he pushed her away, sausage and tomato splattering the table.

'What are you doing, are you stupid woman? Feed the boys.'

133

'Jump this way or that, you will always be wrong,' Bianca thought, looking down at her empty plate. Mia turned to catch Benito picking bits of splashed food off the tablecloth and passed a bread roll to each son. Sitting down she looked at Bianca who whispered, 'What about me Mamma?' Mia silently hushed her, heaping spinach leaves on to her plate, two small slices of a sausage secreted below.

'Wine,' Vittorio interrupted without looking up.

When she returned with the opened bottle, Bianca had put some of her leaves onto Mia's pristine, untouched plate.

'It was hard today, Papa. Sofia and I went everywhere to find provisions,' Bianca attempted a pacifying comment.

At the end of the table, Vittorio's face remained unmoved, no acknowledgement. Bianca's knife and fork hesitated in mid-air as she looked around the table, her brothers digging into their portion made good with bread, gloomy eyes regarding her with minimal interest. Mia carefully watched her husband.

'Your father is deaf my dear, he can't hear you.'

'Papa, I'm talking to you. Why do you punish me so? Why won't you feed me?' her voice raised a little, dissolving into plaintive plea.

His face remained impassive as he casually leaned back in his chair stretching, savouring his wine. She turned to her mother.

'Why is he like this Mamma, the boys don't have to go out and find food, but he feeds them, why is it only me?' Her tone escalated as the constant ache of rejection and starvation flooded the hollow within. With no response her desperation soared.

'Why does he have to have the major share of everything? I will die if I don't get food, what would happen then, where would he be?'

As his hand slammed violently, dishes bounced and smashed off the table.

134

'You can hear when you want to, can't you?' she heard herself say. A stout water glass flew across the table towards her.

'How dare you speak to your father like this,' the bellow firing off the kitchen walls.

'It's not fair Papa, the boys get more than Mamma and I, and they do nothing,' her attempt to deflect his anger coming to nothing as he flew along the kitchen, her chair falling as he grasped it, propelling himself towards her.

'You cancerous excuse for a daughter; you waste of my sack!'

On her feet, Bianca backed towards the window, escaping his grasp, then dashed towards the storeroom. He slipped on the water from the glass that had glanced off her forehead, as he lunged at the door. The key was on the outside, of course it was. She started dragging the shelves of crockery across the doorway as, regaining his footing, he grabbed the door handle.

Benito remained immobile, as Luca screamed, trying to pull his mother away as she clutched at their father's arm. Plates crashed inside the storeroom as Bianca fought to defend her sanctuary. Her father's physical dominance more powerful than her skinny, starved body; he pushed through the gap in the door frame, launching himself at his daughter. Knocking her backward, her skull cracked on the stone floor.

'Thankless whore! He who puts the roof over your head dictates the food on the table. You never complained when Mussolini was our benefactor, car rides to a select school, impressive elegant friends - I got that for you. Me, all me!'

His left hand grasped her throat, legs astride her thin frame as a growing trickle of blood grew on the floor beneath her head.

'I know what you get up to, hanging around Piazza dei Foraggio, talking to riff-raff boys. I know all about you,

135

whore, do you think I don't have eyes everywhere,' a spray of his spittle splashed in her gasping mouth.

'I don't, I don't do anything like that Papa, I wouldn't.'

'Liar!' he yelled

She tried to turn her head from the ear splitting scream.

'Papa I wouldn't, the boys are my friends' brothers, contacts for food, to put something on the table for you, all for you Papa.' His drool splattered her face as she took another gulp of air.

Her eyes bulged, emitting a strangulated cough, as he heaved his left arm across her neck, throwing the full weight of his body on her chest. Horrified, the face inches from hers had taken on an intent she had never seen before. Malignant lust escaped through the usually guarded blank eyes, more dangerous than ever. His right hand slid under her skirt, clawing at her leg. Shock and terror clamped her body, legs rigid, as his fingers grabbed at her underwear.

'Have this, witch, you know about it already I know you do. Use it to get food for my stomach.'

Mia struggled free of Luca in time to see her husband's head lolling over his daughter's ear as hand and fingers mauled at her legs.

A shriek only a mother could emit resounded.

'Vittorio stop, stop now, do you hear me, stop now.' It seemed the very walls of the house shook with her shrieks as she grabbed and tore at the clothes on his back.

Years of easy living, no longer the lithe young man she'd fallen in love with, he twisted towards her, scrambling to his feet. Sweat from his face sprayed a wide arc, she was an easier target. He launched at her, grabbing both wrists with full force, flinging her backwards, the back of her head smashing against the corner of the table. It slid easily across the spotlessly polished floor lessening the impact as she fell motionless to the ground. Sons invisible to him, he stalked out the kitchen.

Bianca crawled from the storeroom, across the broken plates and dishes. 'Mamma, Mamma can you hear me?' her mother's eyes rolled backward.

'Boys get a cold wet cloth,' she cried.

'There isn't a medical cloth here,' Benito replied unemotionally.

'Just get a cloth, any cold wet cloth.'

'There is only a kitchen cloth,' Luca whimpered. She turned to look at them, one motionless, the other awkward.

'Luca, get any cloth, now!'

Her mother rolled her head as the wet cloth bathed her.

The boys eagerly retreated from the area of conflict, as mother and daughter began to recover. As they tended to each other, a man's voice seeped in through the open kitchen window, from the courtyard below.

Clutching each-other, they edged forward. Below, Carlo and Maria stood with Vittorio, his back to the kitchen; they strained to listen. A brief conversation was taking place as the two frowning faces listened to Vittorio's relaxed, chatty tones. Maria surreptitiously threw a glance towards the kitchen window, as Carlo informed he was calling to finish off a repair in the house, his wife simply wishing to tell Signora Mia she had a contact for some meat.

Her father's voice rose, thrown now for his wife and daughter's benefit.

'No, no trouble at all. The women simply knocked over the shelves with the good crockery. You can imagine I wasn't pleased.' Then forcefully, 'No, Maria, they don't need any help,' followed by a firm, and final, 'go home.'

Tension unknotted its wiry hands, as the women watched Carlo and Vittorio stroll towards the workshops, Maria turning to go down the path to her house.

Once behind her gate, she loitered, tidying imagined weeds, furtively checking the kitchen window until the coast was clear, then darted back across the courtyard. Vittorio had locked the door from the outside and had the key, they were trapped. In the silent kitchen, Mia detected the barely perceptible whisper of her friend below, found her key and dropped it out the window, rushing downstairs to let her friend in.

No words were needed, no pleas. Maria knew Carlo would keep Vittorio busy; they had an hour to make good the scene. His pristine, perfect world returned, no opportunity for further punishment.

Bianca crawled onto her stool at the corner window, as she did the day they moved in. She shivered, seeing nothing this time, not even her beautiful city, glistening below. Was she dizzy? She neither knew nor cared. Looking down she wondered what it would be like to fly over the buildings, swooping and dipping like a bird, feeling the cool, soothing air rushing past, elevating and refreshing her battered bruised body. Instead icy cold fingers of sweat trickled down her bony spine, a clasping tension nipping her neck.

The mothers led her to a bath, one each side, arms around her waist. Passing the dull hum of her brothers' asleep usually comforted her, but that day it drilled into her brain joining the ominous drone of the electricity generators next door.

In the power plant the eruption had been heard. As dishes had crashed, the cold inhuman fury was heard as he called his daughter unspeakable names, accusing her of filthy behaviour for just bringing scraps to his table. When he entered no-one looked up from their work, no mention of the incident to each other, even his most toadying of workers was shocked.

Chapter 31

Trieste, Italy, February 1943

Bianca woke to a confusing aroma of coffee. She inhaled the stimulating fragrance, released at last from the weeping, mucus drizzled sleep she had drifted into the night before. Her first conscious thought was shock, then pain along her spine and bruised rib cage. Confusion rushed in, followed by fear, of what? Be ready to fight. Fight what? Mouth arid, eyes dry of tears, where was she, what had happened?

'Mamma, Mamma.' No reply. On her bedside table a tepid coffee in her favourite cup, a slice of bread next to a corner of cheese. Where did the cup come from? Papa had thrown it at her the year before for eating tomatoes while picking them. Her mother must have retrieved, mended and hidden it from him.

The sun outside was risen, yet the house was silent, mother probably attending to domestic responsibilities somewhere. She fought emerging, terrifying visions and emotions. The coffee was drinkable but the food lay in her mouth dry and tasteless as she struggled to find the inclination to chew.

Traumatic memories pommelled her mind, her body aching as shock and disorientation arrived.

'*Get out of here,*' her only thought.

Looking to the end of her bed, a dress visible, no doubt laid out on her father's instruction. More of the previous days' events rushed in from corners of her mind.

Wrapped in a bedsheet she checked the corridor, and made her way to the cupboard of stacked, freshly aired clothes. Picking shirt and shorts from Benito's pile, her numb brain vowed to be a boy, her brothers never humiliated, assaulted or used, always safe, always revered.

Now she would live like a man, a king like him, shuddering at her irrational, hapless plan.

The house remained quiet, only a little movement in the kitchen but she couldn't talk, all energy gone. She would leave, but where could she go? Once a confident, blossoming young woman, now an urchin of war, broken, a shadow disintegrating in tandem with her country.

Mia called to the storeroom, 'Maria, you will need to see if the chickens have laid again,' dashing around her kitchen muttering, 'how am I to put a lunch together out of these offerings, and after yesterday's events?' she threw her arms to heaven. 'I don't know what I'm to do,' and clutched the Mater Dolorosa pendant.

Bianca slipped silently past as they busied themselves. Outside, she turned left down the side of the power station, all energy summoned to be alone. Glancing at the grapevines along the upward slope, effort seeped with every step. The Bora wind threatened urgent arrival but the sun was high and she mustered enough strength to move. The throbbing electric generators bounced in her skull as she crawled onto the base of an enormous stanchion, bending her knees to wedge herself against the concrete wall, protected from the chilly gusts.

A wounded animal's howl rose from her empty chest. Another part of her innocence stolen too soon and at her father's action, the Bora's energy released the shock of the previous night. She looked down at the scratch marks and bruises on her thighs. Grief penetrated so deeply, it distorted, contorting her face, permeating her blood, burrowed into every corner of her being, infecting even the essence of future children within her; a scream released with the pounding uproar of the power factory.

Stepping outside, Maria heard the unearthly wail. Creeping around the corner the wretched sight stopped her short. Glistening brown shoulder-length hair thrown back, gaunt cheekbones slicing the air, an unnatural moan escaped the slouched emaciated body. Sunken eyes peered into nothingness from dark hollows, mouth stretched open, teeth clenching as she sucked in air through usually full moist lips.

'Poor child,' she uttered, rushing forward seeing the boy's shirt hanging loose from her young woman's bony shoulders. Her eyes fell to her bent legs pressing her back against the wall, thighs thin enough to enclose between finger and thumb.

'Come to me,' she reached Bianca's side, dropping her basket, the single egg rolling to the ground. Without waiting for an answer she pulled the skeletal shoulders towards her chest, stroking her hair, tears merging.

'How has this happened, how have you ended up like this? Where does the food go when you get home?' She had a good idea how provisions were apportioned but had never been so aware. She knew Mia went without, giving what she could herself to help her, never realising Bunella was deprived to this extent, and after walking and running for miles bringing home what she could. Foraging wherever, starved in return. She berated herself, *'I chose not to notice, to not interfere.'*

She took off her cardigan and wrapped it over Bianca's emaciated legs.

'Stay there cara mia, don't move.' Lifeless eyes stared back.

'Promise you will not move. Promise me,' Bianca's shoulders convulsing in shock.

Maria recovered the precious egg, placing it carefully in the basket and ran towards the back of the electricity compound.

'That devil will be made to see his daughter's plight. I will shame him,' she swore.

Reaching the entrance at the back of the workplace, she screamed. 'Help me, someone, anyone. Bianca needs our help,waving her arms frantically as she ran into the thunderous, strictly prohibited men's work area, until one after another they heard her.

'Come see! Signor Marchetti's beautiful daughter is dying.' As they turned, she saw Vittorio appear on the gantry outside his office, malevolent anger shot in her direction, fists clenched white on the safety rail at the intrusion, his control challenged.

In an imperceptible moment his posture changed, power regained and he slapped the handrail.

'Bianca, my dear child, what has happened?'

His steel eye never left Maria, her hysteria ringing in the building's high ceiling, surprised at her clever cunning - he had underestimated the woman.

He charged a party to carry Bianca home where she was put to bed by the women. Vittorio loudly allocated the greater portion of his food for his daughter, ensuring his workforce were fully aware of his selflessness, declaring, 'Our women work so hard ensuring we men can protect and put a roof over their heads, they are saints,' carefully observing the impact. 'From this day I refuse to eat all you insist I have, wife. You will take enough for the girl and yourself, I demand it.' He eyed Mia's confusion and anxiety, as she appeared desperately to search for the response he wanted.

Maria, instantly ratified the generous declaration before Mia lost the importance of the moment.

'We salute you, Signor Marchetti, you are a martyr for your kind sacrifice,' publicly praising him and, with his men suitably impressed, he despatched them back to work.

*

'Bianca, are you awake?' Sofia's soft tones filtered through the warm cocoon of sleep. For the first time in a long while, she began emerging from slumber without angry rumblings in her stomach, her eyes falling on her dear friend by her side. She had been confined to bed for days, fed and

142

cosseted by the mothers, time for thoughts to marshal themselves.

The incident made it brutally clear, her mother held no sway other than domestically. Love, respect and duty to her parents had shifted irrevocably. The savagery of life, of her father's cruelty and mother's helplessness had transformed her mind. With no palpable perception of it taking place, her young impressionable senses were altered forever.

Love for her mother remained, but instincts for safety and survival transformed, it was clear she was dependent only upon herself. Her young mind recognised her mother's subservience was borne of her father's vileness, her way to survive; and yet, how could she see her daughter so abused?

The episode scabbed into an ugly scar in her mind, never properly healing, love and forgiveness tugging on the wound, it protected her from feelings. Her vow, *'If I don't love, I cannot be hurt'*, her barrier against pain, Sofia her angel and sanctuary in the maelstrom, the only one she could rely upon.

Chapter 32

Trieste, Italy, late February 1943

For a short time their table was never as bare. In the strictest confidence, news of the incident seeped into the community. Sympathy as abundant as food was scarce, everyone knowing it could have been them and a trickle of goods found its way to their doorstep. Mia shared with Maria, the two families bonded further in her kitchen as the girls on the road had. Eventually, knowing how precious the morsels were, Mia would accept no more valued gifts.

'I will have to work out how to go forward from here Maria, I cannot accept these offerings. Look at what appeared today, this parcel has boar meat.' She opened the paper. 'I caught sight of a Slovene boy scurrying away as I found it.'

'It wasn't the vagabond hanging around our gate too, was it? I sent him away with a flea in his ear yesterday. He said something about birds, what could he find so fascinating about us? The world is mad; what can we expect from one day to the next.'

'I don't know Cara, but I will have to do something about Bianca's footwear before summer, it's a disgrace.' Maria glanced at her friend; they both knew what had happened to her daughter's shoes in the past.

'I would get her another pair, but the money I have must go on provisions.'

'Can we sew some?' Maria looked at Mia's blank face, 'there could be such a thing.'

Mia considered for a moment, 'Summer is coming, we have plenty of outgrown outfits.' She went to the children's clothes cupboard, returning with sailor suits and uniforms, piling them on the empty kitchen table next to needles and thread.

Maria spoke. 'We'll make two piles of light and dark materials and see what we can make.'

It didn't take long and they began unpicking the seams of the larger items, producing stacks of variously shaped pieces of cloth.

'What do we do now, it doesn't look like anything we could make into shoes,' Mia lamented until a fragment of memory drifted to her mind of old Opicina matriarchs, sitting on doorsteps, sewing in the late afternoon sunshine.

'I know what to do. If we sew layer upon layer into thick pads the material becomes stiff, it will stand as a sole for a shoe, we can then sew straps across, or fashion a covered shoe.' Her face flushed with excitement, an unfamiliar smile breaking, and Maria jumped to her feet.

'We need the girls.'

By the time she returned Mia was tracing one of Bianca's shoes on a piece of paper.

'Right girls, we need you to cut as many pieces of material to this size and shape, with a thumb's width extra around the edge.'

They set to the task, all four around the table working through siesta, the hours passing as they talked, even laughed, discussing many subjects. By late afternoon Maria turned the girls outside to work in the courtyard, while they concentrated on the evening meal, their daughters' conversation drifting up through the kitchen window.

'Mia, I think she has recovered, she begins to sound like her old self,' Maria commented.

'Something still broods very deep Maria, she is not the same,' Mia frowned.

'But listen to them chatter?'

'You are not here at night when she screams in her sleep cara, she has changed.' Mia looked away, 'Thank goodness her father sleeps soundly, he would not tolerate the reminder.'

Downstairs the girls held the layers of material, pushing them down over a needle that rested on a stone, penetrating the dense pad. Once it poked through, they tried to extract it, sweaty fingers sliding off the point until Bianca took an old pair of scissors, clamped the needle between the blades pulling it through. Now and again a screech erupted as a needle slipped off its stone. By evening they had created three wads, with concentric circles of stitching forming robust cloth soles. Sewing straps across the top, with enough space to slip in a foot, proved an easier task, and Bianca wore two new cloth slippers to the evening meal.

Later she walked down to Sofia's house, feet sliding under the stretching fabric straps, soles holding firm, feet cushioned from the pebble path.

'Ciao Bianca, Sofia will be a moment,' Maria waved from the kitchen window as she slipped down the path. Moments later the pair left for Piazza dei Forragio, and she was relieved to see them venture outside the family compound at last.

'How are your new shoes?' Sofia addressed the subject.

'Fine, I think. They may need a bit of adjustment, but are comfortable underneath.'

Usually, they would turn left towards the Piazza after the railway bridge, the square their first meeting point. It was the most valuable part of their day, chatting and exchanging information about anticipated food consignments with old school friends and brothers. Sofia watched her friend carefully as she hesitated, seemingly unable to move, sinews contracted, muscles tense. Bianca looked to the Italian army barracks on her right, towering high, once a symbol of their country's anticipated triumph, now quiet and almost empty. The dark eyes of the windows glowered down, defying she should step from the safety of

146

the hill. A gust of wind buffeted her back as if goading her to cross the boundary.

'Here, you sit quietly while I get my brother,' Sofia ran back up the hill.

She obeyed, eyes staring, thoughts disengaged from the world around her, remembering the eager young Italian men preparing for their missions, calling from the garrison '*See me tonight beautiful*', as the girls had walked by giggling, but ignoring their pledges of love. Now the buildings' forlorn panes told of empty soulless rooms. '*Where are those eager young men now?*' she wondered.

Sofia arrived with her brother. She was her dearest friend living in the bosom of a supportive, united family, happiness always within her, and wondered if she would ever be afforded such a reward.

'Come along cara, let's go home,' Sophia whispered. Rousing her, the three lent into the last buffeting efforts of the Bora before the season finally changed to spring.

Chapter 33

Trieste, Italy, late February 1943

'Do you think we are being honest with ourselves, Maria, when the girls are at large, it benefits all our stomachs? Are we selfish?' Mia put to Maria. She remained silent.

The two mothers and Sophia conspired to raise Bianca's spirit, encouraging her back into the world little by little. They agreed that venturing no further than the bottom of the hill would not help her recover; she must be enticed to her friends at Piazza dei Foraggio. Concerned her father was inhibiting her progress, they resolved he heard nothing of their plan.

*

After siesta, Sofia sneaked to Bianca's room to wake her with news.

'You could never wonder at what I know,' she let the words hang to entice her interest. 'Go on darling, guess,' she continued.

Bianca looked up from her pillow, some sort of barrier still between them. She could hear, could see, even touch if she wished but there was no attachment behind her eyes.

'Come, you will be able to guess what my news is. Try.' Bianca exhibited a spark of interest, listlessly making an effort.

'You are getting your hair cut,' she said.

'No, maybe close though.' Bianca had no care, but understood her friend sought to tax her.

'A new coat then?' she offered.

Sofia saw she was beginning to engage with the mystery, and Bianca suggested, 'I think it is something to do with clothes and a lucky turn of events.' As she was edging closer to solving the riddle Sofia's exasperation exploded.

'I can't stand this, I'm going to tell you, and there are two things,' she paused, burrowing further into her friend's detachment. 'First, we have the chance of some finds, real booty.'

Bianca committed to the draw of the game, saying, 'You will have to tell me more. How can I get involved in this mystery if I don't know what it is?'

The second thing first,' Sophia grinned. 'I am allowed to wear trousers, like you. Mamma has said that if we are to travel the roads when the weather is bad, it is permitted. What do you think about that?'

Bianca looked at her happy face as she explained about the adjustments she was making to some men's trousers, declaring once complete she would sport them any time she wished.

'Oh Bianca, the discussion between my parents.... Papa protested that wearing trousers I could be mistaken as a Slovene partisan girl, or Italian informant; that it was too dangerous. Eventually, Mamma won and he relented.' She smiled wistfully. The concession wasn't lost on either girl, the intention to encourage them to forage, again.

'Now the big news cara, my little brother has spoken to Roberto at the cafe in Piazza dei Forragio. He has been informed of a big opportunity.' She hesitated, examining her friend's response. 'But we must move quickly if we are to take advantage. What do you think, shall we go to see Roberto this evening?'

'Why not?' Bianca pressed the pounding in her temples.

'Can you manage it?' she smiled wanly, leaning forward and taking Bianca's fingers in her hand, squeezing them gently. 'I'll be right there beside you, and my little brother too.' Bianca conceded to the inevitability of it all.

'I'll call back later.' Hugging her, Sofia rose to go.

'Don't forget those trousers,' Bianca ventured a weak smile

*

Arriving at the square the small group skirted around the edge, surreptitiously eyeing connecting roads for communist partisans or suspected informants. As soon as Roberto exited his father's trattoria Sophia joined him, laughter ringing at his every comment. The sight of them together moved Bianca. They had all been friends since childhood, living close by, attending fascist summer camps together, enjoying the benefits of Mussolini's vision. She considered how they had all fallen so low, their esteemed leader's plans in shreds. Not only were food supplies erratic, so many young men lost on ill-fated battlefields, boys murdered in their city by Slavs, antifascists, royalists or others, so many factions striving for control.

Sitting alone near the tram terminus she watched the world turn around her. As children, Sofia and Roberto had got on well, chasing, laughing, and always together. Then, as they grew, games became uncomfortable, odd new feelings emerged, inhibiting and embarrassing them, separating them as playmates. But adolescence hadn't lasted, and there was no time now for personal discomforts.

Friends had disappeared, those remaining, knitting closer, bonded tighter, as war forged them into adults far too soon, mutated creatures, adapting to survive. Boys like Roberto took up the reins of responsibility for parents, doing what they could to support the family. She observed he had a newfound masculinity, not un-noticed by Sofia either. *Now they play a different game*', thought Bianca watching her friend's slender fingers comb through her hair when he was near, head tossed back, face laughing to the sky, hand lightly upon his shoulder as he joked. Witnessing the tender affection between two people who knew everything about each other, she smiled; Roberto's eyes rested upon her longer than the shared joke passing between them. His love was palpable. Time stood still as tender eyes told of their future together, too young, living day to day, simple basic needs the only priority. She crossed herself, *'God preserve them from this war'.* Roberto watched as Sophia moved around the square, always ready to catch her eye when she looked up. Their future was mapped out, love, marriage, children, like Sophia's parents, theirs to take one day.

He gathered the two girls together. 'I have news,' he checked over his shoulder, 'The Italian Army leaves Montebello barracks early tomorrow morning, what's left of them'.

The café had given him the ideal opportunity to glean information from absent-minded talk as officers relaxed.

'I'll show you where we can get in. They are leaving almost everything, bedding, clothes, even uniforms.

'There should be plenty for us to use, or barter,' Sofia blurted. 'Bianca, there may be food!'

A spark of enthusiasm ignited within her. Loot was to be had, and no trek to the Karst. Arrangements were made to meet below Sofia's house the next morning by 4:40, hide, and wait for their chance.

Chapter 34

Trieste, Italy, late February 1943

They huddled in the dark as Roberto slipped unseen through the front gate of the barracks, lorries hurriedly driving away. Panicked orders ricochet off deserted walls in all corners of the parade ground, as groups of soldiers scurried to board the remaining transportation, grasping hastily collected belongings. A small assembly of officers alighted two jeeps clutching cases of documents as their baggage was thrown into the back, expressions frozen, blind with uncertainty.

Bianca and Sofia dashed through the gate holding hands as frightened young soldiers in departing trucks watched, ignoring the bold intrusion. Bianca recognised once arrogant, confident young men who had called each time they passed, *"Ciao bella, you like what you see?"* now dazed and terrified.

Among them she saw the soulful expression of a boy who had regularly guarded their gate. The sophistication of Trieste had been alien to him; he had been plucked from his family's farm when army manpower became stretched to its limits. The lad, grateful for her mother's kindness, reciprocated by giving food from the garrison. As his vehicle skidded out the gate something heavy fell at her feet, she looked down at a bunch of keys.

'Sophia look, that soldier, the boy who missed his mother so much, he just threw his keys to me. They flicked through the assortment as Roberto emerged.

'Don't just stand there, find something to break down the kitchen door,' he looked about frantically. 'The news will be all over Trieste in no time, we have to move fast.'

'No need,' Sofia dangled the ring of keys in front of him.

'Blessed Mother of God,' he snatched them and made back towards the kitchen.

The girls set off in the opposite direction, 'Come on, let's see what's upstairs.' Running up, two at a time, they entered the open door of the soldiers' quarters. Every room was in disarray, beds unmade, combs, clothes and letters scattered around.

Bianca stared at the discarded hopes and dreams of the young men, family photographs and personal effects littered about. She was still unable to feel much, anaesthetized by her own life then suddenly snapped too, seeing the blankets strewn on the floor.

'See these,' she called to Sofia, 'We can make coats.'

'What?'

'Iron them flat and smooth, the material will knit like felt. We can make coats, trousers, jackets, anything. Quick fold up and take them,' Bianca, finally animated with excitement again.

'Forget that, just throw them out the window and we can collect them as we leave.' Sophia pushed up the sash as a couple of figures moved in the shadow outside the wall.

'It's too late people are arriving.'

Bianca looked up the hill; Benito and Luca were being ushered down by her mother, followed by Maria and her young son. She called to her, 'Mamma, here quick catch these.' The girls tossed as many blankets and priceless items as they could manage out the window, rushing down to help carry them home.

Strangers had crept closer, grasping hands pulling at their booty as the mothers and sons flung themselves across the pile, kicking at the intruders. At that moment, Roberto came barrelling around the corner, growling as

153

deeply and inaudibly as possible, to avoid drawing more
scavengers, the intruders scattering as stones flew
through the air. He organised the children to be pack
horses to Sofia's house, the nearest safe hiding place, the
two mothers rushing after Roberto and the girls to
search for food.

'It's going to take all morning to find which key fits
which door,' he protested, so they quickly divided the
keys between them and worked their way along the
kitchen wing.

'Plenty of pots for cooking but not much to eat,'
Mia muttered while opening another storeroom.

'I have an idea,' Maria spoke. 'When we've got
what we can, let's sell the keys, or barter each one for
food.'

'No, no, out of the question, you don't know who
might come along, what if it's Mafioso?' Mia panicked.

'Then, I'll run up the hill and get Carlo,' Maria
declared.

'Inform Signor Vittorio too,' Mia twittered. 'He has
friends everywhere.' Everyone looked at the nervous
voice, surprising even herself with her bold notion.

Shortly Carlo, and the biggest physical specimen of
Vittorio's workforce, lumbered down the hill, to manage
the situation. It had deteriorated dangerously, Mia and
the girls endeavouring to protect what food and scraps
that remained.

By the time the women left, under the protection
of the huge man, the sun was rising, people skulking like
animals ever nearer. Carlo arrived home shortly after to
see his heavy colleague calmly drinking weak coffee at
the kitchen table, behind a mound of food and kitchen
paraphernalia.

'I was lucky to get away with my life,' he told Maria
in a carefully controlled tone, 'the place was crawling
like vermin by the time I got out.'

'Do you still have the keys cara?' Maria asked her ruffled husband.

'I was going to barter them and the contents of the rooms but was inundated, I let them go to the man they call Cosa Nostra Milo; it seemed the safest option.'

The mothers looked anxiously as he continued, 'I promised if we had any other opportunities, he would be the first to know.'

'Probably the best thing to do under the circumstances' Maria said.

'Perhaps Signor Vittorio will be able to sort something out with him.' Mia checked herself, horrified at speaking out, she was becoming far too indiscreet. 'He knows so many people,' she twittered, almost fluttering away to tidy up.

Sofia and Bianca looked at the spectacle of the barracks from her bedroom, as if a swarm of insects had descended, teeming everywhere, until the once-loyal fascist police arrived to beat control into the scene.

That evening Vittorio entertained a mysterious new visitor to dinner. A darkness behind his eyes, the old man expressed an interest in the womens' early morning venture.

Chapter 35

Trieste, Italy, March 1943

Bianca hated her father, she hated his friends. Few visited since the heady days of Il Duce Mussolini, but the disgusting old man drew up regularly in his chauffeur-driven vehicle, to sit in her father's office, laughing and talking. She was astonished to see anyone of substance these days, wondering why her father thought so much of the repugnant creature. He appeared more often than she wished, with ostentatious offerings of lean meat for Mamma, initially conducting himself with grace and reserve, as though paying homage to her father, even grateful for his friendship.

Behind closed doors she heard conversations of the Jewish situation, and lamentations of how Trieste had been a centre of culture and tolerance. Raucous tales of the Avant Garde poet and author James Joyce were cited, of how he had settled in Trieste, fleeing when the Great War started. Unlike then, they dared to say, the great city of humanity no longer was a sanctuary of civilised customs. Deliberations drifted into the night, citing the falsehood of western Allies who in the last war tricked Italy to fight, without receiving the lands promised afterwards. How the vacuum was quickly filled by Mussolini's nationalism, Italians embracing their roots, seeking to re-establish a place in the world.

She wondered _"Why are they still talking about it, what difference does it make now?"_

*

One evening, cool dusk air through the kitchen window offset the exertion of ironing blankets to make a suit. Bianca's shoulder and arm ached from the task as purposefully, she created material flat enough to feed through the sewing machine. When finished she turned to help Mamma with the evening meal.

Mia called out to her from the sink.

'Oh my goodness Bianca, go to the door quickly, I can see Papa's associate arriving. Comb your hair, straighten your skirt, be quick, we weren't expecting a visitor, the meal is only just in preparation.'

Mia bustled around the kitchen, folded the material and placed it in a storeroom. She glanced down the corridor, her husband already waiting for his guest.

Bianca was at the ground floor and opened the door, presenting with downcast eyes and guided him to the first-floor office. He always insisted she ascended the stairs before him, her skin crawling as his unsettling gaze penetrated her clothes. Her father stood, hand warmly extended in welcome, and she headed to the sanctuary of the kitchen as they warmly patted each-others' shoulder. Her father's voice echoed behind her.

'Bianca, our esteemed friend has a gift for us in his vehicle, go now and fetch it.'

She turned, hostile at the thought of passing before the invasive flat gaze of the old man again. Maria recognised her antipathy, 'I'll go for you, Bianca, you can help your mother.' Vittorio shot her a glance.

'Now girl. Go.'

She dashed down to the driver as quickly as possible. The smartly attired man opened the boot, reaching for a hessian sack as she wondered, not for the first time, how anyone had the luxury of petrol, never mind a car and chauffeur. The sack moved as he handed it over. 'A chicken,' he said, his blank stare lingering a little too long.

Back upstairs she decided her mother could take control of the creature and retreated to finish washing vegetables. From the sink she could see their scrawny chickens in the courtyard, picking about under the cherry trees as pink blossoms began budding. The old dears hadn't laid well for a while and her father had ordered them killed for food. She had loved and nurtured them as pets, and they had rewarded the family with eggs as best they could. *"How everything was disposable to him,"* she thought. Her mother scurried from the office.

'Bianca, run down again, there's more to this gift.'

The old man safely in the office, she took her time. The driver unenthusiastically leaned into the boot again producing a sack of chicken feed and a parcel, dumping them on the floor, as a gravel voice from a window above rasped,

'Bring the goods up for the girl, cretino.'

Once deposited at the top of the stairs the family gathered to examine and the old man reappeared.

'You need sustenance Vittorio, I've heard of the hard times your girl has had,' his gaze drifted uncomfortably across her again. 'The chicken is for your next meal, the grain to feed your laying hens, and the other little morsels...' he casually gestured at the smaller parcels, shrugging.

Benito and Luca competed to unwrap them, and displayed two bars of chocolate, another of nougat, four oranges and three unlabelled tins placing them on the floor around the man's feet, nudging each-other at the indulgences.

'How could anyone get oranges?' Luca whispered.

Vittorio took the man's right hand in both of his hands, thanking him respectfully. Bianca thought for a moment he was going to kiss the ring on his finger, as the man said, 'For friends, there are always pleasures in giving. Your family is a pleasure to me,' his eye travelled to Bianca's waif-like form again.

*

Meal over, coffee drunk, gifts placed in the kitchen, pleasantries exchanged, the man took his leave. Her father presented himself in the kitchen as they marvelled at the favours. Vittorio stood, feet firmly planted, shoulders back, and chest expanded, arrogant in his self-satisfaction.

'Well, what do you think about that wife? Don't I provide well for you?'

'Certainly dear, you are the finest of husbands,' she replied nervously.

'Bianca, why so quiet, what do you think of such a generous man? A fine provider for any woman, don't you think?' he asked.

'I suppose' she looked down at the dishes she was washing, fearing her true feelings would be revealed.

'Then you like him a lot I think?' More a statement than question.

'No.' Immediately she stopped, 'I mean, he is alright, I don't know him.'

'Well I will give you permission to get to know him. He wishes to dine with you at Hotel Savoia Excelsior Palace.'

Pans clattered on the floor from the storeroom, where Maria had fled on Vittorio's arrival.

'What are you doing woman, pick those up,' he yelled.

'Yes dear, so silly of Maria.' Mia turned towards him.

'Husband dear, why would he wish to dine with Bianca?'

'His wife died some time ago, and he has lived the satisfying life of a bachelor,' he replied, his eyes narrowed in the dim light. 'But in his mature years he is inclined to take another wife, a young woman.'

159

Vittorio turned to Bianca, 'And his attention has fortuitously fallen on our daughter.'

The women stood stunned.

'Think of it Mia, our daughter married to one of the most influential men of Trieste, not to say richest.'

'But how is he the richest dear, how does anyone retain wealth these days?' she uttered without thinking.

Another thundering crash resounded as he slammed the table.

'It is not our business, how anyone makes his way in the world or conducts his business. Girl, you will spend tomorrow preparing for the meeting; I will tutor you in what you will say, and not say.'

'No!' she blurted. The single syllable rend the air.

'I will not, I will never meet with that man. I will kill myself firs,' Bianca cried.

Her father grabbed her wrist, twisting her arm backwards, 'You will do as I command and he wishes as long as you live in my house. You are my daughter, and believe me if you do not, I will kill you myself.'

The sound of workmen below the window came through the window, and he turned on his heel, thundering back down the corridor. An unexpected rebuke sprang from her mother

'What am I going to do with you Bianca? Where will this all end?'

Maria emerged from the storeroom.

'Mia' she beckoned her friend to the privacy of the store whispering, 'Do you not know who that old man is?' Mia looked confused.

'Don't you remember Cosa Nostra Milo, he works for that old man, he is a Cosa Nostra Don... Mafioso. Why do you think he turned up on the day of our finds?' She took a cautionary glance over her shoulder, no one near to overhear. 'He has no mercy Mia, if he tires of her what do you think would happen? She could end up sold on to another, on the street or dead.'

Mia's eyes widened, she steadied herself against the shelves and Maria continued.

'He is so powerful, even the priests bow to him, before they go to the cross. And he wants to dine with your daughter? God save her from him.'

'Let's hope she cannot be persuaded.' Maria looked to Bianca at the sink and crossed herself, 'May Mater Dolorosa, Our Lady of Sorrows, protect her,' she whispered

Chapter 36

Trieste, Italy, March 1943 (the next day)

Vittorio entered the kitchen, the women working towards the evening meal. He removed his jacket, placed it carefully on the back of his chair at the head of the table, removed his tie and turned back impeccably white shirt cuffs. The smell of freshly ground coffee wafted thinly through the air. Surveying the food, his fury was palpable.

'Where is the chicken from our esteemed guest?' he threw a vicious look at Bianca as Mia twitched.

'We haven't had time to prepare it for you, my dear. It's feeding in the storeroom below.' Vittorio grunted. She added, 'Tomorrow we shall have a supreme dish for you.'

'It's still alive? Why is it not slaughtered?'

'We've never wrung a chicken's neck before.' Mia looked at her sons,

'It's a man's work,' Bianca interjected, 'the boys should do it.' She still festered from the horrendous relationship he intended for her.

'They are too young, my husband, maybe you would....' Mia bleated.

'It is not for a man in my position to stoop to farm work,' his palm slapped the table.

Each looked one to the other. None of them wished the role, to take the creature in their hands, wrench the life from its' warm body, see its last breath, it was abhorrent. Even starving, no-one wanted to place themselves so close to the death of another creature.

'You will do it, daughter, it will be your punishment for defying me,' Vittorio spoke.

'You don't need to tell me.' Something within her had altered, she was determined to take control, be the architect of her own actions.

'I intend to do it anyway.' She glared defiantly at him, 'I will be the one who provides again, the one who does the unpalatable, again.'

Her brothers watched silently.

'I'll show you all, I alone have the courage of a lion,' she declared.

Her father turned to the perfectly set table, his cup of coffee placed before him. He stepped to his chair clamping his fists on the backrest. Fury radiated up his arms and shoulders, culminating firmly in his chin.

Mia moved to dissipate the tension, fussing at the other end of the room, extolling the deliciousness of the food. The table was set, his side plate to the left with spotlessly white napkin carefully folded, a small freshly baked bread roll on top. He sat as Benito and Luca shuffled uncomfortably into their chairs. Luca looked to his mother, Benito, sneered at domestic matters, outside his sphere of interest.

Bianca brought her father a warm plate, as Mia placed the serving dish alongside, anxiety crossed her already distressed face as the delicious aroma was revealed to consist of a thin sauce around vegetables and meat. Vittorio scanned the table for an alternative.

'What is this?'

Mia laughed nervously. 'It's all we have been able to get today my dear. It's good, very nutritious. Not what we would have had in the past, but the girls brought herbs, and we used a tin of tomatoes from...'

'Tinned tomatoes! You think this is a suitable meal? Why haven't you found more food?' Bianca shrank back; she hadn't seen her friend Bird Boy for some while, foraged foods of the Karst were sparse.

'No matter dear, I am not hungry,' Mia chirped, 'I've already had ...' then attempting distraction. 'Drink your coffee dearest, while it is hot'.

Vittorio picked up his coffee, 'This is cold'.

'I was making sure it wasn't too hot for you, dearest.' She turned to her daughter, 'Bianca child, bring some water.'

She placed a jug and glasses, spreading them around to fill the table as best she could, as Mia ladled out the biggest portion of stew on her husband's plate, pushing another bread bun forward with gushing words of taste and health. The remaining food was distributed to the two boys with a final tablespoon placed on Bianca's plate, a portion remained in the dish for Vittorio should he wish, his recent generous declarations of food distribution already abandoned within the privacy of their home.

Abruptly a fork and spoon crashed against crockery as a thin tomato liquid sloshed over the pristine linen tablecloth.

'This is foul. How do you expect me to work with this rubbish in my stomach?'

His voice rose and they fell silent at yet another outburst. 'You got one tin, why didn't you get more? If there was one, there must have been others, why didn't you get them?' he glared at Bianca. She was exhausted from war, of trying hard to do the right thing, of danger and constant chastisement.

The ensuing eruption resounded down the corridor, as dishes clattered. He called his daughter "a thankless bitch to be so ungrateful" accusing her again of filthy behaviour with men yet only bringing meagre scraps to the table. Mia threw herself between the two, muttering words of apology to avert another frenzied outburst, and he pushed her away.

Vittorio swore at Mia's incompetence at not keeping "her" daughter in check, shoving her away and stormed towards the corridor, then turned. No-one moved, holding, waiting. He scrutinised them, then spoke.

'It was because of me you lived a good life. I provided and put the roof over your heads,' he thumped his chest, 'I am sick of insignificant food like tomatoes and eggs. Your lives, everything depends upon me, you should be grateful and do as I say. Did you not lead the life of Il Duce's chosen ones? Because of me! I made it my business to cultivate the right people, to ensure there was the best of everything. And now this daughter has the audacity when presented with a strong, wealthy match, to question and challenge me!' As his agitation grew, Iva broke in,

'Please Vittorio, I beseech you, please take a rest, you work so hard.'

His authority recognised he swept from the room, 'I don't want that filth, bring me Schnapps.' The tension broken, everyone dared inhale the shallowest breath.

Bunella gasped, 'I hate him. After all I've been through,' she sobbed, 'he called me a bad name again. I will never bring anything home now.'

Iva rushed round the kitchen, 'Boys, find the Schnapps and put it on a tray with a linen cloth.' White-faced, Benito and Luca hastily brought it, while Iva scraped food off the plates and table, making a passable dish, and hurried out the room with the offerings.

In his office, Vittorio loudly professed to not being hungry, Mia pleaded and cajoled in quiet monotone, beseeching, until calm descended, and she withdrew.

The scene in the kitchen was devastation; food stained the tablecloth, dishes overturned. Mia sent the boys to their bedrooms with tumblers of water and the

165

juice of the oranges the old man had brought, to fill them.

Bianca, turning to her mother for solace, who snapped, 'There is no food for any-one now, because of your outburst,' displaying the nearest to anger Bianca had ever seen. 'You know your father's word is law in this house. He must always come first, and to question his rule has done you no good at all. He fears the consequences of you rejecting the old man's attention; you don't know the power that visitor commands,' and rushed back to his side.

Bianca had no comfort for the dreadful things her father said, or thanks and consolation for the dangers she sometimes encountered. She stood again, numb, overcome with terror in her own home, as bad as anything she had encountered on the road.

'My contribution only ever seen as derisory at most expected at least, my brothers who do nothing, protected and cosseted,' inwardly berating herself. *'I should know by now, it's the way it will always be.'* Silently tears fell as she ran from the kitchen.

She dashed to Sofia's house, body hardly keeping pace with her spindly legs. At the door she explained her mother's need to placate her father's anger with nourishment, before he reached a drunken rage. Maria immediately dispatched her with Sophia to Piazza dei Forragio. Running, hand in hand across the rough grass they steadied each other, hearts pumping inside bony chests. Together against all odds they got through the worst of things, always by each other's side. Reaching the railway line, they crept across the track.

At the square, they burst into Roberto's trattoria and hearing their anguished gabbling, he rushed from the kitchen. He guided them to a side table away from the few customers that remained, instructing his mother to bring water. She recognised the difference in him since her husband's health had declined but reacted with indignation at his order to bring a luxurious torte.

A heated discussion started as his mother remonstrated at his frivolousness, declaring they needed all resources for the business. Roberto directed her out back where the argument continued. Having kept the café going by his own efforts, organising, and sourcing, instructing staff of duties and keeping his mother's nervous disposition under control he had prevailed, the seventeen year boy had officially stepped into his father's shoes. He asked what Bianca's father had already eaten and returned with a bottle of wine wrapped carefully in a white cloth, parcelled the tort and several slices of pizza.

Sofia clasped the bottle, decanted from his finest, and a little of the precious liquid seeped through the cloth. A red smear stained her fingers as she held it close to her breast; for a moment she and Roberto were lost in another time, eye to eye. He understood the fear she had for her friend's safety and peace of mind, and she responded with unspoken gratitude and shared affection.

As they left, Roberto's mother watched subdued, acknowledging her boy was truly the man of the family now. 'If you need to placate the big man at the power station son, then your word will stand. It is your decision,' and turned away.

Almost as fast as they had tumbled down, gangly legs and fear of retribution powered the girls back up the hill to Sofia's house and they slid under a curled up corner of the fence surrounding the power station compound. Waiting at the foot of the stairs, Maria called to inform Mia at the arrival of provisions.

'Heaven bless you both,' Mia called as the girls entered the kitchen.

'A little acknowledgement at last,' Sophia whispered, as Maria pulled her daughter from the scene.

As they entered the safety of their own home, Maria's hand fell to the red wine droplet stain, just above her daughter's heart.

Chapter 37

Trieste, Italy, March 1943 (the day after)

Breakfast measly again. Bianca went down to the storeroom by the entrance where the chicken clucked and rummaged just as Maria arrived for daily duties.

'Signora,' she asked, 'if we eat this chicken will I have to marry the old man?'

Maria melted at the desperate girl before her, flowering on the verge of womanhood, presented with marriage to a man old enough to be her father, essentially bartered for a good meal.

'Heaven forbid my girl, our Sorrowful Mother the Virgin Mary would never permit it, I am sure.'

She ran her hands over Bianca's shoulders and arms catching her hands in hers. 'Don't worry child, I am sure it could never happen.' Leaving the forlorn teenager, she hurried to the kitchen muttering, 'May God save the poor girl.'

Moments later Sofia arrived to see her friend sitting at a potting table in the courtyard, chicken beneath an upturned bucket.

'What are you doing cara, that bucket sounds angry?'

A sigh emanated from her friend. The spring air was fresh and Bianca wore a thick woollen ribbed jumper with rolled collar, black skirt and thick woollen socks turned at her knees. Her hair was dark from no winter sun, full waves fell chaotically escaping any effort at style, matching the turmoil in her head.

'I have to kill this thing,' self-loathing emanating from resigned eyes.

'Are you sure? Can't one of the workmen do it, or your Papa? I'm sure he could get a worker from the plant,' Sophia reasoned.

'He won't. I was tricked into saying I would dispatch it, Sofia. I defied him , 'she jabbed a thumb at the house, 'about marrying the old man. He knew how to push me into a corner and punish me.' Her eyes looked to the ground, 'I'll just have to.' Sofia ran up to the kitchen, returning moments later.

'It seems you are right cara, your Mamma was trying to get someone to do it for you, but your father has forbidden it.' They looked up at the office window as a figure turned away. Again she lifted the edge of the now quiet bucket in the hope the animal had died of ill health, but luck had deserted her. Eventually, Benito and Luca came out informing that Papa had left for the city, and the mothers followed.

They milled around the table, bucket and unsuspecting chicken, until Luca, attempting to alleviate his mother's distress, said he would kill it.

Released from captivity, flapping and clucking, it was quickly established he was incapable of even holding it. A discussion ensued to determine an efficient way to despatch the animal, concluding wringing its neck was the only possible solution. Benito, asserting his position, declared he would perform the deed, and the creature was placed under his arm. His grip was weak, the chicken struggled and he hysterically resorted to banging its head against the potting table, eliciting shrieks from everyone.

Bianca squeezed the pounding in her temples between her hands. *'No help is coming,'* she declared to herself, *'there is no escape, I am to be responsible.'* The others shrank back as she tucked the chicken resolutely under her arm, took the chicken's neck in both hands, closed her eyes wringing it as firmly as she could and

170

dropped heavily onto the seat. For the briefest moment it struggled to flap, she wrung again until her knuckles showed white and the head fell limp. A desperate heart still beat against her lap, an eye stared into hers. The boys ran to their mother, Maria clasped her daughter and Bianca carefully placed it on the table backing away, sickened. As hungry as she was, she abhorred a world that made her do this.

Feebly, she sat alone in the courtyard as they took the hen for preparation.

'I know some are cooking rats these days Mia, maybe that day will come for us too, but for one night we'll eat handsomely because of your daughter.' Maria's voice trailed.

Bianca sat alone, thinking, *'I am the daughter of pre-war fascism, trained to be a good wife and mother. Now, only old men and boys remain from that ridiculous idealism we believed in, all dependent on girls like me.'*

Chapter 38

Trieste, Italy, late Spring 1943

Sofia moved away as they entered the piazza. Bianca stood aside watching Roberto gravitate towards her as they settled on a bench together. Watching, she thought of the exploits they shared as the world's contours and boundaries crumbled and fell.

How misguided they had all been. The bourgeoisie claimed now they always knew it a mistake to interfere in the world's chaotic designs, they had never embraced Benito's doctrine lamenting, _"We had to go along with it. Why, if you weren't with him you were his enemy and suffered the consequences"_. Intellectuals pontificated; nationalists maintained inflated pride and fascists were vigorously and brutally trying to re-enforce the old doctrine. Royalists were plotting, no reason yet to enmesh further in international plots, and all the time the Vatican remained silent.

The world and factions swirled around her, head swaying in and out of awareness as she looked around the square. Fewer friends congregated, some sent away for protection, others safe within walls of once sumptuous homes, others simply disappeared without notice.

She remembered when her school had encouraged pupils to rally in Slovenia communes, to remind those "lesser" nationals of Italy's superiority. She had defied her mother, carried on a wave of nationalism by her father seeking to make him proud, a pawn in the fascist machine, and was bused to Opicina. Arriving at the outskirts they had set off en masse to the Obelisk, in high spirits, singing songs of summer camps, _"Italy victorious, Italy supreme"_. They swept along the road on a cloud of youthful ignorance, marching, heads high, to remind occupying Slavs, the town was firmly Italian now; they must bow to Il Duce.

It had appeared quiet. *"Look, comrades, they've bolted, they're frightened of our superior race"*, a self-important boy called, everyone cheering in response, marching on. As they penetrated deeper into town a murmur grew. *"Watch the side roads, I heard movement"*; some sniggered, others cautious. They began filing into the piazza, chanting Benito's nationalistic doctrines when a hush descended. The exits were blocked with peasant carts as figures silently emerged, surrounding them.

Zealous youths yelled, *"Have no fear, they will not dare harm Il Duce's children, they know the consequences"*. The bravest attempted a rousing rendition of a favoured verse, rippling uncertainly through their ranks.

Slovene resentment was tangible.

A boy came forward and spat at them, Mussolini's young leaders attempted rebuke by imperiously stamping the ground before him. A stone flew through the air landing near Bianca, shouts and insults following. The crowd had closed in, the mood of Il Duce's little soldiers altering dramatically. Still infused with her fathers' encouragement, Bianca had thrust her chin at the crowd in defiance. An old woman had reached forward and grabbed her hair. Twisting to be free, her assailant's grasp brought her to her knees, hair still clenched in the old hag's grip, their eyes locked. Hate and poisonous phrases of loss and pain dripped from the woman's lips, until someone grabbed her wrist shaking her free.

Boys and girls at the back had already retreated, some caught by inhabitants grabbing their clothes, school mates dragging fallen friends away. As they

173

reached the edge of town the riotous inhabitants melted back into side streets; youth leaders went amongst them checking for the missing. Starting back towards their buses, those who had made an early escape emerged from vegetation, no more triumphant songs rang out, only stunned, bruised, silent.

When she had finally returned home, her mother had chided her fiercely for her hateful actions and dishevelled appearance, no clemency at her explanation that father had delivered her to the bus personally.

Looking back she wondered at her foolish daring. How misguided they all had been, no-one questioned the brutality metered out to opposition of Mussolini's regime then. Consequences were quick and vicious if you failed to comply then, easier to ignore the barbarous system when benefiting from its' rewards.

She looked around now at her rag-tag friends touting for hints on finding potatoes. It seemed these days they were harvesting the penalties of their general unwillingness to resist Mussolini's vicious rhetoric back then.

Life was what it was now. More than half million of Italy's best swallowed up. Aligning with Nazism had taken so many more. If only they had known, their self-proclaimed invincible leader had spurned translators when dealing with Hitler, his ego such he inexplicably signed indecipherable German documents, an act of supreme arrogance, his vision now unravelled.

Chapter 39

Trieste, Italy, July 1943

Maria awoke to unscheduled trains arriving at the railway station above Montebello Garrison and her home. Anxiously she made her way to inform Mia, the Germans were preparing to occupy. The mothers, Bianca and Sofia worked around the kitchen table as usual while Vittorio, equipped with binoculars, stationed himself in a storeroom to observe, all still reeling from news that Sicily was invaded by the Allies.

'Maria, Germans, Allies, what will it all mean?' Mia tried to make sense of their disintegrating lives and the future.

'I don't know cara' whispering over clattered dishes. 'I think the King has made a definite pact with the English and Americans, an armistice. We must keep our heads down, stick to what we know, feeding the family.'

They were interrupted by Vittorio calling Mia to him. She returned, and began grinding coffee beans. Maria bustled to her side. 'Did he hear us? What did he want?'

'No Maria, just coffee.' She checked over her shoulder, straining to hear any movement from the storeroom. 'I did hear something last night though.' Maria's turned to her.

'Tell me, you must,' she urged.

'The driver of our esteemed visitor was talking.' Discretion was everything these days, no names spoken, no opinions given, never knowing who would inform on whom and whispered, 'About *"the German"*,' she checked her friend understood. Maria mouthed *"Hitler"*, Mia nodded. 'He has taken control of Italy's destiny.'

'And?' Maria moved closer.

'And "*our Italian*" met in the Dolomite mountains ....'
she had committed the cardinal sin, using an identifying
name. Maria urged her to continue, 'Go on.'

Uttering the words had released some sort of anxiety
within Mia, the simple act of sharing a physical release, and
she couldn't stop.

'Apparently the German wishes only to occupy the
north, our area Maria,' she stared wide-eyed at her friend,
'and let Italian troops continue alone in the south to fight
the British and Americans,' she paused. 'There were
recriminations against Il Duce and he has been deposed"
hesitating wide eyed, 'by those beneath him, and all
happening while the Allies bombed Rome.'

'Oh heaven above,' Maria hastily crossed herself.
'What has happened to the Pope, the King?'

'I only know that when he spoke with the German, it
didn't go well cara, our leader was treated as an inferior, a
fool.'

Bianca and Sofia at the kitchen table eyed each-other
at their mothers' crude attempt at code. Having existed on
rough roads, their families closeted safely away, Bianca
wondered how her family would survive if things continued
to spiral out of control, and they too became exposed to the
dangerous elements outside the compound. She resigned
herself again, everything may soon come to depend upon
her alone, quicker than she thought; she would have to be
ready, and returned to the vegetables.

Chapter 40

Trieste, Italy, late July 1943

The city, once a showcase, ws barely surviving, unrest permeated every household, every basic in short supply even to Vittorio.

The old man still called presenting a smaller selection of gifts. Vittorio at last submitted to Mia's pleas, casually dropping into conversation, negative comments of his daughter's foul nature.

Not even her beauty engaged the Don any more, national events distracting both men to contain conversations to the office. No arrogant laughter any more, only ominous murmurs seeped under the door followed by episodes of silence and blunt oaths.

'What are they talking about?' Maria asked, 'if anyone knows what's happening, the news will find itself first at the source of the city's electricity.'

Mia flinched, concentrating on domestic duties, thankfully never called upon to discuss wider issues. According to her husband, a woman had two uses only. She had subjected herself to his will over the years, had never revealed her hope to leave him in the early days, and in return been protected in the compound by Vittorio's position, her and her sons' saviour from the chaos outside, at least.

*

Mia and Bianca walked to Piazza Unita d'Italia to meet Claude on the dock for news and hopefully fish. She shivered recalling the heady days when Il Duce visited.

He had retained his position on the quay, with a small boat harboured in Canal Grande and permission to fish in his spare time, supplying fresh delicacies of the sea to whichever officer requested it. The moments of freedom put a little extra on the table at home too. Salvo was still missing in Africa, and Rocco a diver in what remained of the Italian navy. She valued their meetings.

She and Bianca reached the impressively large square fronting the Adriatic. Avoiding the huge empty space they skirted around the edge for safety. Bianca's mind wandered to the many fascist and anti-Slav rallies that had been held there.

She heard her mother's call too late, stumbling over the pinstripe suited man at her feet. Dark congealed blood had spread across the pavement from his head. Mia recoiled in horror at the crumpled article before them, face down on the pavement, body knotted, limbs twisted. Bianca took a step forward to see his face as a voice called quietly from a side street.

'No point doing that,' the faceless figure backed into the darkness as they peered towards it. 'Been there for hours.'

'Poor mortal, where are his family they should be told,' Mia couldn't hide her horror.

'Don't be a fool and get involved,' the shadowy figure muttered, 'even if you know him, walk away, forget you even saw him.'

She strained again to see the speaker, not sure man or woman, as Bianca stood transfixed. She had stepped in the thick sticky gore and wherever she placed her foot it left a hideous reminder, and stumbled backwards.

'And forget me too,' the figure, a bundle of shapeless clothes, seemed to dissolve into the bricks of the dark narrow street.

The women linked arms tightly, stepping away quickly, Bianca checking over her shoulder that the murderous footsteps did not follow. As Mia tried to look back, she jerked her face forward, dazed, white. She had heard of innocent passers-by trying to help at such times, only to be dragged from the streets by militia from one faction or another, their trap sprung. They turned away, no appearance of concern, just wanting to meet with Claude, always wise, always strong.

*

The quay was eerily quiet, the brutal experience compounding their unease. Claude met them at their usual cafe, face more lined than usual, and persuaded the owner to provide decent refreshment in exchange for a little fresh fish. When seated Mia spoke,

'You will never believe the terrible experience we have just had brother, a dead man laying, blood from his face everywhere, no-one to claim him.'

'And, a voice from the shadows warned us away, when we looked, uncle. What horror.' Bianca looked down at the streak of blood still visible on the edge of her shoe, dragging it across the floor to scuff it away.

'It happens,' his bland reply, 'Mia there are many unspeakable things around us all these days.'

'Something bothers you, Claude,' she said.

Bianca looked at her mother's rare directness, calm and concerned, her opinions welcome here.

'I can't tell you, sister.'

The weathered lines of the sea embedded deep on his face, become chasms. Mia moved closer, placing her coffee cup so close, they touched; her hand discreetly upon his.

'You've always been there to protect and help me Claude, tell me. Let the words flow, release them from your mind.'

Bianca feigned disinterest to examine her shoe.

'I've done something ....' he whispered.

'Something bad? Not you Claude you would never....'

'Not bad, but dangerous Mia.' His once broad, rangy frame shrunken.

'Dangerous, have you hurt someone, betrayed your family?'

'No Little Bird, I am not that man,' he glanced sideways at his sister's worried face, 'but something else.'

'Tell me cara, you can trust me, unburden yourself.'

He lowered his voice and looked around the empty room, 'I helped some people.' Mia's confused expression seemed to alarm him.

'Don't Mia, don't look at me like that, you'll draw attention.'

'I don't know what else to do cara, I don't understand. You have "helped some people" but it was dangerous, it doesn't make sense,' she reached for her cup again.

'I helped someone escape, Mia.'

Despite Bianca's affected disinterest her ears pricked up; something significant was coming. A pause followed while her mother and uncle looked into the dregs of their coffee cups, until Mia spoke.

'I am sure whatever you have or haven't done, was for the right reasons, cara. You could not do an evil deed, for your life,' she inhaled righteously, unconsciously touching the Mater Dolorosa medal at her throat as Bianca's shoe clattered onto the tiled floor.

'It was a Jewish family,' Claude spoke. 'The father asked me to spirit them away, and I did.'

'When was this?' Mia interrupted.

'Don't say uncle the less we know, the better,' Bianca blurted.

'She's right sister, forgive me for telling you, I should never have burdened you.'

'Oh Claude, you know me, I can't remember anything but a shopping list,' Mia twittered.

Bianca looked at her usual timid mother, hardly recognising how such artful guile directed the conversation, his shoulders relaxing.

'The father came to me, Mia I couldn't refuse. I knew his face, and could hardly recognise the tortured mask of the man I had known. He was terrified for the life of his wife and child. You knew her as a girl Bianca, the family would visit your home Mia.' Bianca covered her ears. 'I had to help. All he wanted was for me to take them out on the sea before dawn and leave them.'

'I don't understand, and you mustn't tell me anymore,' Mia shook her head, 'no more details.'

He couldn't stop, 'I took no money, only this,' he slipped an envelope onto the table. 'I can't take it home, you know the situation in Opicina, Slavs everywhere, and soon the Germans; it isn't safe.'

'Throw it away,' Mia trembled.

'I can't, what if someone sees it. Take it Mia, please, take and hide it.' Bianca edged open the flap to reveal two antique, beautifully carved coral earrings, Greek ladies heads above pendulous drops, suspended from rich golden hoops, and muttered, 'They are beautiful.' Something stirred in her memory, a glimpse of a past life, a laughing friend and well-heeled mother gathered in their courtyard, sunshine glancing of golden rings suspending beautiful goddesses that kissed her cheek.

'What if they return one day, Mia, I'll need to give them back. Please take it,' pushing the envelope away.

'What were their names?' Bianca whispered. Claude looked at her, she wanted to know which of her old friends had been spirited away this time.

'The Hertzfelts,' he whispered.

'Stop now, forget the name, forget everything,' Mia babbled, adding, 'Claude you are the finest of men, I won't let you be exposed to more than you already are in Opicina. Come, Bianca.' She dropped the envelope into her handbag, a shudder travelling through her slight frame, as she stood. 'We have to go.' A blank expression bled across her face, Bianca watching her return to the timorous creature of home. Supporting Claude had shown a glimpse of the woman she could have been, evaporating now before her very eyes.

Claude passed a parcel of fish to her as they stepped into the daylight. She dashed after her mother as rainbow memories of long ago days drifted through her thoughts.

*

As they entered their home they were still silent, Maria greeting them with the flip-flop of her homemade cotton slippers on the pristine corridor floor. Mia jolted back into reality, 'I didn't know you were here.'

'I can be invisible when I want to be,' Maria shot a glance at her friend. 'Mia you've got to speak to your husband. Something terrible is happening out there, we need to know what it is, and what we should do.' Panic shot across Mia's face with the added strain.

'How would I demand such a thing from him?' traumatised already. Maria recognized it was hopeless and resolved to find another way.

*

Carrying laundry from Sofia's house later the girls passed the chauffeured vehicle in the courtyard and made themselves scarce. Clattering upstairs boisterously, their scheme was to irritate the old man's desire and repel his attentions. At the top, the office door opened, and the old man stepped out. To their relief he ignored Bianca and walked straight down to his waiting car; her father looked uncertain, almost disorientated as he stood in the corridor. Finally, he looked up.

'Child, fetch your brothers. Sofia get your mother and fetch Carlo too. Bring them to the kitchen immediately.' He turned, slamming the office door.

The sombre group gathered around the kitchen table, Mia producing passable coffee predominately for her husband, grainy dregs for the rest. The youngsters stood, backs to the window that overlooked their beautiful city, black shadows against bright evening sunshine. Vittorio finally arrived in shirt sleeves turned up, collar open, tie loose. An ominous mood held everyone motionless, air thick with anticipation.

'I have news,' he paused, his usual self-importance absent, lack of direction lasting a fleeting moment, and began.

'News has reached me via our honoured guest,' he shot an irritated look at his daughter. 'We are lucky to have such esteemed associates, who care to keep us informed of events outside the perimeter of our small world.'

Carlo looked anxious at having been pulled from work, as Vittorio talked at length, ostensibly about nothing in particular, until they caught the formidable words,

'.... as the Grand Council of Fascism has decreed.'

'What?' Carlo roused, looking up, Vittorio surveyed the terrified gathering.

'As I said, King Victor Emmanuel lll, and his cronies....' quickly adjusted his words, '....his associates have moved for a vote of no confidence, and Il Duce, Benito Mussolini has been deposed.' The silence that followed defined not so much confusion, rather uncertainty at how to respond.

'How did this happen?' Carlo regained his tongue, the others speechless.

'There will be a radio announcement this evening.' Terror began to permeate the air.

'General Commander Mussolini attended a meeting yesterday and was presented with his council. I cannot tell you how I know this as no stenographer attended to record, no guards were present, however....' He paused to fully inhabit the greatness of the moment and his place in history, informing of the monumental news before any other lesser man.

'Il Duce spoke eloquently of the current situation, the position of our esteemed Italian troops, of "the dilemma", whether war or peace, and requested comments. A member then spoke at length, ending with Mussolini's own citation of 1924, *"Let perish all the factions so that the Nation can live"*, whereupon Il Duce declared a postponement be called for. At this moment his opponent vehemently confronted him, stating that to rest was unjust as Italian soldiers lay dead, and dying.' The eyes of the group gathered in the kitchen widened at the audacity.

'Despite his wrath, Il Duce allowed a continuation. Never before in twenty years had anyone ever asked for a vote.' Vittorio looked around the room, bending slightly at the waist, adopting the persona of storyteller to a fairy tale. 'Then at midnight, they all stopped for light refreshment.'

Bianca noticed her brothers' eyes widen with intrigue at the tale, fear leaving their young faces. The past years had taught her that anything may lurk beneath the surface of a story and she curled her little finger around Sophia's, as they rested against the windowsill.

Vittorio recognised he was successfully steering them from the tragedy that was Mussolini's downfall as he informed them everything had changed, much worse than he let them know. He was aware Il Duce had attempted a meeting with the King and been refused, had tried to contact the Allies about a truce and been unsuccessful; that he had telephoned his mistress at her luxury villa, and sought to seek out his opponents. But the King meant to replace him, and the unthinkable happened, he was arrested. Vittorio realised his job now was to be on the winning side and having turned Mussolini's downfall into a caricature, a harmless episode, he could turn it back if needed.

The gathering dismissed, Carlo was instructed to let minor details seep into the workforce, to lessen the impact, that nothing had changed and they would continue their work. When he himself returned to the workplace no questions were to be made of him, and there was no place for gossip in his workplace.

That evening he requested wine, usually reserved only for visitors, and the best the women could prepare to be served, there would be no mourning or celebrating, no issue at all, just acknowledgement of family standards. Bianca's head, already reeling from the days' events, baulked at the veneer he smeared across their reality, greedily accepting the extra portions nevertheless.

Chapter 41

Trieste, Italy, early September 1943

The following weeks brought more terror and uncertainty for them. Though the old man's visits had all but stopped, Bianca's father was absent more often, mysteriously disappearing into the city before evening meal. As he left, she would watch him from her vantage point at the window, skirting around her friend's home and disappearing under the railway bridge to re-emerge near Montebello Garrison. After he passed the barracks she could only guess where he went.

On the old man's final visit he revealed an armistice was to be signed with the Allies ending Italy's war with them and separating Italy from Hitler. He himself was moving south as was the King. It was expected Hitler would not accept the situation without retaliation.

'I strongly advise you to move now Vittorio. I can give you details of safe houses in southern Allied occupied Italy,' he offered.

'It is impossible my friend, I have obligations here. Anyway, I am the only one who can guarantee power to the city. Whoever arrives will need my expertise,' he confidently predicted.

The old man stepped back observing his friend. Respectful of Vittorio's wily ability to negotiate his way out of menace, he also knew Germany was capable of navigating its own brutal path through a mere local institution like the power plant. He himself, with all his capabilities, would not take the chance of surviving the wrath that was to come. He took Vittorio's hand in his, cupping his free hand over it in friendship.

'I don't know when we shall meet again my friend, and if we do, I am not sure I will recognize you, you understand?' he raised his brow. Unspoken words passed between them, their friendship was nothing, when survival was your necessity.

'You do not wish me to take the girl?' The old man tried one last time at securing Bianca's favours. Looking down he shook his head, 'No you are right, it is better to travel light.'

They slapped each-others' shoulder one more time and he left. As his car drove away the man considered what he had withheld, that Germany had already begun an indiscriminate massacre of Italian troops. He wondered if he would ever see Castle Miramare from his palatial villa overlooking the ocean again, and whether Vittorio or his family would survive.

As he disappeared, Vittorio retreated to his office to plan his strategy. He recalled the freezing conditions he'd endured tunnelling in the Great War, of sacrifices made, and his ability to manipulate for his own best outcome. But now, he had this collection of family members that would also require his protection, sons, wife, and daughter, and considered, she may still be of use.

Italian forces were now obliged to conduct action against the Nazis. Trieste could not expect support from Slovenia. But the family had the cachet of having lived in Opicina, Bianca born there, something of a shield to protect them from Slav partisans.

Vittorio understood some of their soldiers had already turned weapons over to Italian partisans, others unwilling to take the chance, had joined forces with the Germans. Trieste's huge seaport, the last bastion of the western world before communist rising Slovenia would be fought over he knew. He needed to secure contacts and cultivate his protection. He would visit the Cathedral of San Giusto and seek the support of its worldly representatives, rather than God himself.

*

SS Colonel Odilo Globocnik swept back into the city in September. It was a cruel irony that this son of Trieste had risen through Hitler's ranks, so dedicated he achieved a position of commanding influence in racist repression and anti-partisan operations. Born an Austro-Slovenian, he had lived in the city, child of a lowly official and on moving to Austria had worked his way through the Nazi party with zealous enthusiasm. Succeeding where they had not he had made many enemies within the party which had provoked plans by colleagues to oust him, but by his mid-thirties he had been involved in the worst killing operations in Poland.

The beauty of Trieste hadn't changed. He noted the large triumphal square that opened onto the ocean as his cavalcade passed old Porto Vecchio, recalling the steamy day in 1922 when he had arrived back by train to be instructed in hydroelectricity, ordered then to carry suitcases. Now, every being lay beneath his command as he contemplated his distinguished team; experts in the Final Solution gathered from every corner, officers trained to perform his every uncompromising wish, his stock in trade initiating industrial extermination. He would await colleague Christian Wirth to arrive shortly, and begin business.

Chapter 42

Trieste, Italy, mid-September 1943

Bianca watched the delegation of German vehicles wind up the hill from her corner window, sweeping around to the front entrance of their home. It wasn't unusual to see a military visit. Once, proud young men of their own army had protected them. Now the Nazis had arrived, their guards already stationed, but that night the visit was different.

She moved to overlook the courtyard, observing her father. Any fear on his part, undetectable, dignity and respect in his every movement. She considered how he was so well able to avoid anger against the usurpers; there were no outbursts for them, saving his bile for the family. His projection of power and respect was almost tangible, pervading the still evening air. Perversely, the Bora calmed momentarily as if bowing to the invading force. Vittorio displayed consummate professionalism, no clash of creed discernible between him and the new authority, simply a coming together of malevolent practices.

Bianca shrank behind the blinds for fear of being noticed as the principal German emerged from the open-topped car, but was unable to turn away. September, usually chilly, the evening hung heavy as the tableau of characters seemed to move in slow motion through the thick atmosphere.

Her father stepped forward in his finest suit, chin raised, confident, but without pretension. He approached the stranger with polite, respectful deference, awaiting the German officer's indication to advance further.

'What's happened to all-mighty Papa?' she thought. _'Brought to heel at last?'_

The tall well-built man glanced at his surroundings, turning in her direction. Hooded dead eyes looked from what could have been a handsome face, penetrating, unemotional, as if incapable of recognizing the difference between life and death. A second less athletic man alighted from the far side. He had a round bald head, bespectacled and with a sharp moustache in the style of his leader, preferring to stand back and survey. A translator spoke in deferential tones, as the first man cast his eye around the courtyard Mamma had tidied that morning as adored sons had dragged sulky feet in defiant resistance. Inevitably the work had fallen to the women to create their finest impression.

The second man was detached, unaffected; a chilled atmosphere somehow passed over everything he looked at as suddenly he stared up at Bianca's window. She fell back from the hypnotising, snake-like stare, unable to disengage. Below her father confidently ushered the visitors to the front entrance, passing a small parade of nervous, sweating technicians in ill-fitting suits. He summarily dismissed them, and terrified faces quickly dashed through internal corridors to the power plant, heels clicking on pristine tiles like scattering cockroaches.

Watching the guards, Bianca began assessing who she could befriend or pursue for contraband, but this deputation was different. The car was re-positioned ready to leave, guards scanned the area; she felt uncomfortable. Being young and attractive had its uses, but events had taught her, "listen to your instincts"; discreetly studying the environment was embedded in her core, a marker for the rest of her life.

*

Earlier in the day her mother had been busy preparing, and perpetually jumpy, but relieved when Bianca returned with an exquisite cured ham and bag of durum wheat flour.

190

Somehow, news of the Germans visit had spread throughout the neighbourhood, appeasement uppermost in everyone's minds. A neighbour had brought two steaks, fresh and bloody, peering like gouged eyes on the chopping board. As he mentioned one of the Germans was called Christian Wirth, Mamma had expressed relief at the connotations of his divine name, crossing herself vigorously, eyes to heaven.

'We are saved, thank you for your blessing, Mater Dolorosa.'

'Signora, I beg to correct you,' spluttering, 'he is widely known as "Christian the Terrible" or "The Wild Christian", a little man, with eyes like an animal,' he anxiously struggled to rectify her mistake.

'Maybe he is a hunter,' Mia fretted, baulking at her own ridiculousness. Years of anxiety had driven what was left of her mind to a petrified place.

White with fright the man fled at saying too much, beseeching God, their bizarre exchange would eradicate memory of his presence, precious steaks lost. Mia stood before them, rooted to the spot as they stared back gruesomely. Bianca gently led her to a stool, wrapped the meat and placed it in the cool store, and joined her. For once they allowed themselves an unsanctioned coffee, talking casually of the autumn Bora before relaxing. The incident transformed into a rare moment of affection for them, as a little light laughter eased itself from Mia's tight chest. Bianca leaned forward to lightly squeeze her mother's hand as she pulled it away, jumping to her feet and retreated to domestic duties. Left alone by the window, the bittersweet moment had been abruptly terminated, Luca's footsteps advanced along the corridor, a gangly, growth-spurt figure whining for food.

*

191

The air was thick with tension, after glimpsing the second visitor in the car, infamous SS Major Wirth, the awkward conversation still haunting her. Despite the atmosphere, Mia survived, calling on her experience of heady fascist banquets.

Fine brandy and Schnapps was provided in Vittorio's office, revamped to represent and enhance his standing. An attractive classical painting hung on the wall borrowed from the Cathedral's archives, two more in the dining room. The last thing he desired was for the eminent visitors to think him a simple lowly workman. Posters endorsing the power of electricity and of German military might, surrounded a new prominent portrait of Hitler. A handsome desk was positioned so visitors would have the most comfortable view of the image, and a modern cupboard now housed crystal cut glasses. The scene was set, to represent the best of Italian endeavour while respecting and honouring Hitler's military supremacy. Vittorio wished to be viewed as elite, useful, never a trouble maker. His position was clear, he upheld their ethos, was a faithful servant, and ruled his workers, and all within his orbit, with the same precision and authority the Germans would expect and respect.

*

Mamma had picked up the finest white linen, borrowed from Hotel Savoia Excelsior Palace, and proceeded to the dining room. Table completed, she entered the office and offered the guests an aperitif. Vittorio's strategy was to lure Odilo into companionable repast, marking himself down as both impressive and useful. Returning to the kitchen, she prepared a tray with a cut-glass dish of olives on delicately embroidered linen, and returned, knocking on the office door. It opened and she entered. Mia's muffled entreaties could be heard from the kitchen, followed by Vittorio's yells of derision as the glass dish of olives was hurled into the

192

corridor. Bianca, skulking near the storeroom, turned to see the tray and exquisitely embroidered napkin flung after it, her mother grovelling to pick them up, as she rushed from the room.

'Quick, find glasses, and plain napkins. Our guest has brought refreshment to his own taste.'

No matching napkins to be found except a precious keepsake belonging to Mia's grandmother and two presented to Benito and Luca that morning, still unused. They were quickly pressed and refolded to be presented to the esteemed guests, the oldest to her husband, tension stabbing at their temples the women polished crystal tumblers to accompany.

Mia, spirit pummeled, returned to the office with abject apologies, a rough abject dismissal the response, hearty laughter leaking under the door. The women in the kitchen remained alert; only the translator's monotone was audible, as he relayed information between Vittorio and the officers.

Bianca picked a crumb of cheese from the slicing fork, the temptation too much again, placing it delicately on her tongue, turning it, skimming her bottom lip, savouring the creamy texture and salty aroma for the briefest moment. Mia screamed and she jumped back, the sliver falling on the gleaming floor. Bianca dropped to her knees retrieving and swallowing it quickly. Her mother collected the remaining crumbs and wrapped them in white muslin, to find themselves in a sauce or garnish, nothing wasted. Bianca backed against the wall shamefaced. The entire shave of cheese would have covered no more than her little fingernail and her stomach cramped and moaned at the sudden digestion of the rich, unexpected morsel.

The men continued their convivial discussions, the interpreter conveying Vittorio's dictatorial management methods, all seemingly comfortable in each other's presence. Emboldened, he took his advantage, directing

193

his new masters to understand how he reflected Nazi attitudes.

".... whomsoever holds the power station, holds the city...." His men were, ".... completely subservient to me, if not they lose their job, their families starve ...." They thought him "vicious, of course they are frightened of me, I rule by fear...."

Listening from the kitchen, that much at least was true Bianca reflected.

"It doesn't matter if they dislike me, I delight in it. It is myself alone who matters," adding hastily, "for the greater good of the grand scheme of course."

'Here you could insert Germany, Italy, Yugoslavia, Nationalists, the Pope, the bourgeoisie or Royalists' she thought.

The women breathed a sigh of relief at the slow measured responses of the Germans, seemingly nothing to displease them, and as time and refreshments passed, the men relaxed, turning to talk of women. Mia sent Bianca on an aimless errand, in the far reaches of their home for her protection.

From her parent's bedroom window, she saw the smaller officer, who she now knew as Christian Wirth, step into the car and disappear towards the city. Returning she hesitated on the stairs for the briefest moment, stopped in her tracks. The one known as Odilo was talking to her father in Italian, chatting comfortably about the power station. No-one was guarding the corridor, she listened.

'I recognised you as soon as I saw you, Vittorio,' he remarked.

'And I you old friend. It isn't discourteous to address you so, is it? I would cut off my right hand before impropriety,' a rare moment of reverence from Vittorio.

'Do you remember those days I was sent here to train, as you joined the company? That insufferable old manager,

194

so out of date, we had his life to undermine him,' the German commented.

'Behind his back,' Vittorio responded, laughing.

'You have done well for yourself,' Odilo paused, 'and, if you continue to embrace the new regime, which I'm sure you are capable of, things should go smoothly.'

Vittorio comprehended; his position was not guaranteed, but he had found an ally, and would work well with him.

'Do you remember the whores at the docks?' Vittorio attempted a more intimate line of conversation.

'I remember you were press-ganged into marriage,' Odilo said.

'Yes, and the child died. But the mother has been a good worker, and causes no disturbance to me.'

As laughter rumbled out from the cracks around the door, Bianca returned to her business, the information closeted away in her mind.

His position consolidated, *'The paintings can go back to the Cathedral vault tomorrow'*, she thought.

Chapter 43

Trieste, Italy, late September 1943

Sitting alone in her room, Bianca knew the exact moment everything changed. Thirteen years old when Italy had invaded Albania, only a year later Il Duce declared war on Britain and France, and her life took a different trajectory. Long hair then, braided into pick-tails, curled into loops hanging from bowed ribbons at her ears, her young innocent face laughed easily, gangly legs outgrowing her child body like a thoroughbred foal. She was cosseted by middle-class life, an advantaged existence at the power station. Papa's standing firmly established, unquestionable, workers as obedient as his household. Life was orderly, it was good.

Mussolini had been strong. An alliance with Hitler was natural, the two forming a coalition following the depression of the Great War. Vittorio, vowing he would never endure the discomfort of the Ortler Mountains again, was a willing follower. The two leaders shared an enthusiasm for nationalism, Hitler developing grim practices redirecting the lives of selected peoples, Il Duce re-establishing Italianism in all its forms and territories; similarities endorsed their unity, they were on the winning side, all differences invisible to them.

The Italian Jewish community was not threatened then, a city Mayor among their number, with finance and commerce on the shoulders of established eminent families, their influence unassailable. Vittorio entertained Hebrew colleagues at his home and business continued undisturbed by violations against Slavs in outlying communes. Efficiency and good business were the cornerstones of Italian nationalism, Jewish citizens aligning themselves with the fascist party. They had been naive to the cultish fervour Mussolini would unload upon the city and country, dividing inhabitants, loyalties abandoned, his Black Shirts crunching dissenters beneath their boots.

Things had turned. The throngs of pilgrims who had joyously passed through the Gateway to Zion were gone. Assets of prosperous Jewish businesses were transferred to the state, the once loyal, thriving community abandoned by the last passenger ships.

*

Bianca dared to go alone to Piazza dei Foraggio, considering, *'Where else would we go but "animal feed square"?*

Sitting alone, waiting for the ever shrinking number of friends, she overheard someone mention cabbages, and called out,

'Hey you, is it Savoy?'

The informant looked over his shoulder, hunching his back against her.

'I said, is it Savoy cabbages?' Her mother's favourite dish of the season being braised cabbage, what a treat if she could acquire some.

She studied him as he passed, ignoring her, hauling exhausted feet. He had been rewarded for his information with two cigarettes, and looking at her empty hands had moved on. She jumped up and made her way back up the hill, grasping the ropes slung along the side of buildings to help bear up against the Bora. She didn't need to know the exact location of his secret, she knew his hamlet on the edge of the Karst. The next day they would make their way there, and see what they could find.

Cloth shoes were no longer of any use in the worsening weather she thought as she called at Sofia's house to rest and tell her the news. As the door cracked open against the wind she could see her own mother gripping Maria's hand, Carlo by the window, her brothers, uncertain.

'What's the matter, what's going on?' she burst in. They looked back with troubled eyes.

'Cara, there's been a development,' her mother spoke.

'Not just a development Bianca, it is Mussolini, he's kidnapped!' Maria rushed to explain.

'Not kidnapped, rescued,' Carlo anxious to plough a furrow of calm through the frightful news.

Her mother continued, 'Your father has informed me,' she trembled as the toll of war continued to wring all sense of normality out of life. 'The Germans are all over northern Italy now, God Bless them.' She looked uncertainly to Maria for reassurance.

'Continue Mia, it's alright,' Maria squeezed her hand.

'Paratroopers have been reported.'

Bianca looked blankly. 'German? Why would occupying forces parachute in anywhere, what does it mean?'

Carlo took up the reins. 'Your father has been told that German paratroopers have rescued Mussolini from arrest, he is to head what will now be called The Italian Social Republic. under Hitler's protection now.'

Worried eyes darted one to another, unsure what to do next, how to feel, who to swear allegiance to? He continued.

'The King has agreed an alliance with the Allies, who are creeping up the country with the might of the world behind them. Now the Germans have Mussolini, he will be obliged to them. Where it leaves the people, the man on the street, you and I, I don't know.'

'How will we survive with no recognisable system in place?' Maria asked.

Carlo hung his head, then looked up.

'We carry on as before, wait until we know which way things will go, keep our heads down, bother no-one, agree with no-one,' he looked at the two girls. 'The winter is coming and we will have to try and get stores together as best we can. I have work with Vittorio, and electricity is a necessity. By God's blessing we will have some sort of income.'

He looked angrily at Mia. It wasn't he or his wife's responsibility to rally them into the unknown. Her husband, the most secure, distancing himself again, while enjoying most of the spoils, then relented.

'Mia, hold yourself together, your children depend upon you. You must be their shield against the unknown, you know that don't you?' Her eyelids fluttered uncontrollably.

Maria took over, 'You have us cara, we are here for you and will support you. Don't worry, things are what they are, and we are lucky to be under the ....' she paused to choose her words carefully, '....under the security of your husband's employment, it is essential and that is something.' She shot a glance at Carlo.

Bianca understood his irritation, it was her father's job to buoy everyone into the uncertain future.

'Mamma, let's go home, maybe we will be able to get more information.' She slipped her hand under her terrified mother's arm and lifted her from the seat. 'Come on boys,' she beckoned her two brothers, their safety even more tenuous now.

She was seventeen years old, and would have to assume the leading female role, her mother barely able to do anything, except cook. It was already known that Slav partisans stole into the city to murder young men every day, their bodies displayed prominently. In retaliation, Italian youths and soldiers had joined partisans, hoping to rain havoc down in defence of their city, against all and any sides, hiding as best they could.

Walking home she laid out the rules for her mother.

'Mamma, the boys are never to leave the compound at all, do you hear? Not even to take a message to Maria's house.' Her mother nodded obediently, 'and you and I?' she paused, 'well, we do what we can.'

As they approached the compound gates, the boys entered and she whispered.

'The Germans are very close to us Mamma; it will seem to the outside world, we are their friends. We will be polite and efficient to them, and also to neighbours or shopkeepers, we trust no-one.' She paused, 'Always courteous we make no comment, none at all.' Her mother stared blankly.

'We don't say we like a uniform, an outfit, a hairstyle, nothing about anyone, do you understand?'

'But our friends...'

'No-one, do you understand. We no longer have friends Mamma, only Carlo, Maria and Sophia. We can't know who else we can trust anymore, we have only ourselves,' she pleaded. 'Mamma, which way things will go now is up to the fates. We have only each-other. Promise me, you will try?'

Her mother looked up at her daughter, a young woman now, willing herself to understand the confusion that was erupting around her, finally whispering,

'I will do my best daughter, I know you will guide me.'

As they passed into the front vestibule Bianca watched her mother retreat into her domestic world, avoiding the outside forever. She sighed, she had control over her own life at last, but no benefit of decision.

Chapter 44

Trieste, Italy, July 1943 (some time ago)

Trauma and horror inhabited the ether of the city, gnawing at the life force of every citizen, permeating every wall, rupturing lives, exuding an essence of sadness.

The sun would not rise for hours, yet they would not sleep. The mother and father sat motionless watching their 4 year old daughter slumber on their knees in their once luxurious home. He held his wife's hand gently as sleep tried to take them. They could not succumb, too much at stake. As one drifted to slumber the other awakening them with a squeeze.

She looked around where lavish furniture and opulent textiles had adorned the large space not so long ago. Tall windows overlooked the central square as the hour for departure crept closer. Her mind touched on the desecration of their synagogue the previous year, and the many assaults on Jewish friends since fascist legislation had been imposed. It had been incomprehensible, their families citizens of Trieste for generations, for centuries, had lived harmoniously, contributing richly to the fortune of their beautiful city.

Watching her daughter's light breath come and go, her thoughts drifted to life-long friends, gone, disappeared, no word given or trust in them exercised, they were abandoned, their Jewish population now half its size. Initially, some had left legitimately, others had converted to Catholicism or married into Italian families, hoping to save themselves. But no protection existed for anyone against the fascist regime. She and her husband had remained; they had faith, so entwined within Triestine culture, born in the all-embracing society of the city, until Il Duce had decreed they be turned upon. Many

Italians had refused the call, spiriting Jewish friends away, but they were left alone among the diminished society.

As the night drifted by, she thought about her friends, houses abandoned like empty boats drifting on the sea, tables carefully set, household silent, people gone. She recalled school days in the company of her Italian friends, no difference between them as they laughed and joked together, mixing freely, loving the same films, playing in the same parks, eating at each other's homes. She remembered playing with the daughter of her father's colleague a long time ago, too troubled to recall her name. No difference between them as they danced in the sunny courtyard, ate cherries from the trees and chased the chickens; she had pretended to be mother, cosseting the little girl as her baby.

A cold draft blew through the windows, damaged when her home was looted. Their artwork was confiscated, her finest furniture removed. Grit, splinters of glass and debris, littered the floor where her exquisite Oriental carpet had lain. Across from where she sat, she eyed the dustless square on the cabinet where their modern gramophone had stood. It had been a gift from her father when she married, her precious records housed below, the last item to be stripped from her home, cupboard door hanging on a hinge now, brittle shards of shellac disc scattered across the wooden floor.

Her dear husband had ventured out earlier that day to check on friends, returning suddenly with horrifying news of a Jewish shopkeeper dragged from his store. He had hidden in the crowd, never daring to show his loyalty, as the man was unceremoniously thrown into a truck. No formality, the practice now to remove without notice. They had no choice but to act fast. He had given her instructions, she was to make ready urgently, and had left again.

*

At the allotted time the three emerged into the starless night, giving thanks for the cloudy, moonless sky, and took to side streets. The little girl stumbled sleepily as they passed down narrow cobbled passages, vigilant to their surroundings. Reaching Canal Grande, near where Jewish citizens had solemnly lined the quay to board liners to anywhere, they kept silent.

There was movement as a fisherman prepared his nets at the side of the canal.

She cloaked her daughter from view beneath her coat, pressing her body close against an old dock building. They waited as a truck passed with a Nazi patrol, cool eyes surveying but not seeing them. The father looked at his watch, silently counting. He turned to her.

'Ten after three. When you see the fisherman there,' he pointed at Canal Grande, 'go, run as fast as you can towards him, don't stop, don't look back.' His wife looked up into cloudy eyes.

'And you?' she questioned.

'Whatever you hear, keep running. If there is trouble, whatever happens, just keep going.' He kissed his wife on the forehead for a long moment.

'Now,' he touched the head of his daughter. 'Go.'

As the woman dashed towards the small boat, the child's feet hardly touched the floor. Other figures silently manifested like ghosts, gliding tentatively, as the fisherman reached up and pulled mother and child in.

'Where is your husband, my arrangement is with him?'

The mother, cowering, looked up as the fishermen grappled with people trying to get in his boat.

'You, jump in.' he shouted at the father, pushing back the intruders with an oar. 'Go, there, try them, I am full, you're not with me,' the fisherman waved towards other *small vessels further along the canal. A thud followed as the father landed on the sparse bundles next to the family, and together they managed to push away from the quay.*

'Get down,' the fisherman hissed, 'The Germans expect only me in the boat, there may be searchlights,' coiling the mooring cable, and manoeuvred his ketch stealthily along the canal and out to sea.

Looking back towards the dim quay the fisherman could see figures stealing silently down from side streets as if they hardly existed, no sound, just traces of people. Fathers heads darted every way, along every alley, around every corner, each carrying what precious items and money they could, business and property deeds sewn into clothes, to return after the war. Mother's faces streaked with silent tears they dare not reveal to their children, family jewellery, prized memorabilia, photographs of those who would never now leave, crushed into bags. Bleary, bewildered children clutched one small precious toy, instinctively silent, no fuss or histrionics. Desperate visions that never left the city, or anyone who witnessed.

Chapter 45

Italy, Trieste, October 1943

'Do you remember when we were at school Bianca, how the boys took Il Duce's war games so seriously?' Sophia asked. Only alone did the two friends speak of those times.

'Some boys were allowed to take guns and bullets home, reinforcing ambition to be good fascist soldiers,' Bianca answered.

'My God, how they postured, strutting around; and that boy dropped his gun, it went off and sent us scattering across the piazza terrified, thinking we'd be killed,' Sophia laughed involuntarily.

Passing the garrison now, German boys called after the girls as they dropped their heads shyly, Sophia tugging Bianca to look at some non-existent item by the path instead. The girls tested the soldiers' interest in them, waiting to see if they would throw cigarettes, or promise treats. Looking up, Bianca recognized a boy who guarded the entrance of the power station, not much older than her, and tossed her hair prettily away.

'He's only recently conscripted, Sophia, not much older than us, but one to know.'

'But some' Sophia retorted, 'they are zealots, too eager to do unspeakable things, you can tell. Not like the young ones who are here only because they've been conscripted to make up for losses.'

'I suppose, those already brutalised by what they've seen, would be cruel in return, and we are no more than tasty morsels to them,' Bianca tried to be generous.

'That's what Papa said,' Sophia added, 'they lack empathy for unworldly people.'

*

At night, Bianca avoided the guards at the gate by bending back the bottom edge of the link fence at the back of the compound, slipping under to visit Sophia. They would sit outside the kitchen window talking or listening to Maria and Carlo, cunning and spying everywhere, part of their daily lives.

'Have you heard the latest of the massacres in Yugoslavia?' Bianca asked.

'Hush,' Sofia's young brother entered the garden. He hurried around his task, disappearing to the kitchen and she continued.

'I heard Slav partisans were being thrown into foibes, dead, or left to die in there,' Bianca said.

The girls sat silently for a moment contemplating the horror; how unthinkable life had become. On the one hand, a lesser number of communist partisans to kill them or their Italian boys they thought, yet the shocking news lay heavy on them. Bird Boy had trained them to avoid the dangerous sinkholes and pits himself. He was Slav and their friend, just trying to stave off starvation, like they were. The three had talked so many times of the madness erupting around every corner, impinging upon every part of their lives, three young companions in their strange oasis of normality.

'What will we do, how can we get back on the Karst?' Sofia seemed to read Bianca's mind.

'I'll have to try and find out from Papa. Remember when he left us to work out what to do next when "you know who" was captured? I'm going to confront him. He can't stay removed from the difficulties of life forever,' she replied.

'Bianca that would be foolish, haven't you learned yet how he is, he must be treated gently,' Maria said.

'He doesn't deserve delicate treatment,' she frowned then replied, 'but you're right cara, I need to treat him carefully. I'll see if I can get anything out of him, though you know what he thinks of trouble, that's our job.'

They hugged each-other goodnight and she made her way home, distraction and habit leading her along the path to the compound gates. Inside, a German soldier loomed within the dark sentry box, rifle drawn.

For the longest moment, the young man stood looking, Bianca a statue of terror, until thick clouds drifted to reveal a half-moon glow. She saw he wasn't expecting to be confronted with a visitor, and sprang to her advantage.

'Oh my, I'm so sorry.' Arms spread open, she lightly curled her fingers in the links of the gate between them, innocent in submission, swaying gently towards him. 'I lost track of time tending an old lady. I really should have been home before curfew.' The barrel of the rifle was shaking as he gingerly stepped out towards her, eyes darting around. She dropped her arms presenting no danger, and smiled engagingly, saying, 'Haven't I seen you down at the barracks?'

'I was on sentry duty last night, you saw me then.' He appeared affronted she hadn't remembered him. 'And you are supposed to be inside, I saw you earlier,' lack of imminent threat emboldened him.

'Oh no,' she sighed, 'I took two eggs to the old lady over there,' she waved vaguely in the direction of the hillside, 'you were busy taking instructions,' and sidled up to the gate. The young man struggled to argue against the pale grey eyes shining in the moonlight, when the sound of a comrade came from the side of the house.

'One moment,' he marched towards his colleague around the corner. Bianca breathed a sigh of relief; she wasn't inside, but was close.

He returned as the clouds shrouded the sky again.

'Quick come in, I've sent him to check on something. I know you live here.' She slipped through the barely opened gate as the steps of the German returned. 'Get in the sentry box,' he pushed her towards his shelter.

Her heart thudded, this was not safe for either of them, when from an upper window the sound of her brothers arguing drew the other soldier, who turned, cursed, and walked back.

'Wait here, he'll use any excuse to sit in the entrance instead.'

'How are you speaking Italian to me?' Bianca asked, rationality seeping back as panic faded.

'I was brought up in Italian Switzerland, we ended up in Germany with my father's work, and when he died we were stuck there. Hide, he's coming back again.' Bianca slid into the tiny box as he backed in pushing her against the wood. Guttural words passed between them, the second German sniffed and walked back to his comfortable place in the house entrance.

'How am I to get inside?' she whispered.

'He must not know I let you in, but if I can draw him back around the corner, you can sneak in,' he turned to look down at her lovely face.

'I'm so grateful to you,' she murmured, liquid eyes glistening in the scudding moon-light. 'But I am so tired and hungry, I might not be able to get in so easily,' she would pursue her advantage as far as she could.

'You said you took eggs to an old lady, why did you do that if you were hungry?' he replied.

She shifted her slight body and shivered. They stood face to face, bodies pressed against each other in the tiny space, hips engaged, and she lifted her face to his.

'I just thought it was the right thing to do,' she whispered, feeling the connection between her and a man, understanding her father's course words for the first time, and lowered her eyes.

'I can't stay here Mamma will worry, I have to go,' she tried to wriggle free.

'Wait, you can't go yet,' he caught her thin arm. 'Listen, I am on duty again tomorrow night, I'll try and get you something, it might be left-overs, will that help?'

'That would be wonderful, I'd be so grateful,' she smiled.

'What's your name? 'he asked.

'I cannot say. My father wouldn't approve.'

'You're right of course, I know he is an eminent man.' She looked at him. *"What could he know of her father?"* she thought, as he continued, 'He has powerful allies in the city.' Looking down, as she attempted to step out, his lips brushed her cheek, then dashed to his comrade reporting a noise from the far side of the building, and lifting their rifles they rushed away. She ran to the front door as he threw one last look and disappeared inside.

Chapter 46

North Africa, October 1943

'What you gonna do when you get home?'

Ted wondered why Taff asked the same question every morning. He seemed to live an early morning habit he couldn't shake, which included him. Daily, when he made his way to the wash tent, Taff would appear from no-where, razor, soap and towel in hand, ready to make smart for the day; it didn't matter that no-one would see them, regulations and standards were rooted deep within the British soldier. He wondered not for the first time, where Taff was billeted, he never saw him any other time.

'Not sure Taff, visit me Mam I suppose,' his reply always the same.

'What do you make of action with the Italians then?' Ted was knocked sideways, he had never heard Taff initiate a different topic of conversation before, asking,

'What you talking about?'

'You know the Italians, we've just about sorted them out over here haven't we? Taff commented.

'I don't know, and I'm not prepared to talk about it,' Ted replied.

'Don't kid about mate, you don't think "loose lips sink ships" applies out here do you mate, we're in the middle of a desert'

'It's none of my business Taff, I just get on with what I'm told to do.'

'God Ted, you're more Welsh Baptist than me. Never wander too far from the righteous path do you?' he chuckled, then, 'ouch, cut myself.'

Ted couldn't argue with his logic. The stability of his Welsh grandparents, the only he had ever known, their sense of responsibility and duty, ran thick in his blood.

Combined with the armed force's discipline, it was the scaffold he hung his life upon. He met Taff in Cairo the night he bumped into Arthur, it had been quite a night, and had never set eyes on him again until they both turned up together at morning ablutions, in Africa. What a life.

A shout went out, and they ran to present themselves for instructions.

*

Tents were struck, poles and groundsheets folded and piled high as scores of soldiers presented kit for movement. As lunch approached, a stream of trucks arrived, Ted instructed to attend at the NAAFI for provisions. By the time he assembled back at equipment, the first troops were moving out. Taff joined him as recent tent-mates moved off, waving and shouting, 'See you in Rome Ted'. There was something in the offing.

A truck slowed alongside them. As it pulled away, he saw Taff running after it to suddenly disappear into the back, to calls of 'Come on you little bastard,' as he was dragged in and passed over the shoulders of his mates, his feet the last thing Ted saw. Looking around there seemed only him and the cook left.

'You two get in that.' Ted was delighted at the prospect of not being thrown about for miles in the back of a truck, only to discover, travelling at speed in an open Land Rover had its own drawbacks.

Their route circumvented every obstacle on route, arriving at their destination at dusk, rows of tents already erected as soldiers bivvied down for the night.

'Don't worry mate,' the cook whispered as some big-eared officers departed, 'Come on, I'm NAFFI, I'll get us a good supper,' and they took off for the cook tent.

After enjoying dinner from officers' rations they wandered back towards the tents to bed down. With no-one to instruct, they walked up and down the rows, all bunk-

211

downs taken, until on the outskirts they saw a small abandoned building without a roof.

'Come on let's give this a looking at,' cook said. Ted followed and they dropped their kit-bags to examine. 'It's made of biscuit tins filled with sand.'

The inner floor was lower than outside, boxes piled about six foot high. 'I wonder why no-one else is using it, it's freezing at night,' Ted queried.

'Top drawer' the cook approved. 'I'll get a tarpaulin. We can pull it over the top for a roof. We're going to be warm tonight mate.'

As they secured the waterproof sheet, a couple of soldiers sauntered by and shouted, 'Wouldn't do that mate.'

'You're only jealous' the cook yelled back.

'Please yourselves,' and they carried on.

The sun set rapidly, temperature dropping as they slid into their cosy lair. Silence descended on the camp with only the occasional barked instruction in the distance, as they relaxed in their comfortable hollow.

Ted thought he had been asleep for hours when something alerted him. *"Ignore it, you've been through worse, go back to sleep",* he told himself, then hearing a scuffle from the cook's bunk-up, something touched his leg, and the cook yelled, 'Get off you daft bugger.'

'What you talking about, I'm not doing anything,' Ted answered.

They lay silent, holding still for a moment as a clicking started.

'Yaaa! It's on me,' the cook screamed as his blanket pitched through the air like a seagull. Ted scrambled to get his lighter, flicking it on. Two pale faces gawped open-mouthed out of the dark, as hundreds of scorpions skittered out from cracks between the biscuit boxes. Running on loose sand didn't give much purchase either as they both headed for the narrow exit, creatures underfoot and flying through the air.

'I stood on one, ah man I'm gonna die,' the cook screamed as he escaped.

Out in the night air, some tent flaps had opened and yells of derision filtered out.

'Daft buggers, what were you thinking?' accompanied by shouts of, 'idiots,' and laughter.

As they twirled in the sand trying to see if they had brought any of the creatures out, a straight-backed, broad-shouldered sergeant major strode purposefully towards them, swagger stick in hand. He deftly flicked a scorpion off Ted's shoulder with a muscular swipe of his hand, yelling,

'What did you two bastards think you were doing? Think this is a bloody holiday camp?' scowling at the sagging canvas roof.

'We didn't know where we were supposed to go....' the cook spoke.

'And you thought you'd have a nice comfy time in there while the rest of us put up with tents eh?' he paused. 'So no-one let on, hey?' A barely distinguishable twitch to his moustache disguised a wry smile. 'Why do you think it's abandoned you halfwits?' He pushed his face into theirs, 'Because it's toxic.' It was getting cold.

'Get your stuff tomorrow, bring your blankets,' he turned to go as Ted and the cook stood looking at each other.

'They're in there,' Ted hazarded a reply.

The sergeant stopped in his tracks, a heavy sigh emitted from his general vicinity. Turning he marched to the entrance and straight down into the den. First one blanket and then another flew through the air, landing at their feet. As he emerged, chin firm, mouth tight, they gingerly shook them, just to be sure.

'Bivvy down in a tent along here,' he indicated the closest row.

Mocking laughter and catcalls still emanated along the line. 'What's the matter girls, don't like your lodgings?'

Hoots and cheers of 'stupid buggers' followed, the best entertainment of the day.

'Shut it!' the sergeant shouted and indicated the nearest tent, 'Get in there.'

'There's no room Sarg, we're full up,' from within.

The sergeant stuck his head through the flap, 'I'm sure you children could do with the extra body heat,' and grabbing the cook by his shoulder, pushed him in. Ted took the opportunity to enter the next tent unescorted.

Inside, he stepped over complaining bodies, until he managed to slide in between the last two of the row, rolled himself in his blanket and lay on his side. Adjusting to the light he saw two glistening eyes inches from his face, and alarmed, asked,

'What you looking at?'

A voice behind him murmured, 'Don't worry, he's show business mate, used to be on the stage.'

The face before him smiled.

'What's he staring at me for?' Ted whispered.

'Probably fancies you, ducky,' a guffaw broke out from the rest of the tent.

'You're safe with me sweetheart,' an eye winked and closed.

Ted chuckled, it didn't matter where you went, what you did, you were always part of the Army family, no harm meant, no offence taken, and you met all sorts. He was a long way from Redcar.

The sergeant-major retreated back down the line to his billet as comments and jibes settled, only one sound emanating from his direction.

'Stupid twats.'

Chapter 47

Trieste, Italy, October 1943

Odilo was oppressive, the air almost dank in his presence. It was clear her father knew him from early Trieste days, and the thought chilled Bianca, a scaffold of tension grasped her frame, appalled to inhaling the same air. After his initial visit, he called less, but despite stories of his methods, they devoured any food he sent. She was sworn to secrecy from telling Sophia, even keeping the scraps from Maria, but life continued, their daily chats vital.

'What is your Mamma hiding today?' Sofia asked, neither genius nor fool. Bianca grimaced, how could she lie to her friend?

'I can't tell you, please don't ask.'

'I know all about it, or at least I can guess.' Sophia leaned forward and confided, 'My mother has two sausages hidden in our linen cupboard. They stink, but the bedsheets smell delicious,' she displacing their shameful lies with a joke, friendship too precious to lose. The girls looked at each other, no wedge of deceit was to come between them and they shared their mothers' secrets.

'I've been told to try and get some flour for pasta,' Sophia said, 'no doubt I'll find it in the sentry's pocket.' Bianca laughed, a blessed relief comforted them, and she had a real contact.

'Cara,' she said, 'I know where I can get some flour ground from chestnuts, it is as good as any other. I went to Opicina with Papa yesterday, saw the Bird Boy and managed to speak to him. He said if we meet this afternoon he has access to a huge bag, but he needs brandy in return.'

'Will your father allow it?'

'I know my mother will spirit some away, Odilo keeps sending such things to my father.' She looked away, 'I can hardly believe he accepts them, Italy is supposed to be at war with Germany now.'

Sophia looked as her friend gazed blankly into the distance. The strain of everyday existence rested heavily upon her like a shroud across her lovely face.

'I know it's difficult for you Bianca, keeping your mother's spirits up, watching your brothers as they sit in their rooms playing with toys,' Maria said.

'And you know who provides those expensive toys? That German, Papa's friend, Odilo!' Her cheeks flushed, 'My father is a donkey.'

'Don't say that, cara, it's wrong.'

'Is it?' she snapped.

'It is wrong to say such things because it's dangerous. Have you not heard the stories of his deeds, the horrors he orchestrated?' She mouthed his name. 'Your Papa probably just doesn't want to upset him.' Sofia tried to sooth Bianca's war-weary mind; life was hard, their aim always to keep each-other calm, spirits up.

They set off, glad to be away from the stifling atmosphere of the compound and made their way to their secret meeting place with the Bird Boy. Halfway to the Karst they rested and looked back down at Trieste, spread out in the clear autumn air, a jewel of a city, the azure sea chopped into grey and white slivers, disappearing into a misty distance. There was much activity as German transport dashed purposefully around, no-one taking any notice of two scrawny young women that day, important business for the Fuhrer elsewhere it seemed. They pulled a small platform on wheels made by Luca in one of the workshops to transport their booty, and the military activity offered protection to travel, unmolested by anyone intent on stealing their treasure.

*

On returning she recognized the German sentry at the gate, Sophia flicked Bunetta a knowing look as they dragged their loot to the front door. Another soldier ordered him to carry the sack upstairs for them.

'No, it isn't necessary, we can manage,' Bianca tried to stop him. She had no objection to flirting with him at his post, but the stark reality of his military uniform in their kitchen disturbed her. Outside he was useful, inside a discomfort. Thankfully he delivered the sack to the top of the stairs and politely left.

The front door closed with a noticeable snap as measured haunting notes sounded along the corridor from the kitchen. The opening violin strings of Act V, La Forza del Destino mournfully drifted, stopping the girls in their tracks as her squabbling brothers scurried to their bedrooms, Luca saying, 'I'm choosing next time, this is rubbish.'

'What's going on?' Bianca called, as her father appeared at the kitchen door.

'You girls have done well,' her father looked at the sack, leaning back on his heels, chest expanded, his favoured pose of self-satisfaction, a good mood taking the girls by surprise. Bianca could see he expected some kind of recognition for the new acquisition in the kitchen.

He elaborated, 'The gramophone? Simply a gift for efficient production of electricity, nothing more,' he modestly informed. 'There is a good supply of stylus needles and a variety of recordings,' he paused to observe the girls' awe, Mia creeping nervously from a storeroom, followed by Maria.

'Wife, you may have this ornament in the kitchen to ease your working day, I have no need for it in my office and it would be unthinkable in the workplace. You will benefit from your husband's enterprise again,' he declared.

Bianca realised immediately, her father needed as many people as possible to know he was responsible for provision of the luxury.

Benito and Luca returned to position it on the wooden table next to the coffee grinder and examined the shellac music disks on the table.

Mia dear,' Maria quietly drew her away, 'don't let the boys play that again.'

'Why cara, it is so mournful and beautiful, a little like the day I think?' Mia said.

'My friend you know I wouldn't want to deprive you of your pleasure,' she paused, 'but that opera is cursed.' Mia's eyes flickered warily as her friend continued.

'I am sorry but the music warns of harm, of death. Please don't play it again,' Maria implored.

Mia knew their lives followed a perilous path, hurriedly crossed herself and grasped the Mater Dolorosa pendant at her neck, whispering to The Sorrowful Mother, and sent the boys to the hall.

'Bianca dear, please remove and record, and slip an embroidered cloth under our new gramophone, it looks commonplace like that.'

Sophia and her mother left. She lifted the corners of the elegant wooden case to carefully slip an old linen serviette below; something scraped, obstructing her task. Sliding her fingers along the underside, she felt a piece of paper curled over on the base where aged dried glue had lost its grip.

'Where did the gramophone come from Mamma?' she asked casually, 'how did Papa come to have such an item?'

She gripped the paper between two fingers manoeuvring it a little as it dislodged and came away in her fingers.

'It was delivered just before you returned dear, by a German car.'

Bianca's shoulders tightened. She turned the slip of paper over. It was old, with bold, flowery words written in fading ink.

"Purchased - to be delivered to Hertzfelt, June 1930, on the occasion of their marriage"

The slip of paper fell through her fingers to the ground.

Chapter 48

Trieste, Italy, Winter 1943

Night wasn't a good time to walk but Bianca fled the dim glow of the kitchen grabbing her blanket coat. She stumbled into undergrowth at the side of the power station, hearing Papa talking to Odilo. Her father had entertained many odious creatures, old men, rich men, religious men who should all have been thin as they were but were fat, and now this German. Her father managed to provide tobacco and wine, and if possible a little something to eat, flattering, agreeing, extolling whatever view they had, and satisfied, they left gifts, of meat, spirits or cosmetics.

That day she had watched the Monsignor waddle in through the entrance, saluted by the sentry; her throat constricted, she despised him. She knew of a local mother, a good woman, whose son died in Greece, husband not working and with six surviving children, every year another one to feed it seemed, and had sought advice and support from the priest. Almost dying in childbirth twice already, unable to feed those she already had, her children faded before her, and her husband demanded his carnal rights still. The fascist regime in disarray, women were no longer obliged to produce children, and her smallest babe barely clung to life; if the mother died, who would care for them all? As she had listened to the tale Bianca was sickened at the priest's advice, *"Put your faith in God. Be dutiful to him, and your husband."* There had been no compassion for the woman as he sat in his comfortable closeted world, padding around with a healthy girth, undisturbed by war, fascism or Nazi occupation. Every time the priest visited her home she cursed his lofty disregard for the women of his flock, all vestiges of religious belief withered within her.

She had asked herself, *'How can God exist in a world where his patrons suffer so, demeaned by men who thought only of their own needs.'* She often saw her mother clutching the blue Mater Dolorosa at her throat, her dependence pitiful. She swore to rely only upon herself, unwilling to trust a deity that so badly abused half of its flock. Dear Sophia, the only exception to her rule.

She felt sure the sentries guessed she crept away sometimes, they couldn't have missed the irregularity in the links, but they liked her. She was beautiful and friendly, young like them, unaware how duplicitous a desperate young woman could be.

As she squeezed through the gap her army blanket coat snagged. The Bora was light, skies not harried by clouds but gathering inland, a strong wind would follow soon, and snow covered the upper ground.

Months had passed since jackboots marched up the hill, a familiar sound now. She had seen soldiers beat old men and women with rifle butts, their ominous presence seeping like a virus into everyone's life. No-one knew who to trust any more, any neighbour might report his best friend to defend themselves or gain favours or food. Trips to Piazza dei Foraggio too dangerous now as Germans congregated in Roberto's trattoria.

It wasn't simply that soldiers amassed in the Italian barracks at Camp Montebello below, but they infested every corner of her world like a plague, itching and scratching, becoming intolerable. Like the story of the mother and priest, every tale chiselled harder into her mind, no coping space left. Her head was a warehouse, every wronged event, every torture her father inflicted, every danger she'd encounter, every fictitious favour her eyes had promised to gain food and fear of retribution was noted and stored. Her mother remained in the sanctuary of her kitchen making gnocchi out of crumbs of bread and stale old flour, brothers hidden in the workshops near generators, out of sight. *They are no threat; just little boys playing with bits of wood, making puppets*' her mother bleated if anyone asked.

As she entered Sofia's house, shaking off the dampness of the undergrowth she noticed a silence unusual for the loving, friendly home.

'Sofia?' She looked to her friend standing near the window.

'Come away now,' Maria yanked her daughter roughly and dragged the curtains closed, locking the door.

'What's happening, I don't understand, Maria? Bianca asked.

'Why would you care, you live up there in your citadel,' the words out of her mouth before she could stop them. Bianca, stunned by the outburst, Sofia went to her side.

'It's not her fault Mamma, please don't.'

'They live in their ivory tower, untouched by the world, entertaining the great and the mighty...' Maria crumbled to tears.

'Mamma that's not fair, Bianca has suffered everything I have, maybe even more.'

'Stop that now, your father doesn't embrace the Nazis,' Maria spat.

'Mamma, Signor Marchetti gave Papa his job, it has kept him from the war front. We are friends, we all work together.' Maria collapsed onto a chair at the table, tears gushing as Sofia turned to her friend.

'Cara please don't judge Mamma. We've had terrible news, and she's hitting out at everyone, blaming anyone.'

'What is it Sofia, what has happened?'

'My little brother sneaked into town. He should not have, it is too dangerous, he was in the wrong place at the wrong time. The Germans were clearing the streets, taking partisans, gypsies, Slavs, anyone who looked like trouble,

222

rounding them up....' she looked at her mother, still weeping.

'He hid and watched as they were locked in a bus at an old garage, fool that he is. He thought they were going to be transported and wanted to know where they were going,' Sofia gasped.

'And?'

'The Nazis made the bus tight, switched on the engine and locked the doors to the garage,' she started to sob, 'and waited until it was over.'

Silence cut the air, punctuated by Maria's sobs.

'What happened, where is he now? dazed.

'He's in bed, Mamma has calmed him. He was hysterical when he got home, but sleeps now. Can you imagine what the repercussions would be if they find out he was there, he should never have been outside. He knew of the danger if the Slavs found him,' she looked at her mother again. 'There is more Bianca, he saw our cousin,' tears welled, 'he was one of those locked in the bus,' water rolled silently down her cheeks.

'But why did they take him, Maria?' Bianca turned to her, another abhorrent image squeezed into her uncomprehending mind.

'Because he is Italian, young, and they are frightened he would rise up and fight against them.... I mean - he was,' she looked away. 'God bless you child, I'm sorry. I know you would never have anything to do with the Germans, it is only your father,' a bitter flash crossed her face. Bianca knelt at her side.

'My troubles seem insignificant compared to yours Maria, I am so sorry for your loss,' Bianca drew back. 'I'll go and tell Mamma.'

'No, she need not know. If necessary I'll tell her myself tomorrow. It would have been better if you had never heard what was said here tonight,' Maria cast her eyes around her kitchen, 'it's dangerous to know anything, forget you were here.'

Bianca stepped outside pulling the blanket coat tighter, Sofia joining her for the briefest moment. Embracing each-other, warmth radiated from Sofia through her coat. She wanted to cling to her forever but they pulled apart, both turning without looking back, her friend returning to her mother's distress, she into the growing Bora, as flakes of snow began to fall.

Chapter 49

Trieste, Italy, Winter 1943/44

As she entered the kitchen her brothers were gabbling excitedly to their mother.

'It's true, every word. It is!' Benito related a tale as Luca tried to interject, her mother as uncomprehending as the rabbit she was skinning.

'What are you two jabbering about?' Bianca had no time for their childish antics, time they grew up, not cosseted and treated like babies any more, but looking at her mother's confusion knew she needed to step in.

'I said, why are you bothering Mamma, can't you see she's busy?' They continued excitedly.

'We overheard it, yes we heard; well we didn't see anyone of course, but that's what they said,' Luca blurted.

Benito added, 'It was someone in the power plant, we were in the small instrument workshop.' Bianca took control.

'Look what are you doing to Mamma, don't you see you're frightening her with your silly stories?' she thought of the real horrors just outside their compound. 'Can't you leave her alone?' She turned to hang her coat, the boys followed, still babbling.

'Oh, for goodness sake, what is it?' They gathered around, talking at the same time as she carefully placed the blanket coat on a clothes hanger to prolong its precious life.

'Benito, you tell me,' she demanded. He assumed an expression of satisfied superiority and adopted an appropriate stance.

'As I said we were in the small workshop,'

'And as I say now, you should not have been,' Bianca attempted a semblance of authority over the excited boys, as they led her down to the basement workshop.

'Huh? Well we were working very quietly in case anyone caught us, when we heard a couple of the men in the corridor outside, so we crouched down not to be found, and signalled to each other to be quiet, like in a cowboy film....'

'Benito, please get on with it, we haven't got all night.' A slight smirk manifested on Luca's face as Benito continued.

'We heard them talking about the Moroccan Goumiers....'

'The what?'

'Don't you keep abreast Bianca, you really should know?' Benito chided.

'I would if I had spare time like you,' she snapped.

'They are French Algerian tribesmen, they fight for the Allies and have been crawling over Italy since the summer. They are brave and fearsome fighters, who wear earrings, and a cloak over their uniforms.'

'Alright, so what's the problem? They are brave soldiers, and fight against the Germans right?'

'Well yes, but it's what else they do. The men outside the door were saying strange things we didn't understand; the stories were.... they were, like the movies.' She considered the statement.

'Just tell me what you heard.'

'Around their necks they wear necklaces of ears from their victims.' The information stung the air.

'Benito, just tell the story!'

'I'm trying to. I'm only telling you what we heard. I'm not too sure what some of the words mean, but they *"raped and pillaged"*. What does it mean?'

Bianca froze, comprehending her mother's distress.

'Tell me everything you know.' Her heart sank at the further atrocities assaulting her country. He continued.

'The barbarous warriors walk into villages, taking anything they want. In the mountains few men are remaining as you know, only the old and infirm, mothers and daughters trying to feed everyone, but when the Goumiers arrive they steal the wedding rings and rip golden earrings from their ears, and the Allies, they do nothing to stop them.'

She was exhausted and resigned, 'War is a terrible thing Benito, there are many prices to pay.' She thought of Sofia's cousin and her childhood friend's gramophone in their own kitchen. 'At least they have their life, and don't you remember when Italy joined with the Allies, there were celebrations?'

'Ah, but what those men said, I don't understand.'

'What don't you understand? Surely you know what pillaging is? It's what has happened to Italy since the Nazis arrived: fine furniture and luxuries stolen from our Jewish friends, food taken from Italian citizens for their troops, people turfed from grand homes and places like Castle Miramar to house the upper echelons of their army. Look out of the window Benito, they are housed this minute in the barracks of our army. They gorge on our resources and steal our artwork, that's what they do, these supposed supporters of Mussolini. He is just a puppet, dancing to their tune now,' she stepped back gasping as her brothers started.

'I only wanted to know what "raped" was,' Benito asked. 'The men outside were cursing, they said some mothers and daughters had died from the "rapings". If the Goumiers couldn't have what they wanted they shot their guns to frighten them, and not just the mothers, sometimes men and priests were "rapinged" too.'

'Stop, stop it now.'

'And some mothers and daughters jumped off cliffs, killing themselves instead,' Luca added.

'I'm telling you, stop it. You don't know what you are talking about, just shut up'

'I only wanted to know what all the fuss was about,' Benito's face slumped to a familiar sulky expression.

'It's something not to talk about,' she saw Luca's eyes water. 'Listen, boys, things are happening that none of us should ever know. Try to forget what you heard, don't repeat it to anyone, and please, please, never get involved in anything. Stay in the compound. Listen to no-one and nothing. God willing....' She scolded herself for entreating a higher plane. 'hopefully, our lives will be returned to us soon.'

Rebuked, they left, everything on her shoulders again, she would have to handle these things her Mamma could not bear. Sitting alone in the workshop, the horrifying words crawled around her aching mind, shaking her inside, tears flowing. She laid her head on the workbench against the smooth wood, face wet from tears, the damp, sticky sensation alarmed her. How would she ever escape this nightmare?

*

In a temporary camp beyond the devastation of Monte Cassino, on route to Rome, the USA Commander Lieutenant General lifted a generous whiskey.

'My God they were ferocious, in two days wielding knives they swarmed the hills with merciless zeal, the German posts could not withstand them. If it wasn't for the Goumiers, Rome wouldn't even be within sight.'

The irritated British officer repeatedly tapped his swagger stick on the table.

'Nevertheless, what the French General told them before the assault, was uncalled for,' he said angrily.

'Come now, do you think they would have stormed their prey so savagely had they not had the incentive, that everything they plundered was theirs without reproach?'

The Brit blasted, 'That no-one be punished for what they did? Do you think that it is a justifiable incentive?' he slapped the table again, amber liquid sloshing from their glasses 'It's not decent, or right!'

'They proved their value.' The American had the last word.

Chapter 50

Italy, Spring 1944

'Monty's went then?'

'What you talking about?' Ted stared at the sapper beside him, scraping mud off his boots in the dripping tent.

'Well he has. It's common knowledge. Back in Blighty by New Year, they said.'

'Okay, that was ages ago,' Ted replied.

Grinding against the worst Italian winter in generations, rain poured constantly, mirroring their wearying attempts to mend armoured vehicles stuck in mud. Exhaustion taking its toll, conversation limited, favoured topics regurgitated regularly.

'What's your problem pal?' the sapper piped up again.

'Loose lips sink ships,' Ted attempted banter to introduce a new conversation.

'We're in the middle of Italy mate, what's gonna sink here other than tanks?'

'The saying stands, and you shouldn't forget it,' he flicked a wry look sideways. His mate bit.

'Who's it I'm gonna tell? There's only you and me, and my Ma in Liverpool I writes to. Who's she gonna tell?'

Ted considered the logic and found it sound, but decided to push the tease further.

'Well if you tell your Ma, it'll be all down Liverpool High Street in no time.' A piece of wet webbing swung past his ear followed by a boot.

'Get out of 'ere ye daft eejit, we don't live near no High Street.' The storm continued to blast the sides of the tent. 'Jesus this rain, when's it gonna stop, it's a bloody bog out there?'

Ted and his Liverpool-Irish oppo had been slogging all day to dislodge a tank from the swamp, to start mending track. They had been assigned together since landing in Sicily, trudged up the boot of Italy, slowly making their way, placing temporary bridges and mending anything of use to the Allies. He continued,

'Bet you feel at home, eh?' Ted said, a bit of ribbing might pass the time.

'I'm gonna get a right cob on with you pal if you don't give it a rest. It's only me Ma' is Irish, I've never seen a bog in me life.'

Ted dropped the subject. Usually, it was his mate who was having a go at him, calling him "Geordie", and for the hundredth time, he would have to remind him he was Yorkshire through and through. It was all in fun, something to pass the dreary dullness of torrential rainy days, while unable to achieve almost anything in the torrent.

'Hey Geordie,' he was at it again, 'How come you never swear?'

'All the effing, cussing and blinding from you is enough for both of us mate,' Ted replied.

'Alright Geordie,' he paused,' what do they call yous, from Yorkshire then?'

'Tykes I suppose. But I'm Yorkshire northeast coast, lived in Redcar by the sea most of my life, except that summer we were in Wales after dad left. Why you asking?'

'Just looking for something to needle you with,' he ducked as a wet sock, courtesy of Ted, landed on his shoulder.

'Yer divvy,' he laughed.

Light was fading fast as a head poked through the dripping flaps of the tent, 'You two, Army numbers,' it demanded. They recited them without thinking, they could do it in their sleep. The Sergeant grunted. 'Make ready to move tonight.'

'Where we off to? We're supposed to be getting tanks ready for use,' Scouse asked.

'You should know better than that, son,' their informant, a regular soldier old enough to be their father, water ran off his helmet onto their drying uniforms.

'Only asking,' the Liverpudlian piped up, 'What time?'

'Get yourself over to the NAAFI truck at water point 4 after tea, you'll be issued with rations and be off. Where's the rest of your troop?' he shook his wet list over them.

'Outside, left along for about three rows,' Ted keen to assist.

'Don't break camp.' The Sergeant disappeared leaving flailing tent flaps wafting in more rain.

'Yer such a brown nose, pal,' Scouse quipped.

'Saves you having to be,' Ted countered.

They began meticulously checking kit, no excuse for losing anything even in war. Wet socks were rolled next to wet overalls, dry things at the bottom, wet at the top with anything they could spare to form a barrier between. Come the allotted hour, in full uniform and wet greatcoat, they assembled, waiting for the food truck to squelch into sight.

'Oh, Christ,' Ted groaned as it pulled up.

'What's yer problem mate?' the Liverpudlian scanned the scene.

'The cook on the food wagon, not exactly my best friend.'

'Since?'

'Since I pulled his leg about Yorkshire being "God's Own Country", and him being Irish Roman Catholic, through like a stick of rock, didn't like me taking the Lord's name in vain.'

'Forget about it, what's yer problem?'

Ted turned to him, 'I'm hungry, I can't tell you how cold I am, and he always gives me short rations. I'm telling you, I'm not kidding'

'It's God getting you back for what you said to me earlier,' Scouse threw his head back to laugh, water running off the back of his helmet, down his neck.

'Come on, I'll prove it to you.' Ted joined the line, awaiting food for the journey. Reaching the front he tipped his helmet over his eye, mumbled his number and waited. A cough and enthusiastic clearing of the throat preceded a spit, which landed at Ted's feet.

'You eh?

'Aye me again, what's on the menu?' A bit of light humour might thaw the Irishman, who turned to a crate in the back of the truck, rummaged, and passed a thin sandwich to Ted and nodded him away, 'Tea and water over there.'

Returning to Scouse, Ted peeled back the bread to reveal a sliver of bacon rind. 'Told you.' His mate rubbed cold wet hands together.

'Right, leave it to me.'

He shook his shoulders and strode casually to the front of the queue, 'Scran at last,' winking at the offending cook.

'Ye'll have to wait yer turn mate,' the cook nodded towards the line.

'No problem, just loving the smell of yer butties mate, ah nothing smells better than pork in a fine sandwich. What you got there, bacon?'

'And sausage,' the cook corrected.

'Feckin wonderful,' he closed his eyes, inhaling the satisfying aroma, 'Just like me Mammy makes.' The cook took the bait.

'You Irish, you have a Scouse accent?'

'Oh yes, living in Liverpool now, but me Mammy's Irish born and bred, would live there still if she could. I write to her every week, don't I?' He paused to take advantage of his position, 'Now then, your accent....' he let the half asked question hover before the cook.

'I'm County Galway aren't I, just outside the city.'

'Didn't I know it already, I was just going to say so. Me Mammy's from Galway too.'

'Ye're messing with me! What's the chances, and you say she's in Liverpool now?'

'Aye, had to move there when I was a kid, well you know?' another half-spoken comment implied, some nodding of the head and a serious look to the ground.

Scouse continued, 'What's yer Mammy's name then, mine might know her. I'll write and tell her I've been speaking to you.'

''Tis Helena, so it is,' the cook's eyes clouded with the look of a loving son, asking, 'and yours?'

Scouse gulped, getting in a bit too deep with details, but there was a big prize to play for.

'Er, I'm Patrick.'

'Well Patrick,' he pulled his new Scouse friend aside, 'now we're acquainted,' he indicated for him to open his pockets wide, 'Here's your scran for the night and pushed in two double size bacon buns.

'Now that's very generous of you, and I'm fair starving so I am.' The cook shushed him, looked over his shoulder at the waiting line, all eyes down in the rain, and leaned into the truck and took another generous handful of sausage sandwiches, wrapped them in a bit of paper and indicted his military duffle bag.

'Now then, when ye next write to yer Mammy, you let her know you were talking to a Hennelley from Galway.' The cook patted his new mate on the shoulder.

Scouse slipped to shelter between two trucks and slapped Ted's shoulder.

'Here you are mate,' handing him a proper bacon sandwich, then opening the top of his duffle, 'and, something for later on,' he winked as the delicious savoury smell made it through the rain.

'How'd you get these?' astounded, but not surprised, Ted examined his face.

'Just a bit of craic that's all,' Scouse stopped short of detail. They were both skilled mechanical engineers, but

234

Ted knew Scouse also owned a mighty talent for persuasion.

'You've not been lying to get these have you?' Ted's hunger conflicting with his need for good conduct.

'More like spinning a yarn me old mate,' and pushed the food into Ted's hands. 'Life's very black and white for you ain't it?' He admired Ted's beliefs, '.... but sometimes, when needs must...' and smiled innocently.

Ted had to agree, 'Cheers mate,' and hungrily tucked into the bacon delight.

Chapter 51

Trieste, Italy, May 1944

The rumble of German traffic started early, as usual.

'There they go again.' Bianca sighed, listening to the German motorcade pass in pre-dawn darkness, accompanying Christian Wirth's car.

'That mad man, you know who he is, don't you?' she looked at her mother nibbling a meagre breakfast, as she put her knapsack together for the days' forage. Mia looked nervously down the corridor.

'He visited last autumn with my husband's....' She struggled to describe his associate, ' that is, with Odilo.' She shot a look down the corridor to see if anyone was within earshot. Bianca continued.

'Despite his character, Odilo has a type of handsomeness to him, but this one, what do they call him, Christian the Terrible? He has the round pursed features of a sour fruit with evil beady eyes behind those spectacles. I wonder if he has ever smiled in his life. He looks as if he's capable of anything, and wouldn't even take pleasure in that.' The conversation was a rare moment between them. She hadn't seen the friendly sentry for days, and with no packages or scraps was forced to go to the Karst, cursing all Aryans.

Maria would arrive soon to keep an eye on Mia's diminishing sanity, still angry because they benefited from her father's friendship with Odilo; it was all too much, the tension suffocating, she needed fresh air. In the laundry pile, she searched for an outfit. Rifling through ironing, the first pair of trousers she pulled out were her father's and threw them on the floor, stamping and kicking them, deciding these were the ones to take the brunt of any dirty business that day.

Leaving, she paused outside Sophia's house. Maria suddenly appeared at the open door and a breeze whipped into the house. Instead of a homely kitchen, the crimson door curtain flashed across the scene. Bianca strained to see her friend inside behind the table, her skin white against the gloom, her usual easy countenance dazed as the curtain filled the door-space, flapping like a blood red warning flag. The wind snapped a freezing bolt of cold, pushing past Maria. Again the curtain blew above the table where skinny fowl lay gutted. Time stood still as the ruby drape hung in the air for a moment, a corner suddenly slapping down on the marble chopping board where neatly stacked entrails slid to the edge and slithered to the floor.

Maria forced a self-conscious laugh and the spell was broken. Inside, the kitchen was warm again, filled with the aroma of stock on the stove as Sofia turned to her mother.

'Mind what I say, cara' Maria grasped her hand as she turned to leave, her eyes betraying some undefined fear

'Not again. Every day? I know what you're going to say Mamma,' Sophia lamented.

'Well mark it well daughter,' still clinging to her fingers. 'Be careful of the vegetation because the foibes and sinkholes....' Sofia rolled her eyes heavenward.

'We know. They are hidden by plants and bushes, the entrance to bottomless pits and potholes, with no escape, 'she was given the same warning every time. Maria squeezed her.

'You are my precious daughter, I have to warn and protect you. Wherever you are, even when not by my side, it's my duty.'

Bianca flushed. No-one seemed to worry for her safety, and another stone lodged in her heart. She knew her mother loved her children but her brothers were obvious favourites. She struggled alone, only Sofia to support her through the madness.

Maria laughed nervously, holding down her billowing skirt, 'Get on your way girls, go and seek some tasty morsels for us.' Bianca looked back; the gruesome scene of gizzards and blood seemed to ooze out through the doorway after them.

'And no chatting to soldiers, or strangers,' Maria called.

'Unless they can give us food,' Sofia giggled when out of hearing.

The scene in the kitchen stayed with Bianca. She struggled to abandon the image of her friend amid the red flag roar of wind, as if bloodily savaged. Had the others not seen it, felt it, wasn't her mother affected by something? Unsettled, she pushed the thought away, pulling her friend up the hill in the early light.

'Let's go to Opicina today Sofia, the Karst is too dangerous, there were Germans setting off in that direction earlier. We can turn off at the road and make it in good time before day-light and my grandmother may have fish for us.'

'Why not Bianca? Mamma thinks we are going to skirt the Karst, but a fish soup for tomorrow sounds delicious.' They linked arms, striding purposefully towards the road.

'The Nazi purge the other day will have satisfied their evil lust for now,' Bianca said, 'and their trucks passed very early, they must be going somewhere much further afield.'

'Then it's agreed, it's better to head to the safety of your Nonna's house.'

*

They edged out the city, avoiding occupying troops, then onward to Opicina. As they approached, frenetic activity on the roads forced them to take to the undergrowth. German trucks dashed by, suddenly turning away, back towards Trieste. On the outskirts of Opicina they found themselves buffeted by the few residents on the streets as they scurried inside, slamming doors behind them.

Outside Nonna's home, a jumble of residents dashed around the corner pushing Sofia to the ground as Bianca knocked on her courtyard door. A muffled whisper emerged through the crack as the gate opened, a rough hand grabbing Bianca's coat by the chest, dragging her in as she tried to grasp Sofia. Then the door locked shut as a troop of Germans clattered into the entrance of the narrow street. Her grandfather's gnarled hand clamped, clumsily around her mouth and nose until she wondered if she might die.

On the other side of the wall, garbled Slovene protests and scuffles echoed, as if dragged away. Bianca tried not to squeal.

*

Sofia scrambled to her feet as Bianca disappeared. Skidding on hands and feet on the flagged ground, she was yanked into a small depression in the wall behind an overgrown tree. The two crouched behind the vegetation, as jackboots marched by. Screams sprang up all around as people were hauled along the paving, scratching and squirming. Rifle butts thrust at faces, stocks smashed splattered flesh and heads to stifle the hysteria.

As people were corralled towards the square, Sofia dared to look at her saviour, their friend, the Bird Boy. She opened her mouth to speak, but again he communicated without words, indicating with one finger cutting his throat. Then scanning up and down the street, he pointed towards the edge of town. A salvo of rifle fire ricochet from the square, followed by screams and cries of pain. With one, two, then three fingers flicked, he grabbed her hand and ran.

They skirted the edge of town, making their way along his invisible tracks to the Karst, climbing through early summer vegetation, then along rocky escarpments, finally resting in one of his hiding places.

'What's happened, why were they dragging people off the streets?' She gasped exhausted after their climb into unfamiliar Karst territory. He turned towards her.

'One of the Germans charged with eliminating Jews and partisans,' he paused, 'he's been terminated himself. Shot this morning by Yugoslav partisans.' He leaned back and stretched his neck, taking out a small skin water container and passed it to Sofia. 'They are taking anyone they can get their hands on in retribution.'

Sofia convulsed in shock at escaping by the slimmest odds. The high pitched ping of the bullets ricocheting off walls in Opicina, thudding where they hit their mark and resulting screams reverberated through her mind. He continued.

'The foul murderer, The Terrible he was called, he was so confident of the fear he projected he drove about in an open-top car. They couldn't let it go, he had to die.'

'Who was responsible?' Sofia hazarded the question, 'No don't tell me, I don't want to know.'

'I'm not involved,' he said, 'but if you keep quiet it's surprising how quickly people forget the insignificant boy in the corner, and how much you learn.' He stared into nothingness, 'Last month when the Germans shot seventy Slavs at Opicina shooting range, do you know what they did with them?' She didn't answer. 'They took the bodies to the concentration camp they've built at San Sabba rice factory in Trieste, and tested their new crematorium. Burned them all, men, women, and children. They have no mercy, indiscriminate, just like today.' Sofia sat open-mouthed, there was so much she didn't know about him. Looking at his crumpled dirty exterior, she knew he was kind, generous and non-partisan, but this was new, he had integrity, a command of languages and impressive vocabulary. She wondered how she had missed so much.

'I do know,' she struggled, 'when we smelled the stench we were confused, we couldn't take it in. I think we just chose to pretend it wasn't happening; it was too horrible.

After a while, he spoke, 'Listen, I'll go back to Opicina and get a message to your friend, tell her you're safe hiding up here, and when I return I'll put you on the road back home.' She gasped.

'Don't leave me, please don't. I'll be frightened here alone, and it's dangerous for you down there.'

'You'll be fine, no-one knows this place, I travel all over here and no-one ever sees me. I'll bring you a message if she's still there, and get you home.

Despite her protestations he left, pressing the skin water pouch into her hands, her dirty fingernails digging into the bloated skin. Panic and exhaustion took her, as the sights and sounds of the day tried to assimilate in her head. It was mid-day as he slipped away through the long grass, as almost instantly, sleep saved her from her thoughts.

Chapter 52

Opicina, Italian Territory (same day)

Pressed against the white-washed wall, chest-bursting, Bianca and grandparents hoped the Nazis would pass by. Her eyes tight closed against the wailing and crunch of weapons on bone out in the narrow street. She ached for Sofia, what had she done, how could she have left her?

Nonna grasped her hand as they silently crept towards the kitchen door, her grandfather between them and the gate, backing towards the house, eyes fixed, ears alert, every hair, each sinew primed for danger.

Inside, her grandmother held her close to her chest, 'My dear, my darling, what a day to visit, we never expected you?

'Where is Sofia, I've lost her, why didn't Nonno let her in?' sobs mixed with words. Her grandfather joined them.

'Child you were lucky I reached you when I did. If I hesitated for a moment, you, your friend, Nonna and I would all be lying in a sea of blood now. Did you not hear the gunfire?'

'I heard, but what has happened to her, where is she?'

'There was someone hiding out there, I heard them. Hopefully, she is safe.'

Nonna looked to her husband, 'What will we do now?'

He dashed to the kitchen, 'Quick, help me move this, and don't scrape the floor.' He wheezed as Nonna grasped one side of an old wooden cabinet he was shifting, the contents sliding noisily. 'Careful, noise could give us away,' for once he commanded in his home, weathered, wrinkled skin revealing long unseen muscles.

Outside, German troops were moving from house to house.

'Quick woman.' He carefully located a handle sunk into the floor, prying it loose to reveal a small trap-door to an underground chamber. He leaned all his weight backwards, veins flushing until finally, it opened. Inside the walls were dry, dust and splinters of wood scattered over the base.

'Quick Bianca, get in.' She looked up through tear soaked hair stuck to her face.

'Are you sure, husband, is it necessary?' Nonna, begged.

'If we do not hide her, and they find we have an unknown person in the house, it will be the firing range for us all.'

As a shaft of light came through the kitchen window, a creature of the chamber scuttled out of sight.

'What's that?' Bianca hesitated.

'No time child, get in,' jackboots were near, as screams went up from neighbouring homes.

She crouched in the shallow cavity, her grandmother throwing her knapsack in after her. 'Don't move cara, don't utter a sound, your life depends on it,'

As the door to her prison silently closed, a last glimpse of sun highlighted a scorpion, scrabbling among wood debris at her feet.

Hunched in the tiny underground cubicle, she couldn't move, hoping for air, dreading to breathe, longing for her old life, or just survival. She would embrace her father, forgive anything just to be in the world again. A slight movement crossed her trouser, transferring to her jacket. *'Maybe just close your eyes and wait for God to decree your fate',* she thought as the creature crawl over her.

She could hear objects hurriedly replaced in the cupboard above as Nonna exclaimed and something fell to the floor. Wisps of flour sifted onto her face through the gaps around her prison door, as pounding released heavy boots into the rooms above.

A German voice screamed as Nonno uttered quietly in reply. She didn't understand the words as her grandfather's calm tones drifted through the commotion. No pitiful pleading, only composed, tempered tones.

The footfalls retreated, then one set returned to the floor above her, a boot scraped across the floor and flour dusted her face again, then another authoritative voice forcibly ushered her grandparents out. The cupboard was dragged from its place above her, the man sighing as the other angry voice became more remote, and the scorpion crawled from her shoulder to the wall. She held her breath. Which way to go now, heaven or hell, life or death? Either in this hole in the ground. The hatch ring was clasped, and the German soldier heaved it open.

Light from the kitchen window dappled against the ceiling from a swaying olive tree outside. The light coming and going, casting a ghostly image and silhouetting her captor. She closed her eyes and waited. Hell did not reign down, and she dared to look she looked up. Looking down at her tear-streaked face, the German sentry from home stared back, bewildered, alarmed.

Her life pivoted on this moment. He had tried to get close to her, even given her presents and food, and she'd spurned him politely with her finest aloof pout. What would he do, take his revenge out of spite, or because it was his job, or forgive her rejection? The commanding officer shouted from the front door. This was it, which would it be? His face twitched.

The hatch slammed closed as he spoke to the approaching footsteps. German speech passed between them as they moved away, the only recognisable word "scorpioni" accompanied by guffaws and a snort of derision.

Chapter 53

Opicina, Italian Territory (that evening)

Bird Boy sat in a ditch outside Opicina until dusk, waiting for his opportunity. Eventually, a tomb-like quiet descended, the streets still bearing signs of the day's violence, odd shoes scattered, walls scuffed, doors smashed.

Adept at moving un-noticed, he gingerly stepped into the street, sliding along walls, diving into the vegetation where he and Sofia had hidden earlier.

From the upper floor of her grandparent's home, Bianca squinted through the wooden shutters. Earlier, too risky to leave, her Nonna had gently rocked her until slumber came. Having faced life or death in a single stroke, her sentry had saved her; she knew the risk he had taken and wished for his safety as she drifted to a downy sleepy haze, safe and free.

Having woken, she needed to watch and wait. If the Nazis returned she had to be ready, every fibre of her body primed. Memories of the sulphurous odour that drifted from the old rice factory a mile from home, the month previously, wouldn't leave her. Her family had gathered at the window then, looking down, confused by the charcoal bouquet of grilled meat. The Germans had converted it to a holding camp for what they considered the waste of society, Semites, gypsies, partisans, the old and infirm. When her father caught them he had slammed the window shut, barking orders to confine themselves to domestic matters, his solution as simple as that. It had been the concentration camps' first use of the crematorium.

Sitting at her grandmother's window now she thought of her favourite spot in the kitchen at home, overlooking her glittering city. Now viewing the remnants of the brutal day outside, hell moved ever closer.

*

In the gloom of dusk, she saw a slight movement, just beyond the outer wall, gone in an instance. Did she see something, a cat, a German helmet? She shrank back. Street patrols had stopped, the streets were silent.

The black shadow bobbed above the white-painted boundary of the yard again, it was a hat, someone stalking the streets. She wondered if it was a fool trying to get home, or an informant on a mission to ingratiate themselves and acquire favours.

An explosion of activity smashed into her consciousness as jackboots shattered the silence, descending upon the creature. This was no informer. The hapless figure was pulled from their hiding place, feet sliding on the floor as he swung around trying to escape. A second soldier screamed unintelligible words, landing a knee in the victim's back ejecting a shriek of pain, contorting the figure, face thrown up to heaven.

She could never be sure whether the sound that escaped her could be heard outside, but at that moment the tortured face turned. Bird Boy was descended upon by German soldiers, revenge still surging through them.

A hand clutched her heart, only the shallowest, silent, gasp breaking free, her friend dragged away. The soldiers' spirits appeared high, another capture, another animal for the crematorium.

Motionless, fresh tears fell. How was it possible she could still cry, that her body still reacted to horrors she could hardly even comprehend? The Bird Boy, their friend in times of need, his unwillingness to be involved in brutish partisan activity, confining life to feeding his family, how could this happen? Why was he even in the street outside her grandparent's home? Surely it could be sorted out, the Germans would understand, he would be released?

Chapter 54

The Karst (that night)

Boots crunched the undergrowth waking Sofia. It was night. Reality exploded, she was hiding, waiting for her friend. Harsh Slavic voices became louder, an argument taking place. Something familiar in her memory, someone she had encountered before. As the growl came closer she remembered, it was Bird Boy's brother and cowered lower.

How could she have slept so long, her parents would be alarmed she wasn't home? Whether communists, royalist, fascists or imposed curfew, she had always managed to get home. Now she was lost on the Karst, no-one had come to take her home, and terrible sounds surrounded her as she burrowed her face to the ground. A hand suddenly grasped the back of her collar, hauling her up by the neck.

'What have we got here?' the fearsome voice spat rough Italian words. 'Let me see better.' His huge fist hung her out in front of his sweaty, grime streaked face. She coughed trying to catch her breath, hands clasping her throat. Another comrade muttered and he dropped her to the ground.

'I know you. You're one of those snooty Italian girls my brother hangs around with.' She couldn't speak. 'He thinks I don't know what he gets up to when we are doing men's work, taking back what is ours.' He spat. Sofia fell to her knees, grasping the fastening of her coat, releasing pressure from her neck.

'So you're not going to speak to me, baggage?' he bent over until his twisted, hateful, face was eye to eye with hers. Involuntarily she pulled away from his foul breath.

'You don't like me? Well we've a good use for you.' He grabbed her collar and dragged her to flat ground.

She curled up in a ball as a dispute between the Slav men erupted, the others pulling at his arm as he stood over her. None of them wore wedding rings at night, a golden glint could betray a hiding place, but she could see they were older, family men, fighting for their beliefs. Bird Boy's brother took off his gun belt and holster unbuttoning the top fastening of his trousers, salivating, protests ignored.

There was concern on his comrades' faces as peasant cloth slipped over his hips, filthy undergarment revealed, one of them pushing him in the shoulder. His trousers fell to his knees as another flicked her a hasty glance while his attention was taken, pointing her away. She took her chance and dashed to escape as he lunged, catching her ankle, his trousers now around his ankles. She writhed, kicking off his hand, his companions offering ineffectual attempts to aid him but helping her as she dashed out of sight.

'She's not worth it; she's not the reason we fight for our rights.' The last words heard as she jumped over a precipice, into the dark. She skidded down a scree for what seemed like an age, obscene oaths drifting from above, gravel ripping her trousers until she finally stopped on a small plateau.

The Karst fell silent. She was lost. Regaining her breath, she cautiously surveyed her surroundings. She had never been out alone at night, everything was different, frightening, disorientating. Shivering from a dark hollow, a glimpse of rationality surfaced as she stumbled and fell through undergrowth, no thought of cavernous pits, hardly able to think at all.

Exhausted, she sat to rest. In the black night curfew, a few stars above, she began to make out dim city landmarks on the horizon. The Bird Boy's words echoing, that was how she could make her way home, walk towards familiar places. In the black night, the power station had a few visible lights, as did the garrison on Via dei Montebello. She had picked up the scent of home, quarry no more. With luck, she could find her way home.

*

Maria stood before the cross on the kitchen wall, promising every devotion for the safe return of her daughter. The sun had set and no cheery tousled haired daughter had appeared telling of exploits on the road, throwing a bag of produce on the table. The air hung silently, with only a drift of hope behind her prayers to sustain her.

*

At the power station, there was news. Vittorio was informed that Christian Wirth had been murdered by partisans. As a result, retribution was being sought throughout outlying communes, people indiscriminately dragged from the street, destined for San Sabba, a new intake for the crematorium. He did not inform his wife or Maria. Let them think their daughters were suffering only damp and cold in the wilderness, for now.

Chapter 55

Trieste, Italy (early next day)

Stumbling along back lanes and pathways Sofia reached home. Her eyes saw nothing as she approached the door. The violence of the night had taken every part of her senses, sliding down limestone banks, slipping over edges not knowing whether a pit or a slope three feet or fifty, walking all night. As she touched the front door, her last vestiges of reason fled, all senses disengaged.

Through the window she saw her mother sobbing at the table, head in hands. Still fractured from the scene, Sophia stared, as if in another place. Only a couple of days previously, she and Bianca had gone about their duties, now everything had changed. As she nudged open the door Maria yelped, Carlo frantically wrapped his arms around his daughter, weeping until she gasped for air.

'I thought I'd lost you, I thought you might never come home,' his hair dishevelled he clung, shoulders shaking, turning to his wife, finally telling her.

'Mamma, there was trouble at Opicina, patrols ripping people from the streets, and our daughter's home, safe.'

'You were in Opicina?' she stared at Sophia. 'Why, you stupid child? The Germans are everywhere.' shaking her.

'Mother she is home, how can anyone know where Nazis will be, leave her be.'

After being submitted to a cursory examination by her mother, Sofia withdrew to her room. Door closed, she slid down the wall and sat on the floor, shoving her arms beneath her thighs, hugging them tight against her chest as if a faint would release her. She dug her nails into flesh through the rips in her trousers, the pain relieved;

scratching hard, the discomfort negating images she couldn't shake.

Looking up she saw muddied socks, scuffed shoes, blood caked on legs and trousers, scratches and dirt up her arms. Below, her parents argued, then a fellow worker called to summon Carlo to work. There was an exchange of information, the loathsome name of Wirth mentioned, and a food parcel dumped on the kitchen table, and she drifted to sleep.

*

Maria listened at her door, and hearing fitful breathing, entered placing a bowl of hot water on the chest beside her bed.

'You were sobbing cara, how are you now?' A sudden gasp awoke Sophia, she trembled but didn't reply.

'Tell me what happened dear, give me your pain,' she coaxed softly, putting her to bed.

As Maria stroked her hair, Sophia muttered odd words, and dreams took her to another place, where....

"White organza draped around her in a classroom, perfect unsullied confirmation dresses, pure and unblemished hung everywhere, she was tangled, couldn't move or escape through them. The immaculate image of a favourite teacher momentarily appeared before her; could she reach her, be safe? Fragrant, feminine air engulfed, it was another time. Was she safe? Was it the plentiful days of other summers? One of the garments crept around her, clinging to her legs preventing movement, the others swaying gracefully in dappled sunlight."

She awoke with a start, her mother in the kitchen again, and crawled to where she stored her precious confirmation gown from school. Taking it out, she stroked the unsullied fabric, straightened folds and wrinkles, and hung it on the bedroom door, an untainted guardian against the world outside. She was safe.

Returning to bed she found refuge looking at it, protecting her, until half-sleep returned.

"Why did Bianca leave me? Where is she? Why didn't Bird Boy come back?"

Horrifying thoughts crossed her mind as downstairs her father returned. Maria snapped.

'Those at the house dare not speak to me for their shame.' She had been home all day, yet no one had called. 'Sending food as a bribe to forgive, what other explanation is there?' she spat.

Carlo ignored her anger, wanting to see his daughter, but she made him let her sleep, telling him what little she had found out of her ordeal. When he said Bianca was still missing she couldn't hear him, only cursing the name of Marchetti.

*

Sophia woke at dusk, to movement below. Maria was talking to herself below, discussing the meal she was preparing, a treat for the family to celebrate her daughter's return, remembering how her children laughed when times were good. She hoped with the prospect of a full stomach they would be animated again, free for one night.

Above, Sofia pulled her energy together and looked around the room. In a dream-like haze she scooped cold water from the washing bowl, watching it dribble down her legs, the mud and blood trickling away in dark ruby rivulets, then noticed the white dress. *"How did that get there?"* Somewhere a notion emerged. Covering her body in pure white she would be protected.

Neither thinking or feeling, hardly seeing, her hands gently swept over her nakedness, soothing her anguish like the creases of the dress, then reached in her drawer. Fingers slowly slid across this garment and that, the coolness of cotton discarded, seeking the smoothness of her one silk item, the confirmation petticoat. Pulling it over her scratched, bruised, body it eased her stinging flesh; every tissue tortured she wanted it cleansed; God would do that, wouldn't he? Taking the childish dress from the hook it slipped over her wasted arms and hips without effort.

She slipped silently down the stairs as her mother bent over the oven, quietly exiting the door. A glowing light leeched between the curtains as she turned towards the muted clatter of plates and cutlery. She saw her mother placing a special dish for Papa, a smaller one for herself. But nothing really registered, her hands unconsciously clenching the child dress on her woman's body.

The warmth of the day gone, her bare feet stepped onto the path and she looked down at the city, the slow, calm sea beyond beguiled. A light wind flicked her hair as she passed under the railway bridge, turning away from the barracks.

In a trance she walked towards Piazza dei Foraggio. An old man, spied her from the other side of the road,

'Ciao Sofia'. No response.

'Hey, I said hello. Where are you going, does your mother know where you are?' He turned, shouting, 'It's cold Sofia, you should be in the home making dinner with your mother,' muttering, 'that child what's her trouble, her manners are all gone?' and hobbled on, shaking his head at the trudge home from cleaning at San Sabba. *"Maybe it's my work at that hell hole that makes her ignore me. It curses me, please God forgive, I have to eat,'* he crossed himself. *'If I don't comply they will throw me in the ovens too,'* he thought.

But Sofia was no more aware of him than anything else, only one thought floated through her hollow mind. At the empty Piazza dei Foraggio, she stopped and sat on a bench, no-one congregated, all closeted in the hopeful safety of home. She was confused, was it yesterday or the day before she was there? It seemed such a long time ago. What has happened since then? She fought to remember.

Roberto glanced up from inside the cafe, only a few customers occupied seats. He caught a glimpse of a wisp across the square, wondering for a moment was it his imagination playing tricks, the waif-like ghost looked like Sofia. Straining his eyes, the skin seemed transparent, as if life beneath had already left, not like his beloved Sofia, always laughing, warmth to his eyes.

He turned to a call from the cafe. Looking back, he leaned forward for a better look, it was gone. Something about her white dress disturbed him, it was short and tight. His Sofia would never appear like that. He conceded he must have seen someone or something else, a glimpse into another world, a sprite, it couldn't be her. Soldiers entered to sample the new German menu that close proximity to the barracks had inspired, it was a saviour for the business, keeping him safe for the moment, and his regulars melted away.

She continued along tree-lined streets until grand Austro-Hungarian structures loomed above her, dark giants, crowding in bigger, closer, almost burying her as they rumbled above.

As she reached Canal Grande the sea opened up beyond. It breathed slowly in tandem with her, then expired gently, heaving and hollowing. Darkness pervaded the grey heavens and sea alike, spreading gloom as the dream-like waters gasped in ecstatic rapture, craving her.

A man hurried along the canal, unwilling to encounter any patrol, stopping short at the sight of her. A girl in a white dress almost gliding, as though in a trance,

"What is that girl doing out at this time of day?" he thought.

'Hey there, where are you going? What's your business at this time of night?' he called.

As she approached the canal her head turned, sightless eyes gazing back. He stood and watched as she continued, unmoved by his call. He wondered, had he seen a spirit.

'A ghost! What nonsense. Get yourself home you foolish man. These barbarous factions fighting for the city have spooked you,' he mumbled. 'When I get home and lock the door I'll shake off these fanciful thoughts,' reassuring himself.

Sophia looked back at the canal leading to the open sea. Gunmetal grey waves flicked clouds of white into the air out at sea. An eerie shape like a building seemed to hover in the distant white mist as dreary clouds began to gather soothingly together, and the light changed.

Buildings seemed to radiate a sombre white hue while the sea darkened; pulling in, swaying out, calling her, then hardly moving as if holding its breath. When the clouds could resist no more it rolled tenderly in gentle beguiling motion. Tendrils reached down from the sky flicking the surface of the sea, sending tiny little taps and brushes at the edge of the canal.

Claude heard the muttering man pass as he stowed nets in his boat. Given the weather, he would not put out to sea, the Germans would have to go without fresh fish. Looking up he traced the man's eye-line. A strange spectre was walking towards the quay, white dress, feet bare, something familiar. All at once he recognised the apparition.

'Sofia, Stop!' She continued in her trance-like path towards the sea. He jumped onto the canal-side and ran towards her. The grey skies were gathering momentum, it was becoming unseasonably cold, bleak.

'You shouldn't be out dressed like that, you'll end up in San Sabba as a vagrant,' he shouted.

He reached her within yards of the quay-side, grabbing her waist, vacant eyes staring out to sea with painful longing. As he pulled her back along the canal he could detect faint murmurs and stood directly in front of her.

'Sofia child, look at me,' he shook her gently. 'I am going to get something from my boat, don't move.'

'Will you take me to the sea? I'll be safe there.' she whispered.

'Where is your Mamma, Sophia, surely she can't know where you are?'

She looked back blankly as he threw a bundle of dry fishing clothes on to the canal side.

'Here' he tried to put them in her hands as they dropped to the floor. Anxiously looking around, he was sanctioned to be there, but she mustn't be seen. He implored her.

'Lord bless us Sophia, please put these on, for your life, for both our lives.' She still stared into emptiness.

He managed to persuade her to raise her feet and get the trousers onto her and pulled the old jacket on and across her chest, securing it closed with a piece of rope. He took off his fisherman's cap and rammed it down hard on her head, pushing her hair inside. Nervously he looked around, her feet bare still. Quickly he got a small bundle of netting and wrapped it in a sack, and grabbed her elbow. It was almost dark. Leaving the quayside, keeping to alleys, avoiding cafes that might entertain Germans, they turned into a road near the barracks and a small patrol approached. Claude straightened his back.

'Show no fear,' he whispered to Sofia.' She was still in a trance as he tapped the back of her head holding it up as the soldiers approached, raising their guns at them.

'I have fish for Signor Marchetti, he entertains your Major from San Sabba I believe.' He wafted the malodourous sacking in their general direction. 'With all respect, I must get this to his kitchen immediately, they may be waiting as I speak.'

The soldiers were familiar with the power station manager and his association with their fearsome Commandant and fell back immediately. As Claude dragged Sophia under the railway bridge, he breathed again, muttering,

'Thank God for watching over us,' adding to himself, 'the stink of fish might have helped.'

At her home, rapping on the door brought a terrified face to the entrance. Carlo opened it, confused to see Vittorio's brother-in-law with a ragamuffin. Claude pushed his way in pulling Sofia with him.

'I found her on the quayside walking towards the sea as if to throw herself in.' Carlo and Maria were astonished as he pulled the cap from her head, untying the rope to reveal the white dress beneath.

'I thought she was upstairs resting. I didn't want to disturb her. I thought she needed to sleep,' Maria exclaimed.

They grabbed her as Carlo dashed to the door.

'I have to go, I've taken a chance coming here after dark, I'll try to get into the compound and stay the night with Mia,' he looked at them as they stripped Sophia of the fishing rags.

'I'll take them; they shouldn't be here in case a patrol comes looking.' He bundled them inside the old sack.

'Where are her shoes, why did you make her walk bare-footed?' Maria snapped at him.

'She didn't have any, she was just white dress and bare feet, walking to the edge of the dock muttering about heaven taking her. You will have to find that out for yourself,' he answered sharply, and pulled angrily away.

As Sofia's mother guided her to the stairs Carlo turned to him

'Forgive her Claude she's had a shock too, her mind isn't working any more. I know you took a terrible risk to bring her home to us. Thank you, my friend, I'll never forget you saved her.' He turned the light off, opening the door a crack.

'There is a fold in the bottom corner of the perimeter fence just there,' he indicated twenty feet away, 'the guards are very young and can be quite lax, unless there is an officer visiting. God protect you.'

Claude slipped out, no light to reveal him as the door closed.

Chapter 56

Trieste, Italy (that night)

Claude crept to the fence, finding the turned-up corner of
chain-link hidden by grass, and the weather changed. He
carefully curled it up and squeezed through, crouching low
in the vegetation the family had grown high there.
Moonlight broke through, coating the compound in clear
star-lit white light, as he lay face down in the earth.
Suddenly a lonely scud of cloud crossed the moon, he took
his chance and dashed to the plant workshops at the side,
found a door unlocked and made his way inside.

Inside at the top of the stairs, he approached the
kitchen seeing Bianca eating at the table, and his father
beside her in animated conversation, Vittorio interrupting
as sister Mia fluttered about. Astonished faces greeted his
bedraggled appearance.

'Good Lord above what has befallen you, son?' his
father rose from the table.

'Papa, what are you doing here, you're the last person
I expected to see tonight?' Claude replied.

He took his fisherman's cap off and threw it on top of
the gramophone on the side cabinet, flopping down into an
empty seat asking, 'Mia dear, please tell me you have
something I can eat.' Bianca quickly protected her bowl,
cupping a hand around and pulling it close. Vittorio bade
them be quiet as he left to find the offending door that had
allowed Claude access, and check on the sentries. He
returned with schnapps as Mia presented soup, bread and a
little grated hard cheese and they listened to his story of the
waif he had caught before she stepped out into the ocean.

'Poor blessed girl,' Mia muttered, eyes darting

'What do you know of it woman?' Vittorio demanded.

'Nothing, I mean, very little really.'

'Speak,' Vittorio growled. 'If there's something you know, you tell me now,' he slapped the table, shaking the crockery.

'Take care, man,' Mia's aged father rose angrily. He had delivered his grand-daughter home safely from her hellish experience, and now saw violence in her own home. 'Mia doesn't respond well to such a tone. I may be an old man, Vittorio, but you will not speak to my daughter like that.'

'I hold the safety of everyone in this building in my hand, I deal with every faction, every military, every individual who wishes to lord it over us. If something has happened I need to know.' Vittorio defended himself, 'what brought you creeping in here?' turning toClaude.

'I told you, he said, 'I rescued a young woman about to throw herself off the quay,' he looked around at the faces before him, 'it was Sofia.'

Bianca's spoon clattered to the floor, 'My friend, my dearest darling, what are you saying? She was about to kill herself?'

A strangled cough came from Mia, and all eyes turned to her.

'What do you know, woman?' Vittorio's tone adjusted, and she replied.

'When the girls didn't come home, and Maria didn't come to work I sent her food and she thought it was from you husband. That's all.'

'But you know more.' Vittorio ventured more gently.

'Only what the workman said, that Maria was relieved when Sophia returned just before dawn, but that she languished in her room, and wouldn't speak. Surely, Carlo told you?' she looked at him anxiously.

'I don't discuss personal matters with staff.' He turned away angrily.

Bianca couldn't contain herself.

'What could have happened to her? Nonno, we should have made sure she got through your gate, she will need me, I'll have to go to her, explain what happened,' rising from the table.

'Sit! You're not going anywhere.' Vittorio turned to the window overlooking the courtyard, 'Eat your valuable food. You can leave when the Germans unlock the gates tomorrow. There will be no more unauthorised coming and going here tonight, nothing more to draw attention to us. Tomorrow morning Bianca, you will create a diversion at the gate, and Claude will slip out the back, and your grandfather will leave as he entered, when permitted by the Germans.'

The rest of the evening was spent retelling the events in Opicina and the few details Claude had of Sophia. Exhausted, Bianca withdrew to bed, but was unable to sleep. Her grandparents had been loving and kind, Nonno bringing her home safely, but the terror of being recognised by the German sentry ravaged her mind, preventing all but the briefest of rest.

In fitful slumber, she heard her father put a record on the gramophone in the kitchen below. A mile down the hill, engines revved at San Sabba, almost masking the screams within, when suddenly deafening music from the camp added to the melee. They likely intended a warning to all Triestians that this could be their fate too, rather than simply attempting to drown out the last horrifying howls of the poor souls within.

Chapter 57

Trieste, Italy (next morning)

Bianca awoke to the flip flop of her mother's cotton slippers along the corridor to the kitchen. Times changed but habits remained. Every morning she collected a jug of fresh milk straight from the cow, delivered warm to the front step. Never as full as the old days, but such was her father's standing they always got something.

She turned over, eyes sore from lack of sleep. Visions of Sophie had invaded her night along with the music down the hill, now replaced by coffee beans, ground, rattling up from the kitchen. What could have happened to her darling friend to make her so desperate? She had to find out. Through everything they had endured; Sofia was her only true ally and confidant, they protected each other. When she had been dragged into her grandparents' yard, they were sure she had escaped. Bianca had to find out, put her arms around her, comfort her, it wasn't her choice to close the door.

She grabbed some clothes and went to her mother, 'What do you know of Sophia Mamma, tell me?'

'Nothing cara I haven't spoken to Maria,' cups clattered as she prepared coffee for the sentries.

'Why do you do that, do they deserve our provisions?' Bianca demanded angrily.

'I'm trying to do the right thing,' her mother twitched, 'if we are nice to them, maybe they will be kind to us. 'Bianca thought of the sentry who had protected her, putting his own life in danger. Conflicted and angry, she stalked out.

Striding directly towards the sentries, she waved her arms demanding the gates be opened. One of them spoke.

'No Signorina.'

She snapped, without looking up, 'You opened it for the milk, you can open it for me,' then saw it was her saviour of two days earlier.

The other sentry sniggered and stepped out of the sentry box raising his rifle, slowly aiming it at her. Her German friend clipped words at him, indicating the side of the building where the vines grew, and with one last sneer he turned and walked away.

Awkwardly her friend approached her.

'Apology Signorina,' he tapped his watch. 'I cannot open the gate, there is much trouble here.'

They exchanged awkward glances, but the absence of the other fellow relaxed them a little. Seeing her mother appear with coffee Bianca snatched it offering a cup to her companion, satisfied when the other returned his would be cold.

Concern clouded the sentry's face as Bianca turned to him, saying. 'I want to thank...' He instantly cut her off

'Don't talk to me,' he said.

She ignored him, 'But I ...'

He glared back at her. 'There is nothing we can speak of,' he paused, 'for you and I, there is only danger.' Absent-mindedly she glanced at the cigarette packet in the pocket of his uniform. His unpleasant comrade was still at the back of the power plant as Claude made his way along the link fence and exited under the wire, as the sentry took a cigarette out, lit it and gave it to her.

She was making mistakes. The last few days had sent her off-balance, out of kilter, demanding to be let out and speaking of risky things. Inhaling the cigarette smoke, she closed her eyes. Turning to him again there was a need to ask one more thing, maybe she should not, but she had to know.

'Please tell me if you can....' he looked irritated. 'The people taken from Opicina,' his eyes clouded, 'what happened to them?' The cries of Bird Boy being dragged down the street were still fesh.

He remained silent, and she resolved if begging was necessary, she would. 'Please.'

He turned away looking at the ground, whispering two words only.

'San Sabba.'

The words echoed around her brain, the sounds of night assaulted, nausea taking her, recalling the first time they had become aware of the ovens. How they had baulked at the unfamiliar smell of metallic charcoal and rancid fat, charred and burning, the stink hanging in their nostrils for days.

'But they can't, he's innocent ...'

'Innocent, who's innocent?' the German demanded. She turned away.

'Oh nothing, I saw someone.'

The soldier's face told the story; he was being drawn into the beautiful Italian's web again.

'You know someone from Opicina that night?' he questioned her.

'I saw a young boy, he was taken,' she made her words as innocent as possible, 'he may be Slav, but he's a good boy, not a partisan.'

'Don't say it again, I don't want to hear,' he turned away.

'But he is a good boy. Could you help him?'

He turned his back on her, 'No-one can help anyone at San Sabba.' His eyes were the saddest she had ever seen, then heard, 'forget him.'

Her eyes beseeched with every ploy she could think of for her cheery, brave, harmless friend of the Karst until the sentry grabbed her arm.

'He goes to San Sabba - he's gone.'

Around the corner the arrogant sentry approached, stomping imperiously through the gravel, indicating a small detail of soldiers were coming to take their position. Bianca and the sentry turned away from each other. She let her hair fall over her face, discarded the cigarette, and waited for the gate to be unlocked, leaving distance between herself and the departing soldiers, then made her way to Sofia's home. Surely, if she held her hand, explained, she could make it alright. They meant everything to each other, she would do anything to heal her, and concentrating on that would displace the grief she felt for their Bird Boy. They would heal each other.

Chapter 58

Trieste, Italy (the same morning)

She strode towards the oasis of Sophia's home. Outside she could see Carlo and his young son, deep in conversation, hand on his shoulder, reassuring the troubled boy. In the distance, on the other side of the railway line, Claude disappeared into the city.

'Morning Carlo,' she managed to produce a sound she ventured to cut cheerfully through her despair.

He turned as she walked towards the door, saying, 'Bianca, where are you going?'

'To see Sofia,' she paused. Had her mother made her wait too long, was it was too late, would Sofia think she didn't care, was abandoned?

'She's not available cara,' he said.

They had been inseparable since first meeting, Sophia her sister, and as Carlo put his arm across the threshold barring her she was mystified, admission to her only sanctuary denied.

He knew their bond, and doubted his wife's belief Sophia's condition was Bianca's fault. But Maria had never left their daughter's side as night terrors revealed how she had been left in the Opicina street when the soldiers came

'Bianca child, she is resting now, her mother was with her all night.'

Her grey eyes misted, imploring, 'Please, please, can I see her, I need to explain. My grandfather dragged me inside, he stopped me going to her.' Carlo hung his head.

'I know you would never intend such a thing,' Claude explained, 'and she was spirited away by someone.'

Bianca thought of Bird Boy in the back lane later that night. Was he coming to tell her she was safe, risking his life to help, only to be dragged to San Sabba and his death?

The door swung open, Maria screeching towards her, fingers drawn like talons as Carlo grabbed her.

'You cruel soul from hell, you left my daughter to her fate, looking only after yourself,' she screamed.

'That's not true Maria and you know it,' Carlo said as she struggled to be free of him.

'I know nothing of the kind, you went with my daughter and she returned a ghost, a shadow, no life behind the eyes, no laughter, no smile,' she collapsed sobbing. Carlo reached to lift her. 'Why didn't you go to the Karst as you were supposed to? Only you would change arrangements without consent. If you had done what you were supposed to, she would have been safe.'

'Mamma, we don't know the whole story,' Carlo said, 'we only know they went out together and returned separately.'

Maria threw his hands off her.

'She came back with a loving grandfather, my daughter came back alone, and....' she couldn't go on.

'I swear I did not leave her, it was out of my hands, Nonno slammed the door. I would never have abandoned my dearest darling, I would have died for her....'

'Die for her? You, the spawn of that animal up there?' she flung her arm toward the power plant. 'Save your own skin more like.' Her face contorted as the words clashed against the truth she knew. But recognising only that someone must take the blame.

'Maria, get back to our daughter, you're distressing yourself and the child,' Carlo commanded her.

'Child? Do you see how she looks at the soldiers, she's a whore.' The word slashed like a knife to Bianca's heart. Carlo stepped forward.

'And you eat the product of those looks, as we all do. She, like everyone else, uses anything they have for sustenance.' He was angry, they had all benefited from the flirtatious games the two young women had to play out.

'And if you think she is like her father, your daughter's predicament has blinded you. Get in the house and compose yourself, look after your daughter,' he yelled. The two families had trod a precarious route together, the Primavera family, friends, but also servants to Vittorio. With Italy's decline the bonds between friends clouded ever more, basic existence all that remained for everyone.

The door slammed behind Maria and he turned to her.

'Don't take what she says to heart, she's confused and frightened.'

Bianca gasped, how she could live without the warm love of her friend and family. All life was drifting away from her.

'I believe there is more to know of Sofia's experience, things will be better when she can talk,' he said, turning back to his boy.

'Son, you were seeking to go to the city, and take up Sophia's task to find food?'

'You said I was not allowed, Papa,' disappointed, he kicked the ground. Carlo looked at his eleven-year-old boy, stunted by lack of nutrition.

'I think we can find a way for you to help,' he looked at Bianca.

'Take him with you to do the round of bakers and grocers, hold his hand, he only looks about seven years old, no threat to anyone,' he stood back in the hope he was right. The boy beamed at the chance to help the family, be a man like his father, and Carlo knew, if there was no family member involved in the search, there would be no cut of the spoils. He ruffled his son's hair pulling strands over his face to disguise his features.

A slight movement from the window above their kitchen drew Bianca's eye. Behind the glass the curtains moved slightly, and a white face loomed out of the shade. Sofia's emotionless eyes bore out of black circled hollows, a single finger lightly touching the pane. Bianca gasped at her friend, a stranger hiding from view. The finger slid lightly down the glass, she knew Sophia had recognized her, the stroke the most effort she could summon for a tiny wave, and suddenly she was gone. She hardly heard Carlo's instructions.

'Just take his hand Bianca, he is your baby brother for the task, no offence to anyone. And you,' he turned to his son, kneeling on the grass before him, 'no clever behaviour from you,' he instructed. 'Be guided by Bianca, she will keep you safe, and bring home a treat for us,' he kissed his son's forehead as the boy pulled away embarrassed.

*

She dragged her eyes from the bedroom window and the two walked down towards the railway bridge. Beneath the arch, there was a small group sheltering; she instinctively scanned them, trouble makers or innocent bystanders? Straining into the shadow, she could see they were youngsters more or less the age of her new companion. Excited chatter informed them that unguarded horses were wandering on the ground in front of Montebello Garrison, some with saddles. She sneaked a look.

'What are they doing there?' instantly in hunting mode, 'whose are they?'

The children explained they had been wandering towards the railway line, and had spied the untethered animals and hidden under the bridge to hatch a plan. Everyone had tasted horse meat since the war, and the thought of taking home such a prize created much excitement among them.

'How are you going to achieve that?' she asked, as some of the bravest declared they would take the horses to the piazza, and barter them.

'I think not, they must belong to someone,' she said, 'and they're right outside the garrison,' she warned.

270

'No, they must be abandoned, where are the owners?' the children argued.

'If you had a horse would you leave it? If you lost a horse would you not look for it?' she sneaked another look and turned to the expectant audience. 'There are four or five, but I can tell you, it would not be sensible to charge in there and take them. I suggest we see what happens, see if anyone comes.' The young hunters submitted to her experience, and they all sat beneath the bridge to wait.

Grey clouds skulled overhead, and neither soldier nor person came, all remaining quiet, and a plan was hatched to casually walk up to the horses, stroke them and if no-one objected, casually cut one from the group and bring it back to the bridge.

The motley group of Bianca and children emerged from their den and turned coolly towards the barracks as if unaware of the horses, whereupon caution suddenly evaporated and desperation for booty filled the young childrens' minds. One, then all, burst into a run towards the animals. The disturbance panicked the horses, and they began to rear, every child it seemed harbouring a thought of taking one home, pulling and grasping at them.

With all judgement lost as the children ran past her, Bianca made a beeline for one with full saddle and tack.

'I'm just want the saddle,' she called, considering it easier to hide once cut up, and priceless for mending shoes, and grasped at the reigns flicking loosely on the ground,

A crack burst from somewhere, then again, the sound like stones spitting up from the ground and the children scattered.

She had been grappling with the under belly strap as the horse skittered around between her and the barracks. Glancing up, there were no leering soldiers, windows sashes open only a few inches. She tried to calm it. As she strove to hold onto the flighty horse a stone flicked up against her upper thigh. A warm ooze crept down her leg.

271

The horse jerked lightly in a circle pushing her backwards towards the barracks as nausea took her, fingers loosening, hands sliding from the saddle. Muted voices called from behind her, the hill in front now. A chemical compound filled the air as more sounds reverberated; loud cracks bounced off the wall behind her, legs vanishing from beneath, she slipped to the ground, mind floating, warm molten liquid seeping down her leg, as the horse fell.

Red clouds obscured her vision as a mighty hand grabbed the back of her coat; unfamiliar sounds, shouting, smoke, more cracks fractured the air from every direction, as she was dragged away, a long stream of crimson seeping into the ground in her wake.

Chapter 59

Trieste, Italy (later that same day)

'Hell-fire devour us, what makes that sound?'

Maria turned to the kitchen window as her son ran up the hill, mouth gapping in a dribbling wail, arms flailing, legs buckling beneath him, Sofia roused to consciousness above. The commotion reached the power plant sending the workforce scattering and Carlo edged along the perimeter fence to their hidden gap, eyes fixed on home.

'She's dead, she's been shot,' the boy collapsed into his father's arms as he stretched to catch him, whispering soothing words and taking him inside.

'You are safe with us, son, calm yourself.' The boy sobbing into his father's shoulder.

'She's dead Papa, she was shot.' Carlo began to understand. Maria spoke.

'Bianca, you mean her?'

'Yes Mamma,' a simpering whine escaped between hiccupped gasps, Maria's anger revived.

'The devil, she took you into danger, and look where it got her.' Carlo shot her a look.

'Stop now woman,' he shouted, 'we don't know what happened, only that our son had a shock, and she is not here. Have you lost your mind completely?' Maria stepped back.

'I....' she faltered, 'I only meant....'

'Even you know the hell we all go through, none less than that young woman. When has she ever treated any of us as anything less than family?' Carlo took his anger out on her, as she on Bianca, cradling his son tightly and sighed, 'Instead of arguing, let's see to our children.'

'Well yes, I just don't understand....' Maria stuttered.

'I know dear, none of us do, but we stick together. Think of it, if what he says is true, your best friend has lost her daughter, and we still have ours, whatever happened.'

A knock at the door brought Carlo cautiously to the window to see Roberto, anxiously pacing. Entering, he couldn't hold back.

'I heard the gun-shots, children running everywhere, screaming. I've come to see if....' he hesitated, then taking a deep breath, 'if Sofia is safe.'

'She's resting Roberto. But what do you know of the rifle fire, did the children say anything?' Carlo looked at his son, exhausted in his father's arms and Roberto took up the story.

'All I know is there was a standoff between Slav partisans, who'd taken possession of the railway station, and the German garrison below it. And then it erupted into gun fire.' He looked anxiously around the room, lowering his voice, 'There's been no talk of Italian partisan movement recently.'

Laying his son in a chair, Carlo turned to him, 'The boy said someone had been shot, was dead. Do you know anything about this?'

'The children said they were trying to steal loose horses for food, and a young woman wanted a saddle for leather. Is someone missing?' Carlo looked at Maria.

'Yes,' she answered.

'But Sofia is safe? unable to contain his concern.

'She wasn't there, she rests above. Bianca is the one who's missing.'

They stood motionless for a moment until Carlo spoke.

'Roberto go back to the café don't mention you've been here, even to your mother, or that you heard anything from anyone.' Disappointed, the young man turned to leave, until Carlo added.

'If you wish, you will be welcome to call on Sophia in a few days, if she permits it. When she wakes we'll tell her of your concern.' Relief washed across his face. 'Say nothing of Bianca, the incident, or the children, and especially that our son was there, do you hear, or we'll be compelled to deny all knowledge and that could put you in danger? Do you understand?' Roberto nodded and left, content he could call again.

'Now Mamma, put our son to bed. It starts again, we tend to our children our casualties of war, give them all the love we have, and mend them if we can.'

'What about....' Maria nodded towards the railway bridge, reason finally filtering through her hostility.

'I'll call on Vittorio, see if he knows of Bianca's whereabouts,' he replied and left. From her bedroom window, Sofia's shadowy figure watched her father on the much-trod route to her friend's house.

At the compound entrance, nervous sentries examined Carlo, searching his pockets and body for weapons, despite his familiar face. Eventually allowed to enter he found Mia as always in the kitchen, her sons close by.

'I need to talk with your husband, is he in the house?' Carlo asked. She nervously touched all the dishes on the table for reassurance, dithering, almost chattering to herself.

'Oh, he is attending to business. The noise, and the rifle fire, is most disturbing....' Carlo guided her to a chair, speaking softly.

'That's why I'm here Mia, I need to speak with him.' Her eyes darted nervously.

'I wouldn't disturb him, no I would not.' He adopted a different approach.

'Is Bianca here, I haven't seen her since this morning?'

Bless her, she is doing the rounds of bakers and grocers,' she paused, eyelids flickering, 'the battle you know....' trailing off.

'So she hasn't returned yet?' he asked.

Mia replied in disjointed muttering, hands trembling. 'So close you see, so close' staring up at him. He squeezed her hand and made his way through the house to the power plant, finding Vittorio barking instructions at his workforce.

'We need to speak about your daughter.'

'That firebrand, she's nothing but trouble for me,' ignoring Carlo's indication of privacy, and walked on.

'Now, man! She's your child,' no longer tolerating the disregard for his daughter. Vittorio spun around, curiosity casually crossed his face and he followed Carlo to his office.

Moments later he dashed out, followed by Carlo, sending him back to work. Entering the house he shouted, 'Benito, Luca here now!'

The boys assembled as directed outside their father's home office, and loitered, powerless to wander off. Telephone conversations were made by Vittorio and calls received, his clipped tone heard in short conversations. Eventually Benito drifted closer to the kitchen, disappearing to his mother's side. Luca remained obediently sat on the stairs, eventually twisting to recline his head on the spotless tiled tread, ear pinched flat, arm across his body as tedium eventually drew him to a doze. Snapped words roused him, "Odilo" and "Swiss Red Cross Station" clipping into his consciousness.

His father burst out of the office surveying the scene, his eldest son absent.

'One of you will do, you the youngest!'

Luca sprang to attention, astonished that his brother's absence was not being punished. The situation must be severe.

Vittorio glanced into the kitchen at his wife's clattering, 'You boy, look after your mother,' calling to Benito, turned on his heel and grabbed a jacket. He threw another at Luca and strode down the stairs and out of the compound, no acknowledgement to the sentries, Luca running after him.

He had been instructed it was safe for him to travel the streets, and proceeded urgently. As they passed the dead horse Luca managed a slight detour to better examine the animal. It lay, still with saddle and reigns, eyes bulging, flies hovering already. Adjacent, a collection of women huddled near the bridge, large knives grasped firmly in fists, arms crossed under shrunken flat bosoms, awaiting the right moment. Small children hung around their knees with hessian bags. The other horses were gone and the railway station abandoned. After Vittorio and Luca passed, a flurry of activity burst out behind them, making the boy jump. Without looking, his father held his son's head firmly to the front.

'Don't look,' Vittorio snapped. Luca accepted his disappointment, as wet slashing sounds slurped the air and the women grunted over the carcass behind them.

They reached the door of the barracks housing the infirmary and were permitted entry as rounds of gunfire began again further along the wall, Slavs re-positioned.

After many hours they were allowed to leave. Passing the partially butchered horse carcass, Luca noticed among the entrails and blood, an odd piece of women's clothing lost in the chaos, a shoe, a scarf, abandoned in the stampede to escape as the battle recommenced.

Chapter 60

Trieste, Italy, May 1944 (later that same day)

Father and son strode silently up the hill; Vittorio hesitated outside Carlo's house, then hammered on the door until Maria opened it.

'Well?' she still hadn't forgiven Bianca for her daughter's suffering, and even her father's presence could not stem her anger.

'You haven't been to work and my wife needs you in the kitchen,' he commanded.

'And I will not attend. My daughter needs me here,' she retorted.

Uninvited, Vittorio entered, Luca settled on the window seat outside, looking in as his father began, fist clenching.

'I've been to find Bianca as you might imagine. She had been reported shot,' he instructed.

His eye never left Maria, rooting her to the spot. 'And I should imagine you are keen to know yourself if she is dead?'

'Bianca, dead?' a voice from the stairs drew them. Sofia stood, a wisp of a person, barely audible. Maria flew into a rage.

'Bianca this, Bianca that! You see my daughter, the state she is in, all because of your precious Bianca?' she screamed. Vittorio erupted and Luca pressed his nose to the window.

'Cretina,' he flung his arm in her direction as she backed away, clutching the edge of the table.

'You think your daughter's plight is my child's doing? Without her you would not eat,' he slapped the table.

'Do you not hear me, woman, she has been shot and you don't even ask if she lives,' his raised forefinger slashed the air, spittle discharged from bared teeth.

'Well my daughter, my Sofia....' she started.

'Your daughter? She came home, and she sleeps in her bed. My daughter lays in pain, no anaesthetic, she could die, have limbs amputated. Do you see her here with me now, no, because Bianca is kept from us in the Swiss Red Cross Station.' Sofia swayed.

'Well, I thought...' she muttered.

'You thought what? That your daughter's life is more valuable than mine? Well, let me tell you, this whole family is worth less than that boy out there.' Maria wilted. 'If I wanted every creature in this house out on the street, it would happen,' he turned his back on her. 'Your loyalty to your husband's employer is lacking woman, and you forget yourself. Don't you think half the city would like your position, your own house, a little light housework here and there in my home, a husband in safe employment,' he turned glaring. 'All at my pleasure. If it wasn't for the bond between our daughters, and my wife's affection for you, I'd have some other creature at the sink,' he paused, 'I say again, your daughter is safe at home, mine is not.'

He advanced further into the kitchen, Maria backed against the wall. Outside Luca looked as Sofia descended, her long white nightgown catching his eye.

'Mamma?' she murmured, her brother cowering behind her.

Vittorio flicked his hand at her, then, 'Get to bed children, your mother wishes to know how our family is - ours!' They both backed up the stairs.

'And I inform you woman, my daughter lives, only just, too sick to be released to her family, shot but not fatally.'

Luca backed away from the window, sliding to the far end of the bench as his father suddenly re-emerged, slapping the door frame, swinging to face Maria again. As they stood face to face, an amused expression flitted momentarily in his eyes.

'Listen to me,' more gently now. 'My wife will expect you tomorrow. Your daughter will recover,' he gestured gracefully with his hands, 'so will mine.' He caught her sharp expression, adding, 'God willing,' reasserting his control. 'My wife is a gentle being and values your company,' emphasising, 'though I understand it not,' the verbal barb hitting its mark. 'So you will be there.'

She stood, silent. Everything he said was right. Without his protection, and his grotesque association with Odilo, they could easily be incarcerated in San Sabba concentration camp, the oven their next resting place.

'Certainly Signor, I'll attend as usual,' she lowered her eyes.

He finally stepped away, clicking his finger at Luca to follow.

'Bastardo,' she whispered, closing the door, shooing her boy to his room.

Sofia stood immobile on the stair, palms outstretched, raised heavenward, face bathed in pain, a perfect vision of the Sorrowful Mother. It took Maria's breath away. She stood at the bottom, looking up at her and sighed.

'And,' a tear fell on Maria's face, 'the only word you will speak is, *"Bianca"*,' and wearily climbed the stairs.

Chapter 61

Trieste, Italy, May 1944

Food coupons issued were halved and then quartered putting pitiful rations on tables. Fascists had diverted petrol supplies, strangling the supply, but it was acquired from somewhere to power the car Vittorio had access to.

Bianca was treated by the Swiss Red Cross, operating from a German unit. The bullet had exited her leg, but lack of medication prevented early return home. When sufficiently healed she was released to her father. For weeks she had benefited, not only from medical care, but their strange nourishing food and genial company. Upon collection, her father dictated status required a formal departure and she reluctantly prepared to leave.

'Bianca, these people are not your friends, behave with decorum, don't forget your position.'

She looked at the imperious stance of her father among the hard working Swiss volunteer medical corps, inwardly sighing, he would have his way. She graciously held out a limp hand to the kind senior medical officer.

'Thank you for your time, Signor, I wish you well.' The middle-aged doctor read the situation and squeezed her hand warmly.

'Thank you for your kind company Signorina, it has been a pleasure.'

The remembrance of his warm smile stayed with her all the way home until old realities arose within her. As they neared Sofia's home, she strained to see if anyone was visible until her father barked,

'Sit still, you can no longer go about your life consorting with the lower orders.'

Pain, discomfort and a knowledge of her father's nature left her in no mistake, what the status quo was now.

'Don't forget Bianca, they live under my protection and to cast aspersions upon a member of my family,' he snorted, 'is intolerable.'

'Papa, what are you saying? Do you intend to send them away?' She could not contemplate life without her sister-friend, her only ally.

'Carlo will continue to work and as long as he meets his obligations, the family can stay. Maria will be responsible for our laundry and food preparation in her home but will not be permitted to come and go any more. It is you who shall assist your mother in domestic duties.'

She was stunned, her father had reorganised all their lives with no consideration for any of them. Silently she looked down towards the city as they entered the compound. He had at least spared them a home, and Carlo his job, and maybe there would be an opportunity for her and Mamma to see their friends again.

'What has happened to Sofia, father?' During her confinement, she had clung to the thought of their next meeting, just to know she had recovered from her melancholy.

'Maria continues to claim sickness, with weakness in the head,' he shot a look at her. 'You would do well not to associate with people of that calibre.'

They reached home and he called Benito and Luca to assist her to bed. There had been no discussion and their lives were decreed to a new pattern dictated by him. She was to be a prisoner in her own home, a domestic servant.

*

She watched from her favourite position in the kitchen, hoping to see Sophia.

'Come now Bianca, there's more to do, come away from the window, cara,' her mother said.

She knew her mother meant it for her own good, it didn't help to wish her life away hoping for a glimpse of her friend. Her mother attempted further distraction.

'How are you today dear, is there better movement in your leg?'

'Yes Mamma, it improves a little each day, but still hurts.'

'I know what will take your mind off it. Today most household functions are completed and I have a gift for you.' She went to the storeroom and brought a paper package, carefully unwrapped it at the table, and presented several yards of plain white cotton material. Bianca gasped at the purity of the fabric.

'What do you think cara, would you like to make yourself a new summer dress?'

'It reminds me of the dress Sofia was wearing when she ran away.' Bianca said. Mia's face crumpled. 'Oh Mamma, I'm sorry, I didn't mean to upset you.'

'It's alright dear, I'm fine,' she stuttered, 'I just thought it would help you to be occupied with something special for yourself. I know you miss Sofia, I miss Maria too.'

'Does she speak much, Mamma, when you deliver laundry?'

'Maria is softening day by day, but still very protective of her daughter.'

'Have you seen Sofia, is she well?' she asked.

'She stays in the house, but I did see Roberto calling again. He takes great risks, a young man out in plain sight during the day, but he loves her so, he cannot help himself. He says no-one congregates in the piazza any more,' leaving Bianca to her thoughts.

She missed the camaraderie of her friends, chatting about food and opportunities. She contemplated the irony of the meeting place again, the "Square of Forages", no-one foraging for information there any more since Italy's remaining young men were enlisted to fight for the Germans, on the Russian front.

After dinner, she brought out the cloth again, settled at the kitchen table, and spread out the pure fabric. It was easy to draw a pattern, cut, pin and tack, and a modern culotte skirt and matching blouse started to take form.

An explosion of rifle fire clattered outside the house.

Her first reaction was to run to the window, see which direction the onslaught was coming from. Looking into the courtyard, the sentries ran to reinforce their position, guns pointing, eyes scanning the hillside above. Then an eruption down the hill from beyond Sofia's house, and more rifle shots shattered the windows, sending the family flat to the floor.

Vittorio took charge, 'Boys, mother, are you safe?'

'Yes Papa,' her brothers slithering backwards along the floor to the inner safety of the corridor.

'Daughter?'

Falling to the floor had dragged at her injuries, she winced as blood oozed through her dress, 'Yes Papa, I'm fine.'

Through glass shards they all retreated to the corridor, huddling until night fell and the German soldiers regrouped.

At breakfast, Vittorio joined the family, fatigue evident on everyone's face, Bianca attempting to lift the mood with a suggestion of at least sourcing supplies.

'If you deem it safe, Papa, I think I will try some exercise outside today.'

'That depends, if you stay within a safe distance of home,' he replied without looking at her. She attempted a bold move.

'I thought I would try to walk into Trieste, go to the Red Cross Centre and,' she needed the company of a friend, and had a good excuse, 'try and access medical supplies for the family, in light of last night's assault?'

'No,' the unequivocal reply.

'No? But Papa, it would be useful to be prepared.'

Her father hesitated.

'The Centre no longer exists.'

'Then I'll go to where it's moved to. Please, father, they know me, they will help and it will be good for us.'

In a rare moment of consideration, he replied.

'I know you wish to help the family Bianca,' he paused, 'but when I say the Medical Centre no longer exists,' without looking up from his coffee he said, 'they are dead, murdered last night by the Slovenes.'

Everyone at the table stopped, shocked at the coldness of the statement. The Swiss Red Cross was independent, assisting anyone in need, any creed, any nationality, they were innocent of allegiance. It was senseless.

Her mother gasped. 'Dead? Surely not, they are.... were, so kind.'

'The Slavs thought otherwise. They saw only that they helped Germans and Italians, enough to finish them off.'

'What will happen now Papa, where are they, can none of them be saved?' Bianca asked.

He rose from his coffee cup, unwavering, direct.

'They are dead, all of them, what difference does it make?' and left.

Chapter 62

Trieste, Italy, August 1944

Sewing had distracted her, a time to concentrate on something, the bright, white material refreshing. She crafted a long-sleeved blouse with collar and cuffs, matching culottes, two pocket inset to the front. The sun shone and her hip and leg healed well, but the abnormality of being alive, and a virtual prisoner in her home remained. Having lived as a gypsy on the road, the monotony of domestic chores was barely tolerable, and she missed Sophia so much, needed to see and know she was safe.

Listening at his door she knew her father still had good lines of communication, even with fascists disrupting where they could, battling with any opposition and each other. His finger seemed on the pulse of change, before it even happened.

It was her birthday and Bianca felt better than she had for some while. She wore her new outfit and Mamma's gift of a new permanent wave hairstyle, buoyed her and that evening, her father had news.

For a year the Allies had battled their way up the country, citizens aiding to liberate their beautiful country, while others struggled to maintain fascism, and communists concentrated on capturing Trieste, last port of the western world in Europe.

Despite provisions still being sparse, her father was uncharacteristically subdued as he eyed his paltry meal; unease permeating the room.

'Mamma, bring brandy,' he spoke. Mia rushed to the storeroom swiftly placing glass and bottle before him. During the meal gulps of the liquor alternated with mouthfuls of food as he began to mutter quietly. They all looked to each other.

'Husband dear, does something trouble you?' Mia asked.

'You don't know the burden I carry,' he murmured.

She ushered her sons from the room.

'Tell me, can I help?' she pleaded.

Bianca watched as her mother's concern, duty to husband overriding everything.

'You help me? Hah!' Leaving her parents to talk, she lingered in the corridor.

'Mia,' he looked into his wife's eyes, 'you've served me well, done what you could with this brood. Soon there will be another world, another onslaught on our lives.' Her mother sat obediently by his side. He turned towards her, clasping her hand.

'The Pope himself has appealed to the Allies for help,' he sighed deeply. 'Do you understand what this means to our country, our lives? After our contact with the Germans, we may be finished off by the Allies?

'My dear,' she nervously adjusted her position, 'we don't know that, we can only pray we will be delivered alive.'

'Do you know our soldiers have surrendered in hordes Mia, citizens embracing the invading armies. The war has destroyed every aspect of our lives, and now the Catholic Church surrenders when previously it maintained independence.'

Outside, Bianca curled her lip, *'And the priests maintained their safety while innocent women and children starved, and worse,'* she thought.

'What about Odilo dear, can he help?' Mia asked.

'Him? He will be the downfall of us all. I've courted him, licked the feet of partisans, appeased the fascists and consorted with royalists and bourgeoisie....' he trailed off.

'You are a good husband, you cannot be despised for doing your duty to the city.' Bianca dashed a look, taken aback by her mother's rarely seen insight and intelligence.

287

'I'll tell you about Odilo,' her father continued, 'he was present at some of the most heinous murder of Jews in Poland,' not waiting for a response he unburdened himself, 'that's why he was sent here. It's well understood among high German ranks, it's hoped people like him will be liquidated by partisans, eliminate the embarrassing problem, no-one left to tell of the concentration camps.' He looked at Mia. 'Don't look at me like that, yes, they existed, and still do. Look at Christian the Terrible, they got him didn't they?' he started to slur. 'Driving around a partisan country in an open-topped car, with only a few guards to protect him was an act of the greatest arrogance. Or did he choose to die by their hand, and look how we all suffered afterwards,' pouring himself another drink.

Listening out of sight she thought, *'When has he ever shown compassion for anyone? He's only thinking of himself, and now Mamma panders to his manipulations.'*

Another block in the wall settled into place completing the shield between her and the world, only tiny cracks remained through which to reach her.

*

Night-time wasn't a good time to walk, but she fled the dim orange light of the corridor. Her new outfit discarded, she grabbed a hat and boys clothes and left through a workshop entrance. Stumbling into the undergrowth at the perimeter she sat, waiting to see if anyone would drag her back. Thoughts rushed through her mind of the rich old man, uncaring priests, and Germans, all parading through their home. They had provided for them all, she and her mother working hard and going without to make him look like the big man he wanted them to think he was, now remorseful, for himself.

She'd heard it so many times, he was "important", "if it wasn't for me, the city would be in darkness". He managed the power station with fervour. It was his project,

288

he'd watched it being built and manoeuvred himself to the position of controller. Thinking back to her childhood she remembered how he guided them to embrace the fascist lifestyle, streets teeming with commerce, industry, and culture then, it was the jewel in Il Duce's crown. Now the power he produced fuelled the Nazi holding camp, lit the lights that watched over tortured innocents like Bird Boy, enabled the gas chambers to do their abhorrent work.

Huddled in the undergrowth she thought of him moaning about his lot. He called her sullen, but she was frightened and lonely; the things she had seen and experienced intruded and tortured her mind at the most unexpected moments. She looked down at her spindly legs, bullet hole scar stretched painfully, face tight from salty tears.

Pulling the cap down over her eyes, no-one would know what she was thinking. Looking at the rough grass beyond the fence, they used to catch rabbits there, all gone now, pointless to set traps any more. She crawled under and set off down the hill. It was strangely cold, cutting into her neck, the cap pulled down so tight it felt like a hand gripping her skull. She didn't want to be in the world tonight.

In the distance, drifting up from San Sabba, engines revved, accompanied by blaring music in another pointless exercise to mask the screams. She covered her ears, walking towards Sofia's home, drawn like a spell. As she approached the garden a shadow flickered across her path from behind, she spun around, as a cloud swept across the moon.

Then a scratch of gravel. She turned again, the vegetation made her jump. She sensed something, there were ghostly forms all around, air on her neck moved. Bending forward, she propelled herself to Sophia's home, danger everywhere. Glancing over her shoulder, the shadow of the bushes were wrong. She started to run and a hand grasped her, another round her throat as she flailed to be free. A fist gripped her mouth as she was flung to the ground, kicking, writhing.

Half-starved and fearful, still fighting her captor, her escaped arm became a scratching claw. A sickening thud to the side of her head slammed her body sideways as spit and something warm shot out of her mouth. The blow reverberated around her head as blackness flooded in.

*

A gentle hand slapped her face, a vague vision of Roberto hovering above. For the second time, a hand covered her mouth as he looked down at her, he shook his head indicating silence. She closed her eyes again trying to gather her sensibilities.

'What are you doing here? Are you mad coming out after curfew?' he whispered, 'you ran into Italian partisans Bianca, you're lucky your throat isn't cut.'

'Why would they want to hurt me, I'm no threat to anyone.' He leaned back.

'It's no use to them if they are planning something, and you come along and see what they are up to, is it? How would they know which faction you belong to?' He crouched beside her as she sat up.

'Roberto, how do you know this sort of thing? And what are you doing here?' she quizzed.

'Let's just say I was visiting a friend whose wellbeing I care about.' Bianca noticed a maturity and attitude previously lost on her.

'Sofia? Have you seen her? Is she alright, I miss her so much? Her mother still forbids me, she blames me for what happened in Opicina.'

'Well, can you blame her?' he snapped.

'I don't understand, I never denied her entrance, and I was nearly taken to San Sabba myself, I could be dead now. Anyway there was no hiding place for two, we would both be ash on the gas chamber floor now,' she gulped. 'I never wanted anything to happen to her.'

'Then you don't know, do you?'

'I know she was found at the quayside, out of her mind.'

'And you don't know what drove her to that madness?'

'No. I would have done anything to protect her, and she me; after everything we've endured I would have shielded her with my life.'

'She talks a little now, I think she is recovering,' he hesitated. 'Your friend the Bird Boy found her and took her to the Karst for safety and returned to tell you she was safe. It's thought that was when the soldiers took him.'

'So it is true, it was him I saw dragged from the street,' she whispered.

'And Sophia knows this? She must be heart-broken, responsible for his capture. He was such a friend to us.'

Roberto snorted. 'You have no idea do you, she doesn't know that, and never will? Being left on the Karst was only the beginning. The boy's thug of a brother found her, fell upon her and....' he took a deep breath, 'and tried to rape her. She only escaped by throwing herself down the escarpment.'

Bianca's mouth hung open as she tried to take it in. 'I must go to her, beg her forgiveness, she's all I have in the world.' Muted sobs escaped through her hands. Roberto looked at her, no more the haughty young woman, and relented.

'Listen, Bianca, the war has made monsters of us all, things will change, the Allies are near, Italy is with them.'

'How do you know this?'

'Let's just say, working in a café, you hear nothing but learn much.'

'I'll go home. Tomorrow I'll stop at nothing to see her, my world revolves around her Roberto. I know you two will marry one day, but she will always be my friend, my sister.' He leaned forward.

'Do not, Bianca.'

'But why? I have to plead for our friendship, I'll make it up for the rest of her life.'

He grasped her shoulders, whispering, 'She won't be there.' His look penetrated her befuddled mind as he continued. 'Don't come looking for her, or me, it will draw attention.' Bianca looked confused. 'If you love and care for her as you say, don't go.' The thunderbolt hit her.

'You are a partisan, aren't you? she said.

'Don't ask. Don't even think of it if you value your life, and that of our family. Forget you said that, do you understand?' he shook her. 'Just know, she will be with me and I will make sure no harm comes to her. You won't see her again until all this is over.' He shook her. 'You have to be strong, Bianca, as you always have.'

'I can only be strong with her,' she sobbed, 'she's the rock that made life worth living up there,' she jabbed a thumb towards home. 'We've been two together since childhood,' her head fell forward, no more sound came.

'Then remember that, and look forward,' Roberto whispered, 'life cannot go on like this forever. Now, go home without being seen, all our safety depends upon it.'

The arid cracks within her sealed completely closed, she would allow no-one else to touch her heart again, no man to be loved, no child embraced. He lifted her chin.

'I will tell her you risked everything to see her, I know it will mean something to her, now go.'

She climbed the hill, the clouds obscuring the moon, sky black. Looking back before crawling under the fence there was nothing but empty wilderness, he was gone.

Chapter 63

Apennine Mountains, Italy, Autumn 1944

'I can't believe this crapola.'

'You Yanks have an interesting turn of phrase,' Ted shouted at the U.S. soldier ahead of him. 'What's your problem?'

'Ok Blighty Boy, how we gonna get across this ravine, we're supposed to be over there by now?' the American pointed up the escarpment.

An officer marched through the servicemen, bunched up at the chasm before them. 'What's the holdup, I've mechanical and infantry stacking up?'

'Ravine sir, obstruction.' The American soldier snapped to attention as the officer examined the gulch before him.

'Call that a ravine soldier?' he turned, 'It's a gully, get it bridged now.'

Ted found it hard not to snigger, it wasn't the first time a gully had become a ravine, a pile of stones an avalanche, a stream a torrent. The rest of 13 Corps group were pushing through the crowd of miscellaneous soldiers and vehicles.

It hadn't been easy, trudging over rugged terrain, through rocky bluffs, over sharp ridges, but he knew his detail more than able to bridge what he considered no more than a cleft in the terrain. The throng parted as men, machinery and supplies made their way through to get to work. By the time they'd made good across the span, autumn mist was whispering across the Apennines again, it was to be expected. During the night troops continued onward and upward.

*

'I said, bringing your light coloured summer coat was a good idea,' Roberto turned to his companion. 'A tight fit over your woollens, but see how we blend into the landscape, no one can spot us in this snow.' High in the mountains, the two figures surveyed the drama spreading below. When the fog drifted away, moonlight behind them prevented reflection on their binoculars as he noted impressive new German defences below.

'Come on Roberto, we can't stay here for the night, we're not prepared.' He ignored his companion, continuing to scan the activity.

'I can see movement beyond the Germans, further down the pass, the Allies are coming,' he rested the field glasses on his crouching knee, contemplating the scene. 'When they get over the next set of cliffs and inclines, the Nazis will have them in their sights, and well within range. They'll be obliterated.'

'Listen, Roberto, you're the brains, I'm the guide, we go now before it's too late for us too.'

*

'Take down the bridge and break camp? We've only just finished reinforcing it.' His Scouse friend was becoming more belligerent the colder and more haphazard everything got.

Ted and his mates were dismantling links and bridges, as troops and equipment hurriedly retraced their tracks, back down the scarp. He looked at Scouse.

'It's not for us to wonder why,' he muttered as his comrade cussed, flinging tools into a truck, as it turned round and retreated.

'Listen, mate,' Ted took him aside, 'we've just got to jump to it. It's all part of a greater plan, got to be,' he looked at the bedraggled miserable lump of sinew and bone in front of him. 'We don't know why we have to go back down the mountain, but there's got to be a reason. Better we turn back and live, than freeze or die; there'll be a NAAFI somewhere down there won't there?'

'Aye pal you might be right, come on,' his mate replied. Ted patted his shoulder as they began to trudge, rain falling heavier. They lifted the handles of two wooden barrows laden with the last of their tools, turned up their collars, threw duffle bags and water bottles on top and started the arduous slog pushing them down a waterlogged sodden track.

'Never mind mate, tomorrow's another day eh?' his friend's spirits lifting.

'Tomorrow's nineteenth of October, my birthday. Wonder what me mam and sister are doing?'

As they pushed on down, his mind drifted to the scenic, windswept beaches of Redcar, his mother cheerfully striving to make ends meet and Cissy engaged to Arthur. Thinking of his lot, he considered, he'd seen a good bit of the world, more than the likes of the scornful farm girls back home ever would. Army reports 'Exemplary', and 'Hard-working'. Promoted, then promoted again, he appreciated his place and enjoyed the banter and camaraderie. But the deluge continued.

Next day, driving rain and intense artillery brought the day to a close. Ted kept his head down, obeyed orders, jumped to it, whatever needed. Twenty-two years old, no time to wonder about celebrating a birthday. If there was a job to be done it was completed to his best. Three square a day, usually a roof of some sort over his head, sending money home to his Mam, all because of the Army. They deserved the best he had, and he gave it willingly.

Further up the incline, the mountain erupted along the route they had just come down, revealing a huge hidden German stronghold. Bombardment after bombardment tried to make its mark upon them but falling short. They thanked God they had been pulled back.

'I wonder how they knew to withdraw,' Ted said.

*

In the following days his head throbbed, he lacked sleep existing on wiry muscle, determination and handfuls of grub. Casualties were ferried in all directions, but they had the upper hand and there was no giving in. Booming explosions, disorientated, functioning on trained automatic body responses, mind exploding, eyes sore from smoke, rain soaked, the Allies responded and then some.

Sat in a dugout Ted prayed, thinking, *"Brits, Yanks, Canadians, African Corps, We're all blown to bits the same, brains smashed, limbs ripped out"*

The downpour continued.

"Persevere" he vowed.

Chapter 64

Trieste, Italy, December, Winter 1944/45

'The German sentries have left Mamma, their replacements were late.' Bianca had been to check on the chickens for breakfast eggs.

'Mamma I'm talking to you, why don't you answer?' Her life revolved around domestic obligations, washing floors, cooking, mending, ironing, only leaving home in the company of a parent. She was numb, only kitchen drudgery registered in the small fissure that remained of her mind.

'Cara, it's no matter to us, just put the eggs in the store and grind coffee.' As usual, her mother concentrated on the confines of her domain. Then a glimmer of interest flickered in a desolate corner of her mind.

'Has it happened before Mamma?' head misty. Sophia gone, now she was alone, deserted.

'It may or may not, I haven't noticed.' A fluttering of activity came from her mother at the sink.

Something started to reignite within her, an ember of recognition for her surroundings, her mother's nervous activity a sign of something, but without energy to concentrate she applied herself to the coffee machine. Benito and Luca entered the kitchen, drawn to the warm smell of bread her mother was taking from the oven.

Breakfast progressed as every day, her father neither looking at, nor talking to anyone at the table, mother fussing and serving, brothers surreptitiously needling each-other just out of Papa's gaze. As her father left, and she collected dishes for washing, the boys hung around the gramophone,

'Can we play it Mamma, please?' Years of confinement to home had narrowed the opportunities for fun. Luca had taken to model making in the basement,

Benito reading articles in old magazines about movie stars, the rest of the time lounging around or looking out the windows.

'Oh heaven's children, if you must,' her mother scurried out of the room with laundry to store. Something creaked in Bianca's mind, something was going on and she affected an interest in the heavy 78 rpm records the boys were looking at.

'Boys, careful now, don't crack or break anything, you know mother loves these. What are you going to play?' Benito looked at her sad eyes.

'What do you care, we're only doing it to annoy you, and send Mamma out the kitchen.' She ignored the attempt to needle her.

'What's the idea, why do you want Mamma out of the way?' she asked.

Benito checked the hall then quietly slipped into his father's office, returning a moment later with binoculars under his woollen jumper as Luca selected recordings.

'Got them, Luca, come on, leave the gramophone, let's go,' he said.

'Papa put those away, what are you doing with them,' she asked.

'He never uses them, and he'll never know unless you tell him, but you won't, will you?' Bianca looked into his eyes, something of her father made her shudder.

'I don't care,' she retorted.

Benito escaped up the tiled stairs two at a time as Luca returned records to dust sleeves. She took her chance to find out.

'So what escapade are you two up to Luca, what do you need binoculars for?' using mild interest to tease out details of their adventure as she washed dishes.

'Benito has become sentry for the house, he's watching and writing down the comings and goings at the barracks, and railway station and needed equipment.'

'Comings and goings, like what?' she asked.

'Well during the day, because of course, he can't see anything at night.... but you know like when the communist partisans come over from Slovenia, but that's during the night so he can't see that or track their activities and murders then of course.' Bianca winced at his childish ramblings, thinking of Roberto's warning.

'Does Papa know about this?' his silence told her he did not, and she continued. 'Luca, don't you know how dangerous this action is? To spy on things you should not, it will make us all accountable,' she grabbed his arm.

Luca wrenched free, 'You're hurting me. I only wanted to make puppets in the workshop, and a candlestick holder for Mamma, a gift for the Feast of the Immaculate Conception. Go and tell Benito.'

'What have you seen, Luca?' she shook him.

'Just that at the barracks, there doesn't seem to be much activity any more, a lot of the soldiers have been transported elsewhere, probably to fight Slav communists I should imagine.' Luca looked pleased with this presumed knowledge. 'They're everywhere now you know, attacking convoys, bodies turning up in the city, supplies diverted.'

'Luca, where are you getting this information from, you shouldn't know this sort of thing.'

A wave of realisation washed over her, things forgotten suddenly remembered, the veil that had been protecting her consciousness, evaporating. Her mind, hidden from horrifying memories, healed, she could think now, no longer in a trance. Luca was talking.

'.... and then when they changed shifts outside I heard Carlo telling this other man about the attack.'

'Luca, forget now you ever heard Carlo say anything, you mustn't tell father you know these things. If the wrong people find out they could take you away, take us all away.'

He stared, immobile, broke away and ran down to the workshops.

All-day she wondered how to divert Benito from his perilous occupation. Luca was sufficiently scared off spying, never really committed anyway, but Benito would be difficult to influence.

That evening they congregated in the kitchen as usual. The expressive, dulcet duet "O Norma" by Bellini melodiously playing on the gramophone as Bianca turned the conversation to her brothers' excessive energy.

'Papa how these boys challenged me all day.' Her father's interest slightly aroused.

'How so, daughter?'

'They grow Papa, every day more,' surreptitiously she checked her father's attention. Of late she had been docile and withdrawn rather than irritated and disagreeable, her brothers watched her gentle exchange.

'Papa they are maturing, they have energy to spare and no occupation to use it upon, confined to home as they are.'

Hypnotic tones drifted from the gramophone in the background....

'Look at your dear children, of yours on your knees. Be moved by pity for them, even if you do not pity yourself'.

Vittorio raised a penetrating eye to his daughter. She dropped her gaze to the plate before her, could he read her true intent to divert them from their spying game? Stealing a glance, it seemed he did not identify deception on her part, concentrating on the gnocchi tossed in mother's excellent preserved tomato sauce with sautéed fungi from their mushroom farm in the basement.

Courage failed her, loneliness and isolation had taken their toll. Once she would have continued, brazenly challenging her father to pay attention, confidence coursing through her. Losing Sophia, life had fallen apart, she had retreated into a replica of her mother and the subject was dropped.

*

They celebrated Christmas midnight mass at home, her mother earnestly clenching the blue enamelled Mater Dolorosa as usual, her brothers looking sideways at each-other, father deep in contemplation, face raised piously to heaven. The next day they would make their way to church. It held no credence for her any more, but she would attend to despise the priest's wide girth and mourn the injustices that had befallen her city.

Recently she had been accompanying mother to town as she had with Sofia, searching for morsels to supplement provisions, and had grown a little more confident to go on her own. She buried fear and fatigue beneath her blanket coat, walking further afield, hardly noticing the icy sting of the Bora as she clung to the chains and rope along streets. She knew the best opportunities fell to the bravest who ventured the furthest. Pursuing an ever-widening course occupied her, but as reality was creeping back she thought how a bicycle would shorten the journey and bring better spoils.

The sixth of January 1945 arrived, the night of Epiphany, when gifts were bestowed upon children. Her father implied he had picked up the concerns for her brothers' welfare, hinting at extravagant gifts. From her favourite vantage point she caught a glimpse of wondrous rewards being secreted in through one of the side entrances.

*

The moment came, the family congregated in the kitchen, anticipation in the air. In her drudgery, Bianca hoped for help in her daily grind, and propel her back to the modern woman she had once been. Her gift for her father was a leather wallet for cigarettes, hand-sewn by herself; the delicate tiny stitches had made her fingers bleed.

'Boys, Bianca, your father is coming,' Mia called, Benito and Luca looking excitedly at the kitchen door as footsteps and voices ascended the stairs with something heavy.

'They're carrying something, it must be big,' Luca speculated.

'Shush, have some decorum,' Benito assumed a senior position.

Bianca positioned herself at the far end of the room. She could hardly contain herself, awaiting the gifts that represented his regard for them.

He led the small procession into the room, standing aside to allow full view as men wheeled in two bicycles. A third man placed a small bundle of parcels on the table and returned to the landing.

'So boys, you are nearly men, as your sister has suggested, it is only fitting that my sons display themselves as people of substance in the city. For you two,' he swept his hand in the direction of the cycles. The words barely out of his mouth, the boys ran forward excitedly. With back to the window, she strained to see the worker behind them, with her cycle.

'Papa?' she asked.

'Why do you not collect your gift, it is here,' he replied, sweeping a hand towards the table, 'you show no gratitude?'

'Papa, thank you,' but didn't move. 'Those lucky boys,' she spoke fast, could she make some advantage for herself. 'They will be able to get about the city now, if they are allowed out.'

Her father's cold eye surveyed her, a slight curl to the corner of his mouth. 'No daughter, they will not. You know well the dangers for them outside the compound; they will ride them here, but word of their acquisition will filter into the community, and as you intimated they need an occupation. They will grow strong and healthy.' His steady gaze never left her.

She moved towards the table fingering the paper parcels, considering another approach

'But of course, if they are not using them, then I could perhaps borrow one? I could travel the city quickly seeking food further afield, be back sooner to assist Mamma?'

She fingered a tiny parcel with her name, wondering if it was from a jeweller.

'No.' The word boomed.

Disregard and punishment washed over her again, every crevice once tentatively occupied by love and affection, hardeneding still by the demeaning regard he had for her. A fist of resentment clenched her heart. She stood for a moment, the war had taught her emotion denotes weakness, show none, as her mother spoke.

'See your gift from Papa, I'm sure he has thought just as deeply about your situation,' she twittered vaguely.

Bianca opened the parcel, and two even smaller packages fell out. Unwrapping one, a small metal capsule rolled onto the table, the outer case stamped with a wispy pattern, a small pink tassel at one end. Pulling it apart, in the middle a tiny cotton reel with several sections of different coloured thread, contained sewing needles at its' centre, a thimble over one end.

'So daughter, you have the means to remain smart wherever, no excuse for lost buttons.' Her father looked pleased with himself.

The second tiny parcel was one small piece of paper carefully folded over. Bending back each crease, in the centre, a metal disc lay. Turning it over, so small she had to hold it close to read the inscription. On the reverse side she read the words engraved. "Pray for me".

'And to assist your journeys, a St Christopher charm.' His eyes never left her, 'You see daughter, I care for your welfare.'

He continued, 'Mamma, here is your gift, a friend for you.' Inside her package, a small collar in finest white leather with matching lead, and small woollen coat.

The assembled group stood curious, as a workman made his way up the stairs. Still she hoped, maybe there would be a bicycle for her now. The man entered, a brown and white pup skittering along the shiny tiled floor. Excitement filled the room as the boys teased it and Mia fussed over her wriggling new companion.

'Husband my dear she is delightful, you continue to spoil us all. I'll call her Lola'

Her father had won again. Her position firmly established somewhere above the local cats, possibly, but definitely below the dog.

Chapter 65

Apennine Mountains, Italy, Early Spring 1945

'My God, look at these defences,' Ted shook his head.

They had battled across the Apennine mountains. Crumbling and abandoned German observation posts and machine-gun fortifications littered the way. The Axis troops had received little protection from them under Allied gunfire, and were in retreat. Word from Italian partisans had revealed the poor quality concrete supplied for Nazi battlements had been deliberate. Italy pillaged, citizens made to be slave labour, food diverted for Germans, artworks stolen, they sought retribution where they could, producing sub-standard concrete for their defences.

'What the hell are you going on about workmanship for Teddy boy; haven't you got something better to talk about, like say, the women?' Ted chuckled and replied,

'The Germans are supposed to be craftsmen, aren't they? Well, there's little evidence here.'

'Mate, I've never come across anyone so concerned about standards.'

'That's just it, Scouse. Rules, right and wrong, you've got to maintain them otherwise the world'll go to hell in a handcart,' he laughed.

'Let's get on with it then. We're on the move shortly and rumour is it's the last push,' Scouse said.

As his mate spoke, sunshine broke through grey clouds, revealing a mountainous landscape surrounding them.

'There you are, the sun shines on the righteous,' Ted cast an eye at his companion, 'I told you, it pays to have standards,' and laughed.

'You daft bugger,' Scouse said, 'these hills are probably wick with partisans watching, so watch your step.'

Within hours an extraordinary unseen military force of Allied soldiers emerged from crevices, formations gravitating towards each other, a huge potent, fighting force. The push was on, banter over.

*

Bianca's eyes cast listlessly across the hillside above their kitchen window. Debris from last night's battle was being cleared away by returned to post, German sentries. They nervously looked over their shoulders for unseen dangers.

'What are you doing daughter, there is cleaning to be done?'

Her mother's domestic lamentations, about floors and cooking, depressed her, already fatigued from loneliness, isolation and bad news. The night's trauma had come from Yugoslavian partisans, who had skittered down the hill like an infestation, scattering around the electricity compound, to the railway station and barracks below.

During the battle, family and workmen had barricaded themselves in basement workshops facing the city. From the long narrow windows below the ceiling, she'd watched white flashing explosions play out, the noise so loud it drowned the hum of generators. Everyone had curled up under thick wooden workbenches, white and red flashes splattered on the far wall until, head buried under her coat, exhaustion finally took her, as perverse crashing lulled her to sleep.

Back at the sink, she saw movement further up the hill. She looked out at the two Germans clearing the road outside the gates.

'Mamma?'

A solitary crack resounded, a puff of smoke rose from the rocky ascent, a moment's silence, until one of the soldiers fell to his knees, then on his face, death trickling down his neck, from the entry wound at the back of his head. Bianca looked up the hill. Only a gentle cloud of dust fell on dry spring vegetation, no footfall or person. She fell back against the table.

'Mamma?' clutching the table, falling to a seat, eyes wide, as Mia ran from the storeroom.

'Cara, what's happened, I thought I heard....' She ran to her daughter's side, 'it sounded like.... surely...., not during the day?' She bent across the sink to look out the window.

Bianca grabbed her arm, dragging her back.

'Don't look, Mamma, you're not strong enough.' Her mother shrank back as her sons ran into the room. Bianca took control.

'You two, stay together, go directly to Papa, speak to no-one else. Tell him.' she emphasised, 'the Germans need to clean up their mess. Now!' The boys raced to the stairwell.

*

Arriving minutes later, the womens' pallid faces told the story, and he hastily made his way to the window, then courtyard. Approaching the two Germans, he grabbed a coat from the sentry box and ordered the other stunned boy to cover the body. When he stood shaking, Vittorio threw it over the dead youth and ordered him to report back to the barracks immediately. Still immobile. Vittorio stepped forward and slapped his face violently, shrieking instructions into him and pushed him away from the compound. The traumatised lad stumbled down the hill as his body tried to keep up with his legs. Her father adopted a stance of arrogant victory, and scanned the hillside, smirked, and dusted his hands dramatically as if to rid himself of the Nazi stink. If any Slovenian partisan remained, he demonstrated his unpalatable disregard for the German invaders, his allegiances elsewhere, clear for any communist to see.

*

'Ted old mate?'

'Oh right, what you want then?' he looked at Scouse.

'Just wondering if you had any smokes to spare?'

'What'd you do with your ration, smoke them all at once?'

'Just askin, it's been a difficult day.' Ted looked at his mate. They had been shaken about all day in the back of the truck, heading north to join the rest of the Corps.

'Difficult, how? You've been fed, the sun's shining, we're not stuck up a mountain any more, or in the mud, no-one's shooting at us. Generally speaking the natives have been pretty welcoming, wouldn't you say?' Ted summarised their progress.

'Alright smart arse, have you got any tabs or not?' Ted flicked open his packet and tossed him two. 'You owe me.'

It was getting late, but warmer than for months as the line of trucks pulled into a field, a sergeant shouting.

'Okay, you layabouts out and set up camp, NAAFI in one hour by the northern corner. Don't be late or you'll get nothing.'

They jumped out stretching their legs. A human chain formed instantly, passing tents and kit bags, creating another neat line in the canvas village. Placing bed rolls inside their bivvi, Ted and Scouse made their way, enamel cup and plate in hand in the general direction of a food smell.

'My God, if the Bosch don't know where we are already, they'll be able to find us by the smell of that stew; just like something me mother made, vegetables floating in a sea of water that someone has waved a bit of beef at.' Ted grinned at the memory.

'Got any fags?' Scouse pipped up.

'You still after a smoke, what happened to the other two?' Ted replied.

A rugby ball rolled in front of their feet, followed by a sapper tackling it.

'Sorry mate. Have a game later eh?' he tucked the ball under his arm and ran off.

'Aye much later, see you in Venice,' Scouse yelled.

'Should you be saying that?' Ted teased.

'I was just jesting.'

'Me too,' Ted laughed, getting a dirty look back. 'Even so, you could be pulled up about it.'

'I suppose,' his mate replied.

They walked in silence as Scouse thought about Ted always keeping an eye out for his welfare.

'Looks like there is something big about to happen though, look at the numbers here,' they took in the enormity of the huge, busy field.

'Hey, let's have some of your Mam's stew to set us up for the fight then,' Scouse chirped, rubbing his hands together. They took their place in the queue as dusk fell, contemplating the coming days.

*

No-one talked at the evening meal Mia had managed to make, and Vittorio brought a bottle of wine from his much-dwindled reserves. Even her brothers were subdued, with foul murder on their doorstep until Benito spoke.

'Who was it, Bianca, that friend of yours?'

She almost choked.

'How do I know? Do you think I looked at the hole in the front of his head?' she snapped.

Their father rapped the table.

'Desist all. This is not the time for arguing amongst ourselves.' The room fell silent.

'We continue as always. Know nothing, want nothing, dislike nothing, do you hear me?' He spoke slowly, quietly, sharp blue eyes scanning the table for weakness, any chink in their defences.

No one spoke again.

Chapter 66

Trieste, Italy early Spring 1945 (later in day)

'_The Germans must be regrouping_' Bianca thought.

No sentry at their gate since the morning incident and much activity near the barracks. At least moonlight provided some guarantee of a quiet night, no partisan would venture out then.

Laying on her back, eyes open or closed, no sleep reached her, still awake as a clear moon crossed the sky shining on this wall then that one.

After activity in the home stopped, her brothers' slumber drifted from their bedroom meeting her father's snoring, the night seeming deafening to her. Her eyes sore, scraping downstairs grew more irritating as she tossed to find a cool place on the pillow to soothe her head. The incessant grating didn't stop, she knew it wasn't their dog Lola.

'_I'll go down and break that branch off myself if it doesn't stop,_' she chuntered

Kicking at the covers angrily, consciousness began to seep in.

'_There is no tree near the door, it can't be a twig._'

Laying stiff as a corpse, eyes wide open, she realised there was something outside.

'_It can't be Germans, they would pound the door, and partisans would have kicked it in by now._'

She struggled to make sense of it, deciding,

'_I'll go to the kitchen window and look down, maybe I can see._'

Grabbing cotton slippers and a jacket she crept to the kitchen sink overlooking the courtyard. Quietly shifting the shutter slats she bent until her breath clouded the glass. Shrinking back she saw a bundle at the entrance door, a dark lump on the floor. Looking again a shaft of moonlight showed a contorted white face looking up, a grotesque, hunched horror. She silently crept downstairs, the faint whimper of an injured animal penetrated the wood. Rushing upstairs, two at a time, she entered her parents room. Gently rocking her mother awake she whispered her discovery, when despite his contented snoring, it seemed her father never slept as he spun round demanding explanation.

Going to his office he took a gun from his desk, and the three quickly gathered behind the front door. Vittorio listened carefully.

'Wife, open the door,' he hissed, standing in the darkness of the hall the weapon raised. The women were armed only with kitchen utensils and Bianca flattened herself against the wall just out of sight as her mother put her hand on the handle, and turned the key.

As it opened, a sick old man slumped against the door fell into the hallway.

'What do you want, vagrant, get away from here?' her father commanded angrily. 'Why are you bothering good citizens, be gone with you.'

He waved the gun at the body on the floor. A barely audible gasp spluttered incomprehensible noises. Vittorio repeated his orders.

'Get out of here, take your ramblings elsewhere, go,' he kicked the body.

'Papa?'

'Be quiet,' he snapped.

'Papa, his clothes!' They looked at the fouled rag of a uniform he was wearing with its' Italian army insignia. Vittorio stepped back.

'Who are you old man, what do you want? How did you get the uniform of our army?'

The cracked voice grew stronger.

'Don't you recognise me, Signor? I'm your sentry, from not so long ago,' he flopped on his side.

'Don't trouble me with your lies....' Vittorio bent before the creature on the floor, lifting his head by the dirty white hair, then spun around to Mia.

'He cannot stay here.'

Bianca came out of the shadows.

'Where have you been, what happened to you? Your name is Angelo isn't it?' Her father pulled her from the crumpled heap spitting, 'You don't know his name, you've never seen him before.'

'I was only a young boy Signor, seized by Slovenians, captured and starved. Please let me stay, please.' he implored, 'I escaped with my life, don't let them take me back, I beg, I beg,' finally slumping in a heap again. Vittorio pulled the women back as Mia spoke.

'What's happened to his hair husband, it was thick black curls, now white straw?' innocently. Vittorio responded instantly.

'Forget you ever saw him, he cannot stay here, we could all be murdered for protecting him, he has to go.'

Bianca moved towards her mother.

'It's true Mamma, we dare not protect him,' the women mortified at their heartless choice. Vittorio pulled them aside again.

'I am going to bed, you two do the same.' He hesitated on the stairs. 'If food goes missing, no-one would know. If some of Benito's clothes are gone, then the boy will have lost them, and if we need to burn rubbish tomorrow from the battle, it would be understandable.'

He turned towards them. 'What is unacceptable, is if you know or remember anything of this night, you take it to your grave, both of you. I will not tolerate involvement by anyone. I have seen nothing, I sleep very well and never wake at night.' He looked at the boy on the floor, 'now clean this mess up women,' ascending the stairs.

The woman understood he was their responsibility, and half-carried him to the kitchen, the moon allowing them to act. They worked swiftly, bringing cheese, bread and wine to fortify him. Bianca boiled eggs and wrapped them in an old napkin with a piece of ham they were saving for morning.

A swish of footsteps on the stairs brought Bianca to a halt as a dark terrifying figure loomed out of the stairwell. She reached for a knife, her mother immobile as Carlo silently entered the kitchen.

'Oh Carlo, what are you doing here, you frightened us?' Mia moved between him and the boy.

'Move, you don't hide anything,' he pushed her aside. 'I'm night watch today lucky for you,' he looked down into the hollows where bright young eyes once shone.

'Carlo?' Mia was confused.

'It didn't take much to catch your shadows creeping around the kitchen in the moonlight, I waited until it was safe to approach.' He looked at the boy, 'And lucky the Germans are too busy to post sentries.'

'Bianca, get your Papa....' Mia instructed.

'You will not.' Carlo commanded, an authority neither had heard before and stunned they obeyed.

'What have you got for him there?' He quickly examined the pile of clothes they had gathered, picking items and casting others aside.

'What food do you have?' Bianca pushed the small parcel wrapped in the old napkin.

'Soak the bread in any sauce left from dinner, it will give him extra strength, get rid of this,' he flung the napkin away. 'Do you want a trace of yourselves with him if he's found?'

For all her previous experience, Bianca was ashamed at her lack of judgement.

'If you have some leaves, even from the rubbish, that will do,' he expertly wove a parcel, placing it in the pocket of an old jacket the women had brought.

'I'll get some hot water for him to wash,' Mia went to put a pan on the stove.

'There's no time,' Carlo was in full control. 'Paper and pencil!' He quickly tore a strip and began writing. Bianca couldn't resist straining to see,

"RS, the baggage is safely delivered and approved, no charge. Padre"

Addressed to "RS", the note confirmed the holder as a safe person with clear instructions to be helped. Bianca couldn't believe her friend's father being so entrenched in partisan activity, even an authority. Carlo looked down at the terrified young man.

'I've seen unspeakable things, Signor,' the boy, unburdened himself. 'Slav partisans, they starved and tortured until I never knew from one day to the next if I would live. They would take us to the deepest foibes, stand us in a line on the edge, some they pushed in, others not, sometimes throwing a mad dog in too. The screams, I could bear it no longer and took my chance. They had us lined up, and were using us as target practice on the Karst, as my neighbour fell I dropped beneath him and played dead. When they left us for a moment I managed to creep into the vegetation Signor, I vowed I would die escaping rather than remain. Please let me stay, keep me safe, I beg of you.'

Carlo bent close to the boy's ear whispering, 'Courage. If you have that, you may return home safe one day, if not you may be the death of us all,' he lightly slapped the back of his head, then seeing his traumatised expression, gently caressed the straw-like white hair. 'Courage I say, you've had it so far, it will not leave you.' Liquid eyes loomed out of black sockets.

'Now this paper,' Carlo folded it and then again until it was nothing more than a small square and handed it to the boy. 'You will give this to the person you will be delivered to.'

'Who is it?' he asked.

'You don't need a name, but you will recognise when you see him. If anyone else finds you, place it in your cheek so,' he indicated, slipping it between his back teeth and cheek. 'No-one must ever find it, except....' he indicated without words. Glancing at the women, Carlo frowned, turning back to the young man.

'If you should meet a girl whose name is "Sofia", tell her, her Papa waits.'

Carlo faced the women, 'You two, go to bed, don't return until the morning.' He turned to Mia, 'Tell Maria nothing of this do you hear,' Mia shrank back.

'Mamma it's for all our safety, you understand it is very serious,' Bianca reassured her trembling mother.

*

Daylight came, both women exhausted, as on many other days. The kitchen was clean when they entered, a healthy fire burned in the courtyard with timber and waste, their larder more sparse than ever. Bianca looked at her mother.

'Do you think Papa would let us take the blame if Angelo's presence was discovered?' Her mother's expression told her everything; he would not suffer for the deeds of others, even for family.

Mia busied herself with breakfast, no trace of the night remained, except that charred in their minds.

315

Chapter 67

Trieste, Italy, April 1945

Bianca saw the rotund, waddling figure of the Monsignor
exit the front gates followed by his young Deacon, an
unknown swarthy character following. The young minister
struggled with a large heavy parcel as the stranger strolled
confidently behind, one hand permanently clutching
something inside his right jacket pocket.

'Mamma why aren't Monsignor, or the Deacon,
wearing cassocks today? I didn't think they had such things
as suits.' Vittorio entered the kitchen silently, Bianca
jumped as he appeared at her side.

'For safety's sake daughter, the Slav partisans would
kill an Italian Catholic as quickly as a Royalist or fascist,
never mind Italian partisan.' He looked to his wife and
clicked his fingers,

'Coffee Mia.'

'Who's the other man, I've never seen him with the
Monsignor before?' Bianca asked.

'You ask a lot of questions, is it good to know so
much?' he clipped.

'Sorry Papa, just a general interest in our welfare,
nothing more. I don't mean to impose.'

For a moment she thought of all the times he had
been happy for her to wander the Karst without concern for
her safety, but sensed a change in his attitude. He took his
usual place at the head of the table waiting for his cup.
Bianca noticed no swagger as he sat in silence.

'Come sit before the boys come.' He ordered them
with less authority than usual, taking the steaming coffee.
Bianca looked at her mother, something had, or was about
to happen, her chest tightening. Vittorio looked down at the
table and spoke.

'The Monsignor was collecting some documents, and....' he hesitated, searching for an appropriate explanation, '.... and some properties of the Cathedral that he had deposited in my safe keeping, articles of the highest importance he needed to secure away from German looters.'

'What Papa?' She bit her lip at her impertinence. He ignored her boldness, not being of his usual temperament.

'Ancient gold plate used for the Blessed Sacrament, it needed to be saved at all cost, but now....'

'Now what Papa?'

'Bianca don't trouble your father, he needs his rest,' Mia responded with her usual appeasement when he needed soothing.

'No wife, she needs to know, you both do.' The women sat motionless, not even looking at each other, waiting for whatever news he was keeping.

'He is leaving the area for safety, the Deacon will be left in his place, the other man to accompany our esteemed priest to a place of safety.'

'I thought the Deacon looked nervous, he is so young,' she couldn't help herself.

'Yes, daughter, the unthinkable has happened.' He looked up at their anxious faces. 'Two days ago Il Duce attempted to leave the place where he was protected by the Germans, and fell into the hands of anti-fascist Italian partisans.' Mia's gasps punctuated every detail. 'As you know, communication has not always been reliable of late, and today the Monsignor informed me the leader of our nationalist dream is no more.' Even Bianca was incapable of comment. Her mother whispered what they needed to know.

'And he is dead?'

'Yes wife, Il Duce was strung up like a dead cat by his feet, his woman too. It appears the crowd showed no mercy

317

to either and they hang now from lamp-posts in a suburban piazza of Milan.'

Mia stumbled to the coffee pot, placing two more cups on the table. He looked around at his timorous wife and rebellious daughter, two extremes of womanhood both silent, motionless except for Mia's trembling hands.

'Mia my dear, my daughter ....' he had never addressed them with such sensitivity before, and Bianca's chest contracting at the irrationality of it, the world turning to nonsense, what else could befall them. 'Much is happening in the world, the Slav partisans have arrested hundreds, even thousands.' She thought of the white-haired boy crouched at their door a short time ago. 'They will show no mercy in consolidating their position over Trieste. The word is, Italian partisans are joining forces with the Allies to push the Germans out, our city still to be secured and you must be aware, the communists will stop at nothing to make it theirs.' She found her voice at last.

'Papa, I was born in Opicina, it was Slovene before Italian Territory, and Mamma's parents lived in Croatia, can't we build our defence against the Slav threat on that?'

'We will play any card we can, and it is up to us to play them well. The boys cannot be exposed at any time, they cannot be involved in anything, it is we three who hold their fate in our hands, especially you two.'

It was difficult to take in his words. He, as always, put his safety above theirs, and now she and her mother were responsible to protect the whole family.

'Bianca, Mia, the Allies continue to approach, they are in our province as we speak, will reach our beautiful city soon, their soldiers will base down the hill at Montebello barracks no doubt.' He looked at the conflicted, terrified faces of wife and daughter. 'They are almost at our door as I speak,' he slammed his fist down, shaking the women out of their torpor. 'We proceed with caution, treat them with respect, they may command our future if the communists do not command it first.'

Their evening meal progressed as normal, her brothers noticing little of the subdued atmosphere.

'Papa we were in the grounds earlier, there was an exodus from the barracks, Germans loading the train with goods and weapons and then everything went quiet,' Benito commented without much concern.

Luca added, 'Soldiers were leaving the garrison, some were at the railway station.' His bespectacled face looked up, 'they rushed down and caught the last trucks at the barracks, leaving their equipment on the train.' The three adults considered his unusually long discourse. 'I'm not sure they all got away.' Vittorio took the lead.

'It is not our concern, it is their business boys, we will carry on as we always do,' the conversation terminated.

*

Another sleepless night as Bianca's mind floated to her German friend who had saved her from San Sabba's slaughter, and the guard who was shot in the face outside. She never found out who he was, but had never seen her friend again after that day. She tried to tell herself, what was it to do with her? She remembered the innocent Swiss medics who had saved and sheltered her, then shot by the Slavs, murdered. Her dearest friend Sofia spirited away somewhere. Her heart and mind now impenetrable. Never again would anyone breach the wall around her, built by the savage unfettered cruelty of war.

A mammoth eruption shook the building, a red white flash filled the night, acrid air bursting glass from every window. She rushed to her favourite spot overlooking the city, the family in quick pursuit. A mile away flares of fire and smoke rose from San Sabba. A hush across the city amplified revving engines, this time German vehicles escaping the city, a sick parody of their previous murderous use.

Vittorio ushered the boys back to bed as the women stood, transfixed. Throughout the city, dim lights flickered, other citizens at the windows of their homes.

'It's over,' Mia whispered, 'No more engines to drown out the cries. No more the stench of burning bodies, the Germans have blown the place to hell.'

Bianca turned to her mother, as usual clutching Mater Dolorosa at her neck, so much to bear.

Chapter 68

North East Italy, April 1945

Sappers spilled out of the truck, followed by parts of the Skid Bailey. The engineer, first to jump down, rushed to the chasm that barred the Eighth Army's progress, quickly surveying the situation.

'Another crevice, another day,' Ted jumped down to join his colleagues.

You six, get over there.' The officer was eager to rectify the situation. 'There's sufficient bank to act as a platform to roll out the span. One'll do it.' Ted ran over to wait for the Bailey Bridge section trucks that bumped and rattled across the mountainous terrain, dry spring dust along the road indicating their progress.

As the first one swung around presenting the mechanics with easy access, a call was yelled in the soldiers' direction getting no response. As a general practice they were used to tuning in only to relevant instructions.

'Oy, what you gonna do when you get home?'

Like an animal alerted to alien activity, Ted's back straightened.

'You son of a gun Ted, you forgot your old mate from the desert?'

He spun around, straining his eyes at the truck's cab, listening for that Welsh inflection. Barely visible above the steering wheel the cocked beret of a familiar face bobbed as he wrenched up the hand brake and jumped out.

'Taffy mate, fancy seeing you here,' Ted rushed to greet his old friend, companion of desert morning ablutions, 'where've you been?'

'Where haven't I been, more like,' Taff replied, they slapped shoulders, recalling shared hardships and kinship. 'Brought you a Bailey Bridge, me old mate,' he said.

'Last I saw of you was your boots disappearing into the back of a truck. You must have got to Italy before me,' Ted chuckled.

'So what are you doing here with the engineers?' Taff asked.

'Transferred to REME mate, they recognised my mechanical talents obviously,' he laughed, sending himself up, adding a couple of old jokes for old time's sake, until ordered to jump to it and get on with the job.

The crevice was quickly bridged, with troops moving swiftly towards the next breach. Ted approached his old mate as Taff revved his truck ready to go, shouting down.

'Where you off to now Ted, mate?'

'Couldn't tell you even if I knew,' Ted chuckled.

'Same old Welsh Baptist,' Taff laughed. 'We're off to the border with the Slavs, some fancy city called "Tresty" I think. The Nazis are trying to skedaddle and the Commies are trying to take over they tell us. Now there's another kettle of fish if you ask me.'

'Same old Taff, blabbing all over the place,' Ted countered laughing. After sharing the terrors of battle in North Africa, banter bound them together again. Taff leaned down from his cab, as Ted stretched up and the pair grasped each-others fists.

'Get ourselves a lovely signorina each, eh?' Taff winked teasing, knowing the good looking lad never confident in the pursuit of ladies.

'Aye, if you like,' Ted looked at the ground.

At that moment trucks barrelling onto the Bailey bridge beside them, hitting the sharp wooden incline with a bounce. Officers dashed by in a line of Land Rovers followed by a NAAFI truck, notable by the tins of bully beef and plumb duff ricocheting out the back, landing at Ted's feet.

'And that's another good reason for being in REME,' he winked, 'the perks.' He laughed picking up the spoils as

322

the trucks thundered away. With no time to spare he tossed a tin of plum duff and another of stewed prunes up at his friend.

'See you in 'Tresty' then mate, Ted called.

'Ciao,' Taff shouted, hand waving from the cab window as he drove away.

*

Within days Ted's Eighth Army Corp, along with New Zealand Allies, had encountered President Tito's communist partisans, engaging in combat, with one of their own getting "It".

'Can't believe he'd come all this way through the war for a sniper to take him out like that,' Scouse lamented as they ate, breaking the cold silence. They had received so many tumultuous welcomes along the way from Italian citizens. Progressing fast the New Zealand Allies had charged ahead towards Trieste, yet as they had approached from a point in Slovenia one lone gunman, secreted in the crevices of the Karst, had delivered the fatal shot. Ted tried to change the subject.

'You notice the retreating Italians hadn't destroyed any tunnels in the mountains? They're happy to see us, want us to get at the Bosch and sort things out?'

'What about today?' Scouse was still thinking about the madness. 'I mean, entering that village the partisans were chanting *"Down with Tito and communists, up with the Allies"*. Then in the next village, yelling, *"Destroy Royalist partisans, hurray for America and England"*. It's not easy knowing who the enemy is.' A mutter of agreement from Ted accompanied his concentration as he failed to open his newly acquired booty of bully beef with only a knife.

'I suppose it will all come out in the wash,' Ted added, slurping the last of the syrup out of his rare find, a tin of peaches.

'Okay you wasters, on your feet, you're moving out first thing. You're on your holidays boys.' The group looked up at the NCO, bemused. He clarified.

'You've to take equipment and trucks back tomorrow.

'Where to?' a lone voice asked.

'Wherever you're told, son,' the sergeant replied with the inevitable.

*

By the end of the next day, Ted and the complement of soldiers had redistributed their equipment as required, and were billeted on the coast overlooking a calm, enticing, Adriatic Sea.

'What time is it?' someone piped up.

'Time for tea?' another shouted, adopting an upper-class accent.

'Maybe we have the opportunity to partake of a wee dip,' a gravelly Scot's voice rolled over the top of the group, like broken glass.

Ted, duties completed, he made his way to the beach in time to see his mates running out to sea, starkers. Sergeants on the promenade talked together, ignored the spectacle, and he recognised the horseplay was sanctioned, and stripped down to his underpants. A couple of hundred feet out he could see someone floating on his back calling him, as he ran through cool ankle-deep foam, evening sunshine skimming over the tranquil waters. A hand waved again, 'Come on in, it's just like Llandudno,' and he recognised Taff's laughing face.

Ahead, a soldier, having seen Taff floating had decided to join in, his bare backside followed a graceful dive, only to break into angry splashing and cussing as Taff stood up, shallow water lapping around his knees. Looking at Ted, he shouted.

'I walked for half an hour and it's still only halfway up my hairy legs.' The rest of the soldiers, recognising they wouldn't be able to hide their nakedness, grasped their embarrassment and ran back to shore for underwear.

Before long they were all floating in 18 inches of water, splashing and relaxing. For a brief moment, the war drifted somewhere far away.

Taff made his way over to Ted, using his hands as paddles on the sea bed, 'It's all kicking off in Trieste mate, the New Zealanders have been called in. The Nazis left won't surrender to anyone but them.'

'How do you find all this out Taff, you're one step ahead all the time? Are you getting a paper delivered?'

'No-one notices a short-arse mate. I keep my head down and ears flapping,' he winked at Ted.

'So that's where we're off to next then, Trieste?'

'Aye, like I said before, get ourselves beautiful signorinas.'

'Have some decorum Taff,' he tried to hide his painful shyness with distracting splashing, 'these people have been through enough to step out with the likes of us.'

Chapter 69

Trieste, Italy, June 1945

Benito lounged on his bed, studying an American film starlet in the well-fingered magazine before him. Bianca entered and wandered to the window overlooking the courtyard.

'They're still out there. I wonder who'll be sentry tomorrow,' she spoke to him without reply.

Scrutinising the gate she saw three Slovene partisans, two young men and a woman, all dressed the same with guns slung on shoulders, ammunition bandoliers across their chest in an ominous X. The family had woken that day to the rapid crack of gunfire, as their new guards shot randomly into the hill for fun. Communist Slavs were attempting to consolidate control of the city, dictating Italian citizens' rise from slumber any time they wished.

'What a ragged bunch,' the indiscrete words escaped her, and she shot a look at her brother. He took no notice, luridly examining the swim-suited woman in the photograph, tracing a finger down her leg, eyes glazed, concentration elsewhere.

'Benito, I need to go to the market.'

'So?' he flicked to another page.

'Mamma needs you to go with me,' she paused, 'for my safety,' she kicked the bedstead leg.

'Go on your own, I'm busy,' he laid back to better appreciate the image of the pouting actress, holding it above his face.

'Cretino!' she adopted her most imperious pout and slammed the door as she left.

On the stair Luca was sitting with a wooden ashtray he had fashioned in his workshop, turning it over, checking for imperfections.

'Luca, will you come to the market with me? Mamma says there is talk of food getting through, despite disputes amongst Tito's communists,' she looked over her shoulder indicating the sentries outside adding, 'and the Allies.' Luca's expression, a mixture of surprise and anxiety, he remained silent.

'Please Luca, I need to go and the British are in Montebello Garrison now, while they sort out who is in charge of what. They call out to any woman in the vicinity and I really can't stand it, I'm sick to my stomach with it all.'

Luca looked at his sister; pale grey damp eyes, the once confident rebel of the family no longer wandering the Karst with pluck and adventure in her veins. She had shut the world out, alone, hardly even speaking any more. Pity overruled any concern for his safety.

'I can do that,' he mumbled, not looking up, checking the underside of his creation again. 'We go now?' peering emotionless through his spectacles.

'Grazie tanto, thank you so much,' she responded.

'Don't get excited, it is only the market,' her young brother's reserved nature stabilising her.

At the kitchen, she collected a hessian bag and they made their way out. Avoiding the over-excited Slovene partisans at the gate they crept to the break in the fence. As they reached the path above Sofia's home she looked back to see her father slapping the back of two of the guards, camera in hand. He positioned himself between the two men, friendly hands on their shoulders, face beaming. The girl partisan, having been excluded, was assigned to record the auspicious event. Bianca felt like spitting, but at least he was keeping them occupied.

It was usually too painful to peer at the windows of Sophia's house to see if she had returned, and Maria would turn her away if she asked. But that day was different, as they came alongside the front door it opened, Roberto stepping out. She stopped, emotions rising. What could it mean? Was her friend home? His face told another story.

'Ciao?' she hesitated a greeting. He lifted his head wearily.

'Hello Bianca,' and fell silent.

She searched for the words that would tell her Sofia was safe, they two happy together. He looked down at worn boots, then glancing up recognized a fellow lost soul.

'And Sofia?' she couldn't contain herself, Roberto turned slowly towards her.

'She loves another,' his broken heart reached out. 'We were in the Apennines, working undercover, trying to deter German progress in any way we could. I wouldn't let her come with me on a mission, made her stay in camp for her safety, and my caution destroyed our love.' He looked up and she saw his pain as he continued. 'I'm back in the café. My mother's relieved, the strain has all but destroyed father, and Sofia....' He looked at his feet, muscly shoulders hunched, hardly audible, 'And Sofia was seduced by another. Taken from me while I fought.'

She was shocked, it was unspoken they would marry one day and she had been unfaithful to her protector, her love? How the war had changed them all.

'I am so sorry Robert. Maybe in the future, you will find it was for the best,' she attempted.

'She changed Bianca, wasn't the girl I knew, but I loved her anyway,' forehead furrowing.

Luca's scuffle intruded.

'I will have to go, Roberto. Will Sofia visit?' she asked.

'I doubt you will see her soon. I've given her mother the address of his family.'

'Maybe I could....?' She turned towards the house.

'You are not allowed Bianca. Maria still believes you are the architect of her daughter's ruin, and now I am the cause of her banishment with a stranger.'

They parted, he over rough ground and railway line towards home, she and Luca to the underpass.

'Thank you for coming, Luca, it's hard for me,' she said.

His eyes still to the floor kicking early summer earth with his sandal, 'I know.'

For the first time Bianca understood he was aware of the world around him. He had always avoided involvement in anything, feigning lack of understanding or interest, a little boy when the war started, never really stopping the pretence.

As they turned to pass the barracks, newly occupied by stronger, better fed British soldiers, the calls began as a group of girls passed the garrison before them.

'Hey bella signorina, you wanna go danza?' accompanied by whistles and whoops, and, 'mio bene uomo.'

'He's a good man?' Luca chuntered, 'They're neither handsome nor have manners. How could any girl find them attractive?' he huffed.

'And it doesn't matter what they say, they're not engineers like Papa, either,' Bianca added.

As they approached, she prepared herself for a barrage of calls for her attention. Despite Luca's company, she knew it wouldn't stop and she adopted her most disdainful manner to put them off. Throwing her hair back, an open upper window caught her attention. A tall, bare-chested soldier stood. A handsome face with piercing blue eyes and beautiful lips quietly looked down. He never moved, watching quietly. Handsome as Cary Grant, shy as Gary Cooper she thought, bashful, natural and gentle, improbable markers to cause pain or distress. He mesmerised her.

329

Part III

Chapter 70

Trieste, Italy, Summer 1945

Domestic duties the following day were enriched by thoughts of the divine man at the window as her mind wandered gracefully thinking of him. The brief glimpse inspired thoughts of his name, life, home, every imagining, surrounding that one vision. Annoyingly, Lola's bark from the courtyard interrupted her. The communists now thankfully gone, along the path outside the compound, a small detail of British soldiers were marching up the hill, led by a tall, smart soldier, fresh in the rising heat of the summer. Lola followed their progress along the inside of the fence, ensuring they were fully aware she guarded her terrain well.

She gasped. Beautiful lips parted, the soapy dish in her hands slipped from motionless fingers. He was there, directing soldiers, conjured up in the flesh. Agreement must have been reached between Slavs and Allied officers at last, British troops to guard her home, no more waking to random gun fire. Transfixed she traced his route to their entrance gate, blood rushing to her neck, lips swelling, eyes narrowing at this extraordinary deliverance.

Her mother bustled in, 'What is that dog doing?' She moved behind her daughter to view the scene, as tiny Lola continued to stand her ground against the interlopers.

'Go and get her, she is causing a fuss, we mustn't annoy the soldiers.' Bianca hesitated on the landing, biting her bottom lip. She had encountered many soldiers and factions, enticing what she could from them, leaving before they could get what they wanted from her, it had become a way of life then, but something had changed. Descending the stairs, her heart raced, not with the usual tightening fear, somehow this time her breath full and steady, chest expanded in anticipation. It was unsettling, unfamiliar, she wanted to see the handsome man, but uncertain all the same. Inhaling deeply and smoothing her blouse and skirt, she unconsciously ran fingers through her permanent wave, fumbling with the curls, shaking them free and opened the door.

Stepping into sunshine, her confidence failed and she walked directly towards Lola, who continued to harangue the intruders as they presented for duty. The dog bounced and skittered between the soldiers as they continued to ignore it. Bianca, bending to grasp the dog, two lightly tanned muscular arms scooped the animal up. Lola adopted a new strategy, wriggling to affectionately lick her captor. She traced the arms to strong shoulders, a smooth neck and sun-kissed dark hair crowning flawless skin and crystal blue eyes. It was the handsome man. She hesitated as he proffered the now affectionate dog, his eyes locked upon hers.

The moment seemed to last an undefinably long time until he reached forward to place the docile pet into her arms. As he gently rolled the animal into her embrace, his little finger lightly brushed the inside of her arm, her soft gaze widening as a tingle ran through her body. He took half a step backwards.

'Sorry. I mean, sorry....' She shook her head at the strange, foreign words. He took another half step backwards.

'I didn't mean to...' She stared up into the shy, embarrassed face, all she wanted was to touch the tender being before her but, unnerved by the energy between them spun around and dashed for the front door, Lola whining softly, wriggling to re-join her new friend.

'What happened there?' Alone now, Taff backed into the sentry box, already cupping a cigarette in the palm of his hand.

'Oh, God.' Ted was visibly distraught, 'I was passing her the dog, and accidentally stroked her arm.

'Good for you, boyo, 'bout time.'

'No nothing like that, it was an accident.'

'She's a beauty alright, a lucky accident I'd say.'

'She's stunning.' Ted was still looking at the closed door, 'I've never seen anyone like her before, not in the whole of Italy,' babbling, as Taff looked on, grinning. Then as a perfect accompaniment to her retreat, he turned and marched smartly back down the hill.

'See you later, lover boy,' Taff called, drawing satisfactorily on his cig.

*

A couple of days later Taff was on guard duty again when the beauty came out to collect eggs, neither looking at him nor acknowledging his existence. As she went to re-enter he whistled at her. She tossed him a savage pout and turned away.

'Oy lady, come here,' he gestured extravagantly. Bianca couldn't understand this strange new language, but offered the benefit of her company, and slowly walked to the sentry box, Taff's eager face awaiting. When she reached him, he leaned into the back retrieving a parcel and note, and handed them to her.

'Che cosa?' He had no idea what she was saying but pursuing his quest, he shoved it at her. Bianca took the package and seeing two tins of peaches inside, opened the note.

"Sorry if I upset you. Best regards, Ted". Underneath in another hand, a roughly written translation, "Scusa se ti ho turbato, Saluti, Ted".

She looked at the short soldier before her, pointing at him.

'No not me' he gesticulated violently, 'him'. He raised his voice in translation and pointed down the hill making woofing noises.

Realising the handsome man had sent her a gift, she smiled coyly. It was an apology. An apology for a wonderful moment she would never forget.

*

The next evening Ted stalked up the hill towards Taff's sentry box, clearly an unwilling visitor, as his mate grinned.

'So what's the problem, why did you need me here of all places?' shuffling from one foot to the other.

'Now then mate, it's your job to keep an eye on me, isn't it?'

Ted was off duty but well turned out, as usual.

'True.'

As the word left his mouth, the entrance door to the living quarters opened and he flinched. First, a pretty ankle emerged, followed by a slim well-turned calf. He looked anxiously to Taff, who grinned in reply.

'What's she doing here?' clasping and unclasping his fists.

'She wants to say thank you for the tins of peaches you gave her, you know, to say sorry.' Ted's face flickered rapidly from bewilderment to horror.

'What have you done?'

'Well, I knew you wanted to, so I just moved things on a bit, can't wait forever for you to make a move,' Taff winked.

'I wasn't going to make a move ....'

'Exactly Ted mate, so I did it for you.'

The beautiful woman stepped down from the front step and paused.

Better go over then, she was very pleased with the note.' Ted spluttered a cough, he was cornered. The beautiful young woman was looking at him.

'Go on, don't keep her waiting.'

He steadied himself and walked awkwardly towards her. Taff watched from the sentry box as they smiled nervously at each other.

The couple took to the wooden bench at the side of the door, below a window where the face of the formidable manager looked down with a woman. He searched his breast pocket for another fag to give the young couple a bit of privacy, and himself a well-earned break. *'Definitely a well brought up girl'*, he thought, *'hope Teddy boy can handle them two'* looking up at her parents. He chuckled, thinking of the shy straight-laced Yorkshire lad from a poor background. *'Well, he'll have fun finding out'*. He relaxed into another smoke as Ted's fun-loving personality started to emerge, and she laughed.

Above, Vittorio turned to his wife.

'Who knows how long these Allies will remain, but, as long as they are here, we have a contact for supplies.' He turned to leave as Mia looked at her daughter's relaxed face, happy for the first time in so long, and a ghost of a memory haunted her, sadness dashing across her heart.

Chapter 71

Trieste, Italy, late Summer 1945

Bianca continued smiling softly at him, and his confidence grew. As well as army duties there, he found himself drawn to the compound more and more. Looking into her grey misty eyes at dusk as she threw back her head, the setting sun reflecting golden threads in her hair, he had never experienced such intoxication, and wondered how she could be interested in him.

He had watched comrades take to bordellos, as he gravitated to the company of faithful husbands until pals emerged satisfied. Not for him cheap gratification, and now this exquisite woman offered herself in pure innocence, his reward.

'Teddy,' she pointed at him, 'mangiare,' gesturing food to her mouth and pointing at the small plate in her hand. Taff passed sentry duty watching them as the charades began, sitting a little closer to each other, acting out scenes from the day, occasional English and Italian words exchanged. Then walking around the compound, as they turned the corner out of sight fingers entwined. Taff would sink back into the sentry box lighting his first fag of the shift, satisfied it was he that brought about this connection with the sultry beauty.

'At last,' he muttered, 'and about time too.'

*

Then one evening it was different. Ted made his way up the hill, his uniform crisper than usual, carefully carrying a gift of tinned spotted dick, and a plucked chicken. Entering the compound he followed her, disappearing through the front door which closed with a cool, sharp snap. From his post,

Taff could hear Ted's army boots clipping up the tiled stairs, fading into the distance.

As the evening progressed, chatter seeped from the open kitchen window accompanied by the clatter of dishes, and delicious aromas of Italian food. *'Lucky bugger,Ted old mate,'* Taff chuntered, *'Never thought it would go this far.Wonder what he'll get for dessert?'* and chuckled.

*

Over the weeks Ted and Bianca spent more and more time together between duties. After dark one night, curiosity got the better of Taff, and creeping to the corner he saw Bianca leaning out of an upper window, her hair cascading over her face as she giggled to Ted below. She dangled a long white cord down the side of the building to him, and he tied a small handful of cigarettes in a careful bundle. Stifling giggles she pulled the little parcel up to her window, jiggling it over the windowsill disappearing until a white puff of smoke emerged on the warm night breeze from dark pouting lips. In the moonlight, her moist tongue sought a fragment of tobacco on her lower lip that escaped the draw. A little finger gently rubbed along the pout, seeking the shameful spec, flicked off by the tip of her tongue.

Taff withdrew to his sentry box to sit it out until Ted made his way back towards the gate.

'You've got it made there haven't you, mate? She's a right harddwch, right enough she is,' he quipped.

'What you talking about Taff?' Ted replied.

'It's Welsh for "beauty". You've got yourself a right one there for sure. And the family taking you into the bosom of their home....'

Ted watched his friend's slightly crestfallen face looking at the ground, as he stubbed out another fag.

'What's eating you, Taff?'

'You've got it all haven't you Ted, a stunning woman who's got it hard for you.' Ted looked back dumbfounded.

'Well you have haven't you,' he continued. 'Don't look so surprised, mate, she doesn't pass the time of day with any of us does she?'

'She's probably just being nice,' he tried to justify the unlikely.

'For Christ's sake Ted, you're in with them now, round there all the time, eating at their table, and them not much to give away. You've been invited into the heart of the family, and it's no ordinary one either. That father of hers is no man to be trifled with, a rod of iron worse than the Army. If he's let you get your feet under the table, you're on to a good thing.'

Ted was stunned, trying to collate his thoughts and feelings. 'I supposed they were just being pleasant, we're the ones who've helped liberate them.'

'Not quite yet,' Taff butted in, 'don't forget the bodies found every morning, or rifle battles in the distance. This ain't like other outposts of Italy, mate, the war's still going on around here.'

'Well, all I'm trying to say is,' Ted faltered, 'I don't think they're being anything else but obliging, under the circumstances.'

'And Bianca? You think she spends all her time looking out the window to see you coming up the hill, just to be obliging.'

'What?'

'You heard. I've watched her see you go, and hang out of the kitchen window to catch the first glimpse of you coming up as well. For Christ's sake man, it's not just for a few ciggies and no mistake. Think about it.'

Ted left, scanning the upper windows as he made his way down to the barracks, Bianca nowhere to be seen. But Taff had given him something to think about. It was true he lost himself in her eyes, in her presence, went along with anything she suggested, even the daunting act of joining her family for dinner. She seemed to be in his head, all

337

reason and self-control lost. He never imagined there was a chance of anything serious, knew painfully well how elevated her family were, how refined and cultured their home, with a woman down the hill doing their washing. His Mam would be the person doing that he reckoned.

At the underpass, he thought of how far he'd come from the lonely, starving, days in the fireless rooms of his childhood. An NCO now, respected for his devotion to duty and gratified by the appreciation the Army had shown for his hard work and mechanical talent. A sudden clarity washed through him. Being invited into Bianca's family circle had flattered him, thinking it only their wish to appease the current invaders, but Taff's words burrowed deeper, she didn't need to spend so much time with him. All at once he was honest with himself.

He'd never thought a world existed where he could be so fortunate, captivated from the first time he'd seen her as she had passed below the barracks that day. She'd seemed unwilling to draw attention to herself, but there was no mistake, as she turned her head towards his window that day, he bare-chested, lean and strong from hard work, something happened. Her eyes had met his, a connection made, and only now he allowed himself the indulgence of accepting it. Her gaze had penetrated his being that day, denying him release, never shifting her eyes from his. Then, when they met again in the compound, she passed her need deep into his heart, obvious to everyone but him.

For the first time, he understood the unconditional love of a woman.

Chapter 72

Trieste, Italy, late Summer 1945

'Invite the Englishman to dine, Bianca, he may give us another chicken to enjoy.' She looked to her father as he read the newspaper, sipping his morning coffee, his good mood encouraged her.

'There is an American film at the cinema in Trieste, Papa. Ted has said he will take me if I wish.'

'What do you mean, how has he asked you? You don't speak the same language.' Her father redefined their relationship in a sentence.

'He showed me a newspaper cutting. Anyway, we can speak.' She pulled away from the table, bracing herself for defeat, when suddenly Luca spoke.

'They talk with acting gestures, and exchange words.' Everyone looked at him. Hardly a word ever left his lips even to his family, yet here he was interjecting on her behalf. He continued.

'You know, she says "pane" and he will say "bread"; or he will say "hot" and she will say back "caldo",' he muttered, shrugging.

'You will not walk out with an English soldier. It is sufficient that we invite him into our home.' Her father had decreed.

'Do you only allow that for the gifts? He is a good man, you have said it yourself.' She couldn't contain her disappointment as he continued to read.

'I want to see an American film.' For a second time, Luca stunned the group at the breakfast table. 'It is a cowboy story and I haven't seen one before, I'll go with her instead.' Bianca's heart raced, wondering, could it be an opportunity to engineer a meeting between them.

'I suppose I could take him,' she faltered with little enthusiasm, 'we could go to the afternoon matinee.'

Her father folded his newspaper precisely, placed it next to his plate, drained the last drops of coffee slowly, straightened his shirt, drawing out his judgement as long as possible it seemed.

'Maybe,' he hesitated, 'and, maybe I will come too.'

Bianca looked to Luca, who nodded, imperceptibly.

'That's fine, it will be a day out for us all Papa, an American film too, another gift from the Allies,' she said.

The room emptied and Luca lifted the breakfast plates to Bianca at the sink.

'Don't worry sister, he will never attend a cinema full of foreigners and children,' assuming his usual hunched posture.

'You are a wonderful brother,' she whispered.

'You are my sister,' he said simply, and with a slight inflection of his shoulders, retreated to a workshop.

*

The afternoon arrived, and Bianca and Luca made their way down the path, fully aware eyes from the power station followed them, until out of sight under the railway bridge. There they turned left towards Piazza dei Foraggio, avoiding the barracks, allowing anyone who followed them the opportunity to see their innocent course, and return to tell her father.

'Luca you are my perfect little brother, thank you for this,' Bianca could hardly contain her excitement. He shrugged, 'No problem,' hands deep in pockets, eyes to the ground as usual.

'Why are you doing this for me?' she asked.

He looked dolefully through his dark-rimmed spectacles frowning. 'You're my sister.'

'But you have taken a risk to help me. Papa will not be pleased if he discovers the deception.'

340

An uncharacteristically angry reply reminded her, he was his father's son.

'We are going to the cinema to see a cowboy film. I can't be responsible for what happens in the dark while I'm watching John Wayne.' The conversation abruptly closed indicating his involvement ended at the foyer, from then on, she was on her own.

For a moment his snapped retort replaced her growing excitement, until she spotted the silhouette of her tall, fine, English soldier outside the cinema.

'Ciao Bianca' he had been practising, 'come sta? "How are you?' Bianca threw her head back in delight. Every time the exquisite man attempted Italian for her, he added the English translation even if he'd got it wrong, and always accompanied by an earnest expression.

'Ciao Ted,' her fingers crept towards his, as Luca interrupted.

'Herrumh,' he broke between them, groping for money in his pocket.

'Tickets.' Ted produced three stubs without attempting any Italian translation.

'Molto grazie Teddy,' she pointed at him beaming and grasped at the tickets. Luca, was having none of this public show of affection and pulled her hand away, gabbling quickly in words only she understood. She was shocked again by his outburst, reminded of the risk they were taking, and cautiously glanced over her shoulder to see if they were being watched. In her smart homemade cotton dress she suddenly felt foolish. Luca took command and grabbed the tickets, stuffed one back into Ted's hand and clutching the other two pushed his sister into the darkness of the cinema ahead of him. As he guided her away, just before disappearing, the youngster's face peaked out through the double doors nodding his head for Ted to follow.

Inside, the movie world enveloped them to another place of mystery, excitement and untold wonders. Ted found himself standing alone next to Bianca as Luca scurried to a prime seat in the middle of the circle. Together alone at last she took his hand; it was trembling. Looking up she saw glistening blue eyes shine back. Together they made their way to the back row where lovers met, new romances blossomed and old ones reignited in the magical world of fantasy. There were two other couples, seated wide apart at either end of the row. As she stepped over the feet of the first, a movement took her by surprise as Signor Photographer's startled eyes looked up. She noted his companion, a young woman hardly older than herself, and clearly not his wife. It hardly registered as she positioned herself and Ted at the optimum distance between the two pairs. Over his shoulder, as she made herself comfortable, she saw Signor Photographer's sheepish expression in the flashing opening credits of the film.

Within minutes she slid her slim body into the hollow of Ted's arm, snuggling ever closer, until his hand slipped over her shoulder embracing the warmth of her bare arm, his touch gentle, protective, as her fingers reached up to his.

Safe and comfortable they rested in the double seat as cowboys dashed across the screen, horses were abruptly pulled up to a halt, and guns were drawn. Darkness fell on the desert as she rolled her head across to his shoulder, looking up into his face. Eyes glistening, her longing drew him nearer, warm lips meeting, gently at first, then without restraint. Her sun-kissed hand reached up, tender fingers stroked his neck, her mouth open, his eyes flickering with cautious passion. As her eyes closed, her hand lightly brushed his neck, turning into a tender talon skimming the surface of his skin. He tingled uncontrollably with desire, her strong fingers driving deep into his hair, grasping almost to pain. As he pulled her closer, her hips followed undaunted, her slight frame rolled almost onto his, feeling her join with him, no secret concealing their shared desire. The moment was theirs as he submitted, the film, crowd, worries and punishments no longer existed as Ted's arm pressed her ever closer, his thighs resisting her eager body.

*

As closing titles rolled, Luca was the first to rise in the auditorium, making a great business of the film ending, and hesitating in the aisle until his sister was by his side. They hung back until Ted left with the others.

Signor Photographer took no such precautions as he emerged with the girl clutching his arm as she giggled up at him. His attitude changed in the bright afternoon sunlight, and he strove to shake her free, a familiar figure at the kerb.

'Ciao,' there was no hope to avoid. The man by the road nodded, a thumb of one hand hung from his waistcoat pocket, revealing a blood-red satin lining to his jacket, and his other hand held an elegant cigarette, which he studied with interest.

'A good film Signor?' steady eyes turned to the photographer, examining his every move.

'Yes Signor Marchetti, and you did not attend today?'

'Pah! What do I want with painted women, and men's tribulations?' He chose his words well as he stared at the young girl. 'I believe, however, my daughter attended today. My youngest wished to see the cowboys. Did you see her?' And there was the hook.

The Photographer shrugged awkwardly. 'It was dark.'

'Come now, you can do better than that.' Signor Marchetti spoke. The crowd was dispersing, as a few steps away the young woman swung her shoulders side to side clutching her handbag before her.

'I tell you, how would I know where your family are? It's a cinema, it's dark,' he faltered.

343

'You are right of course.' Vittorio paused, 'My wife doesn't like the cinema,' he looked at the young woman, 'it seems your wife doesn't either. Now tell me, did you see my son?' The photographer shuffled, his shoulders starting to droop.

'Yes, maybe. I think I saw him.'

'And my daughter, Bianca, you saw her too?'

'I don't want any trouble, I think she was there too.' A long moment hung in the air as Ted exited onto the street behind him, straightened his uniform and started walking towards the city. Vittorio watched him go.

'You owe me photographer, and this is your time to pay,' fierce eyes bore into him. 'They sat together?'

The photographer looked at his young companion, considering his reply. Defeated, he replied, 'Together, yes.'

'I'm obliged.' Signor Marchetti touched the brim of his hat and made his way back up the hill. The young woman looked up at her companion

'What was that about? I know him, he's not to be scorned I hear.'

'He wanted to know something and in my way, I answered, but didn't.'

'You are so clever,' she giggled, grabbing his sleeve again.

As they walked away, Bianca and Luca appeared in the sunshine. In the distance, their father turned the corner.

'Cretino,' he said aloud to himself, 'Does he think I can't read his barefaced deceit?'

Chapter 73

Trieste, Italy, late Summer 1945

After the cinema, the evening meal proceeded without incident.

The following morning Bianca skipped downstairs to the kitchen, heart so light her toes hardly touched the floor. In the kitchen, Vittorio held up his coffee cup, indicating he required a refill. Her heart was so full with love she placed her hand lightly on his shoulder, leaning forward to serve him.

Placing the cup before him she sat at her place. No sooner had the cup touched his saucer Vittorio shook his paper and carefully folded it.

'Tonight wife, we have a private family dinner.' He paused to let the information reach its target, Bianca turned sharply. He looked away

'We see too much of the Allies and we need to regroup as Italian nationals. No more English at this table.' The family looked at him in various states of interest and confusion.

'But Papa you've always encouraged us to engage with occupying forces, you have encouraged it.' Bianca's heart raced, *'"We aim to reap the rewards of those who seek to dominate us"*, that's what you said.'

'No more.' Vittorio sat with self-satisfied composure.

'You have always taught us to wheedle ourselves within enemy positions, benefit and rule from within ....' she tried, falling back in her chair.

'Precisely.' Vittorio rose, looking down on his daughter, his eyes as cold as she had ever seen and left.

The room cleared as she sat in front of her empty plate. Her mother scurried away on domestic duty, Benito, in his usual louche manner went to his room, only Luca remained saying, 'He knows,' he said.

'But he said nothing last night. I would have expected him to react then, I thought we were safe.' Shocked, she mulled over his words, *"To benefit and rule from within".*

'The devil! He knew all along that I was with Teddy, exacting his revenge in the wickedest way possible. He let me believe our time together was ours alone, perfect, pure with our love. And all the time orchestrating the most malicious and spiteful control over me, denying me the only love and kindness I've ever felt.'

'And me?' Luca remained seated at the end of the table watching his sister's pain, replying in the usual minimal manner, 'I am here too.'

She looked up, her pitiful expression told of love and despair. He was too young to understand, but his once warrior sister was broken again, maybe for the last time.

'Go and lay down Bianca, or sit in the sun. I'll go into town for Mamma,' he nodded in the direction of the barracks.

'You would do that for me?' her heart beat rapidly.

'Of course, you're my sister,' shrugging.

*

On the way, Luca passed Sofia's home. Raised voices seeped out of an open kitchen window and he dragged his feet to listen.

The low tones of Roberto murmured, Maria's voice most prominent, her anger clear, then another less forceful female voice he hardly recognised, it was Sofia. Luca continued down to complete his tasks, and returned with the news as quickly as possible.

Emerging from under the railway bridge and turning right towards Montebello barracks, trucks raced past, converging at the garrison entrance, movement afoot again. They had experienced this so many times, transport, hurried departures, then ransacking the barracks for provisions. With the British on their doorstep, there had been a period of order and calm, hoping it would be permanent. Thinking of Bianca, he rushed to the barracks gate.

Soldiers were amassing kit bags in the courtyard, orderly piles of equipment accumulating. The trucks had lined up along the length of the road. At last, Luca saw the wiry man often smoking on duty at their gate, and yelled, 'Taffs, Taffs.'

He shouted back, 'It's Taff, old mate.'

'Come,' Luca had picked up a few English words himself, gesturing wildly to draw him over.

'Can't stop, we're on the move,' Taff said, a cigarette behind his ear.

Not understanding, Luca gesticulated wildly. 'Ted - where Ted?' Taff ran to the gate.

'I'm busy old mate, we're off to Palmanova. The New Zealanders are coming to sort out this sorry business. Nice knowing you.' He grabbed Luca's hand and shook it, turned and shouted, 'we'll meet again,' and ran off.

Luca understood little, but knew enough to recognise the Brits were leaving. He looked up towards the railway bridge, a heavy goods train rumbling across laden with military equipment and rushed back towards Sofia's house.

As he approached, he could see Roberto in the kitchen. The same age as Bianca, he had the face of a middle-aged man, eyes lost in the devastating experiences of his youth as Maria continued to shout, changed forever since the night Sofia was lost. Luca contemplated the cloistered existence he and Benito had lived, hidden from view within a guarded compound, and wondered whose lives had been damaged the most. Benito lived his life in movie magazines, his own lonely occupation in the workshops. They hadn't experienced the brutality Bianca and Sofia had, but neither had they learned to live, share friendships or bonds, emotionally stunted forever by the war.

He hurriedly raced home. There was big news of comings and goings, but who to tell first? His father would probably already know the Brits were leaving, given his cruel announcement at breakfast. Instead of breaking the news gently, he had chosen to play a game, and break his sister's heart. The decision was made for him.

'Why are you back so early?' Bianca sat listlessly in the weakening sunshine. The Bora was hinting at its yearly visit and Luca realised the sound had blown away the bustle and movement at the barracks below. She sat hunched on the bench she had shared with Ted, a light autumn jacket pulled around her, eyes lost in sadness. He realised she wouldn't know the soldiers were leaving, that maybe Ted had already gone, and it was down to him to tell her. He swallowed hard and made his way to her side. Even in her despair, Bianca saw he had difficult information as he shuffled about. In the corner of her eye, a tear was forming and he knew immediate action was required.

'Well, what is it? Tell me what has happened now?' she asked.

He was motionless for a moment, rising hysteria in her face urging him on; he had to say something but what first, that Sofia was so close, or her love so far away?

'Is it him, what has he done?' she tossed her head towards her father's workplace.

'No, no, but something....' he struggled for the right words as she leapt up, grabbing him.

Despite his immaturity, he understood the whole fabric of her existence was disintegrating.

He recalled when Ted came into their lives the young girl of 1939 had re-emerged in his gentle, kind presence, a saviour from her father. No longer haughty and indifferent, she had become an innocent child once more, clinging to his arm, he bashfully asking nothing of her, she shyly reborn, another chance at living.

'Tell me what has happened!' she demanded. He could avoid it no longer.

'Bianca,' he looked at her wild eyes, 'You must remain calm.' Panic doubled, then, re-doubled in her.

'Please...' she pleaded. The Bora gusted against her chest

'There is bad news,' he hesitated again, 'the English at Montebello barracks, they are moving,' stepping forward to catch her as she trembled.

'But Teddy?'

'He goes to Palmanova, the New Zealanders replace the British.'

Her eyes tore to his, 'When? I must see him.'

Luca shrugged.

Her body convulsed and she ripped herself away from him, and ran towards their front gates.

'It's too late, he has gone,' Luca shouted.

'Never, as long as I live, he is never gone!' There were no sentries at the gate and the realisation registered. No guards meant no soldiers.

'I have time, I can reach him,' she sobbed. A slash of wind slapped her face as she turned down the path that passed Sofia's home. Luca ran after and caught her, grabbing her jacket and swinging her around.

'Another thing,' Bianca's glare said delaying tactics would not stop her. 'Sofia is in the house.'

She broke free, legs tumbling her forward. As the pair reached the house people and words spilled out the front door, Roberto pushing by Maria.

'Get away from here, you spawn of Satan, you took my daughter and now return her to me damaged.' A frail voice spoke from inside.

Bianca stopped dead, her wonderful, lovely, friend was there. She proceeded tentatively as Sophia stepped out.

'Mamma, he is not at fault. You were only too happy to have him take me away from Trieste. What happened next was down to God, and love.' Bianca's heart bent to the words.

'Get back in the house,' Maria screamed, 'you don't know what you are talking about. Love? Hah! What do you know? Walk in the shoes of a mother and you wouldn't talk so lyrically of love then, only of the pain loved ones bestow upon you every day.'

'I am married Mamma, and in the eyes of God I am loved.' Bianca noticed Roberto wince at her words. So, he was not her husband, had risked his life to protect her and was deserted for the act. For a moment she thought of Ted, was this an opportunity for him to abandon her, glad to leave her behind?

Maria stood between Sofia and Roberto, he turned towards her.

'Maria, her husband is missing, believed dead, have compassion,' he shouted above the wind.

A wail followed. 'No, never dead, just missing, and this baby', she cradled her bulging stomach, 'will be here for him when he is found.' Her tears fell, 'His child, his boy. I know it is a boy.' Maria spun round.

'A boy, you know nothing!' she'd lost none of her fire, turning back to Roberto.

Bianca moved quietly forward, raising her hand to touch Sophia when Roberto spoke.

'I came only to say what I have been told,' he said, sad unrequited love still burning. 'I will continue to keep a watch, to try and find out if he can be found and let you know if there is news.' Looking directly at Sofia, 'Only know this,' he hesitated and for a moment, Bianca thought she heard "My love" carried on the wind. 'I will always be here for you Sofia, no matter what. You are my responsibility, I took you from your home, and I will do what I can to keep you safe, as I always have.' He turned to make his way down the hill.

As Bianca leaned forward to touch Sofia's hand, Maria turned, venomous anger seeking another target.

'And you, you dally with any soldier and now you will be abandoned too' waving an arm towards the barracks.

Sofia whispered, 'I am not abandoned, I know I am not. I don't know where my husband is, but he will be found.'

'Sofia, I didn't know you were home,' Bianca added weakly.

Maria spat, 'You didn't know because I kept it from you. You are a bad influence. I don't want you to speak to my daughter.'

Bianca faced her friend's mother. 'You live in your bubble, and ignore the world. There has been no string of soldiers, only Ted and he is a gentleman, a fine, kind generous man, he is everything to me.' She turned to Sofia, 'As Sofia's husband to her.'

'Well he will be gone at any moment, and you will find out for yourself how much he cares about you,' Maria turned to the door pushing her daughter inside. 'Stay away, do you hear, or I'll chase you with a shovel.'

Sofia, war weary, beleaguered, disappeared as her mother pushed her back into the gloom. Bianca caught whispered words from her but heard them clearly.

'Love will have what it needs.'

The phrase tunnelled into her brain, haunting her, repeating over and over, clarifying her pain.

Chapter 74

Trieste, Italy 1945 (minutes later)

Luca dragged his distraught sister to the path by her flimsy jacket, sighing and scowling, more involved in drama than at any other time of the war. A hunched figure sat on a dry pile of dead vegetation down the hill, collar turned up. They stopped short at the sight of Robert drawing on a cigarette, and Bianca went to him. Luca followed with every appearance of a boy frustrated, annoyed and generally fed-up. Carpentry in the tranquil isolation of the workshops seemed a long time ago, and there appeared no point in expecting his sister to stop her quest to find Ted; his patience was wearing thin.

'There's no point going,' Roberto uttered despondently through the smoke.

'What?' Bianca snapped.

'There's no point looking for the English soldier, he's gone. He left with the first cohort, before dawn,' Roberto replied.

'What do you know, tell me,' she demanded as Luca grabbed and pinned her arms to her sides.

Secrets Roberto had heard at German tables in his café, horrors he had witnessed, were etched on his young face, and the habit of collecting information was hard to shake. He had held a pivotal position in partisan activities and seen friends die, even knowing when they would be taken, unavoidable sacrifices to protect their work. His eyes reached hers, their joint pain recognised. Bianca relaxed and Luca moved away from her as she took a place at her old friends' side. When her brother was out of hearing, Roberto spoke.

'Bianca, I'm sorry but he has gone. They have decamped to the old Napoleonic Barracks at Palmanova to make way for the Kiwis in Trieste. They're the only force remaining pockets of Germans will surrender to. You know it would have been out of his hands, he's a professional and would go willingly wherever ordered. You'll have to forget him.' Salty tears fell from her red eyes and he turned away.

She tried to order some semblance of rationality. 'But you know when he left.... how can I get to him.... join him? We can be together.'

The Bora had tested them but rested now, the silence palpable as he turned to her. 'You have to be mad Bianca, why would you take the risk of following a soldier? Your home and family, they're all here.'

Sat before him, everything he felt at losing Sofia, every minuscule movement and whisp of emotion dashing across her face, he could read. For so long he had held all inside, presented himself to the world as a boy, working in a café, innocent, unworldly, invisible, it hurt to see his life reflected before him.

She started to speak, 'I can't let go....' hands fidgeting, staring into nothingness. He placed his hand upon hers, and leaning towards her, whispered.

Luca saw some of what passed between them, despite his efforts to avoid learning any unwanted information. He relaxed when finally she clasped Roberto's hand and kissed it, drew away, and relieved he escorted his sister home.

Passing Maria's home, he hurried ahead, hoping it would hasten their journey. As Bianca approached, she showed every intention of trying to glimpse Sophia, despite Maria's mood, and at the upper bedroom window her dear friend appeared. Gently, Sofia placed her two hands upon the windowpane between them, revealing her swollen belly. Bianca stopped, raising a hand tenderly to her heart then towards her friend, quickly glancing at the window below, for fear of Maria's approach, but none came.

She moved a step forward, raising her hand to blow a kiss as Sofia's lips moved, 'Follow your love, it must have what it needs.'

Bianca recognised her dear friend's words, but in that same instant, Sofia looked sideways and was pulled away from the window, the curtain slashed across the window between them. All that remained was the memory of Sofia's pained beautiful eyes, holding on to hope.

Chapter 75

Trieste, Italy, early Autumn, 1945

Luca left his sister on the stair at home, she ascended to living quarters, he descending to the sanctuary of his workshop. Looking down the stairwell, she was sure he had the slack-jawed appearance of release as he dashed out of sight.

On the landing all was quiet. She looked to her father's empty office, remembering his appointment with a crony in Trieste, a once fascist enforcer, now partisan hunter, who had skilfully embedded himself within Allied authorities. She remembered her father's words at breakfast and realised the source of his knowledge. She understood now her father knew Ted was leaving and could have told her gently, wondering how long he'd known.

Slipping into the office she moved carefully, lifting files, trying drawers until she found her objective. The gun shocked her for a moment, a warning to prying eyes but lying below was what she sought. With only one notion, she gently lifted the firearm, placed it on the desk and took out the vermillion packet beneath. She found her birth certificate and national identity card and removed them. Below was an even greater bounty, another envelope with carefully bundled banknotes. She removed several large notes from each wad in the hope he wouldn't notice, and carefully replaced envelopes and pistol, exactly as she had found them. Then another envelope caught her eye, absent-mindedly pushed down the inside of the drawer. Inside, were the coral earrings Claude had been given in payment for escape, and to her mother to hide. The Greek Goddesses seemed to plead with her to rescue them too and vowing to love and remember her Jewish friend, she placed them in her pocket.

Downstairs a sound echoed up the stairwell. Panicking, she stuffed the notes and paperwork into her camisole, buttoning her jacket to disguise their hiding place, and ran to her room. All was quiet again as she carefully considered what food she needed. The house was strangely silent. No-one came, no-one wandered around the kitchen, a complete lack of activity. Looking down the stairwell, she knew what was going to happen but a gaping chasm of time stood before her. She was untroubled by apprehension, patience and calm swathed her but required activity. The house seemed in silent collusion with her as if the very walls were holding their breath. It had been their family home for so many years, the scene of working, fighting, sometimes even laughter and was soundless, as if bracing itself for the next monumental event.

She drifted to her parents' bedroom, glancing around at the precise placement of furniture, fine white linen sheets pulled tight without a crease, glass bottles in perfect rows on the chest. The room presented like the electricity station, adhering to her father's demands. She wondered what twisted passions her mother had been subjected to in the stark, unfeminine cell to make her the cowering creature she was.

A warm glint caught her eye. On the spotless dressing table, her mother's gold box link chain lay in a small white dish, the cobalt blue enamel of The Sorrowful Mother's shroud smouldered among the stark, expensive, bedroom furniture. She had never seen her mother without it, touching it at least once a day to remind that Mater Dolorosa watched over her, yet here it was. She turned it over, diagonally on the reverse, another reminder of our Lady of Sorrows, a symbol of piety and devotion, the rich gold mount circling the pedant, throwing out a bright light like a halo. She seized it. In the coming excitement, at least her mother's touch would be close by.

The evening meal passed without incident, her father still absent. Her mother didn't seem to notice any missing groceries or pendant, as she scurried around.

They retired to bed early, Papa still absent, everyone eager to relax in the seclusion of their rooms, undisturbed by his demands.

Eventually he returned, the house falling to silence again. She lay on her bed fully clothed, a small case by her side, the stolen money sewn into a secret pocket in her blanket coat until she made her way to her favoured corner of the kitchen. Looking out towards the sea, the beautiful city twinkled like diamonds in the night, looking like some remnants of its grandeur could creep back. Once home to a wealthy community, she wondered if it would ever fully recover, when down the hill she saw the glow of a cigarette, disappear, then reappear to be snuffed out. It had to be the sign. Clutching her case she set off in a state of passion and resentment. For the last time, she would suffer her father's barking, self-serving commands, and unquestioning obedience, submission to his every word; the memory of his assault upon her in the storeroom would be replaced by the loving arms of Ted. The war was all but over and hadn't she served him well? Yet he still considered himself unquestionably superior to everyone, and she his daughter having a domestic value alone, and after six dangerous years, just another insignificant creature under his command.

*

Roberto had only confirmed to her where Ted's 13th Corps had gone, and to meet at the back of his café after midnight. As she left home, she remembered how she and Sofia had cajoled his father into parting with food, excited and nervous at the drama back then. Later taking their chance with all, and no concern for consequences, just to eat. Their

357

lives had become so out of control. But it no longer mattered, she was heading towards the comforting oasis that was her Teddy.

She made her way under the fence clasping a cheap medal, Emmanuel, a Catholic priest torn between religious doubts and the spiritual needs of his parishioners, given by Sophia when they were at school. In her small case, wrapped in socks for safety, the coral earrings and Mater Dolorosa. Her thoughts drifted to the simple note she had left in the kitchen for her mother to find in the morning.

"I love you Mamma but can stay no longer. Your loving daughter, B".

Her father would probably look for her and she panicked at the thought of seeing him again, adrenaline and hope propelling her on.

In the chill air of the narrow passage behind Roberto's cafe, a doubt leached into her consciousness. Had she misunderstood, would he help or turn her over to her father? She pressed herself against the wall by the back door, sliding her small suitcase flat, hoping to melt into the cold bricks as a truck pulled up at the end of the opening. A hunched character shuffled its way down the alley towards her as the lock behind her made the slightest sound, a key turned and Roberto appeared. The air stilled as the figure got closer, she was trapped between him and her friend, bunching her fists behind the folds of her coat in case. Could Roberto be trusted after all he had been through? She saw a wild glint in his eye as he stared at the stranger. Suddenly he propelled her through the bitter night air, her feet hardly touching the floor as he pushed her towards the man, picking up her case as they dashed. They reached the lorry.

Inaudible words passed between the two men. Struggling to understand the dialect she assumed, hoped they were comrades, perhaps fighters during the war. 'He will take you. You may have to be very brave. For this journey, you are his stupid half-sister. You speak to no-one, look at no-one,' he gabbled, glancing over his shoulder, danger etched across his face. Everything was happening so quickly, taking her over.

'Do you understand?' he grabbed her arms and shook her, feet slipping on the stone floor. Her eyes boggled at the frightened desperation in his eyes and knew he too was beyond sanity.

'He has dispensation from the authorities to travel.' He dropped her, scuffing her best leather shoes as she stumbled. With that, he spun around and evaporated into the shadows; she wondered if it was the last time she would see another childhood friend.

She scurried after the driver who secreted her small case under his seat, and climbed in alongside him. Relieved he wasn't inclined to talk, concentrating on driving, she drifted to sleep as the bounce and shake of the truck took them through the city, past the docks, skirting below Opicina and into the future.

Passing pretty Castle Miramare her head jolted. As she glimpsed the haunting beauty hovering by the sea, something was remembered. What? Her mother's arm around her, a trip on the tram, a story of sadness, and madness, a doll. Another jolt, then drowsy compliance as nervous exhaustion pulled her to sleep again.

*

The glow of dawn warmed her face as the driver pulled onto the side of the road, stopping the engine.

'This is as far as you go.'

Startled and afraid Bianca grabbed the door handle. 'It's the end of the road for you, now you walk,' his weary eyes stared back. 'I'm not going to be caught transporting unofficial cargo,' he drew a finger across his throat. She shuddered

Bianca peered through the windscreen. They were miles from the star-shaped, mediaeval fortress city of Palmanova among outlying communes, the heart of her life still miles away. She leaned forward to reach for her case as he threw a pair of flat thick-soled peasant shoes towards her, pointing to the finely crafted leather pair on her feet.

'Give,' he stared at her footwear.

'But I need....' she slid her feet beneath the bench seat.

'If you are stopped, they will know you are not local....' he grunted, not looking at her. 'And if spotted, you will not get further than a hundred yards before they will be stolen from you, maybe with violence, so give me now or walk barefooted later.'

Reluctantly the shoes were exchanged. He put his hand under his seat again and pulled out an old scarf and flung it towards her. 'Here, really be a peasant, it's safer,' an indication of warmth managed to pull across his weary face, and he prepared to continue his journey leaving her on the roadside with her case.

Chapter 76

Italy, Palmanova, early Autumn 1945

The truck growled towards the city as Bianca stood, case at her ankle. Churned agricultural fields spread around, as small remote villages and homesteads stood between her and flawless Palmanova in the distance.

Exhaustion took her, walking in unfamiliar, heavy laced up shoes, plodding towards one of the large entrance gates. The city was guarded by towering, protruding walls, which jutted outward, creating the star formation, magnificent yet daunting, and by late morning she was finally below the ramparts. Allied soldiers had been coming and going along the road in transport vehicles, some jeering or blowing kisses and she managed to slip through the gates in the commotion. The harsh reality of her flight began to dawn as she wondered how to find Teddy among the throng of testosterone-fuelled English troops. She tied the headscarf tighter, pulling the front down to cover her brow, attempting disguise of her youthful appeal from the frisky soldiers. She knew no-one, had no friends, no familiar roads and passages, no buildings to retreat to if danger approached, she was alone. But her feet knew only one action, to carry her to him whatever the cost and she began asking inhabitants for the English soldiers' billets.

'Another prostituta plying her wares,' an aged crone spouted her lewd opinion as she passed. Women were in no mood to accommodate her queries, even the local men shying away warily. Bianca was used to being viewed with hostility by the Slavs, but these were fellow Italians, she wondered at their reaction. Weary from tramping for miles, it was hard to care, she had to see Ted again, continuing to ask for the Tommies quarters. When not spurned, they laughed, her appearance half-deranged and babbling, until a soldier from Montebello barracks noticed her, then returned to his task.

As dusk fell she sat on the edge of the city's huge central hexagon piazza dejected, with no shelter or friend to turn to, this wasn't what she had anticipated. She had visualised being found as she entered the city, the residents sympathetic, the word getting to Teddy. He would be relieved to see her, eager to take her in his arms. Instead, she looked across the vast lonely expanse at the heart of the city, people retreating home for the night. Shivering in the cold emptiness, she plunged her hand into her bag, feeling around for fragments of broken biscotti.

Aware eyes were upon her, she scanned the large square as the odd lightbulb began to flicker on, no figure to be seen until small gatherings started to emerge in the distance. Through the dim light, she couldn't recognise who or what they were.

She felt someone behind her. She swung around checking the side street, nothing, no-one.

'You are going mad, Bianca. What do you think, a ghost haunts you?'

The words jumped across her mind as she sat on a small wall, rocking back and forth when a wisp of air tingled the back of her neck. Again she looked, still nothing. Her gravest thoughts flooded her shattered mind; the Bird Boy being ripped away, his scream playing over and over in her mind, Maria's screech, commanding her to leave, her father's violent assault, the tragic vision of Sophia at the bedroom window, separated from them forever. Then suddenly,

'Eh you, what do you want here?'

A strong Italian female voice cut into her thoughts. From nowhere, a woman stood next to her and despite the resounding demand looked amenable with a jaunty half-grin. On her feet she still wore sandals despite the season, her dress thin for the weather, loose buttons down

362

the front, one lost, baggy in their fastenings, gaping open at the waist, on her shoulders a cheap tattered wrap.

'Come on, give it up, what are you doing here?' she shivered in her unseasonal outfit.

Bianca looked at her bare legs, toenails painted bright red some time ago, chipped and broken, setting the whole outfit in its place.

'I.... I am....' What could she say, the woman was undoubtedly a whore, and Bianca had chosen her patch to rest her exhausted body. Glancing across the square she realised this was their business meeting place.

'I'm going, I was just resting.'

'Oh yes, and where do you go at this time of night?' the woman demanded.

'I'm not sure. I'm just waiting for my....' she hesitated, then love buoyed her courage. 'I'm looking for my Tommie, he is here, and I will find him.' A light came on behind her, catching her sad liquid eyes. Her interrogator shifted from foot to foot finally resting her weight on one hip expertly spreading the high split in the front of the dress. She fumbled for a cigarette in the imitation alligator skin handbag, dangling from the crook of her arm.

'Want one?' she asked.

Bianca turned towards her. It had been a long journey and she hadn't had a cigarette since the day before.

'Go on,' the woman checked her cigarette packet, 'I have a couple left' shaking out the English cigarettes.

To buy a little time before accepting the prostitute's hospitality, she threw a last desperate look across the piazza.

Around the edge, a broad-shouldered soldier strode purposefully. Spotting him at the same time, the woman's back straightened as she re-positioning herself prominently in front of Bianca, presenting her most alluring stance. Both women traced his progress as he passed world weary purveyors of the oldest profession, ignoring them all, both their hearts beating faster as the selective agent approached.

An explosion in Bianca's heart burst like a chrysanthemum firework, sending sensations spreading to every corner of her body. Stunned, she rose to her feet. The other woman with more flair than her colleagues manifested more and more attention-seeking postures to draw him. This Tommie would be hers.

He disregarded every offer en route, determined strides bringing him closer. Within yards he ran the last few feet, Bianca rooted to the spot, a statue of hope and love. Everything she sought before her, all life stopped in that moment.

Ted looked shocked at her gaunt face, legs smeared with dirt and dust, at her being there at all. His Corps had moved out with no chance of sending a message, but she had found him. His arms encompassed her as her head rolled back, legs buckling, pulling her closer, the thrill swelling within.

The watching woman gave up the game, this was no handsome new man to add to her regulars. Taking a last draw on her cigarette she tossed it to the floor.

'What can that skinny kid do for him when he could have me and my experience,' barely audible. She strutted a small circle, eyeing the couple, disappointed, finally hanging back near the wall to observe, a distant memory recalled.

Slowly Bianca's eyes flickered open.

'Is it possible, is it you at last?' gasping words only he could hear, and she understand.

'Where have you come from....' he held her close, face lost in the waves of travel weary hair, chest heaving, their eyes expressing more than the unfamiliar words.

'Hey you two, get off the street, you'll ruin my business.' The woman in the shadow had regained her composure. Faint, tortured strains of Madam Butterfly's

Love Duet drifted from a home in the adjoining street and she bit her lip.

'I said, hey you two,' the lovers turned to the outline near the wall as she stepped forward.

'What you do now, eh? Hang here all night, ruin my trade?' Ted turned towards the fractured English and looked down at the weary figure in his arms.

'Here.' She threw a key at Ted, catching it in his left hand, his other still supporting Bianca. 'Get there for a while lover boy, that my room over café,' she continued in pigeon English and pointed to the glow of a trattoria on the corner, facing onto the piazza. Outside a few people occupied tables and chairs.

'I have good address. I known.' She adopted an air of satisfaction, looking at the café below. 'Owner will say, I good.'

More soldiers were beginning to collect around the edges of the square as he looked down at the vision before him.

'I need to get you off the street Bianca, you have to walk.' He picked up her small case and started to move, her legs like a rag doll, immobile in his arms. He shook her.

'You have to go,' to her uncomprehending face, 'we need to take you inside.' Nothing penetrated, only that she was safe in his arms. He hugged her tight, murmured reassurances, as gradually she took his direction. Under the dim lamplight they walked the short distance to the door adjoining the café. The proprietor emerged calling in his recently learned new language, 'Hey, where Luciana, what you do with her?'

She called to him, 'My friend, they resting a while,' again in broken English as she waved at a young Tommy already heading in her direction.

The café owner raised his eyebrow at the newcomers, but nodded, and turned to an irate woman behind him who complained fervently. Ignoring her he walked back in.

*

Almost dragging her up the stairs Ted and Bianca stepped into the room.

'No, no, this is no good,' Ted tried to pull her back to the landing, her feet dragging. Tattered lace underwear hung on a line across the window above a pile of worn, red plush cushions on the bare wooden floor.

'Just for a moment then, until you get your strength back,' she seemed unable to notice her surroundings.

'Bianca, you're not used to this sort of thing, you can't stay in a place like this, a prosti... a working girl's place.' He looked down at her shivering body beside him, recognising the physical and emotional exhaustion he had seen so many times during the war.

He looked around. The scene wasn't entirely unfamiliar, no curtains at the window, barely recognisable food on a plate, clothes strung around. The only difference to home were the exotic photographs around the iron bedstead against the wall. Above it a shelf with a collection of trinkets supported curled photographs of soldiers of all ranks, advertising the breadth of her success with her customers.

'You can't understand a word I'm saying can you?' He avoided the bed and carefully placed her on the cushions, rubbing her arms for warmth then sat beside her. Eventually, her head on his shoulder, her breathing deepened. He stroked her hair, the dust of her journey disappearing, some shine returning in the glint of the street light. Thinking aloud seemed to make it easier.

'We are going to have to try and find you somewhere to live, you can't stay in a whore's bedroom.' He looked down, no recognition of his foreign words registered. Their feelings had bloomed for no reason other than he was kind, upstanding, handsome and gentle and wanted nothing from her. She had found an anchor, a rock in the tempest. Communicating through mime and the odd word, they had

366

exchanged everything with their eyes. In his unthreatening company, she had found the innocence she had lost, at last finding solace, love and affection. For Ted, the unexpected attention she gave baffled him, devotion from such an elevated beauty filled his need for acceptance, strengthening his fragile self-esteem, their needs, a perfect match.

'Come on, downstairs before she comes back,' he said.

They gingerly took the old wooden steps to the piazza, turning into the café next door. Tommies coming and going, he found a table out of sight. The place was warm, with signs of activity from the back kitchen and locals at select tables. Outside, Allied soldiers passed with women of their current interest as the café owner emerged and Ted called him over.

'Excuse me. Where can we get a room for the Signorina sir, in a good house?' The café owner stepped back to better assess the situation as his wife glared from the scullery door.

In an accent acquired from various occupying soldiers, he ventured his broken English.

'None here my friend. All gone now.'

'There must be something, somewhere?'

'Nothing, all gone now,' he threw his palms heavenward shrugging, and studied the couple more closely.

'What about an old lady who needs a cook or companion?' Ted drove his inquiry on.

'None.'

'Someone, who needs a cleaner?'

'No nothing, Tommy, my friend.' He looked at Ted's crestfallen face.

'This city full, big time' Bianca sat at the table, a little hunched ball of wide-eyed silence, 'you understand, soldiers all here,' he swung his arm towards the piazza. 'Workers come to look after all soldiers,' tipping him a knowing nod. Ted reciprocating with a cold stare. 'No oppo, you no understand. Cleaner, cook, shop people, now all full,' getting the point over at last.

Luciana, passing the open café door with a cheerful sapper called the café owner to her, concern flashing across her cheerful face as she glanced at the sad couple in the corner, and pushing the sapper away stepped in to join them.

'Hey, Tommy what problem is?'

'I have a name, and it isn't, Tommy.'

'Okay, okay,' her bright smile, harsh in the electric light, 'What problem soldier?'

'We need.... I mean she needs a room, and he says there are none,' he pointed at the cafe proprietor.

'Yes, yes soldier all gone, we fit for busting.' Her throaty laugh crumpled the air. 'Everywhere farmers and shopkeepers, cleaners all over, there no room left. Why you think I stay in that?' she jabbed a thumb at the ceiling.

'But she needs to stay somewhere.' Ted's deflated face told of a man who cared for the woman by his side. Something in Luciana's heart made room for their situation and she took the café owner aside, a moment later strutting back to the couple.

'I make arrangement, see?' She indicated the proprietor and his wife arguing in the kitchen. 'Tonight she stay with me, tomorrow we look again for her somewhere. But if she stay, tonight is free, if more I need something, no?' she rubbed her thumb and fingers together.

Ted looked embarrassed, he was going to have to touch on a delicate subject. 'But your business...'

'No worry soldier, I take break tonight. Maybe I take break for good.' She snapped a look at the still bickering couple at the door.

'I insist I must pay for her bed for the night,' he didn't want any misunderstanding and pulled out some notes.

The café proprietor was instantly by his side with three espresso saying, 'My friend, matey, really nowhere else in this place,' and refused payment for the drinks, 'your girl welcome here. What they say, kosha?' he nodded.

As they sipped strong coffee Ted mulled it over. Squeezing Bianca's cold hand, a small smile formed on her lips. Again without words they communicated, it was to be, she would share the room upstairs for the night. Slipping her hand inside her coat she located the secret pocket and took out the money she had taken from her father. Luciana observed, there was more to this skinny girl than immediately apparent, she was independent, smart, and the room was paid for upfront.

Ted looked at his watch. 'I have to go', he took her hand and they stepped outside. Bianca handed the rest of the money to him, closing his hand around it. He unfurled the notes and handed some back, indicating food, nodding towards the cafe.

'I'll put the rest in a bank for you and keep it safe,' he looked at the gathering faces at the café window. She recognised a word.

'Banka, si?'

'Banka, si," he replied.

Bianca drank in the beauty of his clear eyes, abandoned in them for a moment, as Luciana joined them.

'Nighty, night, must go, time for bed.' She had picked up many useful phrases since the British had arrived, and prised the couple apart. 'Bye, bye, see you soon,' she transported Bianca to the doorway of the stairs, whispering in her ear.

Bianca turned and called, 'See you tomorrow my love,' in perfect English. The door closed and Ted looked back at the café, already the proprietor was busy chatting to men at the tables, his wife's frosty face still evident at the back of the room. Upstairs the light came on and wisps of clothing were whipped from the line across the window, a more substantial rag replacing them.

He checked his watch quickly. As he strode back to the barracks his heart swelled then constricted. Bianca had manifested from no-where. *'How long will it be before her father takes her home. You'll have to make the most of the time you have together old son,'* he thought sadly. *'She'll never stay with the likes of you; you're on borrowed time.'* He wondered why she cared for him, didn't understand; she had breeding, status and could have anyone, but chose a poor boy from a tough background. He would sort it out, take care of her, it was his duty. She had given up everything to find him and her money wouldn't last long, what was she to do then?

He wondered what his mother would make of it. Cissy said Uncle Fred kept a roof over her head but it was never there for long, frittering away any money she got taking in waifs and strays. But Granddad was a confectioner on Redcar High Street now with plenty of rooms above, surely he would keep his Mam right. He considered the money he sent home every month, still the dutiful son.

After a long draw on his cigarette the realisation came, it would have to stop.

Chapter 77

Italy, Palmanova, Autumn 1945

Bianca watched as Ted strode away into the darkness, relief washing through her like a cool, calming stream. She had him back, and shelter for one night at least. Turning she startled as Luciana had positioned herself on the edge of her bed in glamorous pose, toes pointed, legs elongated, directing the eye from garish toenails, along her leg to the front split of her skirt, a hard habit to ditch it seemed. Bianca's horrified face snapped her out of her business pose, flopping one over the other she crossed her legs.

'So, Little Bird, what's your story then, the English soldier is yours eh?'

Stories of her mother's ridicule by Slav boys who called her "little bird" angered her snapping, 'That is not my name.'

'Fine, but the man, he is yours?' She hadn't missed the gallant way he'd protected her new lodger, or his handsome clear skin and manly physique, still looking for any opportunity for a more permanent, reliable, boyfriend to take care of her.

In the warmth of the small room, squatting on the pile of threadbare cushions, a trace of Bianca's old self returned. Levelling her gaze directly at Luciana, pulling her shoulders back, tilting her stare down her nose, she was Bianca Marchetti again, not a lost refugee or timid little creature to be taken advantage of.

'My name,' she paused, 'is Bianca.'

'Bianca what?'

'Just Bianca, for now,' not intending to leave clues for her father to find.

'And...'

'And yes, he is my man. Only mine,' holding her stare. There would be no opportunity for Luciana with him, and her new landlady quickly dropped the subject. Though exhausted, Bianca maintained the image of confident self-assurance, and when a light meal was sent from the café below they talked of her journey. Maintaining her place on the bed Bianca eventually sunk into the padded cloud of cushions on the floor covering herself with the blanket coat. Luciana brought towels and her own coat to warm her fitful sleep, as she dreamed of protection at Ted's barracks easing her sleep.

'Not as strong as you would have me think, Little Bird,' Luciana whispered as she looked at Bianca. 'Never mind, sleep well tonight, tomorrow I need my room back.'

*

In the morning Bianca was led to the café below and, far friendlier with the proprietors than she had realised, Luciana had access to all parts of the cafe. At a table she nibbled a biscuit from her pocket, as surreptitious discussions wafted from the kitchen. The voices concluded she had no chance of obtaining a room at the barracks, or even near them. The city was awash with the broken hearts of women seeking their soldier lovers, potential saviours from destroyed lives, all to no avail. Some were tracked down and swiftly whisked home, others completely abandoned hoping to throw themselves on the kindness of a stranger to love and care for them again. Luciana, however, was a whore and not ashamed of it, interested only in profit and gain.

Bianca's tired head nodded forward, clattering the coffee cup on the table in front of her, the shabby image of the café rushing back into awareness.

'Hey,' the café owner came over, taking the cup and saucer, adding, 'you soldier boy sent his oppo with a message. He will call tonight.'

The two other women looked at the crumpled stranger in the corner, her eyes glistening.

'Ay, ay, ay, no tears here, you'll frighten the customers,' Luciana declared.

Bianca looked around the empty café as, never off the clock, Lucianaswayed as she shimmied across the room, taking a place at the table.

'Due espresso, pronto,' clicking her fingers Luciana ordered.

'Life is what it does, you can stay with me.' She leaned forward putting her hand on Biancas. 'Listen, you wouldn't be the first high born girl to be abandoned by....' Bianca nearly tipped the table as she raised her hand to slap the prostitute, stopping and sat down again.

'Okay, not abandoned but....' Luciana considered how to prepare the young woman for possible, if not definite disappointment, '.... for any problems in your path. You are lucky, he has sent a friend to tell you to wait for him, that doesn't happen often. Usually, they just blend into the crowd, never seen again. Look out the window at night, the soldiers have their pick. Young, old, tall, small, brunette, blond, everything is on offer here.' She paused, 'Let's get you something to eat, you can think better then.' She clicked her fingers again.

After forcing down a meal of bits and pieces, swilled down with water, Bianca assessed the food wasn't the main attraction at the trattoria, and they returned to the room above. The prostitute happily shared her space and they organised the area to accommodate a corner for her. They gradually fell into general chatter, and as Bianca relaxed in her experienced easy company, she revealed something more of her story.

She spoke of her father, though not his position, name or nefarious associates. About starving, her German friend, the Bird Boy, the Karst and being shot. Finally, she spoke of Sofia. Unconsciously, tugging her fingers as she spoke, gently drawing from their sockets, then repeating with the other hand, as if the act would draw the misery from her body as she spoke. Luciana, watching from her bed, fell to her knees and put her hands on Bianca's, holding them tight.

'And what of your family, will they look for you?' The restriction to her hands seemed to travel up into her body and she started to shake.

'I can't leave him,' she looked up, 'I would die first.'

'But your family....'

'He is my family, my world.' As she heard her own words, she knew it was all she could cope with in the time and space she occupied, he was her only hope of survival.

Luciana touched her cheek gently, 'Let's think of happier times.' She looked around the room for a distraction, her eyes falling to an unruly pile of clothes on her bed. 'I need to prepare for the evening, I still have to work.' Getting up she began shaking the creases out of her tattered satin lingerie as Bianca's breathing calmed. Looking up she watched her smoothing and pressing the garments between the flat of her hands.

'You need a stitch in those,' Bianca said.

'You don't need to tell me,' she threw her head back and laughed, 'they've seen a lot of activity.' A crooked smile forced its way into Bianca's cheeks.

'Pass them here. Do you have cotton and a needle?'

'Some cotton, no needle,' Luciana replied, tossing the garments to her.

'Can you get one, perhaps from downstairs?'

Luciana didn't need to be asked twice. She skipped down the well-worn, wooden stairs, returning within minutes cursing as a globule of red blood formed on her thumb.

'Here,' she dropped the needle into her new companion's lap, 'Good luck,' turning back to the door, grabbing a coat and exiting.

Below Bianca could hear the muffled, now familiar utterances of the café owner and his wife. She rested her head for a moment on the scarlet cushions then, with no activity to divert her, or friend to talk to, set to work.

*

On her return, slightly dishevelled and with an unfamiliar, sweaty odour, Bianca awoke to Luciana's delighted yelp. On her bed she had laid a neat pile of undergarments, no ragged edges to the lace, no holes in the seams. Next to them her dress from the night before had the buttons securely attached down the front and three odd stockings had the holes in the feet darned.

'You are a genius of the needle, work of this standard will enhance my desirability,' she held the underwear above her head and swung it gleefully in the air.

'I would struggle to have you here, but a man could take me anywhere now if you could enhance my dresses,' she grabbed a handful from a rail in the corner, throwing them in Bianca's direction.

'Tomorrow,' Bianca countered. 'I have to prepare for Teddy, he comes for me tonight.'

Luciana turned towards the naive young woman before her. 'You still think he will come? If he does not....'

'He will, I know it. He will.'

Chapter 78

Italy, Palmanova, Autumn 1945

As evening fell, Luciana left Bianca to prepare for her English soldier, who arrived at the café as she exited.

'Hey, Teddy boy. How you do? Good yes?' in her broken English.

Luciana presented herself to her best advantage, searching for his eye. His stare turned to a frown as he recognised the prostitute's intentions, but Baptist blood still ran purely through his veins, and he addressed her civilly.

'My name is Sergeant Jones. Can you call Bianca for me, please?'

She acknowledged the rebuff with a saucy grin, adding 'I tried. Never the mind Tommy, your girl is coming. Sit.' She indicated one of the outdoor tables, 'you like my talk?'

Ted shuffled uncomfortably. Experienced soldier on the field, less experienced in other matters.

'Erm, very good.'

'I pick up from soldier boys,' she winked at him. He turned away embarrassed. 'You like fancy woman from Trieste, no?'

His features softened.

'Yes.'

'She very special for you?'

He considered the question. His only other girlfriend had been a friend's sister, never able to ask anyone else, childhood taunts punching through his confidence. When the call came to leave Trieste he had supposed a handsome Italian of her class would take his place in due course, their parting for her own good in the long run.

'She deserves the best life, the best man. I can only try and make her happy,' his words were barely audible.

Luciana turned away, her usual bright, cheery eyes cast down. Regaining her composure she swung round.

'I get your lover for you Teddy boy.' He jumped.

'No, it's not like that....' horrified at the suggestion.

Luciana understood at last, not lovers but in love, the purest of bonds, not united by hypnotic desire to repeat and relive moments of ecstasy, so easily replaced by more thrilling offers and affairs. Bianca had followed him simply for love, and he responded with his devotion.

'I get your girl Tommy,' her bright, brassy smile softened for a moment, she sighed and turned to the door, muttering to herself.

'Ay Luciana, that you should feel such love one day.'

Moments later the two women emerged, and the lovers hesitantly came together. Fingers tentatively touching to begin with, then eagerly intertwining, a hand tenderly around her shoulder holding her close, her head on his chest.

Ted turned to raised voices inside the cafe. Luciana was ordering refreshments be delivered to them at their table outside, the older man looked at his frosty wife, no opposition to the command. He arrived at their table placing before them coffee and some small pastry delights. As Ted went for his pocket he gave a slight nod of the head,

'Complementi di casa. Complement of the house'

Ted looked uncertainly to the café interior, his wife glared from the kitchen door.

'My gift for love,' Luciana called from the doorway. Moving closer she spoke fluently to Bianca in Italian.

'My friend can I be assured, you will remain away from the room tonight?'

Bianca's gaze drifted to the stair doorway, 'What am I to do, how long must I stay away?'

'As long as it takes,' Luciana shrugged.

'But I can't stay out here all night, and Teddy must return to the barracks by 10 o'clock, what will I do?'

'What can I say, business is business. Anyway, I've made arrangements; you can sit in the corner of the café. I told her she has to let you.' She flicked a nod towards the angry woman, 'I've said you will do her mending for her, and she should be grateful.'

Uncertainly, Bianca looked again at the sour-faced woman. 'Yes it is true, you will be safe there and I will let you know when you can return.' The old woman returned to the kitchen.

'I'll explain to your love,' Luciana added.

Minutes later she took up her position, pulling the newly mended dress straight, opening the bottom buttons and positioning herself artfully in the warm glow of the café window. After a while Ted took Bianca's elbow and gently guided her towards the piazza, as a clutch of squaddies noisily approached the café.

After a leisurely circuit of the square, they returned, sitting outside at the furthest table from the revellers, and he produced a well thumbed English-Italian dictionary. Luciana was nowhere in sight, fewer squaddies remaining now. Together they flicked through the pages, gazing fondly at each other and laughing. As the time to leave grew closer, Ted took her inside and sat her in the most distant corner. To their surprise, there was a small pile of carefully folded men and women's clothing on the chair with one needle and black cotton.

They had taken their parting embrace away from the glare of the trattoria, and sitting inside he held her hand. Outside the odd soldier lingered, eyeing them as Ted made to leave, peering in Bianca's direction. Ted leaned in towards each of them as he left, his broad shoulders, sergeant's stripes and brief words enough to redirect their attention elsewhere.

As Bianca examined her mending, Ted checked through the window one last time, reassuring himself no other unsavoury attention was being directed towards her, and set off back to the barracks, the old man bringing her a warming glass of grappa.

'Keep out the chill,' he smiled gently as tutting and expletMias emanated from his wife.

In the early hours, the completed mending was examined by the old woman, who seemed to find little to complain about. Bianca was cold and tired, her head resting on her arms when a man called from the doorway in English.

'Eh you, you can go up now,' jabbing his finger to the ceiling.

She wearily left the café, the door locking behind her, and mounted the stairs. Inside, an unmistakable odour from the nights' work hung in the air, Luciana curled under the bed covers, air stale from smoke. Bianca gathered together her old velvet cushions, made a nest to sleep in and fell into her second night's slumber in Palmanova wondering, was this to be her life now.

Chapter 79

Palmanova, Italy, Winter 1945

In the weeks that followed Bianca fell into a routine, leaving Luciana to rise when she wished she'd creep down to the café. Invariably there was a pile of mending on the table in the corner, and the café owner would bring a coffee and a morsel to eat. She was gaining a reputation as a talented seamstress, and commissions started to come in to alter old dresses to suit young brides or make stylish skirts out of shabby men's trousers. It raised her above suspicion of being in the same business as Luciana, and even the old woman in the café no longer scowled relentlessly at her.

She wondered, not for the first time, how her room-mate came to order the old man and woman around. Despite her occupation, she seemed to rule the roost in the establishment. The café was quiet in the afternoon and she took her opportunity to gingerly pose the subject when Luciana finally came downstairs.

'The old man and woman....' then dropped the subject.

Luciana's keen eye snapped in Bianca's direction.

'Go on, you have questions, no?'

'It's only, well I wondered....'

'Don't be shy little one, you have a question to ask, so ask.'

Bianca wasn't sure her new friend was as amenable as she seemed and changed tack.

'Oh, I just wondered why the signora is so against me. She must know by now my business here is legitimate....' Luciana cackled, reached forward and put her hand on Bianca's.

'Don't look so afeared Little Bird, there is a very good reason. This war has been hard on us all, but for some even harder,' she sighed looking into her coffee cup.

'And I have something to do with that?' Bianca thought back to her father's associations with fascists, Nazis and criminals, wondering, surely they couldn't know and be holding it against her?

Luciana continued, 'You remind her of someone, a young woman much like you, who came to a bad end. I think in a way she worries for you too.'

Bianca put her mending aside; the middle finger of her sewing hand was bleeding from pushing the needle incessantly through thick layers of wool material, a drop of blood ready to fall as she sucked at it. The silence between them hung for a long moment. Luciana seemed in a distant place. As blood rushed to her cheeks a teardrop rolled down her cheek.

'She would have been about your age, in love with a soldier like you,' Bianca leaned forward to hear her. 'He was moving on, as they all do, and she went out to see him for one last night, to beg him to take her with him, couldn't bear to live without him. She was pregnant you see.' Luciana paused not looking up, 'Only I knew that, and only I knew she was going out to find him.' She nodded towards the kitchen where the old couple bickered, 'They don't know, and you can never tell them, it's my shame and I have to carry it forever. Well, she never returned that night, and the next day those two found out she was missing.' She rested a minute. 'Many joined the search, even the girl's old boyfriend from school. He'd always been jealous of the attention she was getting from soldiers, but the glamour blinded her and she dropped her childhood sweetheart.'

Thoughts of Sofia and Roberto churned in Bianca's mind.

'She never came back, and it broke them,' she nodded towards the kitchen door.

'She must have found her love, and he took care of her. You will hear from her one day I'm sure Luciana, I'm certain,' Bianca tried to reassure.

'Silly girl,' she turned to her, 'They did find her a few days later, outside the city, dead, raped, mutilated and discarded.'

Bianca gasped.

'She's in a cemetery somewhere now, taken away again, placed with other damaged mutilated creatures from the fighting at the time. The old ones,' she nodded to the couple, 'they went to pieces, couldn't work, and didn't want to live, on the verge of dying. I did the only thing I could.'

'Your current occupation?'

'You put it so delicately Little Bird. Yes, the only thing I could do to feed them. I felt responsible, it was my fault.' Bianca saw the little girl Luciana had once been, peeked out through her woman's eyes.

'How could you know?'

'Her Italian boyfriend left the area soon after too. He looked at us with disgust.'

'Could it have been him?'

'We will never know.'

'But just because you knew what she was going to do, why did you feel the need to look after them?'

'Silly Bird.... she was my sister.'

'And they are your mother and father!'

Bianca paused to take it all in. Luciana had become a whore to feed her parents because of guilt, and they to their shame allowed her to continue sacrificing herself?

'So you see this is all mine effectively. The business was built on my back,' she laughed, her agreeable facade returning. 'I was the only one who held it together, and I worked my way into the right beds to get this property in its' prime position, to get them working again, doing something, just to keep them going. And you, well you remind them of her and you are still here. The old woman, she is angry with you for that. Why should you breathe when her daughter cannot?'

Bianca thought of honourable Ted, standing by her, trying every way to find her a room somewhere in a city bursting with soldiers, residents and traders. Luciana spoke.

'Don't worry we won't be here forever Little Bird, one day my Teddy will come too.'

'When did this all happen Luciana?'

'She was my older sister, about your age at the time, I was still at school then,' she looked down as Bianca, leaning closer, reached for her hand. Luciana pulled hers away.

A movement in the kitchen alerted them as the old man appeared with two bowls of pasta, their sad exchange abandoned.

'See how you are looked after now Bianca,' Luciana commented cheerfully, 'this is the old woman's speciality.' The man left and she leaned forward. 'You see Little Bird we cannot regard each-other as we once did. They cannot look at me as their little girl since I became their ability to live, and I must retain my position as head of the family to keep them going.' She sank back and winked. 'Don't look sad Bianca, you still have your man.'

Shaking her shoulders, and seductively pouting, she regained her cheery demeanour and they began their meal.

'It's nice to have a sister again,' she said and smiled.

Chapter 80

Italy, Palmanova, Winter 1945/46

Bianca unpicked the seam for the fourth time, hands shaking, chest aching, her thumb rough from forcing the blunt needle through layers of material. The cafe door swung open and slammed shut; a hiss of cold weather scattered winter debris around the floor. Without looking up she knew the figure sashaying between the tables towards her.

'You look like an old woman. Why aren't you taking care of yourself?' Luciana signalled towards the kitchen door saying,

'Due café.'

Some months into her new environment, the routine was familiar; Bianca would station herself in the corner sewing for her keep, Luciana arrived when she wished and ordered her parents around. After ignoring her stares for as long as possible, she finally looked up. Luciana continued her lecture.

'Ah yes definitely, I can see it now.... you look like hell. Is it that soldier boy of yours, has he not written to you? He's been gone for how long, two weeks?'

'Over a month.'

'Forget him, he's no good. There are many here who would love you, and you know that.'

Bianca shuddered, 'I haven't been abandoned,' her shoulders hunched, looked down at her sewing.

'Stop that, look at me,' she leaned forward and pulled it from her hands, throwing it onto the floor. 'You must be strong, look at your position, look at what you have, make it work for you.'

It was clear Luciana had one means of dealing with a problem, manipulation and using her assets.

'He will write to me, and I'll be here waiting as he expects. But you don't understand anyway, at least you have your Mamma and Papa, they stay with you, do what you say, they love you.'

'Ha, love?' Luciana pouted, 'Did they love me when they stopped farming and we starved. Did they love me when I brought the first money back for food? Did they? You call that love?'

'But they are still with you, they care about you. I've seen it in your father's eyes, and your mother worries for you. Where are my parents? They haven't even tried to find me and they knew very well how to.'

The last few words disappeared in a blubbering drool as Bianca hugged herself, damp globules of misery falling onto her skirt. Luciana shifted uneasily and shouted to her parents.

'What do you need them for? Why do you think they are good enough for you? Move on with your life.' Two small glasses of brandy arrived as Bianca bent over sobbing. Luciana curled her fingers around a glass, lifting it to her friend's crying lips, Bianca coughing at the vaporous potion, gulped it down, stopping the desperate weeping. Luciana spoke,

'Listen, you don't have to sit here at night while I.... well you know. We can make your bed separate and you can have a little haven in the room. I'll try and stay out until you are asleep and, hey, what you don't know can't hurt you.' They looked at each other.

'I'm just a burden to you, I should leave,' Bianca muttered.

'And where would you go, my dear? Winter is here and even though that famous Bora wind of yours doesn't blow here, there is no relief, no shelter for someone on the street. You have nowhere else, so you'd better make the best of it.' She took the sewing from the floor, instructed her mother in the kitchen, and it was all cleared away for the day, declaring, 'This will have to wait.'

Bianca allowed herself to be ordered to the room above, she and Luciana making it their mission to rearrange the simple furnishings. The threadbare cushions were arranged below the window and covered with cloth to make a mattress, tucked under, mimicking a bed. At the window, scraps of material from Bianca's dressmaking were arranged to cover the bottom half, and the bigger heavier curtain was fashioned into a room divider by Luciana's father. Behind the curtain, which could be pulled across for privacy, Bianca's few belongings were set out. Her small suitcase opened like a cupboard, contents carefully stacked, positioned to prevent any draft from the door. On the top, her few cosmetic pots stood next to a hairbrush and comb. The windowsill now belonged to her to display buttons, sewing scissors and needles she'd accumulated. On the wall below, by her new bed, she took pins and hooked photographs of her brothers, Lola and parents on the wallpaper.

'My, my, I wouldn't want to meet him alone, such a bastardo!' Luciana stared at the mean eyes penetrating from the photo of Bianca's father and saw her anxious stare. 'You did the right thing to follow your dream. Your soldier boy will come back I'm sure.'

The day was spent together. Luciana saw something of herself in her new friend and more emerged of the Karst, Sofia and her father and by evening their bond was fully cemented. She heard how Bianca employed womanly wiles to feed her family, avoided rape and physical injury by degrees so many times, of her father's assault on her in front of her family, and how it was ignored and forgotten by everyone, the normality of it scabbing over, the scar itching at her pain forever.

They slept in the afternoon, waking to a hearty meal placed beside them. As evening drew closer, Luciana dressed for work, Bianca completing her dressmaking.

*

Days and evenings passed, the new system operated to suit them both. Bianca woke early, descended to the café, set up the sewing machine which had been acquired, and was working by 6 o'clock. Fatigue from the growing business, pattern making, creating city designs for an increasing clientele, she would retire early, already asleep before Luciana invited partners to her bed. Their situation was never discussed further, unsavoury from Bianca's view, uninteresting from Luciana's.

Their arrangement was facilitated by the provision of a good sized brandy upon her retirement. The dense satisfying liquid delivered a deep slumber, separating her from the activity on the other side of the curtain.

*

Then, one day a scuffle penetrated her sleep, squeaking springs alerted. Her consciousness fought the intrusion; she snuffled, turned and pulled blankets over her head.

'What the hell's going on here?' a rough voice and boots scraped across the room as Luciana's cooing tones called for the man's attention. The heavy curtain around Bianca flapped, catching her head as a man tried to enter her secret chamber.

'You got yer pimp in here ready to rob me, is that it?' The stench of alcohol penetrated through the curtain as Bianca's eyes snapped wide.

'Changed the room to hide a thief, eh?'

'Oh you English big boy soldier, you come to me, you like me before,' Luciana cajoled.

'Scottish, you cheap whore! What have you got behind here?' The curtain ripped back, the cord snapping to reveal Bianca, cowering, Luciana already on her feet.

'Come to me Scotland, I do you well again, yes?' she pulled at his arm. He stood immobile for a moment, trying to make sense through his alcoholic haze.

'Well, lookee here, two for the price of one,' rocking dangerously. The faint light from the cafe below caught the leering glint in his eye as he grabbed Bianca's arm, dragging her across the floor towards the bed.

Luciana launched herself from the mattress clinging to his back, red nails digging into his face and head as he swung around. Jars and knickknacks sprayed around the room from flailing legs, Bianca, twisting out of his clutch, scuttled on all fours to the wall. The intoxicated soldier fell against the door, crushing Luciana, and losing her grip she fell on the bed. He lunged, throwing out a massive angry paw, clawing at her clothes as he pressed her against the bedstead.

The door burst open, Luciana's father and a customer fell into the room as she pulled a knife from under the mattress, money and documents scattering across the floor. She leapt in front of the soldier, defiant pointing it at his eyes. Swaying, he tried to focus, struggling to comprehend.

'Here what's your game?' he belched. Luciana quickly read the situation, he was legless, and quickly changed her reaction.

'Hey, you big boy. Scotland men best lovers, you pay me now, you had good time,' she told him, digging into the pocket of his half-buttoned trousers as he staggered sideways in the direction of Bianca; Luciana swung him back around.

'Come on, come on, big lover, money,' pulling her hand out of his pocket, his wallet found, and counted out her fee. 'And tip for my friend you naughty boy,' nipping his cheek between forefinger and thumb. She waved the money in front of him and made a big show of putting the wallet back, her father and the customer guiding the drunk soldier back to the street as he did up his trousers.

'Ciao,' she called cheerily to the departing Scott. 'Mamma mia, too much trouble,' she started tidying her half of the room, turning to Bianca, simpering on the floor.

'Ay, Little Bird, you're not used to it are you, come let's put you back to sleep.'

She straightened her bed and lay Bianca down, pulling the covers up around her neck.

'We'll fix everything tomorrow, rest now,' stroking her hair until a soft purr of sleep took her.

As the trauma of the night seeped away, memories of a privileged life skipped through her dreams. Playing with her Jewish friend; rich little girls in front of her home swirled with images of Signor Photographer talking intently with Sofia; then sumptuous meals prepared by her mother, seemingly extending for yards along the kitchen table, and Teddy's lovely face, smiling down at her.

Sleeping late she woke from a loud yell, then realised it was herself, the room crowding into her consciousness. Her cheeks were stiff with dry tears, then sensed the dampness of the pillow on her neck. She turned over, peeling her face from the cloth. Luciana wasn't there. From her vantage point on the floor, she could see the damage of the night before. The money gone, most of the documents relocated, but under Luciana's bed, some papers remained.

She rolled off her cushion bed, stretching to retrieve them, noticing an open envelope. Turning it over, a thud to her chest took her breath away; the handwriting was her fathers, the letter addressed to her. She gingerly pulled out the single page, dated some weeks previous.

No warm salutations, no oaths of regret, no heart-broken pleas for her to return home. One word indicating the intended recipient, "Bianca," followed by a brief business-like acknowledgement she had left the family home, offering a promise to provide a bicycle if she returned, signed with his official signature above his title, "Manager of the Electrical Stazione".

Luciana entered the room as her fingers tightened on the paper.

'Oh Bianca, you should never have seen this,' she attempted to pull it from her fingers. 'I'm so sorry, I just couldn't show it to you, I knew it would break your heart, angel.'

'How long.... the date?'

'It arrived a week ago through a courier,' Bianca thought of Roberto's network of contacts.

'After you told me of your father's nature, I had to check it first. I didn't want him to hurt you any more Bianca, I'm so sorry, I didn't mean to....'

'No matter,' she uttered as the paper fell to the ground, dead eyes staring into nothingness.

'Come, come,' Luciana fussed around her, 'Taff is downstairs, Teddy's friend, he may have news of your love.'

Half dragging, half coaxing she managed to dress and get Bianca to the café, pulling at her blouse and straightening her skirt, manoeuvring her through the tightly packed tables to him.

'Keep lovely girl here long time Taffy boy, I busy.' He looked back startled. 'You free drink, Welshman,' she gabbled a line to her father and resumed her position outside.

During the evening, Luciana noticed a small row of empty glasses gathered before a beaming Taff, as he tried to talk to the blank empty face of her broken friend, sitting silently beside him.

Chapter 81

Palmanova, Italy, February 1946

Luciana breezed into the café, trade had improved further. In her corner, Bianca sat solemnly, fingers working without thinking. A thin sun shone through the window across her pallid face, highlighting her lost spirit.

Hips swaying, she assessed the situation moving towards the crushed creature at the sewing machine, and sighed.

'Bianca my dear, what has happened to you? Where is the beautiful vibrant young woman who walked into Palmanova those months ago? You decline week by week.'

'He is gone. I don't think he will ever come back to me now. All I have is sewing old men's drawers and darning stockings. This is my life now.'

'And you make stylish dresses, silly girl. He hasn't gone away just working for the Army, he will return.'

'But I have no letter, or hope.' She looked at the now glamorously dressed woman at her side, who had taken full advantage of her talents, and a thought reaching her dull mind.

'You haven't received a letter and kept it from me Luciana, tell me you haven't?'

'I wouldn't do that to you dear, I really wouldn't, please don't think that of me. The other time, the only time, I did it to protect you, to keep the mean utterances of that pig from your eyes, I swear it.' A smile almost splintered Bianca's pained expression, but too much effort, she gave up.

'Look at you, you're pale and thin, even forgotten how to think.' Luciana sat back and looked at the waif before her. 'Listen, since we have shared our little room you've seen my life, and we've spoken about many things together... I don't know what the future holds for either of us, cara, I stopped depending on the luxury of friends a long time ago, but we have shared something haven't we?' The affectionate term "cara" ignited some response, and Bianca nodded. She continued, 'Then trust me on this.'

Luciana stood, picked up a pair of her father's trousers and pulled her towards the door. 'Come on, these will do.'

Dragging her back up the stairs she threw them on her bed, 'Put them on. Go on, I said put them on.'

'But these are your father's second best pair.'

'They are clean, and where we are going you will need all the warmth you can get.'

Bianca pulled on the un-darned trousers, fastening them around her thin waist with the belt from her coat while Luciana stepped into a new pair, sewn for her a few days previously, donned a thick wool jacket, and tightened a leather belt stylishly around her waist. Bianca struggled to close her coat over the wool blanket belt. They donned headscarves and left.

'Where are we going?' she asked, hardly caring, only a kernel of interest igniting.

Luciana didn't answer but called into the café; her father exited and walked a short distance in front of the two young women. One of the fortress gates came into view. Her father produced papers and they continued, passing the huge protective moat until a flat expanse of fields lay before them in every direction, small hamlets dotting the distance.

'See what you have been missing Little Bird, this is what you need. Look at the sky, how big it is. Take in a mouthful of that good farm air.' Bianca looked at her, cold.

'Come, he's getting away,' She pulled at Bianca's arm and they bent into the light wind, tugging head-scarfs tighter, silently following the old man as he stretched into a country walk.

He turned off the main road into smaller roads, and narrower lanes, until rural buildings clustered together beside a tilled field. Luciana pulled her aside.

'We won't go any further, let's take shelter here.'

'What's he doing?' Fresh air and exercise had revived her spirits, enough to take an interest in her surroundings.

'Business. I've given him instructions, how much to offer, how much we want. He'll be back in a while.' They settled behind a cluster of bushes. In the near distance, a young man stood with his back to them, surveying the ground around his feet.

'Hey, Paolo, how are you?' Luciana's voice carried on the breeze towards him. Looking over his shoulder, he stiffened when she waved. Pulling his collar up, he turned away, striding towards the buildings.

'You know him, he heard you, I know he did. Why didn't he speak?' Bianca turned, and for the first time saw a glimpse of the sorrow beneath her friend's cheery bravado.

'Oh, I don't know. We used to be friends, played together. I've known him since I was a baby,' she paused. 'See that farm he enters, it was Papa's until.... Well you know the work the war has done to all of us. His family rents it from me now, but he won't talk to me because of my profession,' she gazed after him. 'Yet when we were children he was always trying to get his hand up my blouse.' She shot Bianca a glance, 'He is excrement to me now,' and cracked a defiant grin.

They sat a while, Bianca breaking the awkward silence, 'What is your father buying?'

'Illicit alcohol, cheese, sausage, anything we can sell in the café. The farmer's son,' she nodded in the direction of the disappeared young man, 'he'll deliver tomorrow.'

'Does he know you run the whole business, Luciana?'

'He doesn't need to know, no-one does. You are the only one I've told. If these people knew it was a woman taking their money, and a whore at that, they would run like rats, or we wouldn't get as good a deal.' Another silence rested on them until Bianca spoke again.

'You know you could move, go somewhere no-one knows your circumstances, your past, or even the reason for your parents downfall. What about Opicina? No, that's Slovene. Then go to Prosecco, it's Italian, there are farms, good valleys to grow vines and crops.' Luciana rested her hand on Bianca's.

'Don't worry yourself Little Bird, it will come good for all of us in the end,' she squeezed the woolly gloved fingers, 'you can let it go,' and smiled gently. The old man emerged from one of the buildings, a ruddy complexion to his warmed cheeks and they retraced their journey back to the fortress city. The wind was behind them now, Bianca struggling at the exertion, but refreshed by the exercise.

*

Following their outing, something in Bianca breathed again. Everything continued as usual, sewing and mending, and designing fashionable garments, even Luciana's mother was softened by her respectable trade. But sadness remained as she waited for news from Ted, and despite the food put before her, she lacked the sustenance of his company, becoming ever fragile.

As winter melted into spring she retired earlier and earlier to avoid soldiers and locals relaxing into the peaceful aftermath of the war, unable to tolerate their contentment. Following the incident with the Scottish soldier, another space had been found for her, emptying a cupboard on the landing, giving her a space that was private and safe. There was room for the cushions, sewn together as a mattress, and the cubby hole provided somewhere she could think of Ted and re-examine the one polite postcard he had sent. It was pinned among her photographs even though it painfully provoked her loneliness, testimony he was enjoying leave while she languished in the confines of the cubicle. It taunted her, gave rise to growing insecurity, picked at the edges of her confidence. Did he still care? But she needed it to be the first thing she saw opening her eyes in the morning, the last thing at night, the constant pain bringing a dull reassurance of his existence.

Occasionally Taff took his place in the café, enticed by Luciana's offer of free drinks, to sit with her and attempt pigeon English small-talk. They avoided the emotional subject of Ted, and she accepted his company reluctantly, drifting further into sadness and depression with little energy to resist.

One evening, Luciana positioned herself at the corner, as usual, watching Bianca's sad figure enter the staircase to their separate sleeping places. The door hardly closed when a straight back and broad shoulders caught her eye powering through the crowd of promenaders, soldiers and whores. She ran towards the door, tottering on new stylish platform shoes, and screamed up the single flight of old stairs.

'He comes Bianca, he's here, come quickly. Teddy arrives!'

Accustomed to cutting out the daily comings and goings from her consciousness, Bianca ignored the commotion until Luciana's persistence penetrated her little haven, and she spilled out of her tiny room onto the landing.

'Cara, he comes around the piazza, he will arrive at any moment.' Luciana clattered up the stairs pulling Bianca into her room, grabbing a hairbrush with one hand, lipstick with the other.

'Really?' Bianca turned sharply, 'You wouldn't lie to me Luciana, swear to me it's true?' in a trance.

'On my mother's life,' she crossed herself, looked to heaven then turned her around, 'Yes, yes, you will do well, your waist tiny, hair curled, lips red,' she pinched at her cheeks in place of rouge. 'Quick my platform shoes,' flinching at the thought of giving them up.

'No Luciana, I must be what I am for him, I haven't changed, he may love me differently if I do.'

She pulled out her only footwear, the flat, peasant shoes, and followed her excited friend down to the square, heart thumping. Luciana turned her this way and that, raising her hand to her hip to create the best pose, all to no avail as it dropped limply by her side, still in a haze.

Disorientated, uncertain from which direction he would arrive she spun this way and that until her eyes saw only one vision, her man returned. Anxiously she searched his face for intention, for a clue he still loved her, wanted her. He looked in her direction, and hesitated, stepping back a moment. Her heart stopped, he'd seen her, she feared repelled, her feeble heart cracked.

Ted broke into a run, his face euphoric, a path cleared through the crowd between them. She couldn't move, her farmworker shoes rooting her to the stone floor. He reached her with such vigour nearly bowling her over, his arms encompassed, pressing her to his chest, one arm around her waist the other cradling her head, holding her face to his cheek. Eventually, holding her at arm's length, and then clinging to her again, the moment continued, her tears mingled with his, she giggled, he choked back unfathomable foreign words. Time passed for minutes or hours, they didn't notice. Luciana managed to manoeuvre them to the stair doorway, pushing them inside.

'Take this love to my room.' She eyed them wistfully, 'you'll ruin my business,' and smiled.

*

Perched on the edge of the bed, Ted attempted to explain the lack of messages was the British Army withholding mail, testing the depth of affection between soldiers and their Italian women. He had written many times, but the army's distribution service only forwarded those with the most flimsy of affections.

Bianca tried to tell him about Taff trying to cheer her up, her experience leading to occupying the landing cupboard and her father's feeble attempt to entice her home. Understanding little, he looked down with concerned blue eyes, commitment and responsibility burning within him. His heart ached; how far she'd fallen to be with him, how much she had endured. He regarded their intertwined fingers, clenching and unclenching, jaw set firm. Remembering when they first met, despite the ravages of war, her position was indisputable, the family had standing; now the only thing he understood was she was reduced to farm worker's shoes, living in a cupboard, and him. She was his responsibility; it was for him to save her, and her adoration was his reward.

Looking into the grey mists of her eyes, he heard his tentative English words.

'Will you marry me, please?'

Struggling with the language she sat stunned, his eyes glistening, his face earnest. He went down on one knee before her, taking both her hands in his, trembling. Could it be what she thought? Usually they spoke with their eyes, a gentle embrace, long loving gazes, a light touch to the back of her hand, or tenderly lifting a strand of hair from her face. Each movement, every action charged with love and care. Mimed efforts had left them hysterical, laughter and shining eyes binding them closer. He pointed to her ring finger, leaning down, kissing the rough dry skin.

She leapt to her feet and rushed to the stairs.

'Where are you going, what have I done?' He dashed after her.

Outside she caught Luciana's eye as she was gesticulating sensuously to a passing soldier, and ran to her side demanding translation, be certain, could it be everything she hoped for? Would they be together forever, the answer to all her problems, all her sadness?

A moment's dialogue conferring with Ted, it was true, he was asking for her hand in marriage.

Luciana pushed away the lovelorn soldier, dragging the couple to the café. They erupted into the warm interior adding to the peacetime merriment, her parents bursting from the kitchen at the commotion. A celebratory glass of wine was organised, local patrons, soldiers and their girls joining too.

Bianca had proved it could happen, that a Tommy would take an Italian girl, make her respectable, and bring her home as his wife. Security, food coupons, happiness, it really could happen to any of them.

Chapter 82

Palmanova, Italy, Summer 1946

As spring led to summer, Ted worked to obtain permission to rescue and marry Bianca from the sordid wreckage her life had become. He came regularly, his presence sustained her, banishing forlorn anxiety, doubt melting with every visit. She began to live again, eyes shone, skin smooth from released tension, reassured by his every call.

The sewing business continued, mending and creating fashion, grateful for shelter and food, but, seeing Ted and her dreams of the future being realised, her surroundings began to affect her.

Sometimes, Sophia and family darted in and out of her thoughts, although in his warm and breezy company, painful memories scattered. His unassuming outlook on life and high morals were becoming a reassuring structure to build their future on.

Suddenly, one night, two hands appeared from behind, covering her eyes.

'Ay Teddy, ti amo,' she spun around, his lovely eyes glistened clearly below a furrowed brow. She stood back holding his hands and took a deep breath carefully saying,'I love you.' His straight white teeth grinned back. They began to walk, miming, gesticulating, laughing, a picture of love. Entering a smart trattoria on the other side of the piazza he laid some documents written in English on the table, a brief translation in Italian attached.

"Although married quarters in the usual sense are not available, modest accommodation will be provided for betrothed Italian female nationals, and Italian wives of British forces personnel, and will henceforth come under the care and jurisdiction of Allied Forces. Notification is *given, Bianca Marchetti, is hereby advised of quarters allocated within the original Napoleonic barracks, effective from ....".*

She couldn't contain herself, gabbling in Italian and hugging him, it was happening, she was a step closer.

Rushing back to the cafe she presented the letter to the old man and woman. They had given a generous impression of belief in her impending nuptials, but no jewellery had manifested, no date had been forthcoming, nothing to confirm the English soldier would uphold his promise. Now her faith was rewarded, the proof in her hands. Soon she would be with the other women and wives of English soldiers, domestic bliss would replace the cupboard she lived in, and her cloistered existence among doubters ended. She would sew a wedding dress for herself, no longer mending raggedy old men's draws or designing exquisite garments for other women.

*

The sewing business had boomed, a young girl and elderly matron were found to replace her rapid turnover of mending and dressmaking, Luciana ensuring no interruption to income. As customers waited for quick repairs they had partaken of the café's refined new business, income increased by the offer of dainty cakes and refreshments during the day. A significant reduction of work occurred upstairs while Luciana busied herself elsewhere, and an air of increasing respectability began to permeate the building.

As the two women mounted the stairs, Luciana attempted a tone of disinterest.

'So you are leaving me Little Bird?' On the landing, Bianca turned to face her.

'Tell me the truth, you never thought it would happen did you? You thought his promises were only words, uttered in the heat of the moment,' she said.

The joy of life flowed within Bianca again, confidence growing. She looked directly into Luciana's eyes, 'You know I love him, and he loves me. I have no choice but to follow my heart to wherever, or at whatever cost. There is no life for me in Trieste; my mother, "him", my brothers, none of them cared to find me, and my Sofia lost behind her mother's shutters.'

She took Luciana's hand, 'There has been only your generosity, sheltering me when I had nothing, but I can't stay here forever, this isn't my life. He will take me with him to England and I will make him the best home I can, look after him, and he will love me, I know it.'

Luciana looked away. 'Well, let us gather your things, let's see what we can add for your wedding.'

'I won't be able to invite you, Luciana,' as she said the words, she knew it would hurt.

'I am very busy anyway, why would I expect to ....' Luciana's clipped words trailed off.

'It's the wedding, it will be in Trieste, there is no possibility of transporting guests,' Bianca tried to soften the blow.

Luciana recovered, 'No matter cara, I'll be busy,' she smiled gently. 'Here take these,' she handed Bianca a fur collar and matching cuffs. 'A gift from a grateful admirer.' She stroked them wistfully, 'well he was, last time I saw him.' and passed them over.

*

An army Land Rover pulled up outside the café the next morning and her few belongings were quickly loaded as Bianca sat in the passenger seat. Luciana pulled back the old thick curtain from across the bedroom window and

401

hazarded a wave as her friend disappeared towards her new life.

Following the straight roads of the star fortress, Bianca was soon deposited at her new accommodation, the original Napoleon barracks of Palmanova. In the forecourt, two other Italian women waited to be housed. Despite being united in circumstances, any warm welcome she imagined did not happen. Bianca examined her new neighbours, a shy young woman hugging herself uncertainly, arms permanently wrapped around her midriff, another nursing a baby, scowling relentlessly, bitter eyes surveying her surroundings and everyone in it.

They were all directed up the concrete steps to the walkway in front of rooms on the first floor, and allocated one room each. Dusty, without furniture, dirt at the windows, a sapper left buckets, mops, rags and brushes and the women set about preparing their new homes, the baby passed among them until beds, mattresses and basic furniture arrived. By night time their complaints of lack of curtains were rectified, then NAFFI presented bacon, bread and tea, their corner of the barracks comfortably out of the way of the main cohort of soldiers, new lives beginning.

Within weeks Ted, and the other soldiers promised to Italian women, were sent home on leave and the brides-to-be were obliged to rely upon the angry mother for information. She had learned English quickly and seemed to take bitter comfort in informing them, it was another effort of the English authorities to push them apart, encouraging the soldiers to abandon them. Contact from her baby's father was sporadic, and being constantly called upon to translate or write love letters on behalf of hopeful would-be wives only added to her grudge.

*

Eventually, all paperwork was completed, stamped and signed by the appropriate officer and marriage dates were allocated, only the absent grooms required. Bianca rushed to share her news with Luciana. Arriving at the café her father shifted uncomfortably and directed her upstairs. She burst through the door to see her friend reclining uncomfortably on the bed, back towards her.

'What's happened?' she asked.

'Nothing cara, just the way it is,' Luciana answered.

'Have you been attacked, who did this to you?'

'Much has happened since you left dear, not attacked....' She rolled towards her, revealing a swollen belly.

'You're with baby?' Bianca gasped.

'That's what it looks like cara, I think you may be right.' Bianca sat on the bed beside her.

'What's going to happen, what will you do?'

Luciana laid her hand on Bianca's. 'Nothing that cannot be fixed, dear. What about you? You look like you have good news for me.'

The rest of the afternoon was spent divulging every detail of her new adventure at the barracks, the women, the absence of their menfolk, and continued lack of news from her family.

'So, all is set for you Bianca, your new life lies before you. God bless and look after yourself, cara, you deserve love and happiness,' said Luciana.

As Bianca got up to leave, she noticed her friend's hiding place under the mattress revealed some new secret, and bent to pick it up.

'What's this?' she asked.

Luciana snatched the documents from her, 'Nothing for you to worry about.'

Chapter 83

Trieste, Italy, November 1946

The wait for two women ended, they were to have their wedding. Firstly the shy girl, then Bianca was informed she was to be second; Ted had returned and they would become man and wife. Spirits were high in the women's quarters as other prospective wives were reassured their day would come.

The night before the big day all the women were invited to the canteen where several bottles of local wine and beer were set out on a trestle table and someone took to the piano to play dance songs. Everyone threw themselves into the celebration of the upcoming nuptials.

Women still waiting for their soldier boys to return stayed on the periphery chattering among themselves, until lone soldiers took courage and gallantly asked them to dance. Bianca clung to Ted's arm, the excitement and music intoxicating.

'Teddy come,' she stood, pulling at his hand, unable to resist the merriment, joy overwhelming her. He looked up from his chair through tousled hair, shrugged and turned away, fists clenched on his knee. Bianca laughed, 'You come, Teddy,' she tried again, pulling him as couples swirled past on the dance floor.

'Get off,' he shook his hand free and grabbed his glass of beer. She stood, a lone island of embarrassment in the sea of merriment on the eve of her wedding. Taff, ambling through the crowd, saw Bianca partnerless and close to tears, his mate turned away, sweating. He took her hand and whisked her into the crowd with a twirl, dancing this way and that until she laughed with silly dizziness.

'You know, I've never seen him dance once.' Taff nodded towards Ted, over-exaggerating and pointing, every word a mystery to her.

When the tune was finished, someone struck up the Hokey Cokey, demanding everyone who could stand, could dance, and they all joined hands. Bianca smiled at Ted as she went by, but still he looked at the floor or chatted to the nearest spare man.

For the first time in as long as she could remember she danced in mad abandon at the joy of her life coming together with the man she loved.

A sudden angry scraping of a chair was quickly followed by a clatter as it fell backwards, a figure dashed through the crowd, her arm suddenly yanked away, as a fist caught Taff's chin. Women scattered as soldiers jumped to action, arms pulled back, shoulders pushed between men, oaths and shouts drowning out the music as it trailed off.

Bianca staggered back in horror as Ted bellowed and fought, soldiers trying to separate him from Taff, who despite his stature gave as good as he got, drunken fists punching the air, and missing their mark. A gap opened up around her as the other women shrank back leaving her alone, a beacon of trouble. She rushed to Ted, restrained now by two sappers.

'Teddy, cara ...'

The bitter Italian mother was instantly by her side, eager for once to demonstrate her bilingual talent.

'He says you flirt too much, you should marry his friend.' The woman looked more cheerful than ever before, seemingly delighted as the relationship fell apart at this late stage.

Everything was to be played for, this could not happen, and she would not let it, and Bianca threw herself at Ted, tears streaming. The shy Italian girl led her away as men's voices barked, and a brave soul took to the piano again, playing Roll Out the Barrel in hopeful distraction.

405

In the corridor Bianca was alarmed as Taff fell sideways out the canteen door, careering towards her giggling, ricocheting from door frame to door frame, uttering unintelligible foreign words as he passed her.

'Daft bugger, thought you was after me.' He grabbed the bitter mother's arm as she tried to sneak away. 'Tell 'er,' his beery breath shouted, to enhance translation, as he lit up a tab and exited.

'It's true, the mad Englishman was jealous,' the hostile woman, back to her usual tight expression. 'Apparently, you are too good for him. Too fine, too beautiful,' she looked Bianca up and down. 'He is right, he doesn't deserve you, why would you want him,' and flounced off.

Chapter 84

Trieste, Italy, November 1946

Next day, Ted waited below Trieste's Italian Park of Remembrance at Wesley House, renamed a Methodist Church. Bianca was taken separately to a hotel commandeered by the military, and prepared for the wedding. When ready, she joined the driver in her blanket coat adorned with ill-fitting collar and cuffs. One of the women pinned a brooch with petals to her lapel, but her hand reached for the blue enamel Mater Dolorosa around her neck. She closed her eyes for a moment. Ted had provided money for the dress she had sewn so lovingly. At the last moment she had invested in chemicals for a perm, and as an escaping tuft of frizz lolled on her forehead, she anxiously pushed it away. It seemed to symbolize the unexpected events of the previous night, the memory still raw. They had parted with only the briefest kiss.

Travelling through the streets she thought how she had yearned for this moment, desperately needing him, her only sign of hope. The wedding would show she was cherished, a promise never to leave, her future fully dependent upon him, and he, fully responsible for her. Last night should have been their bright new beginning, the start of their future and now all she could think of was how cold, angry and distant he had been, Taff the only one sharing in her delight. She had followed Ted blindly, wasn't that proof enough of her love? Was it all a mistake? Her family had not bothered to bring her home, drying and frazzling her mind, she could no longer think of anything but him. Family, friends or country meant nothing as she had sought the protection of his warm, strong, gentle embrace. There was only him, only Ted.

*

At the entrance to Wesley House, Taff looked him over.

'Pulled yourself together yet mate?' he pulled a packet of cigarettes from his tunic pocket, offering one to Ted. A woman emerged from the building with flower button-holes for the waiting men. Displaying every kind of embarrassment and awkwardness, he clumsily attempted attaching it to his battledress. No part of him seemed to control his limbs or the turmoil within, churned by lack of confidence, gathering from every low point of his life, reminding him, not for the first time, of the differences between them.

'What do you think she sees in me? I mean look at the life she had,' all differences from the night before vanished.

'Not this again,' Taff was exasperated, 'she chose you mate, you'll have to get used to it.'

Forever cheerful, he winked and continued, 'Got yourself ready for tonight?'

Ted blushed at his friend's attempt to relax him, spiralling further into panic, coughing and spluttering as he inhaled the nicotine hit.

'I know, but she's a different class to me, and she's beautiful, and...'

'And she'll be here in a minute,' Taff looked along the road to see if Bianca would arrive before Ted completely fell apart.

An official from the registration office called out Ted's name, cigarettes were discarded and they disappeared inside.

Some of his friends still milled around the door as Bianca arrived, straining to see if any member of her family had turned up to mark the day, none to be seen. No sooner had her foot touched the ground, a voice cut through the crowd.

'I like your shoes,' an Italian woman drew her attention, 'very stylish, they suit you.'

Witnesses were disappearing inside as she turned towards the kind comments. At the corner the woman, dressed in a sober, fashionable suit, accompanied by a smart young man stood, a baby warmly swaddled in her arms. Business-like she spoke again.

'Maybe you remember me, we met in Palmanova once. You were kind enough to comfort me at the death of my husband,' she paused looking directly into her eyes, continuing, 'I have never forgotten you.'

It took Bianca a moment to place the elegant, respectable woman.

'I married again,' she added, smiling at the prosperous young man at her side. 'I've been blessed, and he has given his name to my husband's child.' She turned to him again, he looked back affectionately and handed her a package, bid Bianca a gracious 'Good day' and entered the Registry.

Bianca stood open-mouthed before the vision of respectability, all anxiety and fear about Ted gone as she spoke again.

'It did no harm, that it was a marriage of commercial convenience for him too,' Luciana winked discreetly. 'By the way, my name is Sofia now,' she smiled gently, 'for you.'

She checked the registry entrance and continued. 'I spent time visiting the graveyards and acquired the birth certificate and Identity Card of a sadly deceased occupant. Don't ask me how,' her eyes sparkled. 'She was younger than me too, which was a bonus.'

She grasped Bianca's cold hand. 'I took your advice, cara, and went to Prosecco, sold my farm and enterprises in Palmanova and bought into a winery. The proprietor was only too happy to marry me off to his son, the dirty old man fancied me too, I could tell. Needless to say, they are ignorant of my past.' A momentary flash of her old brashness flickered across her face, and looking over Bianca's shoulder she continued.

'The business is not in the best condition at the moment, but it will be, I will make sure of that. Mamma and Papa are settling in happily working there too. My new family don't know we are related, but I like to know what's happening behind the scenes,' she winked again.

'Here, I have a gift for your marriage, you see, I keep an eye on your progress with Teddy.' She produced the package containing a large, floppy felt hat, and expensive matching leather gloves. 'You should dress like the lady you are. It complements your beautiful coral earrings,' smiling fondly.

Ted's party started to emerge shouting for her and Luciana turned away

'I don't need him to see me, and I may not see you again Bianca dearest, but I will never forget your friendship when there was none, it gave me the boldness I needed to continue. Good luck on your adventure in England.' She squeezed her hand and withdrew to the corner to wait for her new young husband.

Bianca stood a moment looking at the beautiful hat, far too good for her coat, but matching the leather shoes Ted had bought as a wedding gift. Her tight chest reminded her of the sorrow at losing another friend.

Ted bound over grinning, 'Time to go in.' She looked at him cautiously. He gestured towards the Registry nervous but smiling, and together they walked hand in hand into their future.

*

A short time later they emerged, posing for photographs with registrar, witnesses, and guests, the shy, handsome working-class man clasping the hand of his previously vampish, brave, rebellious, middle class, beautiful wife.

A Land Rover arrived with her few belongings from the hotel to take them to Palmanova for the wedding breakfast. In the Sergeant's mess tables were set out in a horseshoe, at the centre, a tiny three-tier cake on a large board which they cut with a military sword while more photographs recorded the happy event.

*

The poison of the war, that had seeped into her very being, departed as they spent their first tender night together.

Within the week Ted was to be dispatched to England, his term of service in Italy finally at an end, yet another effort by authorities to separate soldiers from their Italian brides. He presented her with a crumpled envelope containing the money she had given him when she first arrived in Palmanova, all of it saved.

'You will need this for bits and pieces,' still speaking through mixed language and mime.

Bianca simply looked adoringly at her love, her Teddy, soon to be parted again.

'Things you'll need for England,' he mimicked a train. She smiled, lost in his kind eyes. 'I'll see you back in England, when you get your papers to travel.' A teardrop ran down her cheek onto the white satin nightdress she'd sewed from scraps.

Leaning down he kissed it, then her neck, her cheek, her fingertips. Her eyes closed as she lost herself in the moment. All thought melted away as she tried to lay down memories of his every touch, every sigh, of their treasured, cherished wedding night.

*

She watched the truck pull away with the shipment of home-bound soldiers. The timid girl gone too, left only with the company of the bitter mother with the child.

411

Appeals for her to write to Ted were largely ignored, no wish to be reminded of other women's happiness, Bianca waited until her travel pass allowed her to visit Trieste to prepare for her journey.

Advised she would not be allowed to exchange her lire or take money out of the country, her only option was to spend it. Along with the money from her father's house, she had her married women's allowance from the Army and was advised to buy gold to take with her, but despite searching, no jewellery or bullion could be found.

Walking the once fashionable streets one shop caught her attention.

Chapter 85

England, Spring 1947

Travelling back from Redcar after Ted had introduced Biancato to Rose and Cissy, she stared out of the railway carriage window. Drizzle ran down the outside, and inside, condensation. Unhappily she wiped the mist away with her glove. The trip had been a disaster. Cissy had taken an immediate dislike to her the minute she appeared in a fur coat. Then his mother seemed to take a mischievous pleasure in insisting on taking control of her food coupons. *"Their old habits die hard"*, Ted explained simply, but did not defend her.

When she arrived in England, there had been a terrible row. Ted said the coat embarrassed him, it was rubbing their bleak, post-war noses in it, and attracting uncomfortable attention everywhere she went. He claimed it looked like she was lording it over everyone, so many still struggling among the bomb sites. He couldn't understand, it was the only thing of value she was allowed to bring out of Italy. Tracing a dribble on the window with her finger, she sat with her back towards him wondering how it was possible to argue with someone when you could hardly speak the same language. His thigh rubbed against hers as the train rattled along.

Her pout was re-established since leaving Italy, time now to coiffure her hair, present only to please, appeal to his growing confidence, poise re-emerging to overcome new difficulties.

Ted laid a hand on her knee indicating they leave at the approaching station, and rose to take their case off the rack.

It was becoming dusk as they arrived at married quarters, their first proper home together. He took her hand to the front door, unlocked it, pulled the coat from her shoulders, tossing it through the door. A cloud shot across her face, as unintelligible words came out of his mouth until he swung her up in his arms, carrying her across the threshold. Sliding her body slowly down his, her toes barely touched the floor and they kissed for the longest time. Light rain on their case interrupted the moment and he pulled it into the hall, closing the door.

Nothing had changed. Love flowed daily from his body into hers, despite pouting sulks. On the first full day he left her, when all their worldly goods were delivered, and on returning in the evening, a wretched child-woman sat cross legged on the hearth rug. Her hair was scraped back under a scarf, legs bare in socks and slippers, cross-legged on a paint-splattered floor. A fire raged ready to warm him, her gaze fallen, forlorn, the saddest thing he had ever seen. That weekend he bought her two puppies, to keep her company.

*

'Hello there,' the woman next door kept speaking, on her brief excursions out of the house, and Ted taught her some new phrases.

'Hello, my name is Bianca.' The woman seemed to take this as an opportunity to chat nonstop, gesticulating wildly in words she didn't understand until she made a nervous retreat inside. Memories of Redcar still worried her. Not knowing if it was because of her nationality and being on the other side during the war, she felt uncomfortable.

However, every evening the neighbour watched as Ted approached the house, striding purposefully, expression serious, fists clenching and unclenching. The house, silent during the day, would resonate with her screams soon after he entered.

'I can't stand this any longer Norm,' she told her husband as her neighbour escaped each night, shrieking, running to the privy at the end of the yard and locking herself in as the man banged on the door, picking her up kicking and taking her back in the house.

'I don't know what he's doing to her, but she's terrified.'

'I've seen him about camp Doreen, seems alright to me,' her husband lit his pipe and settled in for the night.

'What do you know of a woman's trials and tribulations? She's foreign and alone, never talks, frightened to bits, always scampering back in the house terrified. I don't know what's going on,' she stood, arms crossed, 'but I'm going to find out. She needs someone to talk to.'

*

The next day, true to her word, she kept watch at the window until the foreign woman emerged, hair in a headscarf, sad, lonely, thin.

'Hey!' Doreen leapt out.

Bianca jumped at the call, 'How do you do?' she said carefully in return.

'How are you?' Doreen adopted the most theatrically sympathetic face she could to aid translation, and adopted a neighbourly lean against the fence between them.

Bianca recognised the phrase, 'Very well thank you,' hazarding an uncomfortable smile, wondering whether stories of her fur coat had reached her neighbour, as the woman raised her voice.

Doreen was impatient, 'Oh lass, what is he doing to you? Does he hit you? You can come to us if he does.' She lent in angling to see any incriminating bruises.

Bianca smiled weakly, 'I good.'

Doreen began an elaborate mime of a woman subjected to violence, by hitting her own head and

415

strangling herself, yelling "him" and "bastard", vigorously pointing in the direction Ted disappeared to every day.

Bianca stood wide-eyed, unable to speak, only adding further to Doreen's belief there was cruelty at hand, more resolved than ever to get her message across but the foreign wife disappeared inside.

*

Every day Bianca learned new words and the neighbour continued to gesticulate dramatically, adding more swear words until one day Bianca released a deafening shriek of laughter. Doreen stood open-mouthed as the shy bride erupted, holding her sides and crossing her legs to prevent an accident, hanging on to the fence for support.

'Well, there's no need to be like that, I'm trying my best to help.' Doreen, affronted by the hilarity, turned to leave.

'Please, no you go,' Bianca called.

Still hurt and confused, Doreen crossed her arms under her bust, her face set for an explanation.

'My Teddy, he no....' she slapped her own face a little too hard in demonstration. 'Ow!' and burst out laughing again. 'He good man, I love very.'

Doreen frowned, 'But, the screaming?' she waved her hands and ran to the privy, presenting her evidence.

'My Teddy, he trickle me.'

'He what!' Doreen, in a mixture of alarm and confusion.

'No, no trickle,' Bianca concentrated hard, 'he tickle.'

Bianca stood back for a response, adding, 'Monday, Tuesday, Wednesday, tickle, tickle, tickle.' She lunged at Doreen wiggling her finger, squealing.

The neighbour stepped back and adjusted her headscarf.

'Well, that's something if I'm not mistaken,' allowing the new information to settle.

She looked at the foreign bride, eyes shining, the first time she'd seen a smile and declared, 'Well my dear, time for a cuppa I think,' turning to go, beckoning Bianca to follow. 'Well come on then.'

The two women entered Doreen's kitchen, shoulders shaking at the comical misunderstanding, and absurd spectacle at their antics, laying down the first cornerstone of friendship.

*

From that moment on, the two couples shared picnics, visits, cinema, and then many photos and letters when the Army finally parted them. Doreen watched Bianca and Ted move through life, the foreign bride finding her feet in her brave new world, alongside her rock, a modest, quiet man, servant to her vivacious love.

*

In the years that followed, Bianca and Ted, the couple who loved so completely, would face unthinkable highs and lows. How do we judge lovers and people? By their acts, or the lives that made them? Another tale to tell in the coming nuclear age.

Glossary of Names, Places. Italian Words and Phrases
(alphabetical)

1st AGRA	1st Army Group Royal Artillery
Arthur	Cissy's friend/boyfriend
Axis Forces	Germany, Italy, Japan etc.
Balilla	Fascist youth organisation, Italy
bambina	girl
bastardo	bastard
bella bambina	beautiful little girl
bella signorina	beautiful young lady
Benito	Biancas
Bora wind	Annual strong wind from Karst to Trieste
Bianca	Main female character
brutto	ugly
Buonasera	Good evening
cara	dear/beloved
cara mia	my dear
Carabinieri	Police
Carlo Primavera	Vittorio's Friend from old electricity station on the quay
Castle Miramare	Austro Hungarian Castle on edge of Trieste
Che cosa	What
Christian Wirth	SS Officer
Ciao	Hello
Ciao bella	Hello gorgeous
Cissy	Ted's elder sister
Claude	Mia's eldest brother after her birth
come sta	how is he
come va	how are you
Complimenti di casa	Compliments of the house
Cosa Nostra	Sicilian Mafia
crapola	Loose interpretation for excrement

cretino	fool
Due cafe	Two coffees
Stazione	Station
foibe	deep, natural sinkhole often hidden by undergrowth
Grazie	Thank you
Grazie tanto	Thank you so much
harddwch	beauty (Welsh)
Il Duce Benito Mussolini	Fascist leader of Italy WW11
Mia	Vittori's wife/Bianca's mother
Karst	Limestone wilderness
King Emmanuel 111	King of Italy 1900-1946
Luca	Bianca's youngest brother
Luciana	Bianca's room-mate in Palmanova
Mafioso	Mafia
Mamma	Mother
Mamma mia	Goodness me
mangiare	eat
Maria Primavera	Mia's friend
Mio buono uomo	me good man - crude foreign translation
Molto grazia	Thank you very much
Monfalcone	Town on coast, north of Trieste
Montebello	Road below Railway and Electricity Station
Nonna	Nana
Nonno	Grandad
Odilo Globocnik	Higher SS & Police Leader
Opicina	Town close to Slovenian border, to north of Trieste
Palmanova	Fortified medieval Italian town housing Napoleonic barracks
Parenzo	Croatian town governed variously by Austria/Italy
piazza	square (town)
Piazza dei Forragio	Forrage Square -place for animal food
Piazza Unita d'Italia	Unity of Italy Square
pizza rustica	country pizza
Porto Vecchio	the Old Port

Prosecco	Region west of Opicina
prostituta	prostitute
Risiere de San Sabba	Name of the rice factory/site of extermination camp
Roberto	Sophia's admirer/lives in Piazza dei
Rocco	Mia's youngest brother
Rose	Ted, Cissy and Michael's mother
Roy	Ted, Cissy and Michael's father
Salvo	Mia's middle brother
Si, banka	Yes, bank
Signor	Mr
Signora	Mrs
Signorina	Miss
Slovene	Solvenia
Stanley	Ted's youngest brother
stazione	station
Strade di Fiume	River Road/above Electricity Station
The Bird Boy	The girls' friend/Slovenian boy from the
ti amo	I love you
Trieste	Major city north east Italy/extensive docks/borders Slovenia
Verona	Provincial capital city north east of Italy
Via Carducci	Trieste street with classical buildings
Vittorio	Mia's husband/Bianca's father
Zia	Aunt
Zio	Uncle

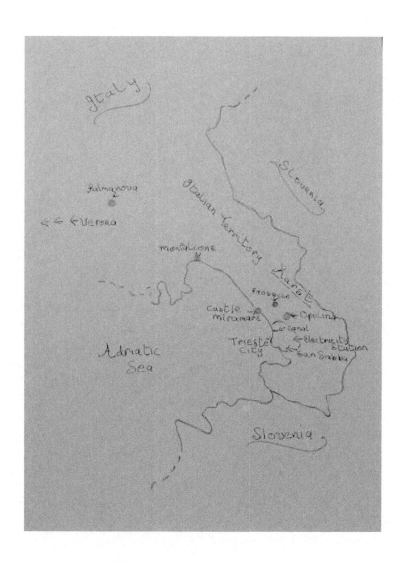

Region of Italy and Slovenia

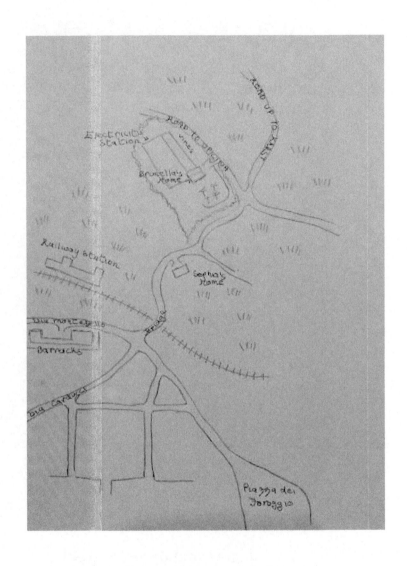

Area of Electricity Station in Trieste

Printed in Great Britain
by Amazon

35377192R00235